WASTED

ALSO BY THIS AUTHOR:

Twinkle

DAVID SILVERMAN

WASTED

Matador
5 Weir Road
Kibworth Beauchamp
Leicester LE8 0LQ, UK
Tel: (+44) 116 279 2299
Fax: 0116 279 2277
Email: books@troubador.co.uk
Web: www.troubador.co.uk/matador

ISBN 978 1848760 882

A Cataloguing-in-Publication (CIP) catalogue record for this book is available
from the British Library.

Typeset in 11pt Stempel Garamond by Troubador Publishing Ltd, Leicester, UK

Matador is an imprint of Troubador Publishing Ltd

Printed in Great Britain by the MPG Books Group, Bodmin and King's Lynn

For Issy, Nicky and Dan

Chapter One

Shame is a malady. Once afflicted it never leaves you. It is a disease for which there is no known cure, a bad smell that hangs about in your clothes that no amount of cleaning can eradicate. You try to put it out of your mind but those puckish summonses catch you off guard, trigger unwanted memories and quiescent organs to somersault. If the shame is widely known you learn to avert your eyes, staring at the ground becomes second nature. Some gain compensation from their predicament, catching sight of loose change.

Helena heard on the grapevine that her sister-in-law Pauline was hurt because she had not attended her father's funeral. Old man Jay had died two months before and it was necessary for Helena to apply the blame for her absence. She sat at the kitchen table, lowered the volume of the television set and bit into a chocolate bourbon. She crunched the biscuit and concentrated on her problem.

Helena was a thorough person, meticulous in her thinking and equally meticulous in her appearance. Helena did not believe in love or humanity, conscience or consideration or anything that discomforted Helena Black. As long as the outside world saw Helena in the best light, the truth and the means were irrelevant.

It took half the packet of bourbons but Helena conjured an alibi that absolved her of any fault.

'Pauline did not telephone me very often and when I telephoned her she was stand-offish. I felt I would not be welcome at the funeral.'

This statement had a grain of truth. Helena was well practiced in manipulating the facts. Yes, Pauline did curtail the regularity of her telephone calls to her 'friend' and when Helena took the initiative and called Pauline, she was unfriendly. These truths

1

were undeniable. The problem was in the timing because these snubs happened after Helena failed to attend the funeral but the grapevine accepted her presentation of the story.

Society today does what it wants when it wants to do it. Fewer and fewer people are taking responsibility for what they do. It is a society that enjoys pointing the finger, allotting blame. The existence of shame is diminishing.

Helena and Pauline Black live in Wyford, a betwixt and between town to the north of the metropolis. Half its population regard themselves as Londoners, which they are not, the other half claim to live in the countryside, which is palpably untrue. Wyford is a reflection of its population: dull.

There are numerous communities tied to the numerous churches, mosques, synagogues and pubs and these cross paths at the Conservative Club, the Labour Club, various Masonic cliques and the football ground.

Wyford is a typical English town.

The box-shaped town centre exists either side of the High Street, a 'posh' population live to the north, in and around Pemberton Park on the Pemberton or Nepsom Estates. Some of those who live on the Pemberton see themselves in an outmoded light and Helena Black revels in this anachronistic fallacy.

Soulless estates spring up on soon forgotten green. Ribbons of artisans' houses crumble until they are re-appointed by the optimistic. Industry, like a leaking tap, puddles into every available gap.

Wyford has cornered the market in traffic cones and traffic lights. Road works abound and every alteration adds to the congestion that blights the oversubscribed town. These well thought out tasks take fourteen weeks to complete and fourteen weeks to undo because the yellow warning signs are pre-printed with that figure. Traffic lights are fitted here and there but no significant change to the congestion is achieved and the lights are hoisted and moved to another unfortunate corner of the borough. Life and traffic go on.

The police station cowers beneath the ugly tower blocks in Junction Road alongside the Magistrates Court, which alone stands proud and a bit baroque amidst this mayhem of concrete and glass, dispensing justice by the bucket load.

The prisoner and guard walked in practiced synchronisation along a corridor pervaded by the odour of human degradation, a stale mixture of dirty bodies and disinfectant. They climbed a short flight of stairs and a pair of oak doors opened onto a clean smell of freshly polished wood. These contrasting smells are a reflection of the debasement and deodorisation that epitomises both sides of the law.

In the dock, Gideon Black was kept standing by his chaperone, his body remained frozen but his eyes wandered in search of sanctuary. None was to be found in the accusing hush as eyes bore down on him, piercing his aching chest.

The spectators saw a boyish man of twenty-five with a dash of disregard and hubris concealing two decades of resentment. Not particularly appealing, with dishevelled hair and exaggerated features, he was attractive to women.

Gideon is the son of Helena and the few genes he inherited from his father have been devoured by antibodies. Easy charm, devoid of accountability, Gideon understands life to have been created for his convenience. Like most men of charm, beneath the superficial lurks a cad. This cad makes bargains and promises he has no intention of keeping.

'God,' he said in silent prayer, 'if you get me out of this I promise not to do it again. I will never gamble again, I swear on my mother's life'.

For what seemed a lifetime they remained transfixed, a pair of waxworks, one a waxen poor, 'Just his rotten luck that Chris could not stump up the money in time. Why is it that registered letters turn up on Saturday mornings after the banks have closed? God, see me all right on this one and I will start going to church regularly.'

The green room door opened and the Magistrate emerged, resplendent in a crumpled suit, missed his step and collided with the furniture. Gideon recognised Alderman Edgar Swan, the old Mayor, who was a friend of his parents.

Alderman Swan, grim and purposeful, was proud of his self-deprecating wit.

'Edgar, where did you get that suit? It looks like you've been sleeping in it.'

'I'm a very important personage, sir,' said Alderman Swan. 'I have someone sleep in it for me.'

3

His wife took the seat beside him dressed in a costume more fitting to the Wyford Players, a suit of antiquated tweed and a deerstalker hat. They both wore grave expressions and Gideon guessed he was for the high jump. He sighed deeply, alarming his chaperone who took hold of his arm more firmly.

'I understand that the complainant has not arrived,' said Swan in an unfamiliar plum.

'No, sir,' said the clerk. 'The solicitor is taking a call outside. He will be here in a moment.'

'This is highly irregular,' Swan complained and confided a word to his wife. In unison they stared disapprovingly at the man in the dock and shared a second whisper. Mrs Swan shook her head, there was no saving him.

'He's going to the devil.'

'Not just yet,' Gideon thought. Was this delay his fifth cavalry, his eleventh hour? God had answered his prayer. 'Good bloke, God.'

The oaths Gideon had sworn were based on flimsy premise. His regard for his mother was tenuous and he would scarcely have cared either way, whether she lived or died. His sporadic attendance at St Marks church was temporarily suspended because of the rebuilding, the original St Marks having burned to the ground. In the meantime, the congregation were attending St Thomas', and Gideon was not welcome there.

As a child he had been introduced to Reverend Rollins, who rumpled his hair and called him 'sonny'. He had bitten the poor man's hand. The bite turned septic and it was touch and go whether the clergyman would lose a finger.

The solicitor asked to be allowed to approach the bench and shared a long exchange of whispers. Swan was obviously miffed and said grudgingly, 'Mr Black, you're free to go.'

'Thank you, sir.'

'I wouldn't thank me young man,' said Swan. 'I'll be seeing you in the near future, different time same place.'

'I don't think so, sir.'

Swan waved him away while consulting with the clerk on the next hearing. The only exit from the dock was back through the police station. On his way out Gideon crossed a pair of officers frogmarching an agricultural youth with more spots than whiskers toward the hatch. The youth gave him a wink and the officer not handcuffed to the prisoner elbowed him in the ribcage. The spotty youth grunted and said, 'Fucker.'

Outside there was no sign of his solicitor. It was half a day before Gideon found out who paid off the bookie.

Chapter Two

The choice for the design of the new St Marks was decided by a competition. There were five judges, but the winner, overriding fierce opposition, was chosen by the Head of the Committee, Ian Black CB, who happened to be Gideon's father.

'Why were you so set on Mr Heath's design?'

'One has to do right by one's fellow Masons,' said Ian.

George Neville Wyford Heath had been fascinated with light from the time he sucked on his mother's teat. He had trained as an architect but failed to prosper in the heady world of Planners, Conservation Officers and Arboreal Experts. Heartbroken, he worked as a salesman for a Middle Eastern lighting company based in Bethlehem. His artistic bent was much better suited to sales, where he could keep his feet firmly planted on the ground.

Subliminally, visits to Bethlehem gave him impetus and inspiration and in his solitary hours he toyed and fiddled with improbable designs for a unique church. He doggedly searched for a design that would satisfy the integrity of Planners, Conservation and most important of all, the Tree Officer.

Heath had learned priority the hard way. At the eminent architects Marshall & Gardner, he formed part of the team that prepared a scheme for the redevelopment of Bournemouth Town Centre. Three months of intensive work was presented to the senior partner who pondered, mused, viewing from every angle while the team waited with bated breath for his opinion. Architecture could be intoxicating. Growing more and more lightheaded, the senior partner squinted, stepped in and looked closer. The great man rubbed his chin, raspberried, frowned, faced each of the team in turn, nodded profoundly and spoke with an authoritative voice; 'Where is the fucking public toilet I asked for?'

Satisfied with the form, Heath contemplated a method by which he might impact on the pious. Egyptians had achieved tricks of light in tombs and Brunel had chosen his birth date as a commemorative day to light the Box Hill Tunnel. Less egocentric, Heath, a romantic, chose love for his theme. He struggled between having February 14th or June 1st for his base date. In the end he chose the spring month because of the likelier possibility of sunshine. He studied the angles of Wyford light throughout the year in relation to the north point.

He left a set of instructions with Reverend Waddingham. This paper provided explicit detail on how to adjust the dais throughout the year according to the solstice. An absent-minded fellow, the Reverend promptly mislaid the document.

Revitalised, with a revived career in prospect, Heath travelled to Israel to hand in his notice. On the bus journey from Tel Aviv airport to Jerusalem he was blown to bits by a suicide bomber and the last thing Heath saw was a flash of blinding light.

The external design of the new St Marks was described by the Head of the RIBA as creditable without being exceptional. In the *Wyford Observer*, Mr Edmund Pook, a resident of the Nepsom Estate, described the new church as a barnacle. Actually he described it as a carbuncle but the fledgling journalist had trouble reading back her shorthand. In the final analysis, however the eye saw the building, Heath's stroke of lighting genius would create an international reputation, a lasting mythology and a feature in the new editions of Ripley's *Believe it or Not*.

Before the grand opening of the new St Marks, the elders were given a guided tour of the new building by the project manager. The group remained upbeat through the tour until they reached the altar. It was here controversy began. Nobody seemed to mind the omission of traditional set pieces such as the screens, hagioscope and apse but one particular inclusion caused outrage.

'Heath was a great humanitarian.'

'Poor man,' said Celia Eddowes. 'What a terrible way to die.'

'Man was a bloody fool,' said Helena Black.

'Helena,' Ian Black remonstrated, 'don't forget where you are.'

'What's this thing supposed to be?' Lord Justice Christie stepped onto a small platform in front of the chancel steps.

The sanctuary formed an arc and housed the pulpit centre

stage, flanked by a handful of grand chairs with a lectern stage left for the reader of the lesson.

Keen to re-establish racial harmony throughout the world Heath saw religion as duty bound to initiate the process.

'How does this thing accomplish that, exactly?' The Lord Justice was growing impatient. Since the boring of the piles, the Project Manager and his Lordship had been at loggerheads.

Lord Justice Christie glared about him at the travesty. He did not approve of arty farty architecture, sand faced brick and timber beams. Tradition was what we British did best, not imitating foreign muck. Foreigners were heretics and hedonists to a man. Christian joy or joy of any kind and frivolous pleasure was for the empty headed.

These Planners had a lot to answer for. The last thing they had on their minds would be classified as architecture, insubstantial men with more than their fair share of dilettante. Now the buggers were interfering with courthouses, designs that should possess grandeur and foreboding were more appropriate to a leisure centre. What a fiasco the new church had been, a wasted opportunity.

Why had he agreed to associate himself with the new building? He had been reluctant, but Lady Christie's constant cajoling and being told that Ian Black CB would lead the committee and soak up the flack, he caved. He had not stopped kicking himself since. There was no denying that Ian Black was a decent fellow but he quickly proved to be a disappointment. He was a fish out of water and a fish out of his depth. He kept rather strict order at meetings but had no conception of architecture. Give the man his due, he openly admitted he had no taste and his home was a monument to kitsch.

Christie had accosted this infuriating bluster ever since he was a junior barrister. Pigheaded fools who thought that they could turn their hand to any issue, floundered but refused to stand down. It was not a syndrome confined to the legal profession, it applied across the board. Why had Ian remained adamant about the choice of architect? Was it some Masonic tie up? The policing system was crippled with secret handshakes.

'Get that man off my back,' the Project Manager complained to the Building Committee Chairman. 'He's holding up the work with his constant griping. If we finish late the builders are on stiff penalties...'

'...and you lose your bonus.'

'That too.'

'As you know, Heath spent a lot of time in Bethlehem. This smaller dais is a tribute to the Jewish faith. It is called a *bimah* or *chupa* and is used for wedding ceremonies.'

'Get rid of it,' said Christie. 'Which of these fripperies is a tribute to Mecca?'

'There isn't one that I know of,' said the Project Manager, 'although, since you mention it, when the congregation genuflect they are facing east.'

'I can't see any harm in this meeting of the great religions,' said Ian Black, reasonably. 'It's only a box.'

'What are these runners in the floor for?'

'The dais is movable.'

'Get rid of it,' said Christie with finality.

* * *

The building was three weeks late. The committee saved the bonus payment and recouped a wad of money implementing the penalty clause. The builders pleaded mitigation, placing the blame with Lord Justice Christie, whose early interference caused a month's delay. Christie had also upset the Building Inspector, a pragmatic man, who was pushed beyond endurance and had inflicted the letter of the Building Regulations law, creating a 30 per cent unnecessary overspend in remedial work.

'Who would be a builder?' observed the disillusioned Project Manager. If it had not been for so many strings being pulled in opposite directions he would have been spending his bonus on the omnibus collection of Mantovani recordings.

Christie called in a favour or two and the builder's letters of mitigation were consigned to the skip and, six weeks after the deadline, on Whit Monday, St Marks keystone, dedicated to Lord Justice Christie was laid in a topping out ceremony.

Sinners of old thou didst receive
With comfortable words and kind
Their sorrows cheer, their wants relieve
Heal the diseased and cure the blind

Though 1800 years are past
Since thou didst in flesh appear
Thy tender mercies ever last
And still thy healing power is here
Wouldst thou the body's health restore
And not regard the sin sick soul
The sin sick thou lov'st much more
And surely thou shalt make it whole

Seated around the pulpit, where Reverend Waddingham stood collating his notes, were the significant elders. Lord Justice Christie, his scatty wife, Ulrike, who talked incessantly, Mayor Michael Eddowes, his wife Celia, proud and prouder, and Ian Black CB, the Chairman of the Building Committee, with his wife Helena, who sang loudly and hopelessly out of tune.

'...Thou shalt open my lips , O Lord and my mouth shall shew thy praise,' said the Reverend into his chest. He lifted his head and scanned the congregation. 'For thou desirest no sacrifice, else would I give it thee; but though delightest not in burnt-offerings. The sacrifice of God is a troubled spirit, a broken and contrite heart, O Lord shalt thou not despise. O be favourable and gracious unto Sion, build thou the walls of Jerusalem...'

Lord Justice Christie was in a bad temper. The box was still in the centre of the aisle despite his instructions to remove it. He leaned forward and glared at Black who, oblivious, was smiling that sickly smile of his at no one in particular.

'Damn the man.'

He and Black started out as kindred spirits.

They were similar shapes, shopped at Marks & Spencer and their paunches caused that unsightly puckering to the front of their trousers. They were in accord on many topics, Queen and Country, the letter of the law and old fashioned values, but it was their egos that had caused the rift. Each was determined to get his own way and Black was winning hands down. Christie was not happy to be bested and sought redress. Unlike Ian Black, the Judge was experienced in the facts of life and he knew his time would come.

Ian's older son was a chip off the old block, a charming lad with the same regard to the eternal verities as his father. An accountant with Getliffe & Quinn International and suitably lacking in dimension, he was doing rather well. The brother, Gideon, was a wayward lad, his name was often associated with scandal, coupled with tags like tearaway, ne'er do well and hothead. The Black boy, a black sheep, had taken up the law. Christie suspected his reason was to keep one step ahead of it.

Reverend Waddingham was another traditionalist. He loved the old hymns, the standard books of prayer, Matthew, Mark, Luke and John. Today he had to stretch to Corinthians for the text of his sermon.

'...We know that if our earthly tabernacle of this house were dissolved, we have a building of God, a house not made with hands, eternal in the heavens...'

Helena Black surveyed the congregation, pleased that every available seat was taken. An unlucky few were standing along the chancel and in the aisle. The Reverend's wife had given up her seat and was acting as door person for late arrivals. Neither of Helena's sons had put in an appearance as yet and time was getting on. It would not be long before credit in creating the new church would be apportioned and she wanted the boys to witness the moment.

Three different types of wives who married successful men were represented on the sanctuary.

Lady Christie was the indispensible woman, who claimed, 'If his head wasn't screwed on, never mind his wig.'

Celia Eddowes, a long suffering doormat, spoke in black country singular, 'We are Mayor for the year and we are going to have to tighten our belts for the foreseeable future.'

Helena Black was on an equal footing with her husband Ian. Any spotlight he was under, she glowed in the same beam. She was not indispensible in the way of Lady Christie, she was entitled by the simple process of living at the same address. It was the sole manifestation of equality and sharing in their marriage. In Helena's mind there was no question that if their roles were reversed and she had gone to work while Ian had stayed at home, she would be the Commander of the Bath. Most probably she would be a DCB by now.

'Anything he can do, I can do better.'

Helena was getting a surprise award for her charity work from the St Marks Ladies Guild and she wanted everyone she knew to be present. The more of her friends and relatives in attendance the further news would spread. If her boys turned up that would be another generation who would know what a special person she was.

A shadow appeared in the church entrance and Mrs Waddingham pulled the door open. It was the local press, who knew to the second when to time their arrival, precisely as the services were ending. She had seen Camb, stained and grubby, hovering at functions with his eyes trained on the free drink. He had not dressed for today's occasion, his blotched raincoat and battered hat, notebook at the ready. The photographer was new to her, a younger man with greasy black hair and an Armani suit. They were directed to the area beneath the lectern and, as soon as the Lothario occupied his reserved space, he began stifling yawns. Before the church doors yawned shut Helena caught a glimpse of her two sons on the pavement outside, arguing.

'This is the last time,' said Chris stepping aside from Gideon's pointed finger.

'30K? I only owed the bastard 20K.'

'That was before you clocked him one.'

'You should never have agreed to damages,' Gideon's finger chased his brother's sidestepping jaw. 'I'm not paying that.'

'I'll stop the cheque,' said Chris. 'It's no skin off my nose. Mind you, when the cheque bounces you'll be back in court.'

'For a debt to a bookie?' said Gideon. 'Don't make me laugh.'

'For GBH,' Chris explained. 'The solicitor reckons you'll get a custodial. You broke the bookie's nose and his genitals swelled to the size of grapefruit.'

'Fuck him.'

'I'm going in,' Chris pushed inside and looked for a spare seat but they were all taken. He took up position leaning against the back wall. Mrs Waddingham remembered another duty to perform and rushed out the side door to the vestry. She had been talking to a chubby girl, who came face to face with Chris and blushed deep red.

Helena did not know anything about Gideon's overnight stay in a prison cell nor of his gambling problem. Helena's life had been edited by her parents, then by her sisters, now by her husband and sons who spared her the seamy data.

'You know me, if it's in my mouth, it's on my tongue,' Helena bragged.

Either way it was rarely in her head. Never satisfied with telling you once, it had to be repeated four or five times to make sure you got the point. Do not bother to respond in kind, your audience is not interested.

Chapter Three

Helena is the youngest of the White sisters and has made a most satisfactory marriage that in no way can be construed as gold-digging. When they met, Ian was starting out on his Civil Service career.

In any group of siblings you expect some similarities, but the White sisters were interchangeable. Their personalities were so alike; snobs, slaves to routine, genii at turning situations to their advantage, none of them could be wrong, none of them were prepared to bend, and this implacability had caused conflict. For some piddling and arbitrary difference of opinion rifts had developed and sustained for a decade.

Each set out to find a partner who was prepared to sit at their feet, obey their every whim and satisfy their every demand. Each husband was loyal to the point of humiliation, backing their spouse, whilst knowing they were in the wrong. Only Emma, the eldest sister and the last to marry, slipped up, her husband was not totally manageable and unable to satisfy her appetite for sex.

The source of this self-conceit was the result of Mr White's indulgence. He treated his daughters with exaggerated reverence and convinced them they were goddesses. A vocation they accepted without question. Emma was the first of the Immortals and those that followed, Jessica, and the youngest, Helena, were self-proclaimed divas.

Her father's indulgence of his darling baby was extreme. 'You don't want to go to school, darling, don't go. You stay home and help mummy.'

'You don't like your school, darling, we'll find you another one.'

The longest absence was six months, before the authorities got wind of it and the Whites were severely censured for the truancy. Helena was made to go to school whether she liked it or not, providing her with a new and unwanted experience which lay heavily in her memory bank. It had a lasting effect on her psyche and never again had she allowed herself to be forced to do something she did not care to.

As a child, having her merest whim fulfilled, suppressed whatever gifts she had been born with. It began with her father accommodating her desires and, after his premature death, the other three women in the household worked in concert to protect her. Fussed over, every wish granted, Helena developed narcissism of the spirit, not just self-absorbed in her isolated oligarchy but able to obliterate the consideration that others had wills or desires. Helena was assured of her divine right at the head of the queue.

If her desires were not constantly fed she could not function. She was a bird of prey's offspring baying to be fed, and grew into a hovering eagle, saw something that took her fancy and swooped. She saw herself as an Olympian deity, worshipped by the multitudes, single-minded, ruthless, tenacious, oblivious to objectivity.

Down the years, Helena had grown more impassive, frigid, except for this incessant appetite. No food was required, just as long as she got her own way. If the need arrived in her gut, the need had to be satisfied. She derived no pleasure from giving and possessed no maternal instinct. No tendency to any emotion besides satisfying her wants. She did not dwell in the past, did not speculate on the future. She wanted what she wanted and she had to have it. Reason, morality and how it will affect others did not come into the equation. Helena Black was number one, top of the spoiled brat poll.

In fact she was christened Helen, but it did not sound grand enough to her ears so she added the extra 'a'. Once again she tampered with the truth and was allowed to get away with it.

Cocooned in this vacuum, Helena created a world of her own. Her lively imagination concocted a game of fantastical sketches that she acted out in her room. What qualifies as unique is that so many of these fancies became reality.

'I'd like to call on Pamela Riklis to make a special presentation,' said Reverend Waddingham.

'Lords, Ladies and Gentlemen,' Pamela Riklis began, 'we here at St Marks are privileged. See the numbers in attendance today to celebrate the resurrection of both our church and community after our sabbatical at St Thomas. I would like to take this opportunity to thank Reverend Rollins and his congregation for taking us in.'

Pamela paused for a short burst of token applause.

'We as a community are privileged and can boast several eminent members in our congregation...' Pamela turned to gesture to those seated on the sanctuary. 'Today I wish to focus on just one among us, someone who works tirelessly for the community, who helps the poor, the needy and the unfortunate in parts of Wyford where the communities are not so blessed. This person, this woman, works selflessly, carries out these charitable works and has done so for more years than I care to remember, without seeking any reward, any recognition of any kind. I and several other members of the Ladies Guild agreed that some sort of acknowledgement was long overdue and we are taking this opportunity to make amends. I invite Emma Telleulin to make the presentation.'

Emma, carrying a rolled scroll tied with blue ribbon, stepped up onto the sanctuary. She undid the ribbon, unrolled the scroll and read, 'We, the members of the St Marks Ladies Guild duly acknowledge the selfless contribution of Helena Margaret Black.'

Helena, so busy trying to attract the photographer's attention, signalling Camb to give the dago a prod, missed her cue. Her belated attempts at shock and surprise fell flat and only those who wanted to believe were taken in.

Ian's staff referred to Helena as the scarlet woman. Her hair, her lipstick, her fingernails, the electric bulbs in the main bedroom were red, and inside her outrageous number of shoes, her toenails were red. She admired and aspired to being Imelda Marcos.

Whereas her eldest sister Emma Telleulin was vain, Helena was particular. She had no claim to beauty but had set unrivalled standards of fastidiousness. Her week, like her sisters', was planned to the minute and she would not tolerate a deviation. Monday was set aside to recover from the hurly burly of the weekend, a little housework, a little ironing, Tuesday, good works for around an hour, Wednesday, tea with sisters or friends,

Thursday, Waitrose. After a week of exertions, Friday was a day of indulgences. Friday was a day devoted to Helena; pedicure, manicure, facial, blow dry and best of all, a captive audience. Friday afternoons were torment, heating the ready-cooked dinner without damaging her nails. These were invariably heated too early. Having promised to finish at a sensible time, Ian returned home around ten pm and his meal was scorched.

Monday to Friday Ian Black ate, lived and breathed his work. On weekends he brought home a satchel full of papers. There were two distractions from the satchel, sport and church. Not a religious man, he enjoyed the cant and mellow of Sunday services and the cant of Saturday afternoons at Wyford FC. There was nothing like a rousing hymn to unite a congregation or football crowd. His greatest love was cricket and he can be seen every summer Saturday at the Nursery End, satchel open on his lap, biro tapping against his upper lip or teeth.

'I need a break from the rigours of office. When I get home from a hard day's work, the last thing I want to do is think.'

Helena was a grass widow but she did not mind in the least. Her husband was an important man. He was a Permanent Secretary at the Home Office, one of the keystones of government. Ian was important, very important. Therefore, Helena had gravitas.

Chapter Four

Tea was served, plates of sandwiches (crusts removed), cakes and pastries bought and prepared by Dorothea Waddingham but served by the Ladies Guild with modest pride, refusing to accept compliments for their altruism. Dorothea made it a point to absent herself from these displays, anxious to maintain her dignity. She peered around the vestry door, checking if it was safe to come out and joined the tea party.

Helena Black was centre stage, her thatch of vermilion hair rotating as busily as a Polish mop, uncomfortably maintaining a smile, her features etched on her grim countenance. The reconsecration of the church was taking second place to her presentation for good work. The husbands, less animated, less shrill, having dispensed the niceties, discussed interminable aspects of football.

Dorothea Waddingham eased her way to the tea table, smiling sweetly. Ian, who took care to save lost souls, accosted her.

'You're looking flushed my dear,' he said, soft and awkward confronted by a comely face.

A flash of guilt clouded her vivid blue irises for an instant, which he did not pick up on, melted into her sweetest smile. It was the rarest of favours because it included her eyes.

'There are so many people and so much to do.'

'Let the Ladies' Guild take the brunt,' said Ian. 'They will claim the credit anyway.'

'I pity poor Mr Light. He's normally worn out by the time he gets here on his bicycle.'

'Old Ronald, is he still going strong?' Ian's face crinkled with affection. 'How long has he been caretaker.'

'Over twenty years,' said Dorothea. 'His job description does

18

not include cleaning but he does it anyway, without moaning I might add.'

'Old school,' said Ian, who was pulled away by Doctor Riklis. 'My brother wants to meet you.'

'Why isn't Ronald here?' Ian asked over his shoulder.

'He wasn't invited,' said Dorothea accusingly and both were soaked up in the clamour.

* * *

Without being asked, Ronald Light, clumsy with arthritic hands, dismantled and put away the trestle tables, swept up the crumbs and cucumber and replaced the pews in perfect symmetry. It was then the controversial discovery was made and started the scandal that rocked the St Marks community. If Ronald had been by himself the matter would have died a natural death. If he had reported the discovery to the Reverend or his wife the object would have been disposed of, but as fortune has it, the first Tuesday in the month is when the Ladies' Guild convenes. Most often these meetings are held at one of the homes of the members, but anxious to make good use of the new church it was decided to meet there.

The ladies bustled in and clustered around the moveable dais that Lord Justice Christie so strongly objected to. One by one they began sitting on its edge. They found its height conducive and the number of seat placements perfect for their number. They were chatting away merrily when...

'What on earth is this?' said Ronald, the volume of his voice amplified by his increasing deafness. He put his hand in the font and lifted out a pair of cotton knickers.

Being passed from hand to hand, the provenance of the item was quickly established and the class of the owner pinpointed. What was not so easy to establish was the age of the person the knickers belonged to.

Helena held the item distastefully between thumb and forefinger and inspected the label, 'George'. 'Who do we know who shops at Asda?'

Conclusively the assembly denied such acquaintance. Helena suggested the panties be pinned to the notice board. After getting over the shock of finding a cheap pair of knickers in the font, their thoughts wandered to who would have done such a thing.

There was an unspoken consensus. One culprit sprang to mind. It would be typical of his previous history but they could not voice their suspicions because his mother, Helena, was present. Once again, the unspoken politesse among those of even a modest association with Helena Black kicked into place, and the real and possible truth was suppressed.

* * *

Gideon sat in the dark and listened to the night noises. Everyone had gone home and he was safe and quiet for a few more hours. Nothing would happen today and there was no point on dwelling on what tomorrow might bring. He would do anything to go back and start over and make a new bargain with God. He composed a solemn promise not to make the mistakes a second time and banged his fist on the desk to confirm the undertaking.

'I'll be different from now on. Forgive us our trespasses,' he muttered and added defiantly, 'as we forgive those that trespass against us.'

He told himself he would not miss the exhilaration. It was not worth the agony and complication that came after. If only he could go back and start afresh, begin again, he would be a new man. These periods of regret and depression were becoming more regular and harder to throw off. Harder to rationalise and explain away. He should find a suitable partner and get hitched, have a baby, settle down.

Sex was better without a condom. He loved the gamble and preferred the rhythm method. He must have some Catholic blood in him. Fucking a girl who was on the pill was no fun at all, there was no edge.

'It's like betting on a fixed race.'

Christ he had had a bad run of luck lately. Everything was going against him.

'You should never shit on your own doorstep.' Uncle Duncan told him that.

He should have listened, it was an obvious rule of life. If he was honest, that was the attraction. What was more exhilarating than shagging a woman when her husband could be home at any minute? Shagging with one eye looking over your shoulder was the best kind of shag.

'Shag your boss's daughter, forbidden fruit, and getting her up the duff was none too clever. Fuck!'

He thought a virgin might be turn on but it was a waste of time. The moaning and groaning was all right but the mess. The second time was not much better and she got knocked up.

'Just my fucking luck, if only I could turn the clock back.'

How he hated the life he led, standing around in pubs getting pissed, going on about how little sleep you got, how wasted you were, and most of it was a pack of lies. He was sick of his own dissipation and bored by the bragging of his friends. Everyone he knew claimed to be 'mad'. It gave the dull a semblance of a personality. He did not need to petition for madness, he had a gift for women, he knew what to say, was easy in the company of females and they were easy with him.

He would wipe the slate clean. He flipped open his mobile and began erasing names from his address book. He would get rid of his regulars and find someone who loved him for something other than his dick. A name scrolled into view that caused a groan of exasperation.

'Fuck, I wish I had never laid eyes on the stupid bitch.'

He had been avoiding her for days, but he answered the call yesterday without checking the name and she started in on him. At one stage he put down the phone and made coffee. He picked up the discarded mobile, sipped the scalding liquid tentatively and listened. His absence had not been noticed.

'Why do you do it? The married ones are the worst, the hardest to shift, they are like limpets.'

He pressed the delete button and her name was gone. If only he could do the same with his other problems, a press of a button and the worry would be over. Getting women to bed was no longer a challenge. Getting rid of them was the challenge. The magic had gone, it was routine.

'Do you love me?'

'Am I beautiful?'

It was easy to say 'yes' and hopefully not see them again.

What dampened his ardour was the flush of irritation these banal questions evoked. The sheer predictability of these inquiries, and the wholehearted acceptance of his blatant lies, disappointed him.

He had toyed with the idea of settling down, finding a worthwhile partner. He understood that some men married a clone of their mother. It was there that his speculations ended, he would rather go to prison for life than marry anyone that resembled his mother.

Chapter Five

Speculation on the ownership of the mysterious underwear continued unabated, except for a temporary digression when it was discovered that there had been no CCTV security included inside the church. There were cameras mounted on all four corners of the exterior, which fanned through 180 degrees, but nothing inside. Blame had to be apportioned and a scapegoat found. Black and Christie spoke gravely about the oversight, their brows were furrowed to emphasise the gravity. In truth, despite their proximity to the criminal classes neither had given the notion a thought. There was a variation order from the architect that succeeded the luckless Heath requesting a fifth camera which remained on Black's study desk, unread.

'Did anyone see any of the assembled guests near the font?'

'...Or on the sanctuary?'

'Do you know anyone who would buy their lingerie at a supermarket? My cleaning woman does and most of it ends up polishing my furniture.'

'Living on Reverend Waddingham's salary can't be easy.'

'Pamela!'

'How could you?'

'Dorothea Waddingham of all people.'

'She used to be a nurse.'

'It's not actually my idea,' Pamela was on the back foot. 'It was Helena's suggestion.'

'I bet it didn't include that son of hers.'

'I know,' said Pamela. 'Wherever there's trouble he's bound not to be far away.'

'Has anybody considered that he brought the underwear with

him and left it in the font as a prank. He has a history of warped humour.'

'That's so clever of you, Jessica.'

* * *

Helena sorted through her collection of plastic bags for those labelled Waitrose. It was Thursday and she was dressed for shopping in a tan skirt, white blouse and red cashmere sweater. She took care choosing her jewellery, a glass bracelet and silver earrings. There was no justification for a necklace, not in the wilds of Barrow Weald. Helena claimed she did not shop locally because standards were simply not good enough.

She parked the 4 x 4, organised her luggage and surveyed her surroundings. As she opened the door she caught sight of her niece, Amy, talking to a middle aged man outside Phil's Cafe opposite and hastily shut the door again. Adjusting the rear view mirror she watched and waited for the coast to clear.

There was gossip about her niece's behaviour, sordid tales about her nocturnal activities. In their teens there had been similar stories about her sister Emma but she had not believed them. Sex was boring. Mouths can be so cruel and convict an innocent on the flimsiest of evidence.

Her husband Ian was prone to say, 'There is no smoke without fire.'

No matter how outrageous the accusation, in his experience there was often a grain of truth. Helena had serious doubts about these pieces of wisdom.

The man touched Amy affectionately, placing the palm of his hand on the side of her face, and his body language suggested he was leaving. He kissed her goodbye and crossed the street into the car park. Helena ducked low in her seat. It was her brother-in-law, Duncan. She waited for his taxi to drive away before sitting up straight and checking that Amy had also gone.

Sure that the coast was clear, Helena got out of the car and made her way to the Waitrose entrance, continued past over a narrow access and entered Sainsbury's.

Helena had a morbid fear of being caught with her Sainsbury's shopping. Ian's dietary preferences were an embarrassment. Here was a man who wined and dined with the rich and powerful, ate at exclusive restaurants, clubs and hotels, but preferred a fry up in a greasy spoon, who mourned the passing of the British Railway breakfast and the demise of the Little Chef.

Helena was not much bothered by food. She cared more about where she was eating than what was on the plate, so that she could regale her coterie with her grand lifestyle. She existed primarily on biscuits and was particularly partial to chocolate bourbons.

Ian was supplementing his dehydrated meal with a tin of baked beans. 'You should take better care of yourself,' Helena told him coldly. 'Take more care with your diet.'

'I'm happy enough,' said Ian blithely. 'You needn't worry about me.'

'You'll regret it,' she warned him. 'You mark my words.' She wanted to add, you don't have to share a bed with you, but thought better of it.

* * *

When she emerged from Phil's Cafe, Emma was in a bad temper.

'Did you get through?'

'Of course,' she answered irritably, in the manner she usually saved for the staff. Amy pulled away and muttered an expletive. 'What was that?'

'Nothing,' said Amy sulkily.

'For God's sake girl, I can't count on you for anything, so don't start playing up at this late hour.'

'It's not my fault your mobile's not working.'

'Isn't that Helena's 4 x 4?'

'Where?'

'In the Waitrose car park.'

'How should I know? I didn't know Aunt Helena had a 4x4. I just saw Uncle Duncan.'

'Did he have a mobile?'

'I didn't think to ask.'

'You are amazing,' said Emma, crashing her palm against her forehead. 'I know which side of the family you get your brains from, you're 100 per cent Telleulin.'

* * *

Helena kept mementos of her beloved father, a fan of embroidered handkerchiefs, a Meerschaum pipe and a treasure box. The box had been a theatrical prop in the 1956 Christmas season pantomime at the London Palladium. That year they did Treasure Island with Duncan Askey and Tommy Cooper, their signatures were on the bottom of the box. Somehow the box found its way to the Portobello Road and from there to Mr White. Helena had used it to store her bottom drawer but that trousseau was not a patch on the one she had accumulated for her daughter.

Throughout her second pregnancy, Helena researched as many old wives tales as she could find and adapted her condition accordingly. She thought 'pink' and decorated the room with rose satin. If she were to carry at the front, she stood erect and thrust out her abdomen. To carry high she bought a corset but this restraint caused her to lose control of her bladder and had to be abandoned. To carry low, she stooped. Having suffered backache, incontinence and a pulled muscle behind her knee, the adjustments were to no avail.

As she came round from the anaesthetic she asked, 'What sex?'

'It's a bouncing baby boy.'

'Shit', was the word that heralded Gideon's arrival and proved to be prophetic.

Cheated of a daughter, Helena took it out on her son.

With Ian working such long hours, Helena, left alone for long periods, did not care for television, had never read a book and struggled to fill her time. Once she had read the gossip column and chosen a frozen dinner there would be four or five hours before Ian got home. During a period of nostalgia, what she started as a dalliance became a daily ritual. The seed of this ritual germinated during Helena's prolonged absences from school.

Eunice White disapproved of her husband's pampering, preferred to be strict with her offspring and as a result was ignored, disregarded or overlooked. Not only did her husband treat her like a doormat but so did her children. What angered her most was that he left her to deal with the consequences of his actions, school inspectors knocking at the door, nasty jobsworths, impertinent, snide, looking down their snippy noses.

'Mrs White?' asked a ferret-faced man with sweat stains under the arms of a grey mohair suit.

Eunice did not bother to answer but stepped back inside, shut the door and locked the latch.

'Are you the mother of Helen Margaret White?' the man spoke through the letter box. 'Open up Mrs White, you don't want the police involved. Mrs White you're leaving me no choice.'

These scenes conducted in full view of the neighbours, the Whites were the talk of the street. Not only was Helena's truancy a subject of gossip but Eric White was equally notorious. Guilt for his philandering was the source of the extreme indulgence of his girls.

Helena would go back to school for a period, but the odd day off would kick start the cycle again. Under scrutiny by the authorities, the Whites were now obliged to cover Helena's absences with proper excuses and pressed their GP to supply them with sick notes. Their GP, a priggish Scot, a stickler for the rule book, gave a lengthy lecture with each certificate. Worse still were the neighbours who seemed to delight in reporting Eunice to the school superintendant. Embarrassed at being confronted in the street, Eunice went shopping leaving Helena alone in the house.

With nobody to prevent her, Helena raided wardrobes and drawers, dressed up in her mother's and sisters' clothing and acted out fantasies. Mostly fairy tales, princesses and frogs turning into princes, which evolved into a crush for Prince Charles and so began a lifetime of social climbing. She studied the society pages in every periodical she could get her hands on and got her daddy to buy her magazines, *Tatler*, *Harpers & Queens*, *The Lady* and *Country Life*. She learned about the influential, the aristocracy, the rich and powerful and used this knowledge for inspiration. She chose favourites and included them in her entourage and glued them into a journal. She saw herself as a queen-like figure, with equerries, servants and intimate advisers. She also augmented a photograph of herself with a crown.

Completely self-taught, in adulthood Helena continued to conduct her life in the same fashion and, unaccountably, her coterie fell into line. She was a Svengali who was able to hypnotise her friends into unbridled hero-worship and conjure a devotion that belied belief.

Helena locked the bedroom door, took the treasure box from

its hiding place behind her shoe boxes and stripped down to her slip and bra. From the box she unfolded a silver lamé dress that her mother had worn to the 1977 Ladies' Night at Wyford's Oddfellows Hall, struggled inside with much wriggling and chipped a nail forcing the zip. She brushed her hair with forty strokes and carefully placed a fake diamond tiara on her forehead. This was another memento of her childhood. She donned elbow length satin gloves and slipped rings onto each index finger.

In a full length mirror she checked out her appearance thoroughly. When she was sure she was fit to meet the Queen she commenced her fantasy. Standing as though waiting in line, Helena imagined she was in the foyer of the Leicester Square Odeon at the opening of a Tom Cruise blockbuster or the new James Bond. She stood between Michael Caine and Albert Finney for years until she found out the latter had refused a knighthood, she replaced him with Ben Kingsley. Making sure she remained facing front, out of the corner of her eye she watched the Queen's approach.

Her Highness stopped for a moment to chat to Audrey Hepburn, and Helena gathered her nerve for their meeting. Finally the Queen stood before her, beautiful in a turquoise dress, and was introduced by some flunkey. Helena curtseyed flamboyantly and burst a seam.

'Whoops!'

She repaired the chipped nail, sewed up the tear and fastidiously rechecked her appearance. There was a ring at the front door. Nobody worthwhile called at this time of day and she ignored it. Next she began her second favourite game, where she was given the MBE for her charitable work. She had begun the preliminaries while sewing the lamé dress. The letter had come from Buckingham Palace offering her the 'gong' and she had duly accepted.

Properly attired, Helena waited in the anteroom for her turn to meet Prince Charles, the first love of her life, who would make the presentation. As much as Helena was incapable of love, her emotion for His Majesty was a close as she could get. It was more reverence than affection. Their eroticism did not venture beyond a brief merging of lips, because there was no way the Prince would do tongues. Deep down Helena truly believed that the royal line was propagated by some sort of an immaculate conception. She viewed royal sex in the same way as most of us regard our parents.

Helena was one of two women in the waiting group to receive their MBE. There was an Admiral, who inquired of a balding man with a tanned complexion what he was being honoured with and why.

'I'm to receive a CB for my work in the Civil Service,' said the man, proudly.

The Admiral turned up his nose with immoderate disgust, turned on his heel and confronted the other woman. 'Why are you here, my dear?'

The other woman's voice spanned several octaves, fluctuated between abstinence and sixty a day, 'I'm the Queen's secretary.' Helena was disappointed that the Queen's secretary was a smoker and so was the Admiral. It was not seemly for the Queen to employ such a person. 'And you, my dear?'

Helena, at her modest best, provided him with her curriculum vitae. The list of her good works was substantial and as she recited them her chest inflated. Sure that she had forgotten nothing, she smiled modestly and her achievement was reflected on the Admiral's face. He was as proud of her as she was.

They were led along a sumptuous corridor and Helena walked on the red carpet as though she was born to it. In the presentation theatre, they were surrounded by encouraging faces. Having been briefed that they were not to touch his Highness, she curtseyed cautiously and stood patiently mute.

It was here that her fantasy faltered. Despite years of practice, their exchange of words was never perfect, never quite matched the greatness of the moment. The one bit of this scene she did not tire of was that the Prince looked into her eyes and was transfixed. Helena did not attribute this chemistry as another of her Svengali conquests but as the meeting of two minds. She was his lost love, a maelstrom began whirling in both their chests and no words needed to be spoken. The Prince broke with tradition, took her hand in his and kissed it. Helena, welling up, excited beyond endurance, collapsed onto the bed, breathless, heaving.

She lay there, recovering slowly, her asthmatic love subsiding. 'Wow,' she said, 'that was a good one.'

What was odd about so many of Helena's fantasies, whether

elaborately acted out or mused over while reading Nigel Dempster or William Hickey or any of the mordant gossip columnists, was that so many of them came about. Ian got a CB and she got a video of the presentation and played it over and over and over, providing hours of diversion. Her fantasies were elevated from a 'gong' to a knighthood and in Helena's life fiction was getting closer and closer to fact.

Helena cleared her junk back into the box and returned it to its hiding place behind her shoes. She opened the freezer and took out the top packet. She read the instructions, extracted the contents and stuck them in the oven at the required temperature. She then set two places on the kitchen table, each with a knife, fork, spoon and linen napkin in a plastic ring. When the meal was cooked, she opened the lid smeared a plate, knife and fork with the gravy and left it to congeal at her place setting. Ian's place was neat and tidy ready for his arrival. She put the ready meal back in the oven on a low temperature, boiled a full kettle of water and poured a cup of Earl Grey tea. The rest of the water she emptied into a saucepan to which she added peeled potatoes and a cup of frozen peas. She put these on a low light on the hob and opened the biscuit tin. She drank her tea and ate her confectionery supper while watching a home being refurbished on the television. She was looking for ideas. It was time for the dining and living rooms to be redecorated.

Helena heard the key in the door and jumped to her feet, turned up the heat on the oven and drained the vegetables. She opened a small tin of baked beans, emptied the contents into a glass dish, filled the plate, carefully separating the potatoes and peas into groups, and dished up half of the ready meal.

She retrieved the packet from the bin to check what she was serving. As she put the meal on the place mat, Ian entered the kitchen. To Helena's horror he was not alone. Chris was with him and had a girl on his arm, a soft squidgy girl with copper hair, and there was she in her bra, slip and housecoat. Thank goodness she had not removed her make-up or tied her hair up for the night.

With a squeal she fled the room. By the time she returned properly dressed, Ian was washing his empty plate. 'You might have warned me,' she said testily.

'They were waiting outside,' Ian explained.

'We knocked earlier,' Chris intervened. 'There was no answer.'

'I was in the bath' Helena lied, and did not appreciate the knowing look her son gave her. 'Who is this young lady?'

'Forgive my manners,' Chris apologised. The girl was not in the least put out by his oversight and did not appear to be enthusiastic about anyone, certainly not Chris's mother. Helena could not explain why but she did not like this person. 'Katy Eddowes, this is my mother.'

'Eddowes. Are you related to the Mayor?'

'He's my father,' she spoke as though on the edge of irritation, as though she had been stopped in the street by a market researcher and was reluctantly answering a survey. She was thinking, 'Isn't that bloody obvious, even to you?'

'May I ask the point of this visit' Helena asked snootily, 'at this hour?'

'I wanted to be sure that dad was home.' Chris took the girl's hand in his own and the girl had to restrain an impulse not to snatch it away. 'Katy and I are getting married.'

Helena inspected the girl with a rheumy eye and speculated that no amount of refurbishment was going to put this child's house in order. To suggest that she was plain was being kind. Get a load of the backside on her, a veritable shire horse. The girl was a frump and would not be suitable for any wedding Helena had envisaged.

The Blacks' relatives and friends who were introduced to his fiancée concluded that Chris was marrying his mother.

Ian Black, a kind but dull, unimaginative fellow, loved set plays. He disappeared for a few minutes and returned with a bottle of champagne and champagne glasses.

'Cheers', echoed hollowly around the bare walls and the cheap fizzy liquid added to the sour atmosphere in the room.

Ian watched his son and prospective daughter-in-law sipping their champagne. 'How happy they were. What a credit to him the boy was. Everything a father could wish for.'

* * *

He so enjoyed Saturdays, waking without the pressure of catching the 7:05 and expectation in the air, a morning's uninterrupted paperwork, walking to the ground with a son on either arm, speculating on the prospects of the match. How he loved crowds, being part of the throng.

Katy was a pretty girl and looked quite fetching in her pin-striped suit. Maybe he would be a grandfather and he could give his grandchild the care and attention he had denied his sons. He could make up for lost time, put matters right.

The method required to create a grandchild gave him pause. The merest recollection of conjoining with Helena caused severe discomfort in his groin. How could he have been responsible for a son like Gideon? They did not share a solitary gene, similarity or impulse. The way his younger son conducted his life was an ocean of trepidation. Trying to understand Gideon left him floundering, and Ian hated to be all at sea, had a dread of water. Helena's insistence on dispensing with a bath in their en suite removed a swathe of dismay and alarm. Life was so much safer amongst the jets of a shower, and none too safe there either.

Chapter Six

Pamela Riklis was a faithful friend and the conversation that had taken place on the *bimah* about Helena gnawed at her conscience. When she told her friend what had been said she had no problem omitting the references to her son Gideon.

'They were shocked that anyone would contemplate the Reverend's wife doing such a thing.'

'Buying supermarket underwear?'

'No,' said Pamela, 'being unfaithful to her husband.'

'Who said what?' Helena listened closely to her friend's recounting of the conversation and stopped her at regular intervals to be sure she understood every implication.

She brooded about what had been said for several days. Helena was a determined woman and nothing motivated her more intensely than being scoffed at behind her back. If necessary she would make it her lifetime's work to prove them wrong. She was like a Rottweiler; once she got her teeth into a problem she would bite down to the bone. If she had this intuition, there must be grounds for it and she would either find them or manipulate the few facts she did know to provide the merest hint that her speculation was true. Years of reading gossip columns had rubbed off and she was well practiced at conjuring a few bits and pieces into a story that would fit her claims. The implication that she was on the right track would be satisfactory enough and one corroborating witness, however much this witness lacked veracity, would be perfect.

Brood as she might, she struggled to recollect any incident at the topping out that would be of help to her.

'Think,' said Helena emphatically, 'surely you saw something?'

'I've gone over it a thousand times,' said Pamela. 'Did you see anything? You're much better at these things than I am.'

She had not noticed anything that would help and Ian was a waste of time. It was not until the *Wyford Observer* landed on the mat that she was provided with the chance of assistance. She was very pleased that her presentation rated a separate mention and a photograph, even though it was consigned to page five. Ian was on the front page handing a trowel to Lord Justice Christie.

'Eureka,' she cried.

That scruffy reporter Mister Camb must be trained to notice minutiae. She would give him a call.

'I wonder if you can help.' Helena offered him her sweetest voice. 'At the topping out ceremony someone left a piece of personal property behind and unfortunately it has no identification. During the tea party did you happen to notice anyone on the sanctuary or near the font?'

'Nope,' said Camb, through a sandwich. 'Is it valuable? There could be a story.'

'Only of sentimental value I'm afraid.'

'I can't say I do remember, but if I think of something I'll let you know. What's your number?'

Helena enunciated slowly and Camb repeated every digit.

'Why don't you check with Pellicci?'

'Who is Pellicci?'

'The photographer.'

'Could you put me through to him?'

'He doesn't work here, lady,' said Camb, his sandwich scatter speckling the mouthpiece. 'Pellicci's freelance, he's got that shop at the top of the High Street, Photos R Us.'

'Thank you so much,' said Helena and hung up.

David Pellicci, the owner of Photos R Us, had a nose for sex. He was highly sensitive to oestrus and inflamed testosterone like some truffle dog and could sniff out a woman on heat at one hundred paces.

Pellicci had studied photography with the Navy, where he had plenty of time aboard ship to observe irregular companionship. A candid shot of an officer with a subaltern got him and the officer dishonourably discharged. Marooned at Devonport, there were few work opportunities. He owned a camera, and a nose for infidelity, so accepted a job with a detective agency. He spent the next two years in and around Plymouth refining his craft in taking action pictures. He could assess a situation in an instant and place himself in exactly the right position to get the complete picture in one shot. This was very necessary for nocturnal work because the flash invariably alerted the protagonists.

He remembered Helena from the topping out ceremony because he had taken an instant dislike to her. Pellicci was a homophobe and her oestrogen count was so low he suspected she was a transsexual. He was deeply suspicious of sex change because it put his nose out of joint.

Helena told him the same lie she had told Camb, but he was onto her immediately. 'I can let you see the proofs but they're £50 a copy.' He guided his forelock into the general mop but it sprang back.

'How much?' Helena was outraged.

Pellicci took out a comb and scrupulously straightened his thick head of greasy hair, 'Take it or leave it.'

'Take it,' said Helena. 'Only if I can see all the negatives.'

'Come back in an hour.'

* * *

Chris and the girl who had been talking to Dorothea Waddingham hit it off. She was a soft looking girl with vengeful eyes.

'What brings you here?' asked Chris.

'Parental duty,' she complained. 'You.'

'The same.' said Chris. 'Who are your parents?'

'The Mayor and his wife. Yours?'

'Ian and Helena Black.'

'Who are they?'

'The pair in the middle, up on the stage, the bald man with the tan and the lady with the vivid hair.'

'The queen bitch is your mother?' she exclaimed.

'You don't like her?'

'Who could like her?' observed the girl unapologetically. 'Do you?'

'Not much, no.'

35

They laughed and their relationship was underway. It was a good coupling because they shared so many traits. Both of them were inept at dealing with the opposite sex, both assumed they would never find a suitable partner and both had serious psychological problems.

'I'm Chris.'

'Katy.'

'It's funny that we've not met before.'

'Is it?'

They talked easily, shutting out the hordes and ceremony going on around them, until Chris caught sight of his brother out of the corner of his eye. His intuitive skills were well in advance of his mother's and once his interest was aroused he was unable to contain it. Despite having the moment of his life to date, his desperation to satisfy his curiosity overrode his pleasure. He continued talking to the girl but the need pulled at him. He was a fish caught on the line and the need to know was reeling him in.

Torn between not wanting to spoil the flow and curiosity was teasing, torturing. He could not have been more uncomfortable if he was bursting for a pee and too embarrassed to ask to use the toilet.

Katy sensed his discomfort and came to his rescue. 'I think I'd better check if my mother could use some help with the tea.'

Chris had already worked out where he could see what was going on, pushed his way to the toilets at the rear of the church and nipped into the spare cubicle. He put the lid down, stood on the pan and carefully opened the window. In the gap he could look down onto the parked car beneath and could see his brother's bare bum pumping and a pair of spread legs, but no matter what angle he tried her face was hidden from his view. He gauged that might be possible from the other cubicle.

* * *

Emma and Ben had a summer house installed at the bottom of the garden. Jessica and Helena followed suit. The children used these summer houses to play in the holidays and no girl who came to play stayed without being relieved of her clothing. Gideon made sure of that and Christopher liked to watch.

* * *

The other stall was vacant. Chris waited until the coast was clear before changing cubicles. He found the seat cover already down and the window already open. He realised that the other user had not flushed. Was he also spying on the lovers? He raised himself slowly up to transom height and saw the woman reaching the edge of her climax. She grabbed hold of the straps either side of the seat and raised her loins to allow easier action. It was done and Chris went back into the main hall of the church. He searched for the girl and found her coming back inside having taken some air. They found a quiet corner before speaking.

'Your brother is shagging the vicar's wife in the car park.'

'I know.'

The photographer had got the picture through the toilet window and was deliberating whether to show it to the androgynous woman. All that hooey about lost property, she was after the lowdown on the vicar's wife. He scanned through his negatives with his loupe and found the snap that alerted him to the liaison and made a print. He would let her have that copy for £50. If she wanted the explicit picture he could ask ten times that amount.

Helena paid £250 for a shot of the vicar's wife with her skirt hoisted but the man had his back to the camera and a tattoo of a pansy on his backside. Helena was outraged that the vicar's wife would have sex with a man sporting a tattoo.

It was her civic duty and when he got home that night she showed the picture to Ian and he took over the affair. Dorothea went home to her mother in Colchester and Ian promised the details would go no further.

'The vicarage will be a bachelor pad,' said Ian attempting to lighten the moment.

The Reverend said a prayer of thanks for salvation and added an addendum, thankful that their marriage was childless.

'What do you expect from an Essex girl?' Helena pointed out to her coterie, and made another stronger point of how she had been right all along.

The mystery of the knickers in the font was not satisfactorily resolved but speculation continued long after the separation. The identity of the tattooed man remained known to everyone but the Blacks. Gideon visited Dorothea at her mother's home but the excitement was gone. He stopped responding to her calls and soon they stopped coming.

A faction continued to suspect Gideon of placing the underwear in the font, but the fact was known only to the prankster. The photographer had taken the picture he sold to Helena from the cubicle window, but the man Chris heard leave the toilets was Reverend Waddingham. He spotted Gideon discover the knickers in his trouser pocket, look round for somewhere to dump them and choose the collection tray. Waddingham rescued the lingerie and put them in the font. It was he that had been on the sanctuary during the celebrations. That is why nobody present noticed anything unexpected.

* * *

Outwardly he seemed such a nice young man, but Gideon was in trouble again and Helena insisted Ian take a firm hand. Ian was being forced by his errant son down an unacceptable path.

Throughout his career, Ian had been called upon and had made some tough decisions. Dealing with Gideon, out of context, rendered him totally inadequate. He was used to dealing with the theoretical, face to face with the delinquent he was at a loss.

'What am I to do with you?'

Gideon glared at him but remained steadfastly silent. It was the emotional overtones that were undermining his judgement and suppressing his vocabulary.

Ian was seen by his contemporaries as man of honour and integrity, power and influence. He prided himself on his scruples. He would never contemplate using his power and influence to further his own career. His son's depravity was forcing his hand and he had to avail himself to reciprocations for past favours.

Lack of schooling had prevented Helena maturing beyond a playground mentality, neither has Ian, for an entirely different set of circumstances. These regressions may have accounted for the neat jigsaw that had become their relationship, that and the tenuous exercise of growing (up) together.

Thirty years ago an innocent stepped through the doors of

that damned institution referred to as the Home Office. This naive, fresh faced lad with a clump of badly cut hair, sensible shoes and a Union Jack tattooed on his heart was determined to sell his soul to the company.

Ian was blessed with good fortune. Not many of us are allowed to find our true niche. He was born to be of Civil Service. Fastidious, well prepared, an adept administrator, he thrived on the prosaic missives. His vocabulary was ambiguous and pragmatic, his demeanour was understated and bland and he kept his tie on while mowing the lawn.

Starting as a dogsbody, ingenuously, bodily and doggedly he climbed the ladder, reaching a level of self-assurance whereby he responded to memoranda with a modicum of wit. His first senior post was secretary to the Junior Minister, John Hay, who was spoken of as a man of potential and a future First Lord of the Treasury.

They worked well together. Hay was a thoroughbred charger, he galloped full tilt at the subject but Ian reined him in. They were principled men and they slipped into a working rapport that extended beyond the tainted walls of the mausoleum where justice was dispensed with.

At the next General Election, Hay's Party was ousted, but Ian made a giant leap. He became a force to be reckoned with. He had power and kudos, honours were a formality. Some day he might be Sir Ian Black. It had a formidable ring, it had gravitas.

Ian Black was orthodox. He did everything by the book. Suits were navy, shirts were white, sensible shoes were black. One walked in hiking boots, mowed the lawn in wellingtons and sandals were for holidays. He was one of those cowardly men who hid behind being laid back and only expressed their true feelings when pushed into a corner. Ian was particularly adept at side-stepping confrontation. It was Ian's most abiding trait that after three decades and three re-housings in the Home Office, wallowing in the excrement of human life, he remained unsullied. He was as callow as the day he entered those grim portals. Calumny remained a sort of fiction that existed on paper. He did not meet with the criminal classes. He somehow did not believe they were truly English. They were faceless *Daily Mail* visions, cloaked in black, wearing broad brimmed hats, and inhabited a nether world somewhere near Glasgow. Minor misdemeanours, like drunk and disorderly, he associated with kilts. There were rules and rules were to be obeyed. Those that broke the rules had to be punished. So it was written.

'Have you any idea how humiliating it was being confronted by that man over his pregnant daughter? Sixteen years old. You will have to pull up your socks my boy.'

Gideon groaned

'What am I to do? What do you suggest?'

'Beats me,' said Gideon.

He got his boy a post in the Hertfordshire County Prosecution Service in the hope that the sober surroundings would guide him in the proper parameters of acceptable behaviour.

Chapter Seven

Ian walked down Great Smith Street clutching his umbrella tightly to counteract the wind that tried to wrestle it free. He liked to use the time walking from Victoria Station to the office to think through his problem for the day but his battle with the wind was disturbing his concentration. The file on his desk related to an immigrant from Somalia who claimed deportation would result in torture and death. Ian was troubled by the veracity of his evidence. He had a problem with citizens of Somalia. Their baby face features contrasted with their inner man. He would have preferred their hearings to be held in the juvenile courts.

In Ian's opinion, humble of course, of the three homes of the Home Office, Marsham Street was the grandest. He believed that the law and government should be transparent and this was reflected in a glass building. He had not been happy in Queen Anne's Gate, housed in that concrete penis. The design was an easy target for ridicule and gave the wrong image.

He crossed to the main entrance, distracted by his recalcitrant umbrella, he stepped into a puddle and water splashed his socks. Gingerly he descended the gentle slope and, despite his discomfort, got a thrill crossing the threshold. The duty officer gave him a nod and a smile and his chest got that warm feeling. On his way up in the lift he decided on the fate of the Somali in his file. He would have to take one of those tough decisions.

The Home Office, like a married couple, has a public face and a private face. Behind the scenes it is not a marriage made in heaven. Visitors see a great edifice that they suppose houses great works, but the truth and nothing but the truth was another matter. Home Office morale was low. Its working atmosphere was heavily laden with some indefinable yolk. A procession of

Home Secretaries had rolled up their sleeves, promised a new broom and swept all before them. These broom heads had not been suitable, because lurking in unreachable corners was a maleficent sprite. It hid until the pogrom was over, crawled out from under a rock and resumed its mischief.

A new incumbent had the clever idea to demolish and set up Home in shiny new accommodation. Forewarned, the sprites bided their time, lingered in the clothing of the staff and it was not long before the new building was as contaminated as the old buildings had been.

In the 1970s the great architect Basil Spence was called upon to attempt fumigation, designed a hideous cep and the Home Office moved house in 1978. In 2004 they repeated the futility, instructing the architect Terry Farrell. Detractors gave his design the soubriquet, the Ugly Sisters. On dyeline it resembled two glass dumbbells with a slatted concrete bar, dedicated to Fry, Peel and the politically correct Seacole. The public handouts claimed a 'vibrant civic community', open 24/7 with 'pocket parks' and employed 'artists' to find ways of reducing the stark and raising morale.

It was a waste of public money, the sprites returned and morale was as low as ever.

Staff at the Home Office, however well-meaning, were a ragged crew. Whether it was the job that attracts misfits or the job that created these maladjusted no one has had the nous to establish.

Ian remained steadfast and uninfected while those around him suffered contagion.

That from heaven, or near it, pourest thy full heart.

Having remained undefiled for over thirty years, Ian's immune system had been breached. Without realising it, Ian's apostasy had begun some time before, but he had not had the wit to digest the fact. He sat in his office like Gilbert Pinfold, listening, hearing a strange burble from the pipes. Had one of the neighbouring officers left the phone off the hook? He tried to work but the burble would not let him and, search as he might, he could not find the offending source.

'Can you hear that odd noise?'

'What noise?' Lizzie, his PA, asked.

'It's a sort of hum.' They stood ears pricked but the offending murmur eluded her. 'Could it be the telephone?'

'I'll get the engineers to have a look.'

No fault was found but at no time did Ian doubt his sanity. Something was going on, he could not fathom what it was but after thirty years in the same organisation you got a nose for change. A foreign body had got into the goldfish bowl that was the Home Office. What was trapped in the jar? A bee, a wasp or a bluebottle? In view of his seniority, there was no one else with whom he could confide. If there was something afoot that he was not party to, he would lose face in the asking. If he was mistaken and there was nothing afoot, he would be suspected of paranoia, and tittle-tattle spread like wildfire. Worse still, if there was a plot hatching that he was not privy to, that would be total humiliation.

Ian was an innocent, a triumph of the system. He was living proof of the democratic way, ensuring fair play and equality. Here was an unworldly man who had risen to the top of the Home Office tree and remained clean of the ordure around him.

There was no plot but nor was Ian paranoid. The reason for the elusive buzz in the Home Office jam jar was the arrival of Suzanne Marks in the fight against terrorism. Suzanne was a linguist and spoke five European languages, four Arab dialects, Mandarin, Urdu, Hebrew and Latin. It was said that she could conquer a written dialect in under a week and a coded message in a foreign tongue in less than a day.

What was most impressve was that she had free access to Peel, fourth floor. Staff pointed her out and spoke in whispers.

To look at her you would never imagine that she was a linguistic genius, you would expect her to be on the front page of a fashion magazine. Her dazzling smile would make you want to buy, buy, buy. She had dazzled the staff of the Home Office. Buds that had failed to bloom for decades suddenly flowered. Ties, were more colourful, handkerchiefs reappeared in top pockets, carnations in buttonholes. Suzanne was a stunner. Jet black hair down to her shoulders, bright blue eyes, her cheekbones and nose sprinkled with the palest drizzle. She dressed in pastels that set off her eyes and she was as slim as a well written memo.

Lizzie said sardonically, 'Like bees around honey.'

Monty Blewitt, one of the token homosexuals, put it more bluntly, 'Like flies round shit.'

Ian felt the need to for a rebuke and advised Monty to

moderate his language, 'She seems like a nice girl to me and she's rather fetching.'

Monty gave him an old-fashioned look and replied, 'You would,' in a tone he found offensive but let it go at that. He did not puzzle over what Blewitt meant by it for long because he was drawn into the horde of groupies that became the Marks Appreciation Society.

Ian, for no reason he could muster, was overcome with a need to supplement his life. Had the balloon of his brain developed a weak spot? Perhaps years of self-discipline, self-denial and self-sacrifice for his country had taken its toll. He was an expert in the school of management, including self-management, and he could not account for this unexpected blip. He felt no great need to rectify his losses nor anxiety about the sands of time running out. There was no seven year itch nor fourteen nor twenty one year itches. There had been no itch of any kind until now. He had passed the signposts of life without recrimination or flagellation, and he carried on as usual. He had maintained the attitude of a male in his fifth decade since puberty and remained an unlikely mixture of man and boy.

This apostasy was not the abandonment of religion, fence or cause but of his very fabric. It began on the 9:10 to Euston. For years he had caught the 7:05, and this morning his alarm had sounded but he ignored it, simply turned over in bed and fell back to sleep. Helena did not notice the time or Ian's failure to get out of bed when he should. She was busy with the wedding. There was a lot of planning to do and when the planning was complete there was a lot of organising to do.

Michael Eddowes and his wife Celia smiled politely when Helena offered to help with the wedding arrangements.

'That's very nice of you but we have money put by for this occasion.'

'Katherine is our only daughter and we've been looking forward to giving her a big wedding.'

'It's very kind of you, I'm sure we will cope.'

Helena simply did not hear a word they said. It was not as if she ignored their preference to organise their daughter's wedding, after all, they were paying for it. None of these trifles were going to deter Helena Black.

It was part of her grand plan that her son's wedding would be covered by *L-O* or *OK* magazines, for a suitable fee. She would be quite satisfied with a feature in *The Lady* or *Country Life*, but someone had to put Wyford on the map. Helena had subscribed to those magazines since inception and not once had a Wyford nuptial received column space. Leafy suburbs around Wyford had been blessed, but not Wyford. Helena Black was going to stop the rot. She lay beside Ian, oblivious of the time, engrossed in her scheme.

Ian was further delayed by having to print a report written on his home computer. He consigned the report to the recycle bin but had trouble eradicating it completely. It did not do to keep classified information.

The 9:10 had no first class compartment and Ian tried to concentrate on his paperwork, but could not overcome the constant ringing of mobile telephones. Why was it necessary for the ensuing conversations to be roared throughout the carriage at maximum decibels? They should provide separate coaches for the mobile user so that silent passengers could travel in peace. They used to have smoking and non-smoking carriages. There should be mobile user and non mobile user carriages. He must have a word with the Minister on that very subject.

A girl, an obvious girl, picked her way through a maze of legs and took the seat opposite. She knew what she had to offer and she showed it. Trusses of blonde curls billowed around her sweet face, a low cut blouse revealed ample breasts, a short bomber jacket with a badge on the lapel and tight black jeans that clung to her unusually long legs.

Ian could not make out the wording on the badge but was mesmerised by the breasts. Unblemished, creamy white, bulging, voluptuous, he longed to touch one, if only for an instant. What had come over him? This sort of impulse was totally out of character, but it would not be denied. He stared and stared like a cat seeing a dish of thick, luscious milk on a window sill, but there was no way inside. She saw him gawping at her and pulled a face which he translated as disapproval. Blushing hot he returned to his paperwork, furtively his eyes returned to that considerable cleavage. She raised her book to eye level and screened his view of her chest.

Pretending to concentrate on his work he scrutinised what bits he could see and wondered why he had never possessed such a desirable object. He could not recall having wanted to possess a desirable object. Attractive women troubled him, he was intimidated by their beauty.

Why now? Why today?

It was inexplicable. Was it to do with power?

There was a rumour that the Prime Minister was contemplating some revolutionary legislation and that his name was on the short list to organise it. If he was appointed to this job surely a knighthood would follow. Would he then be afforded squire privileges? He would order this girl to...

To what?

Go with him to a hotel. Why had the girl looked at him so disapprovingly? Probably his age was against him.

When Helena and he had married they bought a one bedroom flat on the edges of the notorious West Wyford Council Estate. Ian got his car serviced by his next door neighbour, Dennis Sparrow. Dennis' customers parked in every available space and the street was strewn with vehicles in disrepair. Nobody complained because Dennis was a sweet man who looked after his elderly mum. Everybody in the street took their cars to him to be serviced.

Dennis was a small man in his forties with twinkling sad eyes and black grease in every nook and wrinkle. He spoke, bemused, with a castrato voice somewhere in the region of alto.

When Ian and Helena moved into the leafy suburbs they took their car to the local garage owned by Reg Wellbelove, a burly man with an RAF moustache and a voice register down in the baritones.

Ian, the raconteur, dined out on these two men and the gamut of their speaking scale. Some years later he bumped into Dennis in the High Road and Dennis' speaking voice was normal.

His voice had broken.

Ian was over fifty years old and the puberty long arrived in his genitals had finally reached his brain.

Ian's limited imagination made its way slowly up the girl's leg with her tight jeans removed. He made it safely past her knees but when he got to her hips, a strange and unfamiliar feeling stirred in his trousers. It stirred with startling vehemence and he had to adjust his brief case to conceal the fact.

What if he was able to tell this girl that he was 'Sir' Ian Black? Would she be impressed? Would she throw herself at his feet? She might.

This question and others like it were regularly disturbing his equilibrium and no matter what remedies he tried he could not shake them off. He had read somewhere that bromide was the appropriate drug or the taking of cold baths. That would not do, the cure was worse than the disease.

When the train arrived at Euston, Ian got a last look at her glorious cleavage, and saw that she was reading a book called *The Well of Loneliness* by a man named Radclyffe Hall, which meant nothing to him. He followed her along the platform to the Underground, his eyes glued to her gyrating bottom, but she strode nimbly through the crowd and was gone.

In thirty years, Ian had not considered there might be a social life attached to a job in the Home Office and if there was he was not aware of it. He was not an advocate of dissipation, the job came first and it did not do to be seen in public houses consorting with your juniors. Apart from his squash league, cricket and football he was not an enthusiast of extra-curricular activities. He did not miss a Wyford FC home game and he sometimes arranged his travelling diary to be in the vicinity of the occasional away match. This was as corrupt as he could manage.

Ian's life was the job and vice versa. It came before his wife and children. He had ignored them until they showed an interest in cricket and only took them with him when they were old enough not to be a nuisance. Do not get the idea that Ian was a ruthless and determined man. He was a considerate, well meaning fellow but the job came first.

Mornard had walked off with the Fineman file and Ian intended finishing his report before he went home. He found Mornard in the Dog & Duck with a clutch of other men in a half circle around Miss Marks and her chaperone. It was more evidence of how out of touch Ian was, because standing alongside Miss Marks was Lizzie, his PA.

Lizzie was a pale, severe girl with her hair tied back and a suit with badges on the lapel; a metal brooch in the shape of a pink ribbon, a Union Jack pin and a white button with the inscription, 'Say No'. Miss Marks had the same badges in her own lapel. Ian had not thought to inquire what the badges implied and made a mental note to do so.

'Excuse me, Mornard, have you got a moment?'

Accosting Mornard caused a chortle of good natured merriment and he was prevented from his purpose with an introduction to the new translator.

'Suzanne, this is Ian Black. He is one of the Permanent Secretaries and Lizzie's boss.'

He was gently encouraged to shake hands but was unreasonably reluctant to touch this apparition. Her hand felt as sensual as gossamer floating and this touch, erotically ephemeral, punctured his long standing stoicism.

'Ian, you must stay for one drink,' Mornard insisted good-naturedly. 'All work and no play, old man. What will you have?'

Befuddled, Ian's brain had switched into neutral.

'What are you drinking? Gin and tonic?'

'I'll have the same,' said Ian and added hastily, 'without the gin.'

This caused further amusement, but neither girl joined in the laughter.

He sipped his drink and waited his chance to collect the file and go. The girl they were admiring scared him to death. He could barely confront such beauty without wanting to run away and hide.

How did men cope with such women?

It was that question that created further discord in his brain. Miss Marks had an alarming effect on the Home Office population. Since she had arrived on the scene, crabs and snails emerged from their shells.

He retrieved the file, went back to the office but could not concentrate on his work. The girl's image haunted him and more to the point, the look of utter disdain she gave him when they were introduced, played over and over in his mind. Her eyes had flitted, up and down, tip to toe and summed him up in a flash.

'You are invisible.'

In his private moments, Ian saw himself as a man of substance, dynamic, a man to be reckoned with but mostly dynamic. If he had chosen to go into the private sector he would be a Chief Executive earning seven figures, with a yacht and a villa on the Costa Brava. This slip of a girl looked at him as though he was nothing, less than nothing, and he needed to know why.

Chapter Eight

Helena had opened a new scrapbook for the forthcoming wedding. She had searched through back copies of her magazines and cut out everything that took her fancy. She had prepared a guest list, a table plan and rang various halls in the area to check on availability. She had priced cake suppliers, car hire companies, dressmakers, printers for invitations, florists, hairdressers, a favour shop, dress wear hire suppliers, caterers and Mr Crook, the master of ceremonies. As far as she could make out she had left nothing to chance, nor had she conferred with the Eddowes on any of these topics.

'Pamela, it's me, Helena. Guess whose wedding will be the first in the new St Marks Church?'

'Is Gideon going to marry that girl?'

'What girl?' Helena demanded.

Pamela, hearing Helena's angry tone saw that she had made a *faux pas* and nimbly covered her tracks. 'That pretty girl from the chemist. I saw them in town together.'

'Her?' Helena derided. 'That sluttish girl with the enormous chest, I hardly think so. No, it's Christopher, he's engaged to the Mayor's daughter.'

'Katy? How wonderful.' Pamela wiped the perspiration from her top lip with a tissue. 'You must be pleased for him.'

Helena hesitated, wanting to answer but unable to locate one. 'It's so exciting, the first recorded wedding in the new church. It's an honour.'

'I'll say,' said Pamela. 'When's the big day?'

The couple had not set a date but she was going to have a June wedding. It was the only possible month for weddings, only the choice of hall was causing her some concern. Ian wanted the Oddfellows Hall but Helena was not sure it was suitable.

'Do you think the Oddfellows Hall would be a good venue?'

Pamela felt awkward, not wanting to set off her friend's wrath, she was loathe to reveal her true feelings, in case they conflicted. 'It could be very nice with the right trimmings.'

'I think the place is a bit dour, don't you agree?'

'A bit dour, yes,' said Pamela biting her upper lip and crossing her fingers.

'Couldn't you be a tad more definite?'

'Dour? Yes, OK for banquets and Ladies' Nights but a wedding requires an upbeat atmosphere. The Copse Hotel has a choice of halls.'

'So it does. Would you come with me and view?'

'I'd be happy to,' said Pamela. 'Wouldn't it be more appropriate to go with Celia?'

'Bah!' said Helena and hung up.

One thing was for sure, the bride was not suitable being the size she was. How could she subtly get Chris to induce the girl to go on a diet or take some exercise? Any device that might help her shed a few pounds. She telephoned the leisure centre and struck a deal for six months' membership, gave her name as Katherine Eddowes and the Mayor's address.

* * *

The Dog & Duck was an anachronism. It had not changed since the Second World War and therefore had what the guide books referred to as atmosphere. It reminded Ian of the Olde Curiosity Shoppe, bottle end glass in the bay window, dust on the wine bottles, nicotine stained ceilings and welcoming doors. The landlord was a simple man of simple pleasures and there were no frills on tap. No sport, no music, no food that did not come out of a packet pinned to a sheet of cardboard. The Dog & Duck was considered to be unpretentious and served a good drop.

Ian stood slightly back among the men encircling Miss Marks and her unprepossessing friend, Lizzie. Ian noted that her eyes were watery as if on the edge of tears.

Why was she so sad, he wondered?

Lizzie Borden was in love, it was the unrequited variety.

Lizzie was a thirty four year old spinster, a frequent visitor to the Tate Modern, an active member of the First Church of Christian Science (Boston, Mass.) located in Luton, a Sunday School Teacher, supporter of the Luton Temperance League and was saying 'No' to sex before marriage.

Her parents, particularly her mother, were a constant embarrassment. Her stepfather wore a pony tail and a Luton Town FC shirt. Her mother emanated from a long line of Royalists dating as far back as that scoundrel Cromwell. Her grandmother was pressing her nose to the railings of Buck House the day that Queen Elizabeth II was born, her mother, at her grandmother's knee, was in the same spot on Coronation Day 1953. She got soaked through that day and developed weak lungs, suffering annual bouts of pleurisy. Undeterred by this minor setback, she was again at the family spot on the eve of Charles' wedding to Diana. She could be seen every summer, Centre Court at Wimbledon, floppy hat, Union Jack on a stick, alongside a quartet of women similarly attired, waving frantically every time a Brit won a point. Lizzie often saw her mother picked out by the television cameramen and peeped agonisingly through the gaps of her fingers.

'Do you have any questions for us?'

'Yes,' she said, but dared not ask.

Lizzie Borden was interviewed by a committee for the job as PA to a 'Chief Exec', 'Director General' or 'Permanent Sec'. It was not customary for there to be more than one Permanent Secretary in any government department but in a previous administration the new Home Secretary and his guide dog detected the negative smells that polluted the HO halls. He demanded the assistance of a Chief Executive from his previous portfolio who was duly promoted to Permanent Secretary.

On the advice of a consultancy, the current Permanent Secretary, Crest Mornington, had been brought in from the outside. The Director General, who had been passed over, took early retirement and published a scornful autobiography. Top advisers warned the Home Secretary that the appointment of another gate-crasher was not good for morale. To placate the rabble Director General Black was uplifted to Permanent Secretary in charge of Immigration.

Helena did not care for Ian's new title. Permanent Secretary did not sound as impressive as Director General. She would not be pacified until Ian explained that the post of PS carried an automatic knighthood. It was just a matter of time serving and good behaviour.

Lizzie had been appointed to the HO at a similar meeting six years before and consigned to the typing pool. It took five members of the Human Resources section to get it wrong. One digit of this handful spotted the scar on Lizzie's upper lip. It was the result of surgery to rectify a hair lip. This diligent lady detected a nasal twang intimating that there had also been a cleft palate and bragged of her cleverness at seeing what the others had not. That the other four accepted her observations without question was daunting and that they formed a consensus based on the insinuation that because she had been born with these defects she must therefore be a gibbering idiot was more daunting. One of the men lived in Watford and the fact that she came from Luton worked against her.

'Why is the system propped up by meetings?'

'Such as this one?'

She studied the potpourri of fragrant men and women opposite and wondered what they would like to hear. 'Would I receive instruction in the correct approach to working with so important a personage?'

Lizzie sensed an instantaneously favourable response. Her question gave the committee a frisson of self-regard. Choosing the help for a big knob was a weighty task.

'Yes, you will shadow Elvira Barney for a week. She has years of experience.'

'I notice you have not inquired about the supplement to your salary.'

Lizzie knew the rate paid to PAs working for Permanent Secretaries but said, 'I was more attracted by the challenge than the pay increase.'

'Is that all?' Ms Thompson inquired of her and checked with the committee either side. Everyone nodded in agreement. That was all. It was a consensus. They would wait for the door to close behind her, voice their opinions, minutes would be taken and another meeting arranged for the near future.

Lizzie was a resilient young woman and, being pragmatic, she accepted the system. If she was to get a position suitable to her capabilities she must find a way. She must overcome an institution prone to pigeon hole. It took a sledge hammer to undo these punitive assumptions. The majority of those employed in Human Resources were women who had learned little from their subjugation prior to emancipation and did not treat their fellow females with anything approaching equanimity.

She was not surprised or disappointed by the chauvinism of the rest of her sex. It was simply the way the system worked as exemplified by the inherent and unshakeable bigotry rife in the police force. Despite fifty years' reflection on racism, the lionising of Martin Luther King and Nelson Mandela, the black population were still treated with suspicion and regarded as jungle bunnies.

As for the police officers on this particular topic they did not let a day go by without exposing their hypocrisy. A road block was set up on the M1 to apprehend possible IRA or Arab terrorists and of the first hundred vehicles apprehended, sixty-four were driven by West Indians who later declared by the Police Commissioner to be Rastafarian Moslems or Black Irish. Since De Menezes, the Commissioner was safe in the knowledge that the police could do almost anything to 'coloureds' aka terrorists and no heads would roll.

When Lizzie was accepted into Home Office employment, her mother was prouder than Punch's nose. She even gave up *Coronation Street* to sit with her at supper and listen to her daily news.

'Are there lots of typists?'

'A few,' said Lizzie.

'Have you made any friends?'

'Nothing to write home about,' said Lizzie.

Her mother was like most mothers, a celebrity freak, and got a vicarious thrill from the possibility that she had passed the Home Secretary in the corridor.

'What's he like?'

'What you would expect.'

'Does he have presence?'

Lizzie conjured a memory of the Minister, a saturnine squirt with shadowy eyes and a surly temper. He had a premature white streak in his wavy hair and a yellow streak down the seam and slit of his pinstripe jacket.

'When he puts in an appearance he does create an atmosphere.'
'I'd so love to meet him,' said Mrs Borden with a faraway look. 'Does the Prime Minister ever visit?'
'No,' said Lizzie. 'We go to him, he doesn't come to us.'
'Of course,' said Mrs Borden gravely.

The majority of Lizzie's fellow typists took minutes while occupying their minds with the more pertinent aspects of their lives; shopping, fetching, organising children and the evening meal. Reams and reams of HMSO paper were filled with arcane subject matter that was often confined to the shelves.

Nothing in Lizzie's genes was likely to breed an insurgent but she was not conventional in the formalised and rigorous conventions of a government typist. She listened to the content of her dictation.

She was alarmed by the number of meetings required to make a decision, let alone get any tangible work done, and on many occasions where a decision was taken, another party who was not present at the meeting would read the minutes, find a flaw, report back and the whole cycle would start over.

This was not Lizzie's own discovery, Parkinson got in first, some time ago.

Having got past the awestruck phase of her new position Lizzie gained confidence in her own abilities and allowed her regard for her fellow workers, peers or seniors, to find its level.

'It is a fairground ride,' she told her mother with a mouthful of cottage pie. 'You climb aboard, have a meeting, decide to meet again, climb aboard, have another meeting, no decision is reached, arrange another meeting and so on and so on. The only consensus is the joy of setting a future date.'

Mrs Borden was concerned that her daughter's cynicism would get noticed and she would be released. 'They must know what they're doing. They are cream of the country.'

Lizzie discerned the worry in her mother's tone and let the subject drop.

Having spent six months on the first floor of Fry Block she decided it was enough time to be vegetating and applied for a vacancy on the second floor. It was not customary to succeed first time out and following her third interview she climbed the extra flights assigned to an Ian clone in his sixth year of employment working on Prison Building. Sidney Fox, a mother's boy, was proceeding suitably along the Civil Service path, albeit at a snail's pace.

Sidney was a quivering mass of uncertainty and dithered over the wording of letters and reports. Lizzie could not be bothered with his problems, without reference to him edited the letters and reports as she typed. He did not spot these refinements but the upper echelons did.

He was summoned by Ian Black CB to explain himself. Uncertain, Fox quivered so ferociously his innards turned to jelly and he stumbled up four flights to the executive toilets. There he deposited his lunch, followed by his last evening's meal and a good deal of bile. Bile was what he was expecting to be replenished in the impending interview.

To his utter astonishment he was not bollocked but praised for the upturn in the standard of his output. Upon re-reading his reports and letters he could not grasp what the fuss was about. He discussed the interview with his mother and she provided the explanation.

'You have been editing my work,' he confronted Lizzie, using his umbrella as a shield. 'I..I...don't let it happen again, or...or..'

'You read it before it goes out,' Lizzie accused. 'You get plenty of opportunity to change it back.'

'I want this to stop as of now,' he waved the umbrella's spike vaguely in her direction.

Following the days of his rebuke, Sidney wrote everything out in longhand, submitted his paperwork to his mother for proofing before giving Lizzie dictation. His mother was good but she did not have the pithy *mort d'esprit* that Lizzie was blessed with. There began a daily bickering, as Lizzie suggested a tweak here and there but our CS fledgling wanted to keep it in the family.

It was a late Friday evening when a difference of opinion got overheated and Lizzie overstepped acceptable bounds.

'Sidney,' she told him, 'you're a wimp.'

It was difficult to contradict what he was well aware of, but Sidney did so to save face. 'You've gone too far this time. I will be reporting you to Mrs Barney.'

If it had been before 5:30 she would have been sent home early.

She spent a fretful weekend composing an apology, altering, tippexing and grovelling lower and lower. On Monday she was resigned, there was no possible alternative. She had broken the typist's code. She would be asked to leave.

'Good morning,' Sidney muttered almost inaudibly, placing handwritten work on her desk with a post-it note demanding TYPE AS WRITTEN, PLEASE.

This foolishness continued for a week and a half with Lizzie anxiously waiting for the chop, when on the second Wednesday she was summoned by a call from Human Resources. If it was not the sack then she was bound to be downgraded and have wasted ten months of diligence.

Human Resources were quite unemotional and told her to report to the third floor of Peel Block. She was temporarily seconded to Felix Mornard on a trial basis and if she proved satisfactory the move might become permanent. That is how Lizzie learned a mandatory rule of the public sector. If you want to get rid of someone who is making a nuisance of themselves get them promoted out of your hair.

Chapter Nine

Prior to Miss Marks, Ian had two lives, work and home. The differential between the two was becoming less defined, the subject of his conversation less random. Ian enjoyed being the centre of attention, he had plenty to tell and plenty he could not, the latter often added a mystique to his personality. He quoted the Official Secrets Act and obeyed it to the letter and beyond. He would fish with his audience, attaching bits of bait and flicking them into the pond. The catch was that there was no catch. He would make a grave face, purse his brown, bland features and sigh, then he would confess.

'Sorry, I cannot reveal more.'

'It's *prima facie*.'

'It's not in the public interest, etcetera.'

Ian thought it best to leave them hanging.

Left hanging and not in possession of the facts did not prevent his audience expressing their views. Ian applied alternative ploys to cope with these misguided notions depending on the rhetoric it was couched in. For those who moderated their words, he tapped the side of his nose, for the more vehement he smiled beatifically with galling condescension.

Helena revelled in these confidences. She would corroborate Ian's brevity with a sweetly superior smile, when in truth she was as much in the dark as everybody else. Ian did not confide in her on any subject to do with work, especially the more formidable aspects. She could not be trusted.

It could not be denied that mixing in heady circles at the nub of power had turned his head. He had a tendency to be pompous, brought on by his wife's interjections, and he had also come to believe that he was the most interesting person present. This was not altogether his fault either. In this celebrity obsessed society, dining with a CB gave a person some self-worth and fellow diners lapped it up. At the drop of a hat he would hold court until home time. Nobody seemed to mind, in fact the opposite was true. He was treated with respect, a reverence he relished, and his audience hoped to vicariously imbue some kudos.

You could hear them at the office on Monday, 'I had dinner with someone high up in the government and he told me...'

Everybody, that is, except his brother. Dining out with John Hay, Ian's brother Duncan excused himself to use the washrooms. A diner eating at the adjacent table returned from the toilet to announce to his party that there was a man sitting in a stall with the door open reading *The Guardian*.

'I asked what he was doing and he said, my brother bores for England.'

Becoming a drinking pal brought a conflict that Ian, steeped in the status quo, struggled to rationalise. There was the alcoholic camaraderie, which he liked, but losing inhibition brought a familiarity from his fellow drinkers that he did not. He was sharing an involuntary secret, an unspoken nod of acquiescence and a wink that cut the legs from under his seniority. Of the men encircling Miss Marks he was the most senior, by sharing his social time with lesser mortals he was undermining his position. It did not do to be commonplace with someone you had to give orders to or reprimand. From the outset he made it a point not to patronise or prevail upon his work force. He was fortunate to be more able than they were and by virtue of his position and CB had no need to establish his authority.

Another aspect of the drinking culture with which Ian was awkward was the morning after inquest. These phoney theatrics ate into his best hours of output. He dare not leave his room for fear of being accosted at morning coffee to be told exaggerated tales of consumption and hangover. Depending on the age of the story teller the slang varied but the details were essentially the same.

' Whatdyamacallit got pissed...'

'... got wasted.'

'... got blind.'

Whoever was chosen to be the worse for wear would be the

butt for tiresome, supposedly amusing asides that were repeated over and over until the pubs opened and the cycle began again.

Ian was careful not to be in the limelight as a result of drunken reverie. He did not come close to getting wasted, blind or worse for wear. While the others were 'swilling it down' he watched Miss Marks, quiet and diffident, a classic painting in a gallery where a crowd of admirers gathered, silently taking her in. Every man that entered the Dog & Duck, dog or duck, eventually caught sight of her and stared hungrily, longing for a bone or any crumb of comfort.

Ian had a secret he filed away with his personal Official Secret folio. It was not a dark secret and to call it 'dingy' would contrive a connotation that it did not deserve. He firmly believed that no other person was privy to this peccadillo and it was the only skeleton in his cupboard. Ian was infatuated with his sister-in-law Pauline. It was a mild form of puppy love, restricted to yearning from discreet distances. The closest he came to confessing his rapture was on the dance floor on Ladies' Night.

'You look extremely fetching,' he told her.

'Does your brother fancy me?' Pauline asked Duncan.

'He's in love with you,' said Duncan. 'From the first moment he laid eyes on you, just like I was.'

'Can you ever be serious?'

'I'm deadly serious.'

When Ian became a Permanent Secretary he gained confidence enough to pursue a whim or two. He intended to invite Pauline to lunch but to balance matters, he invited Duncan first. He introduced him to Lizzie, showed him around the new building and treated him to a decent meal. There was no mockery or squabble and they parted company on good terms for once. Duncan gave him a lift in his taxi, dropped him outside the House of Commons.

Pauline was shown into his office, wearing a linen jacket, pink top, white skirt and open toed shoes. Her toenails were not painted and curiously Ian felt more drawn to her than ever. He kissed her soft cheek and drank in Chanel No 5. They ate in a secluded corner of his favourite Italian and between each mouthful she mocked him, pricked his balloons in a way he interpreted as affectionate. He watched each forkful enter her mouth and imagined his own mouth pressed to hers, softer than her silky cheek. Could he say something that would draw him to her?

'You look extremely fetching, my dear,' he said, knowing the 'my dear' blew it but keen to give his usual compliment an extra kick.

He was told that women were attracted to the rich and powerful. What was it he could say that would turn her head?

'I'm rich and powerful' sounded a trifle conceited so he told her about the job with its customary butter fingered name dropping.

Self-consciously she leaned forward and whispered, 'What is Number 10 like, you know, inside?'

'Magnificent,' he glowed, but stumbled on inadequate adjectives, traversing a chasm between extravagance and hyperbole, failing miserably to impart the grandeur of the building. He had recently been honoured with an audience with the Queen and from his faltering descriptions of Buckingham Palace Pauline pictured tawdry salons adorned with bling.

He fluffed it as usual, made do with a parting kiss on the cheek and a promise of doing it again. She gave no indication that she had feeling for him, base or otherwise. Having her to himself for an hour or two felt good, for those brief moments she belonged to him. He was grateful to have a job so demanding that it filled the spaces of his mind. If he dwelt on his thwarted emotions he might go insane.

* * *

Lizzie did not realise what she had gotten into until Ian's heart appeared on his sleeve. His obvious attraction to Suzanne hurt, disappointed and clutched her vitals with every reminder. On top of this pain was the undeniable flaunting of her sacred vows, overnight from anchoress to anchorless.

She had adopted the mode of a nun, without habit or wimple. Now she was riddled with guilt and shame for her feelings. Feelings that had crept up behind, stabbed her in the back and penetrated her heart. Sentiments that magnified into love, love because it was involuntary, was all the more powerful.

'Unrequited love is a bore,' she confessed.

'I don't want him,' said Suzanne offensively implying she might check the soles of her shoes for more offending ordure.

'You don't know him,' Lizzie defended. 'He's a sweet and decent man.'

'If you say so,' Suzanne barely concealed her doubt. Men were lascivious bestial creatures, snake charmers with fetid souls. If the deity created life in its own image there was no question in her mind. 'It has to be.'

'What has to be?' said Lizzie expecting affirmation of her heart's mischief.

'God is a woman,' said Suzanne.

Lizzie was disappointed but unsure for what cause. Was it her friend's blinkered self-involvement? She preferred God to be a man. That way if she deviated from the ascetic straight and narrow it would be more forgivable for the adjudicator to be male. No man could truly be without sin and her moment of lapse would merely be a step to evening up the balance.

Later that day, after she had more time to think, she dismissed Suzanne's polemic as a foolish dream. A woman would not own the temerity or conceit required to restrict the commandments to just ten. Nor, for the same reasons, could a woman create the first commandment. Most of the other nine were designed to keep the male population on the straight and narrow.

'A lot of good it's doing.'

Lizzie was a great believer in the axiom that it takes one to know one.

Well-endowed in the wiles of her sex, cunning and deviousness, Lizzie was fortunate to be able to combine these with imagination and patient methods of implementation. She set about getting her maiden's prayer answered and her first ploy was to unsettle her man.

Chapter Ten

Ian was misplaced in the etiquette of pub going. It was outside his experience. He knew how to wine and dine in the flesh pots but public houses were seedy places inhabited by junior staff. Wine bars were a cut above.

Ian went to work, he went home and Helena arranged his social life. Ian did not segment his existence into private or public, his job was sacred and the bits in between were therapy to enable him in his work.

He had not interacted with his fellow men since university. He liked and respected his peers, he would count John Hay MP amongst his friends but there was no emotion involved. These men were attributes picked up on the way to the top.

Did he care for his family?

'Of course,' he told himself confidently, without being totally sure.

His sister-in-law Pauline aroused more sentiment within him than Helena. Did he care for his parents? Would his life be any different if they were gone? His sons were a mixed blessing. Chris was a sound fellow, he could rely on Chris, but Gideon was a bolt from the blue. Where did he come from? His every action was a trial of his father's patience.

Did he love his family? Was there a thing called love? Ian believed 'Love' to be a word people said that was as ephemeral and insubstantial as 'Heaven' or 'Hell'. It was a politeness like 'Hello' or 'Goodbye' that formed part of coming and going.

Ian's reputation amongst his colleagues was of rigid adherence to the rules. His unsocial approach was not seen as stand-offish but as dedication to Queen and Country. Ian Black CB was regarded as a fully-fledged company man. Avuncular Ian could have remained unhurt by this lapse, this open-mouthed fascination for this woman but the Home Office was a jealous beast. In fact, the entire judicial system had green eyes of one sort or another.

'Ian, it's your round,' said Mornard.

Previously, Lizzie would bail Ian out of his predicament and place his order for him. Part of her plan was to expose Ian to humiliation and stop pandering.

Ian got out a note out of his purse and turned to hand it to his PA but she had disappeared to the toilet. Gritting his teeth, Ian placed his elbows on the bar and waved his money.

Miss Marks had a taste for fashionable drinks, white wine spritzers, Martini and Russian or Campari and soda. Ian paid for a round and his order never failed to draw a sarcastic comment from the landlord. Any drink other than beer or whisky was worthy of severe derision and had no place in the post war ambiance of the D & D.

Having overcome that hurdle, Ian said with rash self-assurance, 'Two pints of lager.'

'Carling or Heineken?'

'No,' said the bemused Perm Sec, 'lager.'

This *faux pas* was the talk of the HO for years and passed into HO folklore.

Ian was alarmed to discover that his fellow drinkers were not there to admire this beautiful woman but vying with each other in their intention to bed her. Adultery was the province of the unscrupulous, politicians and the like. For heaven's sake it was a commandment in the bible and the bible was one of the few places above the law.

He continued with the evenings at the Dog & Duck long after he got bored with them. Observing his colleagues hiding their lecherous motives behind a mask of bonhomie, compelled by some mysterious need not to miss out when Suzanne chose a beau.

He knew these visits to the pub had damaged him but he could not keep away. He wanted to be there when it happened and vicariously share the lucky man's joy. He had no real expectation that he would be her choice. No one had succeeded as yet and he developed hopes for a late burst, a final surge that would push him to the forefront, if he could just prevent his jaw crashing to the floor whenever Miss Marks addressed him in conversation.

There was another irony that Parkinson would have revelled in. Ian was spending time in the pub that he would have allocated to work but his absences made no difference to his output. His work got done and on schedule.

* * *

'Good evening, old boy,' said Arundel Coke.

Arundel Reppington Beardsley Coke was a typical Home Office misfit, a throwback to the bygone days when Ian first entered the portals. Government then was not open to the modicum of public scrutiny it is today. Senior men were as described in the novels of Ambler and Greene; dry, taciturn, figures of depth and mystery.

Coke, known alternatively as 'Twinkle' or 'Diet' by his younger colleagues was six feet three inches tall, extraordinarily thin, like a stick insect. He always dressed in conservative kit. A navy or grey pinstripe, Eton tie, a bowler hat, inordinately shiny, wizened beetle crushers and he carried a rolled umbrella in all weathers. He had a ruddy complexion, a dark beard where his blunt razor missed its target, and there were tufts of hair on his sore cheekbones.

Arundel had been at the HO a decade longer than Ian but remained at junior level. He was as inept as his pretension to Eton and had attended a small public school in Hastings. He lived a bachelor life in *digs*, a single room in a five storey conversion behind Swiss Cottage, ironically built and owned by the Eton College Trust.

It is a strange quirk of human nature in the world of labour that those promoted off the 'shop floor' suffer amnesia, effective immediately. One day your fellow workers are mates, the next day they are lesser beings. Those that make it to the very top, after they have readjusted the furniture in their new office, go deaf and blind. Unfortunately, they supplement the loss of these senses by finding a new voice and the egg that houses their ego bursts its shell.

64

Of those left in their wake, some fight harder to climb up the greasy ladder, some bide their time, some massage their envy, some rubbish their superiors, most grumble in a monotone. His friendly greeting did not convey the scorn and envy Coke felt for Ian. The same scorn and envy he felt for those who had undeservedly been promoted over him.

'Where was everybody this evening?' Ian listened abstractedly to what Coke had to say, troubled by his lack of condescension and fascinated by the tufts of hair peeking out of the cuffs of his shirt, above his Windsor knot, out of his ears and on his roseate cheeks.

There must have been a change of venue. It did not occur to him that he and Coke had been left out the loop together, that he was being coupled with an established misfit. It was simply a clerical error.

Ian, unable to extricate himself, yearning for the 'crowd' to turn up, half listened to Coke's foolish prattle on how the legal system was failing because the hierarchy were deaf to their grass root employees.

Finding himself trapped, Ian had slumped into a sulk and accepted a drink so as not to look foolish. Coke continually felt impelled to break the silence. Arundel was a sports enthusiast, especially on the art of *fisticuffs* and would bore anyone prepared to listen on a history of boxing.

'I wonder, is there an active Marquis of Queensbury?' Coke wondered, sipping his red wine, toning up his grog blossoms.

'I've no idea,' said Ian petulantly. 'Was there ever such a title? Sounds a likely character you would find in a Sherlock Holmes story.'

'Conan Doyle was a boxing man,' Coke frothed into a bubbly excitement, 'Wrote a novel called *Rodney Stone*, which was based on the gentlemen's art of fisticuffs. Did you know Doyle was a goalie for Portsmouth FC?'

'Portsmouth?' said Ian, 'the premiership team?'

'Yes.'

'Really?' Ian was surprised.

'I wonder how many of the chaps at the office know that about Doyle?'

'My brother was a professional footballer for a time.'

Coke's eyes suddenly coated over with what looked like a gelatinous substance, a sort of cataract. He blinked and his amorphous brown irises were miraculously cleared. He was touched that his senior would confide a family skeleton of this sort.

'A professional footballer,' he sympathised, why the man might have been much worse, a taxi driver or an estate agent. 'Who did he play for?'

'Wyford FC.'

'Not Duncan Black?' Coke began frothing with enthusiasm and Ian swore that the spots on his cheekbones were throbbing faintly like a *son et lumiere*. 'I saw him play.'

Ian searched for an escape route while Coke meandered through a history of individualism in sport, 'Howard Winstone, Terry Allen were stylists and could maintain their individuality....'

Ian slipped in and out, wondering whether the others might show and if not why not.

'...your brother was just such an individual and that was why he did not fit.'

'Sorry?'

'Your brother,' Coke repeated jollily. 'He did not fit because he was too clever for the other players. That does not sit well in British team sports. You notice the commentators on the Rugby often refer to Gallic flair as though it is beyond the pale.'

'I don't care for rugby...'

'Gallic flair and British clog?'

Ian studied his unwanted drinking partner, suspecting he was in the presence of a fifth columnist. His train of thought was diverted by a long forgotten summer's day.

Ian was an above average batsman, a figure of respect in the Pemberton Cricket Club, opening the innings and averaging thirty runs. One sunny Saturday afternoon, Duncan had brought the boys along to watch and three members of the team failed to turn up. The opposing captain agreed for Duncan and his children to make up the numbers. Young John was thirteen and Toby eleven and they came in at the end of the innings when Pemberton were 85 for seven. The two of them put on 60 runs and Duncan, batting at number 11, hit 70 runs in four overs before getting caught on the boundary. To add insult to injury he later found out Duncan had batted left handed.

'If you had been old enough to see the Pegasus football team you would understand what I'm getting at. They were an amateur team of university students who out-thought their opponents. They disappeared when the ruffians took over the sport.'

'Excuse me,' Ian was incredulous. 'We live in a privileged time. Football is the greatest it had ever been.'

Coke was miles away in a dream of a bygone era, 'I rather feel football has become some sort of Pentathlon because it encompasses so many other sports. Greco Roman wrestling, the two footed lunge reminiscent of the luge. I wonder, is luge French for lunge? It might very well be. Then there's diving, calisthenics, climbing, acrobatics, gymnastics, I wonder if, in a few years, there will be any football content left as we know it...'

'I must use the restroom,' said Ian, picking up his briefcase. 'In view of recent controversies, best take this with me.' They laughed knowingly. Instead of using the toilets, Ian sneaked out the side door.

A man who had been eaves-dropping their chat broached Coke and asked him to elaborate on the work ethic prevalent in the Home Office. Coke happily obliged, in some detail. Some months later a treatise was published on the vagaries of the Civil Service system. This article won plaudits throughout the globe for incite. Sir Herbert Smith demanded a search for the mole that had disloyally spilled the beans but his search did not sink as low as the 'shop floor' and Coke was never exposed.

Chapter Eleven

It was Lizzie's idea for the 'crowd' to try a new venue. Ian took care his exclusion should not be repeated and every evening he made sure he was ready to leave at the same time as Lizzie. They walked slowly through the empty streets and talked easily, she of God and he of Ian. One night she persuaded him to forsake the pub and they found a late night café and ordered coffee.

'Suzanne has brought a lot of the old crabs out of their shells,' said Lizzie. 'Rather pitiful, isn't it?'

Ian was uncertain whether he was included amongst the crabs but nodded agreement. 'You'd be amazed, I've known some of these men for thirty years, we've grown up together, so to speak. It just goes to show you really don't know people.'

'Suzanne's a committed Christian,' said Lizzie with unwarranted fervour.

Ian was unclear what he was to make of this, he hoped for more but remained unenlightened.

'Reverend Rais has taken her under wing,' said Lizzie. 'She looks full of confidence but deep down she is in turmoil.'

'Gilles de Rais? St Peter's?'

'You know him?'

'I sat next to him at Lords.'

'Lourdes?'

'That's what I said, isn't it?'

On the train home, papers on his lap, his mind wandered from the page. What had she meant by referring to Miss Marks as a 'Christian' so pointedly? Lizzie's intent, zealous face rose up before him and smiled. Her widened mouth obliterated the scar, the liquid in her eyes dispersed and they shone brightly.

'Fineman is a known reprobate,' he wrote in his precise script.

'His sworn testimony cannot be relied upon. We must search for more conclusive evidence. I suggest that we obtain DNA, otherwise the prosecution's case will be laughed out of court or dismissed on appeal. It is essential for the morale of the HO that we win this difficult case.' Ian was not happy with what he had written. It was informal and not business like. He started to rewrite but the evening intervened.

'I must go,' she had said and placed her hand over his, causing him to swiftly recoil.

At that moment, everything became clear and he understood what she was trying to tell him, that his regard for Miss Marks was reciprocated. He folded away his papers and planned how he could discreetly precipitate the inevitable. If she lived in Berkhamsted she must use the same railway line. What would be more natural than to bump into one another accidentally?

Ian tried every permutation possible but did not catch sight of her, even from a distance. He rotated the train times, he rotated the carriages, he rotated waiting at the underground entrances at Euston, he waited at the top and the bottom of the stairs, he waited at the top and the bottom of the escalator and he stood outside each of the exits at St James Park and Victoria.

Worried that he would lose his chance and that her ardour would fade he decided to take matters into his own hands. He hung around the Dog & Duck, waited for her to leave and followed her. Thankfully she made her way through the streets unaccompanied. At last he was getting lucky.

Despite trying to appear matter of fact, he was unbelievably nervous and as he rushed to keep pace with her he rehearsed what he might say. She scurried into St James Park Station and he followed behind but when he got inside, there was no sign of her. He hesitated, searched about him, concluded she must have continued on to the platform. He made his way below and found the platform empty and the next train due in ten minutes. Hot and flustered he sat on a bench, cooled his head against the cold tiles and closed his eyes. This was getting too much for him. Dainty footsteps came out of the nearby tunnel and turned along the platform away from him. He was going to give up seeking a change and go back to normal. He had his career to think of and did not want to jeopardise his knighthood.

The soft footsteps began pacing back and forth and picking up pace came hurrying to where he was sitting, he opened his tired eyes and came face to face with Miss Marks.

She was clearly angry and none too pretty, 'You pull a stunt like that again and I will report you.' She turned on her heel and marched away.

Seven of the eight pints of Ian's blood thundered into his face so fast he thought he might explode. He cupped his nose to prevent gushing and fought to control himself, to restore order in his body but he was drowning in his own turbulent fluid. As the blood flowed back to where it belonged, other fluids, irritated out of their warm slumber snarled retribution and bit his plumbing at every change of direction, careering up, as the blood splashed back down, pushing each other aside in their headlong determination to be where they should not.

As the train pulled in, doubling the crashing sounds pounding at his eardrums, he got to his feet and commenced a pirouette, circling in slow motion, and on completing the circle crumpled to the floor. He was revived by a gentle slapping to his simmering jowls.

Lizzie was baffled by the chain of events. Could she have been clearer about Suzanne's indifference to his devotion? There were some yawning caverns between the sexes that can never be bridged.

The way he dealt with his brush with disgrace and ruin was predictable and Lizzie focussed on that. He simply locked himself in a metaphorical cupboard and did not come out. There was an abrupt end to his fraternising at the Dog & Duck, he threw himself into his work and where five sides of paper would be sufficient he produced twenty. Instead of leaving the office at 6:30pm to go to the pub, he stayed in his office (cupboard) until 9:00 pm. Plainly, Ian was back on track.

Lizzie was happy to have manoeuvred control over her target but she was having far less success in the war with herself. Her emotions, which had begun somewhere in the chest area, had spread like a cancer all over her body. Especially one area she did not care to think about let alone mention. These agonies were set off when she least expected. Noticing the tiny hairs on Ian's knuckles, seeing a slither of soap on his ear she desperately wanted to wipe off. This desperation passed but was replaced by a more severe desperation that would have made her 'saving it for marriage' broker blush to the roots of several generations.

Ian remained oblivious.

Lizzie gave Ian time for the humiliation to subside and as they were clearing away one night she rued the passing of their intimate coffee moments. His hopeless reaction to her nostalgia answered countless questions, including the most elusive question of all.

Why do you love him?

It was there, in his eyes, the reflection of the foundation that formed three decades of her life.

As a girl, Lizzie was bullied unmercifully. She was surrounded in the playground like a cornered animal and she developed an affinity for the dumb and repressed. She collected one eyed cats, damaged sparrows, spiders trapped in the bath, and would not dream of squashing a bluebottle.

What she saw in Ian's eyes was the resignation suffered by the dumb and repressed. He was her wounded pet and it would take a unique kind of administration to bring him back to health.

It was at the weekends Lizzie suffered most, forty eight hours waiting without knowing what the future would bring. At work, while he was in the next room, there was a semblance of a relationship. She knew where he was and what he was doing. His weekend life provided no picture for her pedantic imagination. She had considered driving to his address to do surveillance but quickly thought better of it. She had a strong suspicion that if the roles were reversed Ian would be parked across the street.

Lizzie had established a view of Helena long before she met her in the flesh. By some kaleidoscopic osmosis, particles of detail gyrate and flutter through time and settle. These speckles form a whole and, however misguided, represent a complete picture.

Certain component parts of Ian's wife were irrefutable. Helena was a colossal snob and one of those wives that claim credit for their husband's success. Lizzie hated the benighted wives of the knighted who used the 'Lady' at the drop of a hat when even their husbands were embarrassed by the celebrity and the chance to brandish their 'Sir' prefix.

She had also cobbled together other odd facts. In heartfelt terms Ian's marriage was a fraud, one son was a boring accountant and the other a rogue. Ian lived in his brother's shadow and may have had a thing for his sister-in-law.

'She's a very special woman,' he would say. 'I'm very fond of her.'

'Transparent or what?' Lizzie would ask herself.

This was her first experience of jealousy and it quickly grew into loathing. She did not feel such extreme emotion towards Helena because she was not hampered by Ian's feelings for his wife. In the quest for Ian's heart Helena was not a contender.

She met both Duncan and Pauline when they came to lunch. Duncan was kept waiting while Ian finished up some work with Mornard. She kept him company while he waited and was genuinely sorry not to conclude their conversation. As Ian dragged him away Duncan pulled a face.

She took to Duncan but his wife Pauline did not have a chance of any favourable sentiment. Their rivalry was clear when Lizzie saw her with Ian. Her speculation of the worst was palpably obvious. So het up was she over this assignation that it took several days before she could recall what she saw and heard in a rational fashion.

She had nothing to fear from Pauline Black.

The woman teased her brother-in-law and however affectionate a rise she took out of him there was an undertone. Pauline knew what she was dealing with and was keeping Ian at arm's length.

'How dare she ridcule her dearest darling,' Lizzie snarled rather dubiously, because her realisations about her rival were extremely comforting.

One Saturday the gnashing of her innards was so tumultuous she decided a change of scenery was called for. She would attend St Peters for Sunday services, drive over to Berkhamsted and catch Suzanne at her devotions. Perhaps she would get the chance to bend a sympathetic ear.

This was another of her problems, no one to confide in. The only person to whom she confided her feelings was Suzanne and she had soiled the confidence. She felt a need to rectify her friend's opinion of her boss.

As she drove across country Lizzie was filled with misgiving.

Suzanne was a private person and might not be best pleased to receive a visitor, especially an uninvited visitor. She tried to weigh whether she was doing the right thing but the moribund instructions of the SatNav kept intervening. The voice sounded disturbingly like her mother.

Years of Borden household routine had been disrupted by Lizzie's recent change of mood. Mrs. Borden, aware of her daughter's distress, found excuses to visit Lizzie's room.

'Would you like to help me with the shopping?'

'I'd rather not,' said Lizzie. 'Sorry.'

'Your father's at the match,' her mother explained. 'The shopping seems to get heavier and heavier.'

That was her mother's ploy, trading in guilt. Lizzie drove her to the supermarket but refused to go inside. She went to Borders bookshop and browsed. She had no intention of buying a book but for no particular reason the title of a bodice ripper attracted her attention and she left the shop with it. Her mother had still not finished the week's shop and as she waited she began reading. It was one of those clever novels that draw you in from the opening paragraph and when her mother tapped on the window, she had been transported.

'What are you reading?'

'A book I found,' said Lizzie. 'Look at the title.'

'*Lizzie Loses her Heart*,' her mother said out loud. 'That's not all she'll lose if I know anything about books like that?'

She thought of pointing out that it was the 21st century, that she was a thirty-four year old virgin, but her mother was stuck living in 1953. They drove home in silence, the older woman itching to ask and the younger praying she would not.

It was an easy question, 'What's the matter?'

And an easy answer, 'I'm in love,' but Lizzie could not manage to speak the words.

Her mother pulled the rabbit out of the hat, she sighed and said softly, 'He's married?'

Lizzie had to pull the car into a bus recess, crossed her arms across the steering wheel and burst into tears. Her mother comforted her until an irate bus driver forced them to move on. There was no further consoling, the weeping helped for an hour or two, then the aching returned redoubled.

Saint Peters Berkhamsted is a rough stone Gothic looking building on a corner of the High Street. Lizzie was late and the service had started, she searched for her friend but could not see where she was sitting. After the service she made her way to the front and stood at the back of the queue to speak to Reverend Rais.

'I came to see Suzanne Marks but she doesn't seem to be here.'

Rais looked at her quizzically, 'Are you a relative?'

'Friend,' Lizzie qualified, 'from work.'

'Give me a minute to finish up,' he said. 'I'd like a word with you.'

While the Reverend removed his hassock they talked of Suzanne. 'She has virtually disappeared, she helped me with the children, attended every Sunday without fail, then without a word, gone.'

'Have you contacted her?'

'I left a couple of phone messages, called at her house and left a note. I'm truly worried about her.'

'There's been no sign of a change in attitude at work. She talks of you often, as though things are as they have always been.'

'Strange, don't you think? said Rais. 'Quite clearly they are not.'

The street of Suzanne's house was a short drive along the High Street towards Northchurch. She passed a Café Rouge, the last shop in the street, complied a roundabout and turned left up a steep hill. She parked at the summit, applied the handbrake and, unsure it was safe, put the car in gear. As she was about to get out of the car the door to Suzanne's house opened. She and Mornard shared a frosty goodbye.

Chapter Twelve

How Helena and Ian came together was a mystery. It might have been in a fog because neither of them had a nostalgic recollection of the event. Ian's attraction was simple, she was the first woman to show the least interest in him and he latched onto her like a limpet. Did she see potential in this desultory man?

'I work for the government,' Ian explained. 'I'm a civil servant.'

Perhaps Helena was impressed with this speech?

For the devotion he heaped on her during their courtship she felt pity. His foolish declarations, cribbed from a book of poetry, made her cringe. She had chosen him, he had nothing to fear. They married and made two babies, it was part of her grand plan. Sex was not. She did not care for the farmyard snorting or the sticky mess. Ian was so wrapped up in his work he barely had the energy.

They were united in a common bond, the undeniable certainty that there was no such phenomenon as love. The idea of such an emotion was as remote as infinity or nothingness. They shared a void in which Ian claimed to be fond of his wife and Helena listened to this empty claim with scorn.

Helena therefore was not even in love with Helena.

There was no parallel for her in any Greek Mythology. She believed she was the centre of the Universe and had a divine right to put Helena above all others. She was a mixture of revisionist astronomy and terminal delusion. What Helena wanted was the one exercisable commandment and she genuinely believed it to be an irrefutable fact. If, as a result of this self-determination, others had to be sacrificed for her well-being, so be it. If this sacrifice included one of her children, that would be a nuisance but not a tragedy.

Despite his success, she did not respect or revere her husband, just claimed that his elevation was her doing.

Ian and Helena's conversations were rarely resolved, she radical and he on the fence, neither accepted a heated word the other said. Helena grew more adamant and Ian more reasonable. Dealing with some of the largest egos in Britain, Helena, though a worthy contestant, was child's play. She was a strong supporter for the reintroduction of hanging without being discriminate about who to execute. Her jurisdiction covered 99 per cent of the globe. At dinner parties when Ian made his pledge, 'The only reason I would give up my job is if they bring back hanging,' she waited until they were alone and berated him.

They had little in common, Helena detested sport. On holidays or official visits, Ian got out his Baedeker and she trouped around museums and churches, stifling yawns. She was prosaic and that was an end to it, matters artistic were a waste of time and energy and the province of the pretentious. She felt no passion for anything that did not reflect on her personally or would impress her hairdresser.

She was happy that he was tied up at the office, it was a shame he did not spend the weekends there. Now that the boys were off their hands, his absence allowed her freedom to indulge her pleasures without interruption. This period was approaching the zenith of her existence but there were a few minor details left to complete the perfection.

There had been one irrevocable setback. In her grand plan, her son Gideon should have been a girl, and his mother never forgave him. He grew up without love, without a father and had to suffer resentment and hostility. Once thwarted, Helena will not forgive the perpetrator and unremitting revenge is meted out. It may take time to execute justice but Helena, like the law, always got her man.

Chris and Gideon were raised by a string of nannies. Most, pushed beyond endurance, took against the 'Mrs' and gave notice. One departure, Dolly Churcher, caused unexpected rebellion. The Nanny Agency's file on the Black boys had 'Brats' scrawled in highlighter pen across the front page and they sent experienced, hard-bitten women who went about their tasks with ruthless efficiency. Their dogmatic personalities clashed with the 'Mrs' and it became a matter of time and will. Dolly, a sweet middle-aged housewife seeking extra cash to bolster her husband's statutory sick pay, was sent for an interview by mistake. She lasted four times longer than any of her predecessors or successors.

She was a natural with children. Overnight, the boys became easier, their tantrums less frequent and Helena carried on obliviously until a worry nerve began to twitch. What was going on to bring about this major reversal? A pattern was emerging. At the weekend when Dolly was absent, the boys would degenerate. It was time to keep a watchful eye on nanny.

Spying, Helena heard Dolly read stories and found herself looking forward to bedtime. There were pillow fights and giggling and through the crack in the door she saw cuddling up and tickling. 'It might be suspicious,' thought Helena, without knowing quite how or why.

A piece of weekend mischief brought about Dolly's demise. A new water feature installed in the garden had been broken by a cricket ball and Chris and Gideon were sent to bed early. 'It's still light,' Chris complained.

'Do as you're told.'

'I hate you,' said Gideon.

'Me too,' said Chris.

'I love Dolly more than you.'

'Me too,' said Chris.

Dolly was sacked not because the boys loved her more than their mother but out of vengeance for their saying so. What did she care who they loved, because no such emotion existed. What she did not legislate for was the revenge the boys exacted for her spite. Learning that Dolly had been replaced, they carried out a programme of destruction that would have impressed the Brown Shirts. They vandalised everything that was not nailed down, books were ripped to shreds, toys mutilated, pottery smashed including a Chinese motif vase bought at a jumble for fifty pence that Helena insisted was Ming Dynasty, denying the provenance of the extra 'e' stamped on the bottom.

Noting that these attacks were not having the desired effect, they started a new campaign and urinated on her collection of magazines. A truce was called and Ian acted as go-between. There was no way Helena would back down and re-instate Dolly and the impasse continued for a month. It was when they burgled her treasure box and deposited a pint or two of number ones in place of the removed swag that the feud came to a head. Angry, so red in the face it was hard to distinguish where her skin ended and her hair started, she had to be restrained from infanticide. Ian had to lock each warring faction in their rooms to prevent mayhem.

Ian left them that way for most of a Saturday, the boys smashed their windows and Helena cut up his favourite ties with a pair of nail scissors. To pacify the boys he bought them a cricket set and for his wife, copies of *Woman* and *Woman's Own* to restart her soiled magazine collection.

He opened their bedroom door and presented Helena with her gifts. She tossed them carelessly into the bin and brushed passed him.

'Wanker,' she said.

He knocked at the boy's door and asked permission to enter. He put the cricket set on Chris' bed.

'What's this?' he asked.

'A cricket set,' he smiled benevolently causing both boys to conceal their faces beneath folded arms. 'Come on lads let's go play in the garden.'

Chris spoke with venom, 'Why don't you piss off back to work?'

Stunned, Ian stood transfixed and the boys began chanting, 'We want Dolly. We want Dolly.'

They kept up the chorus for several hours but Dolly was not reinstated and the damage was cast in concrete.

Dolly had knitted Gideon a cricket sweater, with cable stitching on the front and green piping at the collar and armholes. It was his security blanket and he treasured it until the day he died.

Chapter Thirteen

Chris' pending marriage opened a closed wound. Helena had resurrected the painstaking trousseau she had hidden away since the birth of her second son. Fondly inspecting these treasures brought back long buried frustrations. If one setback in her grand plan was not bad enough, Helena was experiencing a more insidious rebuff.

At the brief encounter in the late kitchen, Katy, no fool, could see the disapproval written large on the woman's waspish face.

'Nasty bitch,' she decided, astutely.

Helena saw her future daughter-in-law in terms of scale not unlike a Rodin, Lipchitz or Ritchie, not that she had heard of any of these men. In her mind's eye Katy was an inanimate substance to be moulded into shape. Currently that shape was sadly lacking.

'I've joined a gymnasium,' said Helena untruthfully, her eye trained on the girl's face for clues. 'They were doing a special offer.'

Katy, who had confined the Watson Place brochure to the wastepaper bin, was inscrutable and showed no tell.

'We women don't take proper care of ourselves.' Helena dug another spadeful. 'Don't you agree?'

Katy took a large bite of cake and chewed slowly, shrugged to be polite. 'I'm happy as I am,' she gauged this was not the answer Helena wanted. Guessing her motives she added spitefully, 'Chris likes me the way I am.'

Helena, intent on getting what she wanted from her son's non-compliant betrothed, considered another method. She searched for ways of planting a tapeworm into the girl's food. A dangerous game but, 'needs must when the devil drives.'

Ian's brother Duncan had mentioned that Helena was on first name terms with that fellow.

As soon as Chris and Katy announced their engagement, Helena jumped into action. If a job was worth doing it was worth doing properly. The Eddowes put an announcement in the *Wyford Observer*, while Helena's singular book of etiquette stated that *The Times* and *Telegraph* were more appropriate. Her next step was to contact *L-O* magazine.

She got the number off the Internet, 'Please put me through to a senior editor.'

After considerable badgering, the telephonist connected her to a sub-editor who listened silently as she explained why they should be considered for inclusion. Without comment, the girl took down her details and promised to show it to her manager.

Helena waited impatiently for several days for a copy of a contract and financial offer but did not receive so much as a call back.

'Could you please check for me,' said Helena. 'There have been some problems with the post in my area.'

'Sorry, Mrs Black but we've got nothing showing on our computer or on file.'

She demanded to speak to a manager and was told bluntly that, 'It's not for us, I'm afraid.'

Helena lost it, threatened to cancel her subscription and rang *OK* magazine. That inquiry proved equally fruitless and the *Wyford Observer*, who showed scant interest in the event, explained that coverage of the wedding would not warrant much public interest, let alone a fee.

Helena was not prone to disappointment but was outraged by *L-O* and *OK's* failure to realise the potential of her son and his intended. She was so upset that she confided in Ian over dinner.

'I approached *L-O* magazine,' she said. 'I can't begin to tell you how rude they were.'

'What did you contact them for?' Ian said distractedly, more intent on the television picture over her shoulder.

'The wedding.' Helena was indignant.

'What world do you live in?'

Helena, her temper on a low light since the telephone calls, ignited into exasperation. '*L-O* magazine. Do you mean to tell me you've never heard of it?'

'No,' said Ian defiantly. 'I thought it was the title of Leyton Orient's fanzine.'

She spluttered violently, 'You're a waste of space, do you know that?'

Ian shrugged, forked up another mouthful of food and his sorry eyes reverted to the television screen.

If *L-O* magazine would not do it, then she must. Helena found a back copy covering the marriage of the Right Honourable Patricia Welton, daughter of Sir and Lady Patrick Welton to David Groombridge, the son of the Duke of Brisbane. Stealing a photograph of Katy from Chris' wallet she made several copies. Pictures of Mayor Eddowes and his wife Celia were easy to come by legally and using old passport photos of herself, Chris and Ian, she began her artwork.

Helena was a prosaic woman but in a relatively short space of time she had turned her hand to sculpture, and now she was doing cut outs in the style of Matisse.

Using her best nail scissors she cut shapes of suitable size and superimposed the faces of her family on those of the Welton/Groombridge family celebrating in the gardens of the Duke of Brisbane's stately home. She even printed off written texts and name tags and pasted them in. Satisfied with her artwork, she gave the magazine pride of place in her box. Every time she remembered the callousness of the *L-O* staff she would comfort herself by reading her bastardised entry or tinkering with the detail. If she could not have the real thing, fantasy would do just as well.

* * *

Church bells crashed and clanged, the cacophony jangled over the rooftops of the Pemberton Estate and beyond. Alderman Edgar Swan, Michael Eddowes' predecessor, was tending his garden and feeding his budgerigars. As the peels rang out, he stood erect and lamented plaintively as a muezzin, 'I wish they'd quit that bloody racket.'

Sunlight streamed through the windows in equal shafts, light and shadow hanging static in the air, creating a ribcage reminiscent of an exhibit in the Natural History Museum. Busy dust fluttered and danced to the excited murmur of the waiting congregation and the stuttering rhythm of the clanging bells.

There was more dissonance in the gallery where the choir tuned their tonsils. Everyone was determined to be at their best for the debut wedding held in the new St Marks.

The original St Marks had burned down following a vigil for the football club in their hour of need. It was that time of year when the play-offs were once again upon us and Reverend Waddenham, who had long conceded that soccer had usurped religion as the opium of the masses, offered a prayer for success. In his nightly devotions he confessed that, 'a full church is a happy church.' A candle left burning after the church had emptied toppled over, setting light to Benedict Allen's collection of match programmes. For the pagans it was a worthwhile sacrifice because Wyford made it to the premiership for their usual single year tenure.

The blackened bells, dented and scratched in the inferno, were saved and stored in Lord Justice Christie's garage. On completion of the new steeple the engineers and building inspectors declared the structure unsuitable and incapable of supporting the substantial tintinnabulum.

There should have been enough funds left in the pot for the remedial work but for the Head of Wyford Building Control. Upset at being contradicted on an esoteric detail concerning insulations, the Architect went over his head to the Deputy Prime Minister's office and got the HBC's ruling overturned. The HBC vowed revenge and found reason to exhaust the fund.

The HBC was well practiced in retribution. The redevelopment of the Town Centre wasted £4 million of Wyford council taxes, dished out in reprisals

A bell committee raised the necessary funds and the bells were tolled for the least excuse to justify the outlay.

A yellow Rolls Royce bedecked in lilac ribbon circled the estate. Helena had not been able to locate a tangerine or lilac Rolls or a company prepared to repaint. Inside, the bride sat staring nowhere in particular, unsmiling, ignoring her father on the seat beside her.

How dare they tell her how to dress.

She inspected her father's sensible shoes. The mottled leather was dull and drab totally unsuitable to wear with a morning suit.

Parents are a pain.

'It's tradition,' they begged and pleaded.

They did not know which end was up but were full of useless advice. They were still living in the dark ages.

Something old, Something new, Something borrowed, Something blue.

'What kind of nonsense was that? This was the 21st Century and they were out of the ark.'

The driver negotiated the roundabout and the church came into view. There was a gathering of spectators waiting in the sunshine and, as the car pulled alongside, they formed a short cavalcade.

The only thing they had let her do was choose her dress, that with a fight. Now they wanted to ruin it with silly superstition.

The driver pipped her father in the race to the door. As she got out, she raised her skirt slightly above her shoes to save the hem and posed for the waiting crowd. Yet to smile, she took her father's arm and they made their way inside.

The protagonists were dressed in pale grey. Ian flitted among the pews like a collared dove and Helena, a vision in lilac, crowed to all and sundry. On the dais, Celia Eddowes, the bride's mother, was irretrievably glum. Chris and Gideon were sharing a joke when the electric piano struck the opening chords of the *Wedding March*. The Blacks and choir scurried to their positions, heads swivelled to see the Mayor leading the bride down the aisle, while the bridesmaid sowed rose petals from a wicker basket to mark their way. A gasp of appreciation bounced from brick to beam with a hollow echo.

'Thank Christ,' Katy muttered.

Chris was waiting on the dais. It had been on her mind that he might flunk it. In her experience, you could not be sure of men and it was best not to trust them an inch. Dirty little buggers like that brother of his, standing there like the cat that ate the cream. That was men for you, wet as morning grass or show offs with heads too big for their bodies.

She and Chris swapped a feeble smile.

There was the bridesmaid in that awful dress. She had told them, she did not want a bridesmaid, certainly not a bridesmaid prettier than she was.

She was in no mood to be a bride.

'Tell us what you want and we'll take a back seat,' said the parents.

What transpired was, 'You can push off and we'll see you at the wedding.'

Weeks of arguments, hysteria, blackmail, 'Who's paying for this?'

Weeks of Chris shrugging, 'I don't mind. If you feel it's right. If that's what you want?'

What she wanted was to shake some life into his sorry body. That mother of his had squeezed the last drop of essence out of him. Once they were installed in their new semi-detached she would change all that. Everything would be all right as soon as they got a dog.

Katy was not exceptional in any way, nor was her husband-to-be. Having had her hair done, and dressed in a bridal gown, she looked part way to the part. Chris dressed in morning suit and cravat looked close to handsome. They faced the vicar and clasped damp hands, their life to come symbolized by the marzipan figures decorating the top of the cake.

Chapter Fourteen

A shuffle and a dosy-do, the leading characters were on their marks and Reverend Waddenham's budgie voice began chirruping, 'We are gathered here in the sight of God...'

As an antidote to his thin timbre the vicar was a devotee of amateur dramatics. He read the service from a soft diminuendo to a hoarse crescendo and in tandem with his rise through the registers a beam of light radiated slowly, gaining brightness and intensity in harmony with the text.

Waddenham commenced the service but Katy was distracted by a glint on the Reverend's spectacles. She felt burning on her bare shoulders and when she turned to Chris he was glowing. The sheen of her dress sparkled vibrantly and, as she glanced up, she was blinded.

A familiar tongue clicked behind her and the irritation bubbling just below Katy's surface flared again. How she hated that smug, self-satisfied, old bag.

What did she look like? She claimed she was a woman of taste, but she was colour blind. What a row they had the other night, locking horns in the living room, standing up for herself for once and her outburst being dismissed as a tantrum.

'Get on with it,' she screamed. 'Let me know which church, which hall and I'll be there, *perhaps!*'

Hardly any aspect of the wedding was to her liking. The smaller venue forced the 200 proposed guest numbers to be reduced to 110. Katy's and her parents' share of invitations were cut from twenty couples to a mere seven.

Katy, not paying attention to the vicar, came to realising that she was expected to speak. 'I do,' she said flatly. I don't, as a matter of fact, if it doesn't work out I'll divorce him. At least I can say I was married.

'I now you pronounce you man and wife,' said Waddenham as the entire dais was spotlighted in a cone of light as fierce as those that lit up Vera Lynn and the Luftwaffe during the war. The scene was mesmeric for the participants and the onlookers. Feeling a desperate desire to comment, Waddenham chirped, 'It's a miracle.'

Katy Eddowes, now Black, had been so immersed she misunderstood the vicar's reference and took it as a personal affront. 'Who the fuck asked your opinion?' was drowned out in a gasp of exaltation and unified prayer, 'It is a miracle.'

A fleet of limousines conveyed the principals to the banqueting hall and dropped them at the entrance of the Copse Hotel. The guests' arrival at the Orchid Suite was announced by Crook, dressed immaculately in pink livery, twinkles dancing on his rimless spectacles.

Crook was bemused. He had announced the invited in their thousands and was a master of his craft. A momentary glimpse into these eyes and he could peer into the soul of those that were unaware they possessed one. Crook was a troubled man. Icy hearts had thawed, the barren were fecund and the world as he knew it had turned on its head.

'Your host and hostess,' his practiced voice projected pleasantly.

He had been hired by the Blacks for the wedding. He had announced them on numerous occasions and knew they were bogged down with delusion. Today their hearts were grateful and had risen above disapprobation.

It was not until Crook sneaked outside for a quiet smoke and found Lord Justice Christie doing the same that he was informed of the miracle. In the hall it was the sole topic of conversation.

'Was it a miracle?'

'They are such a handsome couple.'

'A marriage made in heaven.'

'It's the least the Blacks deserve.'

'Is there a nicer man anywhere on the planet?'

'Of course it was a miracle.'

Crook, having referred inadvertently to the Blacks as the 'host and hostess' had caused a spat. Celia Eddowes dug her thorny nails into her husband's arm, 'We're the host and hostess, tell him,' she demanded. 'Tell him!'

Crook, unaware of his mistake or the vexation, continued with aplomb, 'Lord Justice Christie and Lady Christie.'

The judge, formidable in wig and gown, looked less so in his ancient dinner suit. It gave him a seedy aspect, more akin to habitués of the tote window at dog tracks. Lady Christie's thickly applied make up in the sunshine lighting of the Orchid Suite had taken on an orange hue and was camouflaged, lost among the orange dresses, orange tablecloths, orange bunting.

'It is not orange,' said Helena pedantically. 'It is tanga-rine.'

There were posies of pale orange roses and orange blossoms on every table and a smattering of lilac sugared almonds with a lilac napkin in the wine glass. Placed at each of the ladies' settings was a fan of delicate lilac paper, specially imported from Japan (via an alleyway off the Shaftesbury Avenue).

'Mr and Mrs John Hay.'

Hay, the Shadow Home Secretary, stood a head taller than the throng. As the diminutive looked up at him, over his shoulder you could see a safety net filled with orange balloons. These would shower down upon the party during the last dance of the night. Before Auld Lang Syne and the National Anthem, the band was instructed to play *Feelings*. It was Helena's favourite song.

'Mr and Mrs Ben Tilleulen, and their daughter Amy.'

Emma Tilleulen, Helena's eldest sister, wore black with Chantilly around the collar and hem. Her short, greying hair was dyed jet black and she wore tinted glasses to protect her eyes from the glare. She greeted everyone with a skeletal smile. The dark clothing, pale skin, and bare arms crossed across a treasure-less chest reduced this macabre grin to the humanity of a Jolly Roger.

The photographer took extra care in posing the Tilleulens and, from the pointed look the bridesmaid gave him, he sensed that the best man was going to be out of luck.

'Mr and Mrs Duncan Black, their sons John and Toby.'

Ian's younger brother greeted them warmly and congratulated them on their good fortune, a son to be proud of, daughter-in-law that was the envy of Wyford. An accountant married to a solicitor, it was a match made in heaven.

'Mr Gideon Black and Miss Lucy Moore.'

'Is it serious between them?'

'I doubt it,' Helena turned up her nose to its more usual position. 'When he brings home a girl with a normal size chest then I'll believe it's serious.'

'His brother is a different kettle of fish.'

'Chris has his feet firmly on the ground.'

'The happy couple look like something out of a Hollywood film, they look so lovely together.'

'I thought the press would be here.'

'The darlings wanted a quiet wedding,' said Helena, 'without fuss.'

'Lords, Ladies and Gentlemen,' Crook tapped the table with his gavel, quite superfluously, he had silence. 'Pray silence for your host...'

Celia's nails scored welts into the Mayor's forearm.

'...Mr Ian Black CB.'

How did it happen? Why did you let it happen? I know you are weak and feeble but this is exceptional, even for you.' Michael Eddowes, blades gouging his skin, avoided his wife's resentful gaze.

Less than a year ago it seemed that they would never get Katy off their hands. She had been a difficult child and wet the bed well into her teens. Puberty forced them to consult a doctor who diagnosed a mild form of spina bifida. The Eddowes, discovering the source of her condition, were not relieved. Keeping overnight bedwetting a secret in a small community was simple, no stay overs, no sleep ins. Having produced a child with a problem was bad enough but to be associated with a disease was degrading.

Katy was fully aware of their new shame. Her incontinence had already made her a depressive with a tendency to mild schizophrenia. She spent the day as nice Katy and the evenings as hideous Katy. She took her resentment for her condition out on her parents and the late discovery that her humiliation had been unnecessary intensified her ire. With the help of drugs she was able to lead a normal life but she had got into the habit of abusing her parents and continued to do so.

Below the beat of the music, Celia's voice droned on, Michael let her go uninterrupted. 'What a fiasco, we're strangers at our daughter's wedding.'

'Sorry, dear,' he hoped an apology would quieten her.

Like Ian, Michael was an absentee father but this was not blind ambition, it was a planned manoeuvre. If he gauged it correctly it would allow Katy plenty of time to run out of steam, Celia would have borne the brunt of her temper. He would return home to find his daughter burnt out and suffer his wife's tirades but they were less hurtful. Meeting Christopher did not alter Katy's disposition in the slightest and he was filled with wonder on how they conducted their courtship.

Michael waited for his wife's bleating to subside and said pleasantly, 'We thought she would never find anybody and we would be stuck with her forever. At least she's married now.'

'For how long?' Celia asked gloomily.

The way young people were nowadays, she had a point. Katy did not seem enthusiastic about getting married. It was not the big step it used to be, couples jump in and out of marriage at the drop of a hat and have babies without a thought given to the consequences.

A brief calm as the band decided on the next number was broken by Celia, 'I just don't see how it's happened. The bride's parents pay for the wedding and they have the majority of the say. We have paid for the wedding and had none of the say.'

He could not deny it. What had happened? They were allotted so few invites they had upset their family. Ian kept insisting that they shared mutual acquaintance, which was true. He also promised to cough up for the discrepancy in the ratio of invites but the bills had been split fifty fifty.

It was her, not him, she was the demanding one and every time they tried to stand up to her she pulled that face of hers, as though you had served dinner and she had eaten something offensive. There the face remained until you gave way.

'How did it happen?' Celia had one last gripe.

'Bride, Bridegroom, Celia and Michael, my beautiful wife Helena, Lords, Ladies, relatives and friends, I want to say how proud I am...' He paused for the applause and cries of, 'hear, hear'.

Ian spoke well in public. He'd had years of practice and deserved attention. Helena scanned the tables to see if he was being given due deference. She started with the table to her right where her coterie listened with rapt attention, as did his friends and work associates and the table assigned to the Eddowes relatives. Starting from the other side of the room she surveyed table by table and was satisfied.

She caught Ben and Duncan, her brothers-in-law leaning in and whispering. They had their backs to her but she could tell they were not paying attention. Duncan was laughing at something that did not synchronise with Ian's speech and, adding to her chagrin, they were not sitting in the seats she had designated.

The table settings had taken a lot of planning, time and trouble and she had managed a perfect blend of boy, girl, boy, girl. Nowhere had two boys been put together. A wave of annoyance swept through her and she could not decide which of their crimes was worse, changing the seating arrangement or ignoring Ian.

'Poor Pauline, she has so much to put up with. Duncan Black is a moody man and must be hell to live with. Poor Emma, she has so little luck.'

Nodding appreciatively Ian continued, '…I want to say how proud I am to be English and privileged to live in this great country of ours.'

Uncertainly the applause restarted, out of the uncertainty it redoubled and, breaking with tradition, the Loyal Toast was taken before dinner was served.

Ian Black had barely changed since adolescence. Heavy set, not quite six feet tall, he gave the impression he would run to fat. Regular squash playing won the battle with his weight until his knees and his blood pressure let him down. Missing out on his regimen there were signs of a paunch. With his Latin colouring he tanned easily, only his lack of hair gave his age away.

Always popular, Ian maintained friends from every component of his life. Whether it was school, Sunday school, summer school or university, his alumni were present. He added to their number down the years, Ian was a people magnet.

'I've not been the best of fathers. Duty called me and I had to make sacrifices…'

Crook, at the host's shoulder could sense the quivering uncertainty. 'Where was the real man standing beside him? Had he had too much to drink?'

Crook's 'hostess' scanned the entranced, amused faces. Good, well-meaning people returning the compliment of being invited, some simply happy to touch the hem of those that play to the gallery.

'...I give you,' Ian raised his glass aloft, 'the Bride and Groom.'

The room came to its feet and bellowed heartily, 'the Bride and Groom.'

In accord with the band, the dancers patent pumps bounded with unlikely vigour, foxtrots and quick steps were fleeter, waltzes more graceful, jiving was hot and cha chas charred.

Helena, dressed in silk and chantung smelling of orange blossom, grabbed Ian roughly and yanked him onto the dance floor. Hay watched them, Ian shuffling his feet while Helena twisted her graceless physique to and froufrou, covering her immobility with elaborate arm swings and finger clicking. Hay went outside for a smoke and found Duncan wife Pauline had got there before him.

'Don't you dance?' asked Hay.

'I've got sciatica,' said Pauline. 'Duncan is dancing with his niece.'

She was a woman of average height, with short brown hair and an enigmatic face. He was unsure if she was pretty until she smiled and then her face lit up like a firework.

'Ian made a curious speech,' said Hay.

'He is a sweet man, but how his children hate him. He was never home because the job came first. People like you should not have families, it's irresponsible.'

'Including me?'

'I'm afraid so. You forsake everything for your work and very few of you are with your original partners.'

'It isn't as simple as you make it sound,' Hay mitigated. 'You start out with the best of intentions but ambition creeps up on you.'

'That sounds a very plausible excuse,' said Pauline thoughtfully. 'Somehow I can't get beyond excuse. Everyone is getting more adept at sidestepping blame.'

Having shaken off Helena's shackles on the dance floor, Ian went hunting, but there was no sign of his intention. He loved these occasions because they gave him the excuse to be close to his secret love. He would dance with her once or twice an evening. Any more often would be indiscreet but it was enough to feed his regard for a month or two. Timing these approaches was critical, and it was essential that the tempo of the music was slow. He would take her soft hand in his own and he would put his nose to her hair. She would make fun of him in her affectionate way and that kept her occupied while he revelled in being close. There might be an accidental bump of anatomy but that was a hope he preferred not to anticipate.

From the day he set eyes on her he was intrigued. The confident smile and vivacious eyes intoxicated. At unlikely moments her image would pop into his thoughts. A glimpse of wrist and he could summon an erotic fantasy of hand-kissing and arm caressing. Her delicate arm, with the finest down, was locked in his memory. In his more daring fantasies he imagined pressing his lips to hers. His hand touched his cheek nostalgically where she had kissed him earlier.

He circuited the hall but she was nowhere to be found. Duncan was in the lobby, staring into space. The Cole's were canoodling outside the toilets. Christie, in conversation with Doctor Riklis, blanked him. At the doors that opened onto the grounds he heard her voice and that of John Hay.

'His children hate him,' she said firmly. 'He was never home. The job always came first.'

Ian slipped away, shimmied past his brother, darted onto the dance floor and was lost in the mass.

Hay, who had divorced and married his PA, admired her bluntness and justified his corner, 'In truth, it creeps up on you. You don't know how ambitious you are until you're trapped in its web, then somehow, there's no going back.'

'It sounds plausible but I don't believe it.'

'I agree,' said Duncan, standing in the doorway. 'The gene is there from the outset, as are the other attributes, ambition, hypocrisy, selfishness and, most important of all, dancing to the company tune.'

'You're calling me a hypocrite,' Hay was amused.

'Oh yes,' said Duncan. 'It goes with political territory.'

'You're not ambitious?'

'I'm a home bird,' Duncan put his arm around his wife's waist and she leaned into him. 'You know that thing about patriotism being the last refuge of the scoundrel?'

'Samuel Johnson.'

'I've always wanted to correct him. Patriotism is the first refuge of the scoundrel.'

'Are you accusing Ian of being a scoundrel?'

'Oh no,' said Duncan, flashing a supercilious smile. 'He's not a scoundrel, just surrounded by them. Obviously it rubs off.

Chapter Fifteen

'How's your table?' Ian asked. 'Not too boring, I hope.'

'Ben and your brother are both amusing. I'm enjoying myself,' John Hay waited while his friend finished at the basin.

'Duncan is jealous of me,' said Ian concentrating on a futile attempt to brush the last vestige of his hair. 'Can you blame him? I'm a major cog in the workings of government and he's a taxi driver.'

John Hay doubted the veracity of this claim. 'What about his new career?'

'Sorry,' said Ian preoccupied with his recalcitrant fuzz. 'This wedding is costing me a fortune.'

John looked at the reflection, wondering what the problem was and how so little hair could occupy so much time. The round open face with hooded brown eyes and the permanently pursed lips, he resembled a cartoon rabbit. It was the contrast between that easy smile and the unsure eyes that hinted at vulnerability. This vulnerability and the way he wore his naive heart on his sleeve warmed the chests of his friends, male and female.

'It's a shame I did not take a job in the private sector. I would be earning millions.'

'You think so?' Hay quashed a sneer. So many pen pushers think they're Alan Sugar. Ian works on the 'nice guy' principle and that would cut no ice in the business world. 'I don't see you coping with the cut-throats that run business.'

'I'm used to dealing with men. I've had to make some tough decisions.'

Ian washed and dried his hands and they returned to the Orchid Suite.

* * *

The air outside was frappé cool, a soft breeze filled its cheeks and blew sporadically, fluttering flags and ruffling her lightweight skirt. She lit a cigarette and pondered injustice. Helena, the least deserving person she knew, invariably came up trumps.

Poor Emma, nothing worked out for her, everything she touched turned to dross. Everything Helena touched did not turn to gold but pretty close. Pauline knew the truth but outsiders gave Helena the credit.

Helena was a control freak and no subject was too small or too remote to animate her influence. Katy wanted a dog but Helena did not let up until she relented. Dogs bred germs and Helena had no truck with germs. When the boys were doing the rounds of parties and returned with a piece of birthday cake it was confined to the bin. Another child had blown out the candles and contaminated the confection with 'germs'.

Now, for reasons beyond Helena's considerable powers of control, her son's wedding had been a spectacular success. Emma's daughter, if she ever married, would be knocked up by a shoe mender and eke out a life above the shop.

* * *

Despite her negative mood Pauline found herself being carried along by the other's excitement. Was it a miracle? However big a fluke it was or was not it had worked to Helena's benefit. It was unlikely that any guest would forget this wedding and if their memory was to falter Helena would give them an action replay. How did she get away with it? No matter what happened to the rest of them, Helena came up smelling of roses.

Was she jealous of Helena? Was she deluding herself pretending to a sense of injustice? Emma did not harp on the disparity of her and her sister's fortune so why was she so cut up about it.

'Aunt Pauline.'

'Gideon,' said Pauline unaccountably suspicious. 'Why aren't you dancing with that voluptuous girl you brought with you?'

'To be honest, she's a bit juvenile.' Gideon stepped conspiratorially close and confided to her ear, 'I would like a cigarette.'

Pauline opened the pack, offered it, shook her lighter to stimulate the gas and held the flame out for him. He hesitated, giving her a chance to give him the sermon, the public health warning. None came and he slipped his hands around the flame, touching her unnecessarily before lighting the tip and drawing in smoke. By repute, lighting cigarettes or having cigarettes lit for you was intimately sexual.

'You've always been my favourite aunt,' said Gideon. 'Did you know that?'

What was this little worm up to she wondered? Surely he was not going to make a play for her? Duncan claimed that Gideon's headboard had so many notches it would soon be splinters. Life was unfathomable, she decided. If Duncan was correct and Ian was sexually naive, how did he propagate this sex addict? He was such an unattractive boy, what did girls see in him? That obvious charm, as superficial as a doctor's bedside manner, but it was not the side of the bed he was after.

'Yes, Lucy is a bit young. I prefer more mature women.' In the crepuscule light Pauline could see the glint in his eye. 'Would you like to sleep with me? I'm very good in bed.'

'I'm glad you're good at something,' said Pauline. She dropped her spent cigarette stamped it into the ground and went back inside. It is odd, she thought, that both Helena's sons resent their upbringing but they telephone their mummy every day. Her boys never called.

* * *

The bride and bridegroom left early for the Honeymoon Suite, the White sisters buried the hatchet and swore undying love, the Eddowes forgave the host and hostess, among the guests allegiances were formed, unions were re-consecrated and the dancefloor was filled for *New York, New York*. Arms waved, balloons and breasts bounced and in the disabled toilet, frenzied activity reached fever pitch. As *God* saved the Queen the photographer reached a climax.

It took over an hour for the guests to say goodbye. Happy and tired, Ian and Helena arrived home at 2:00am.

'Did you see Duncan talking with Ben? Ian asked.

'Not really, no,' Helena was preoccupied, checking her list of guests and making notes.

'They were talking non-stop at dinner,' said Ian. 'I can't imagine what they find to talk about.'

'Neither do I,' said Helena abstractedly, 'I don't know why the wives put up with them.'

'During my speech, they talked the entire time. Poor Pauline,' said Ian.

'Poor Pauline,' Helena mimicked, tilting her head back and forth like a servant from the sub-continent. 'You give that woman far too much credit.'

'She's very bright,' said Ian. 'And she's very good-hearted.'

'What do you mean by that?' Helena snapped.

'Nothing,' said Ian, gauging it was time to withdraw. 'I'm going to my study for a while.'

'Give me Lady Christie's telephone number,' said Helena, putting an asterisk beside her name. 'I must give her a ring.'

'I'll dig it out,' said Ian on his way out. He made a cup of strong black coffee and, too exhilarated to work, watched a video of Wyford Town's 1998 triumph in the play-offs.

Having completed her list, there were asterisks by the names of Lady Christie, Ben Tilleulen, Celia and Katy Eddowes, Pauline and Duncan Black and the vicar. Too excited to sleep she re-polished her fingernails and toenails. This concentration helped her through a complete re-run. The adrenalin sustained for several days, well-wishers sent bouquets and the phone calls were never-ending. Helena was utterly fulfilled, because the wedding was a success beyond her wildest dreams. Ian, reluctant to be so lavish, grudgingly agreed it had all been worth it.

* * *

'How did you enjoy the wedding?' Pauline asked her two sons, who were lounging either side of her, Toby's finger poised over the television remote waiting for a chance to switch on.

John puffed out his cheeks and blew a steady chain of raspberries, 'Weddings are for women.'

'So young and so cynical,' said Pauline. 'I want to see you both married in church, white dress and all the trimmings.'

97

'Rather him than me,' said John.

'That goes for me to,' said Toby laconically, glaring at his mother.

'Don't give me that 'when is she going to bed' look. I'm going to stay up and drown my disappointment.'

'You do it on purpose don't you?' said Toby. 'Just piss off to bed and be done with it. He's already up there.'

'He's upstairs making notes, enough went on tonight to fill three volumes.'

'I've got another one for him,' said John. 'I was in the men's and I overheard a man holding a mobile telephone conversation in one of the cubicles. You know how people talk so loudly when they do that. You're on the bus and someone gets a call and the whole bus can hear the conversation. "I'm on the 275 just passing the police station",' he mimicked. '"I'll be getting off at the Red Lion in seven minutes and it's another four minutes walk from there." You know the sort of thing. This conversation going on in the cubicle was incongruous. The exchange did not jell with the voice so I hung about to see who it was.'

'Who was it?' asked Pauline.

'Uncle Ian,' said John.

'Who was he talking to?'

'As far as I could make out,' said John, 'it was a bird.'

* * *

The theme of *Lizzie Loses her Heart* was about a devout and pious young woman, torn between God and bodily functions, searching for the perfect man to provide the irrevocable token.

Lizzie's mother was proved correct. The eponymous Lizzie not only lost her heart but by the end of the book she had also lost her buried treasure. Not without a fight, though. It was a gargantuan struggle, a journey to the centre of the earth, climbing Everest with her legs crossed, circumnavigation of the globe in a yacht using a soiled handkerchief for a sail.

Lizzie losing heart helped Miss Borden circumnavigate the weekend and Miss Vidange Tacher's other two bodice rippers salvaged another couple. On the weekend of the wedding, when Ian telephoned her from the toilet of the Copse Hotel, her heart swelled to twice its size. Lizzie lay on her bed all day Sunday, selecting snippets from what he said, and her heart pinged gloriously.

Inspired by Suzanne's defection and by the mother in the latest story, who when faced with her daughter's fall from grace exposed a sophistication and worldly side previously hidden, Lizzie confessed all to her own mother. She explained how her feelings had unwittingly crept up on her. That she was now besotted with the man and on the night of the wedding he had called her from his mobile.

'Men just want one thing from a girl,' was her mother's sole piece of wisdom.

In truth, her mother's mindless response was fired by dilemma. Her initial reaction to her daughter loving an important personage like Ian Black CB was queer. The idea that he returned her affection started the glow that ignited the set piece. In the interplay between mother and daughter there were some things that must be said.

'Men just want one thing from a girl' was one of those. 'Dinner and their washing done,' was nearer the truth, thought Mrs Borden, but this was no time for frivolity.

'Do you want to be a home wrecker?'

'He doesn't love his wife, mum. She's not a very nice person.'

'If you take her husband, for whatever reason, you will not be a nice person either.'

Lizzie was cut to pieces by this undeniable fact and resorted to tears, 'It hurts so much,' she wailed through a torrent, spattering her mother's apron.

Mrs Borden accepted Lizzie's slumping body into her arms and soaked up tears and warmth. It had been an age since she had felt that wonderful sense of motherhood. She had created a child and that child was a right thinking person. Lizzie was a good girl who had overcome harsh setbacks and would reap the benefit of her resilience.

'Whatever you decide,' said her mother kissing her sweet smelling hair. 'It will be the right decision.'

Her mother's kind words thrust Lizzie into a renewed frenzy of sobs.

* * *

'Darling,' he said. 'I've realised how fond of you I am.'

Lizzie pulled the mobile away from her ear, the electricity snapped and crackled in every corner of her body.

'Darling, are you still there?'

'Yes, my love.'

There was a long silence while N Power restored order, as waves and currents were zinging their way junctions up the M1 and back again. Abelard and Heloise, Tristan and Isolde, Victoria and Albert, Victoria and David were preparing to step aside.

'See you on Monday.'

'Monday,' said Ian, 'it seems like forever.'

Chapter Sixteen

On the Monday after the wedding Helena was told that a reporter from the *Wyford Observer*, having got wind of the miracle, had turned up at the wedding just as the dancing began. Crook blocked his path and Ian sent him packing. Ian understood that Helena had written off the press and wanted nothing more to do with them.

'You sent him away?' Helena did not hide her contempt.

Ian, confused, said, 'I thought that is what you wanted.'

'I suggest in future you do not attempt to think and allow me to decide for myself.'

The story of the Wyford Miracle, belated though it was, mushroomed slowly, but mushroom it did. Despite being turfed out of the wedding reception, Roger Swope, Junior Reporter, resolutely persisted with his pursuit of the story. He sneaked around the back, cowered in the shadows and eavesdropped. He interviewed Reverend Waddenham. He knew Pellicci, the photographer from the Oddfellows Arms, and he acquired a copy of the guest list from the printers in return for a month's free advertising. The guests were only too happy to describe what they saw.

He gathered his material together and wrote enough blarney for a middle page spread in the *Wyford Observer*. It was thick with juicy detail and its veracity was not in doubt because of the photographic evidence. He was left with two outstanding problems; the paper would not meet the photographer's fee demands and his editor wanted him to interview the happy couple. They were away on their honeymoon in the Maldives.

'Every bloody honeymoon couple goes to the Maldives,' he complained. 'No wonder the place is sinking.'

He filled the time pending publication, polishing, editing and comparing his work to the scoops of the recent and distant past.

Swope was a perfectionist, he was ambitious and wanted to get to Fleet Street or Wapping or 'any bloody where outside Wyford'.

He rewrote his piece three or four times but remained in doubt. Writing up a miracle was a far cry from the Mayor opening the new Holland & Barratt. The reading public relied on reporters to colour their lives. It would not be fair to contain a big story like this in the little world that was Wyford. Why should he disappoint his future public? He desired a second opinion, a critique to be sure his article was inflammatory and that he had stretched the truth to its outer limits. He read the gathered material over and over. With the dais paperwork lost and the Architect blown to bits there was no one to refute Swope's mythical embellishments. Waddenham was happy to believe in miracles in the hope that it would attract more worshippers.

Tears welling in his eyes, Waddenham quoted, 'Church lit but without a congregation.'

Since his wife's departure he had a tendency to cry and his clothing, not properly aired, smelled of damp nappies. Preoccupied with his new found isolation, he had rejoined the lost souls. Although maintaining a suitably benign face for his parishioners, inwardly he was wrestling apostasy not dissimilar to the one disrupting Ian Black. As the great HG Wells, he preferred a woman to God any day of the week.

'Had it happened before?' asked Swope.

'Seeing the light so clearly and not metaphorically?' said the abstracted Waddenham. 'Not in my experience.'

It was when the story went nationwide that Swope came up trumps. Luckily, he was not alone on his magic carpet ride. His unlikely guardian angel travelled with him. He was not happy to go to print without photographic evidence. Thus far, withholding the pictures had given the story an edge and created a countrywide argument between believers and disbelievers, pending issue of the visual proof. Circumstances, due to this involuntary withholding, worked in Pellicci's favour and increased the value of her snapshots. It would seem that everybody was going to make on the deal.

Helena picked up the receiver delicately with a fingernail brush in one hand and a bottle of nail varnish in the other and said, 'Hello.'

'That's what I'm supposed to say,' said the jolly female voice on the other end of the line.

'Excuse me,' said Helena angrily having smudged her thumb. 'This is Helena Black speaking.'

'*L-O* magazine speaking.'

A genie that had dwelled for centuries, dormant in Helena's bottle of varnish, rose up out of the top, bowed low enough for his eminent proboscis to scrape the shag pile, 'Mistress,' he said in a obsequious accent. 'Your vish is my command.'

Helena fainted. After forty years of applying acetone the fumes had pierced her senses and caused a multiple hallucination. As she crashed to the ground, her nose occupied the spot on the carpet that the genie's had vacated. During its plummet her body got caught up in the telephone wiring and wrenched the plug out of the socket.

She came too, entangled on the Axminster, (when they purchased the carpet neither she or Ian had spotted that the label was spelled Axeminster) and remembered those magic words as if in a dream. Frantic to unravel from her bindings and dial 1471, agitation caused her to become more enmeshed. To escape this raging bondage she had to strip. Free at last she re-inserted the plug in the socket and the bell rang sweetly, 'Hello.' She said as though she had eaten a thousand plums.

'Mrs Black?'

'Yes,' she said with a 'u' instead of an 'e'.

'*L-O* magazine,' said the voice. 'Is everything OK?'

Helena resisted, 'Sorry about that.' She pronounced 'sorry' as though it had a fringe on the top. 'The phone slipped.'

'Yes,' said the voice. 'That happens now and then.'

So, as Helena's wildest dream unfolded she stood listening in a pair of voluminous pink knickers and bare breasts.

The soothing voice explained what she wanted and her bare nipples grew erect. What she was saying was not erotic but as sexy as Helena could get. They planned to do a spread of the miracle and a representative would be calling at the house to discuss terms. Terms of business or financial remuneration, in this instance, were irrelevant. Helena was prepared to sub their expenses. This was her life's version of the Holy Grail.

* * *

Pellicci was a happy man. He knew the value of what he had kept from Swope and holding out for a better price had increased the value of the pictures astronomically. Swope had sold the story to the nationals and for the time being the photographer was leaving his messages unanswered. His answering machine was acting as auctioneer and with each ring of the bell the bid grew higher. It was not just the money, he was an artist and the bridesmaid's portrait on the dais bathed in iridescence was worthy of a 'best of' anthology. It was right up there with Robert Capa's dying Spaniard, David Bailey's Shrimpton and Hugo Dixon's Andretti. This was his ticket to the big time, but more importantly his ticket out of Wyford.

When he originally interviewed the photographer Swope had temporary hold of a copy of the proof. He held it longingly and Pellicci had to prise it out of the poor man's hand.

The photographer was a good interviewee, keenly observant, but his adjectives were treacly verbose and his Italian as phoney as a judge on a ballroom dance show.

'It started slowly,' he camped, his Italian ancestry painting his tongue. 'Its luminosity transforming the bride from a dowdy frump into a fantastical vision, *bellisima*.'

Swope disagreed, the sour-faced bride look startled and confused but not *bellisima*.

' ..Time and hymn suspended, the music paused without missing a beat.'

In his recollection of the service, the organist, who did not have the best view seated behind the standing congregation in a corner by the chancel screen, claimed that for two bars the instrument played itself.

'... It was a wondrous service, mercifully short, *To Be a Pilgrim* and a sermon of full fifteen pages lasted just four minutes.'

'Now, that is a miracle,' said Swope and added it to his notes.

'Champagne, and small talk flowed and the band sizzled. Guests were pinching each other to be sure they were awake and danced themselves into a slow frenzy...'

'Slower please,' said Swope. 'I'm having trouble getting this down.'

'...A conga line danced round the grounds and returned with daisy chains. *New York, New York*, arms aloft, swaying in unison. Huddles and kisses, cuddles and blessings, *grazie mi amore...*'

'How do you spell 'mi'? Is it m, e or m, i?'

'...Suddenly, auld lang syne, it was done. M, i...'

'Thanks...'

'I'm not finished,' Pellicci reprimanded. 'The band packed up with that deft, efficient discreetness of an abortionist caught red-handed and slipped away into the bushes. Burnished cheeks flushed with lipstick and glancing blows, hearts glowing with sweet words from sweet lips, hands tingling from clasps and expectation. The parents surveyed the residue of their joyous day. The abandoned room, strewn with streamers, bobbling neurotic balloons, spilled and uneaten torte de la nonna, the drunk, the punch drunk, wondering whether they were worthy of this profundity...'

'You photographed all this?'

'Most of it.' Pellicci replaced his maestro hair with both sets of fingers. 'I missed part of the evening while I was shagging the bridesmaid in the disabled toilet.'

'Bridesmaid?' Swope checked through his notes, 'Amy Tilleulen, the girl in the picture.'

'That's the one,' said the photographer, proud as a peacock. '*Bellisima*, aren't you just a teensy bit envious? *Piccolo*,' he gestured with thumb and forefinger.

'Hardly,' said Swope. 'She's fourteen.'

* * *

Word got back to Helena that Pellicci was going to make a killing on her 'miracle' and sell their property to the highest bidder. 'Do something about it,' she demanded.

Ian wobbled and then prevaricated, 'There is no law that can prevent him selling his own property. Copyright belongs to him, you see.'

'We paid for them,' Helena hands on hips, jutted out her jaw. 'The customer is always right, is that in your statute book? They belong to us and I want them, NOW.'

'Ah!' Ian prevaricated some more and wobbled. 'There is a problem with that, on two fronts.'

'You didn't pay for them,' Ian was positive she was going to clip the back of his head and he ducked into his collar. 'Youuu...'

'Not yet,' he cringed. 'I was meaning to. I thought the proofs were excellent. Good enough for the family album.'

'You never intended to pay,' Helena flexed her fingers. 'Pictures with 'proof' stamped across them.'

'Don't be silly,' said Ian, now so low in his chair his torso was horizontal. 'Of course I was going to pay.'

Helena flounced out, sat on the bed initially too livid to paint and brooded. She would put a cheque through the door in the morning and speak to their solicitor. He was bound to be more help than that feeble skinflint she was married to. Without thinking, she reached for the polish and touched up the colour. Reaching her feet was no facile occurrence. Recently accessing her toes was causing a blockage in her breathing apparatus. No amount of fidgeting gained easier access. She bent over until suffocating, then re-surfaced like a whale, stuck her nose above the water line, breathed deep and dived. The exercise brought on an attack of dizziness and she subsided onto the pillow.

Helena claimed sanctimoniously, what goes around comes around, and there is no such thing as a free lunch. She had huge experience with the probity of these clichés. In manifesting some trivial justification she might embellish her rationalisations with a piece of pure fiction and in less than a week, it would travel full circle – the diameter of Helena's circle was relatively small – and the fiction would be repeated to her, embroidered, enriched with detail as though the story was the teller's own. It was like the *Daily Mail* being read to a blind person.

Although she had decided on a course of action, Helena was not satisfied. Usually patient when applying her control to situations, this problem was on a larger scale with too many outside, uncontrollable influences. She decided she must seek advice. Usually her mother was the first port of call but Helena suspected that she would not be a vigorous ally. She spoke to Emma, seeking ammunition for a settlement and was told of the able goings on in the disabled toilet.

Dressed for business in a dark grey suit, the one she used for funerals, a neat charcoal hat, a choker at her throat and coal button earrings, she shoved open the shop door. A bell rang plaintively for such rough handling but no one came to its rescue. She rapped loudly on the counter with her umbrella and called,

'Shop', in the decisive voice she had prepared for the confrontation. Helena was riled and when she was riled she was a force to be reckoned with.

Pellicci emerged from the back of the shop wiping his hands on a grubby towel, seeing who his visitor was and her demeanour he said cautiously, 'Come to settle up?'

'I hardly think so,' she squeezed in, raised her shoulders and thrust out her jaw. She opened her bag and thumped a proof on the counter. 'Do you know that girl?'

'What about her?'

'She's fourteen.'

The photographer's eyelids grew heavy causing him to stare at the floor, he focussed there for a while hoping that when he looked up she would be gone but she was still there, glaring, unblinking, fierce and implacable. His miracle was over.

Chapter Seventeen

In readiness for *L-O's* photo shoot Helena got to work on the house. She looked over the shoulder of as many *L-O* weddings as she could find and rearranged the furniture. She studied each new layout through the lens of her instamatic. Unsure of the provenance of the furnishings in the pictures, she enlisted the help of her sister Emma, known for her good taste. They visited Heals and Harrods and gradually Helena produced a reasonable facsimile of the decor worthy of a society dwelling. When it was complete, she needed confirmation that she had got it right and invited her coterie to tea. This was an agonising sacrifice on her part. There would be cups and plates to wash and if just one of them spilt so much as a crumb on her new bits and bobs, they would be guillotined.

The day of the tea party dawned bright and sunny. Optimistic that tea would be served in the garden and her new trimmings safe from spillage, whistling happily, she unwrapped the Marks & Spencer catering. As midday approached, the sky darkened, the heavens opened and her concerns mounted. Not only did she have to worry about crumbs and spotting but damage caused by muddy feet. A strong cup of milky tea did not do the trick, there only one thing for it, one certain way to settle her nerves.

Helena had developed an obsession with yachts and spent many a happy hour choosing a name for her sixty footer. They had visited the harbour in Palma and seen such a boat with a crew dressed in Persil white shirts, shorts and socks, the shirts with black epaulettes. That was the yacht for her and her guest list was the envy of the gossip columns. Her fantasies were meticulously detailed and the guests' histories were scrupulously screened, one slip and they were scratched. After Princess Diana's death the

Royal Family were persona non grata. Since that time the Queen had been reprieved but in most cases once eliminated there were no second chances. Such minutiae could take hours of deliberation and she had a sense of her own foolishness because these lists were kept hidden in her treasure box.

Dressed in her lilac dress, a mink stole and tiara she waited in line. She turned to her left and checked to see if Ian's tie was straight. She could see how nervous he was and patted him on the arm to comfort him. A glance to the right and she met the eyes of the Duke of Cumberland. They shared a knowing smile. The Queen was getting closer and closer, greeting the honoured guests with a nod. She stopped fleetingly to speak with President Bush and hurried along until she reached Helena, who, sensing her rush, came to a sudden stop.

Helena curtseyed and the Queen smiled sweetly, 'Lady Black, you're looking well.'

'Yes thank you, ma'am.'

'I've heard the wedding went well.'

'It was wonderful, ma'am,' said Helena, her peripheral vision noting the heads craning to see to whom the Queen was giving so much of her time.

'You must come to tea,' said the Queen. 'I'd love to hear about it. Give my equerry your telephone number and we'll have a chat.'

Helena acted out a few variations of this scene attaching a subtle twist. As she packed her treasure away she felt wonderfully high, stimulated by her new footing with Her Majesty. The telephone rang during the afternoon and despite the party, Helena insisted on taking the call in case it was her summons to Buckingham Palace.

Miraculously, the skies cleared and an intense sun dried the lawn. Tea in the garden was over and cleared away without a semblance of a mishap. The coterie assembled for the grand opening and Polly led the way into the through lounge. Open-mouthed, her friends wondered at her skill for interior design. She was bowled over by their enthusiasm and explained that the refurbishment was for a spread in the magazine of magazines. Not only were they bowled over, they were in awe.

As the adoration reached its zenith there was a ring at the

front door bell. 'Emma, come in, come in.'

'I can't stop,' said Emma. 'I'm with Pauline. She's waiting in the car.'

'Fetch her,' Helena's ego did a cartwheel, she would show that snooty bitch some good taste. 'I won't take no for answer.'

Emma deliberated momentarily but caved in. Helena watched her sister persuading her reluctant passenger through the open door of her Land Rover. Pauline entered the room apologising for being dressed in faded jeans and a loose fitting sweater that sagged to one side, revealing a bony collar bone and a bra strap.

Complete with receipts, Helena began a second designer label inventory of the room for Emma and Pauline's benefit. The latter, having eaten cheese for lunch, quickly grew catatonic and fought to keep awake. She was not a good night sleeper. She suffered from an overactive mind and mild insomnia which, since her sciatica, had worsened. Not only was she tired from lack of sleep but irritable.

Helena's guided tour stopped by the mantelpiece where a picture in a gold frame of Ian being presented with his CB by Prince Charles was flanked by a pair of porcelain leopards. Helena pinpointed the artistic merit and precise cost of these china beasts. The roomful of critics shared her rapture.

Pauline was in awe of the ardour expressed for the porcelain leopards and because they were bought in Harrods made them more than acceptable . She wondered about the obsession for designer labels.

Duncan glibly passed it off as always. 'If you have no confidence in your own taste or ideas, it's safe.'

'It's more than that, you wouldn't understand,' said Pauline. 'People are impressed by what you buy.'

'I know,' said Duncan. 'That's part of the con, you pay twice or three times as much for the same product because of the initials on the label.'

She came to when someone prodded her knee, 'Sorry, I was miles away.'

'Dreaming were you?' said Helena condescendingly. Helena was displeased with her brother-in-law and her brother-in-law's wife. She did not care for their attitude. Helena had a long memory and kept a list of dissatisfactions, the list was growing.

She would manage retribution. Her chance would come. A true Machiavellian, she bided her time. 'I'm afraid it must be daunting for you, Duncan being left in the wake of his brother's success.'

'I hadn't noticed a problem,' Pauline answered cautiously.

Pauline understood that she was different things to different people and that irrelevancies coloured views and opinions. She saw in herself a tendency to be blinkered and fiddle or massage an idea until it fitted with her prejudices.

She tried to like Helena but it was a hard task. She held a morbid fascination for the woman's eccentricity, which had started out as a source of amusement but the joke had worn thin. Helena's dominating company palled.

Helena Black was a phoney. She manipulated herself and her life to impress. She was always centre stage, expressing fake sentiment and regard for her children. She spoke of Ian's work in a contrived accent as though she sat on his diligent shoulder, he the pirate and she the parrot. It was when animated that Helena exposed her true self, a fishwife. Meeting new people, gushing, gushing, until she found out you were nobody and, fishlike, you were forgotten in an instant. Helena Black was a designer label.

Pauline decided her sister-in-law was up to something and gathered her wits.

'Yes,' said Helena, her eyes glinting with merriment. 'I got my husband into shape early on. That's where you went wrong, my dear.'

Pauline did not want to rise to the bait but the room was quiet and expectant and she was embarrassed into a response. 'In what way was that?'

Helena gestured a sweeping and tolerant resignation, pointing out the newly furnished room. 'Settling for second best, sweetie, but then you don't have the same standards as me.'

The telephone rang and Pauline was spared. While Helena was out of the room, she got up to leave and refused a lift home. As Emma was seeing Pauline out the door, Helena appeared from the kitchen, gushing and playful, 'Goodbye, and thanks for coming. I'm sure it was a pleasure.'

Pauline snapped, 'It's always a pleasure to see you, Helena. You're so wonderful.'

Since Ian had received his CB, Helena's fantasies were

becoming more omnipotent. His gong allowed her an honorary seat on the bench of a mythical court. In her head, a CB's wife had far reaching powers and she adjudicated several misdemeanours. Helena had a keen eye for detail. She supervised the empanelling of juries, assisted the lawyers with their cross-examination, made trial notes in a ledger and summed up in favour of the prosecution.

She passed sentence wearing a synthetic mauve wig she acquired from a Zandra Rhodes fashion night. As a side effect of her impeccable care in sitting judgement, her radical dress set a trend in the legal process for women. In the choosing of ceremonial wigs they were able to swap multi-coloured acrylic for horse hair.

It was the sentencing that gave Helena most pleasure. Minor offences were treated harshly and punished with a ruthless streak that made Judge Jeffreys seem as severe as Jane Bennett. Anyone who slighted Helena was put on mock trial and punishment meted out. Retribution became more and more sadistic. She carried out justice for snubs dating back to her school days and avenged a list of grievances perpetrated by her sisters.

Prior to the wedding, Emma had cancelled an appointment to accompany Helena to the dressmakers. She used some feeble excuse about seeing the doctor with Amy and there had been nobody to help her choose her lilac vision. She brought Emma before a tribunal and her shopping rights were withdrawn for a month.

Helena was an indefatigable supporter of capital punishment. She and Ian regularly fell out over the issue and it was the only topic over which Ian was blatantly disobedient. No amount of waspish stares would budge him.

He adopted an affected attitude and spouted rhetoric, 'I'm only obeying orders.'

She noticed that he was only obeying orders when there was flak flying around. Once he was off to cloud cuckoo land, hiding behind that annoying glazed trance, there was no point in persisting and she let the matter drop. Her day would come. It always did.

Outwardly, Helena was fiercely loyal to her husband. Her true feelings about his work were mixed because they were something of a disappointment. She expected the corridors of power to be trodden by glamorous men who drank vodka martinis, drove Aston Martins and beat women off with sticks.

Instead they were excruciatingly boring, colourless individuals who took themselves far too seriously, and 99 per cent of what they did failed miserably or was overturned by the next government. If only these reversals came without recriminations.

'If only they had persisted with the policy for a few more months...'

'If only they had given the new legislation a chance...'

'It's only the incoming minister not wanting the outgoing minister to get undue credit...'

'A new broom tends to sweep clean even to the detriment of good policy...'

...and so on.

After her sycophantic friends departed, Helena nipped upstairs and donned her mauve wig. Pauline Black was brought before her court and found guilty by twelve good women and true.

'Is there anything you wish to say before sentence is passed upon you?'

'You're wonderful, your ladyship.'

'You have been found guilty by a jury of your peers and I sentence you to hang by the neck until you are dead.'

Helena had forgotten to place the black cap on her mauve wig before passing sentence and promised herself a retrial for the following morning. In the meantime she would accumulate some more crimes to be taken into account.

Pauline was not the only criminal and there was another blackguard who showed no interest in her revisions to the house decorations; her husband. Ian was deeply involved in revisions of his own and was oblivious to all else.

There was mitigating evidence not brought up at Ian's mock trial. Ian was oblivious to all accoutrements. He bought dark suits and socks, white shirts and underwear. He was not a victim of designer labels or style. As for the house, a chair was comfortable to sit in or it was not, any other consideration was irrelevant. Ian was oblivious to Helena's refurbishing because she had replaced the originals with exact copies. Ian had not even noticed that the replacements were new because with the care and attention Helena applied to her possessions, the discarded items were almost as fresh as the day they were delivered.

Chapter Eighteen

Pauline Black was a happy person. She got out of bed every morning glad to be alive. Her most endearing trait was her ability to interrupt a conversation at 9:35 am and resume it at 5:45 pm, exactly where she left off. Those unaware of this quirk were left floundering. Dining out with their sons, she flummoxed John to the point he had to look to his father for help, and Duncan duly paraphrased.

'How did you get that from what she said?'

'Thirty years of practice,' said Duncan.

Pauline knew why she and Duncan were so comfortable together. They coasted through life well within their limitations. Not having to stretch, they were free of stress within their relationship. Pauline suffered a genetic need for anxiety, and worried unnecessarily.

Pauline needed to care for something, give it her daily attention. Duncan was hostile to even a sniff of mothering and when the boys outgrew her nurture she lost sleep massaging her superfluous guilt. Meanwhile Duncan slept like a baby.

Her ageing parents were typical of the bread that formed the top slice of the sandwich generation. Selfish, undeserving with an outmoded expectation that their children would provide, Pauline lay awake seeking a kindly way to satisfy their constant demands without causing too much upheaval to Duncan and the boys. It was an unrelenting battle juggling time. In their late eighties, they belonged in a home but her father, an implacable man, grew more recalcitrant with age, and refused to see sense. Her mother moaned incessantly about him.

'All he eats is chocolate.'

Just after his 82nd birthday he got up in the night for a

Cadbury's flake and dropped dead on the kitchen floor.

Packed and ready to move in with her daughter, Duncan drove Mrs Jay to Rose Lodge. The old lady sulked for a few days but it was not long before she was regaling the other residents with stories of her wonderful husband. For over twenty years Pauline had suffered a litany of gripes about her father.

'I don't know how much more of this I can stand.' Her mother pressed the back of her hand against her forehead and slumped. The moment he died Pip Jay, known as 'Popping', was reinstated as the love of her life. Pauline was no fool, she saw the futility. Growing apart was natural progression, easing the path to coping with widowhood.

Early on, Pauline sensed that she did not think the way others thought. Her friends had pictures of Donny Osmond or David Cassidy taped to the lid of their desks but she had Marc Bolan.

It was not their conventionality that troubled her, it was acceptance of facts without question. She had a nose for the truth and, more often than not, that was not the information to hand. As she grew older, she was more aware of the mistruths in her friends, less and less could she find a better side of people and that worried her. She had been a compliant youngster, but found she was getting less pliable by the day and prayed she was not turning into her father.

'What do you think?'

Duncan watched her face carefully. She had been dreading this moment. What could she say? It was good, but...what a 'but'.

She shook her head. Being pulled in two directions at once, she said, 'Are you sure you want to publish this?'

'Why on earth not?'

'You will alienate every friend and relative we have.'

'Nobody recognises themselves, especially in print.'

'I hope you're right.'

'You wanted to move to the coast when the boys were off our hands.'

'I was doing that out of choice, not to outrun a pack of hounds.'

Pauline used to be amused by her husband, the loose cannon, but sometimes his dogmatism was tiresome. He would not read a newspaper because they were ill-informed. He had developed her knack for lampoon and would take few matters seriously.

'I'm not going.'

'You have to,' said Pauline, 'out of respect.'

'There's no point to church or religion anymore.'

'Is there any point in asking why?'

'The meek have inherited the earth,' said Duncan. 'The show's over.'

He believed the things he said and there was no dissuading him. She would attend church on her own and joke about his absence.

It had started with that damn laptop.

John had wanted an updated machine to take to university and left the old one on the desk in his room. Pauline did not get wind of what Duncan was up to for some time. He seconded John's room as an office and used the hi-fi to play music loudly. He did not tell her what he had been up to until he finished the first draft.

As soon as Shirtz reached puberty he discovered emasculation. He was too green to know the word for his discovery but he was aware of the phenomenon just the same. He was aware of exploitation without the means to articulate his findings. It was later he understood that the minority exploit the majority and the majority let it happen because they are afraid. Afraid to step out of the box, afraid to put their nose above the parapet, afraid to be different, afraid to stand out. There is safety in numbers.

This was the personification of Duncan, a man swimming against the tide, who stuck his neck out and upset the innocent with his treasons. He was a maverick among the impoverished, contemptuous of the conventional and unprepared to countenance the prosaic.

Would he ever grow up? Pauline wondered.

People make a life. They do it as simply as they can manage. If there is a roof over your head and food on the table you are a success. Caulfield understood that.
'It takes a bit of effort to find there is so much more.'

*Caulfield knew they laughed at him behind his back, that he
was a figure of fun. His regard for his fellow men and women
amused them. He was risible because the consensus found
him amusing and the majority were always right. He was not
only wrong but arrogant in his persistence.*

Pauline's sister Maureen flew in from Australia for their father's
funeral but returned soon after. When their mother moved into
Rose Lodge Pauline had the thankless task of clearing out her
parents' house. She had to rifle through the pockets of her father's
clothes like a thief before shoving them in a black sack for Sue
Ryder. She had packed their few books in a box, when she found
a photograph of her and her sister inside one of them. She
unpacked the box and riffled the pages.

Inside a copy of *William's Crowded Hours* was a school
picture of Mrs Robinson's class at Orchard School, Duncan head
and shoulders above the rest, hair spilling over his forehead and
his shirt tail showing. She wore bobbed hair, downcast eyes and
a striped frock.

Five years later, she saw him again. It was a church dance, and
she had not wanted to go but Emma White made her. The dance
was organised by the vicar of St Marks and held in the Parish Hall.
Duncan had been dragged home from the park by the ear, kicking
and screaming, made to have a bath and dress in a suit. Escorted
to the door of the Parish Hall and forced inside to find clusters of
gawky kids skulking in corners, girls hiding giggles behind hands
and spotty Herberts holding cups of non-alcoholic punch trying
to look cool.

Pauline's childhood was full of smells. Now life was so
sanitised the nostalgic odours were disappearing. The smell of
laundry, horseshit, urine on staircases, French cigarettes, body
odour, dog and boiling cabbage, girls who smelled of face powder,
cheap perfume with a dash of sweat.

Reverend Williams and his wife made them take partners and
dance to the music of a cheap gramophone, the speakers barely
loud enough for the sound to reach the walls.

Duncan was partnered with an ice maiden. Hair lacquered
iron stiff with sharp points either side of her jaw. Her impassive
face was over made up to cover the fading embers of acne and her

eyes thick with black eye make-up. She wore a heavy mauve suit, white blouse and a silver necklace with a cross. The music slowed and he took her hand in his and electricity travelled along his veins. He could feel the swell of her hip and his head raced for things to say.

'I bet I can guess your name,' he said mischievously.

Her pout was lost to a shy smile and Duncan was surprised her make-up did not crack with the movement, 'Really?'

'Really,' he repeated, slipping into the game of pretence. 'Would I lie?'

'All boys lie,' she said confidently.

'Not this one,' said Duncan. 'Do you want to know why?'

'Because you've already told too many,' she said, her confidence taking his breath away. She did not speak like other girls and the way she talked lit a long dormant pilot sputtering in his head. Ideas, like flames, burst into action and the torrent of questions filled him with curious hope.

'Do you remember we had a vote for the prettiest girl in the class?'

'I got one vote.'

'That was me.'

The look she gave him reignited the boiler and they danced on in silence, each engrossed. He struggled to get up the nerve to express what he felt and squeezed her hand gently in a polite show of affection. She responded by pressing her head to his chest.

Duncan kept the reason for his rebellion locked away for years, until Pauline told her story of how she lost faith in adults. She was about five years old and attending a wedding where her sister was bridesmaid and she was not. Not being a bridesmaid was a galling slap in the face for her. She was too upset to eat and, being much younger than the other children at her table, was being ignored. Bored, she went in search of her father. She leaned against his leg and he patted her stomach.

'Hmmm,' he said. 'I can feel chicken, potatoes and green beans,' causing great merriment at the table.

'Let me check,' said Uncle Basil placing his hand on her tummy. 'Definitely, chicken and potatoes but not so many green beans.'

This was why they were kindred spirits because of some parental foolishness committed when they were children. Duncan had confided a worry to his mother and father and the following week his cousins teased him with his concern. He was six or seven years old when he vowed he would not confide in his parents again.

Chapter Nineteen

L-O magazine contacted Helena and wanted to do the re-shooting of the wedding the weekend following Chris' birthday, depending on the weather. The front page storm clouds evaporated and an Indian summer began on the Wednesday. It did not rain again for a fortnight.

Ian was under strict orders to be home on Sunday, no excuses.

L-O magazine sat arrogantly at home on Helena's precious furniture. One girl with studs in an eyebrow and lower lip kicked off her shoes and tucked her legs under her skirt. Helena was torn, staring at the culprit trying to green ray her displeasure, but the girl was oblivious.

'These oiks are from another planet,' she decided but would not admit any further disenchantment that would sour her dream.

A cocky boy, overburdened with camp, was the 'art director', who introduced himself deprecatingly with two fingers from each hand implying inverted commas.

He looked around the room with distaste and announced, 'I doubt that we will be doing interiors, sweeties.'

'Not this side of Christmas, darling.'

'I hate Christmas,' said the lady in charge, the Locations Editor. She had a pretty face, framed in copper hair, and the body of a welterweight. She was dressed in black and white hoops from collar to tights. Not only was she a humbug but she dressed like one.

'I see what you mean,' she said. 'All right for *Country Life*, I suppose.'

'Or *SAGA*,' said the camp.

Helena struggled to keep her temper, over-compensating to hide her anger, she was morbidly unctuous. Ian was bemused, seeing his wife flapping about, hanging onto these ragamuffins' every word. When the wedding photographs were produced their languid insolence dispersed. Animatedly they handed the snapshots round and rubbished the content.

Openly discussing them as though they were not present in the room, the L-O team spoke of cropping, superimposing and airbrushing their sorry images with a makeover.

'We'll have lose the lilac,' said the Art Director. 'It clashes with her hair.'

'The computer will take care of that.'

'Who chose your colour scheme, Mrs Black? Too awful.'

'Who's that ugly man?'

Helena leaned forward, 'That's the best man, my son Gideon.'

'We won't need him for the re-shoots.'

The reprise of the wedding was a sobering event. The morning of the big day, Helena opened the curtains onto a swirl of light drizzle spattering the windows. By lunchtime the wind had transformed solid cloud into balls of cotton wool scudding neatly between the houses. It reminded Ian of Helena doing her toenails.

Summoned family and production team congregated outside St Marks and, being a weekend, there was a crowd of spectators. Unused to modelling, unaccustomed to taking direction, the wedding party were soon exasperated. With Amy's arrival they were shoved aside and relegated to extras.

Helena was promised a preview copy of the spread and waited impatiently for its arrival. The published article was a big disappointment. Helena and Ian were in a solitary shot of Amy, seen in the background admiring the bridesmaid. When she applied a strong magnifying glass to discern their faces, Helena wore her waspish and Ian his situations vacant.

The centre piece was the picture taken by the wedding photographer as the beam of light was at its most luminous. Amy was looking up to see where the light was coming from and everyone else on the dais had been airbrushed out. The bold text asked, 'Amy Telleulin, bridesmaid or angel?'

There was the standard picture of the happy couple, which upset Katy. They had no choice but to include one of the wedding photos which technology was able to tweak slightly out of focus.

'Katy looks like Doris Day at the end of her career,' said Celia, once again miffed because the Eddowes had been completely overlooked.

The miracle, consolidated by the presence of the angel, took precedence over the wedding, which was glossed over in the general text. Amy was compared to Joan of Arc together with an inset of Ingrid Bergman to verify their claim, and the inset was printed in black and white to emphasise it was the olden days.

To escape the kerfuffle going on at the front of the church, Reverend Waddenham hid in his study and refused to re-pose for the cameras. He took out the picture of his wife from its hiding place and wept bitterly.

'My darling,' he cried. 'How could you?'

Needing to take his mind off his loneliness he began preparing his sermon. He knew the text he wanted and opened his old working bible to the book of St John. He flicked the pages and found a piece of paper marking a previous text. It was the missing instructions for adjusting the dais according to the solstice and the text it marked was St John 1:8.

Helena harangued the magazine with complaints about the feature and demands for re-printing. They hung up on her. She cancelled her subscription.

None of her friends noticed the shortcomings, they remained awestruck. Helena eventually came to terms with her plight and relied on commentary of the event rather than the finished article.

Chapter Twenty

Katy lay listening to unfamiliar noises. A lorry bleated as it backed up to the hotel kitchen. Soft, happy voices cursed, a door slammed and in the next room the television blared. None of this noise could blot out Chris' snores.

Not for the first time in her life, Katy felt cheated. She got out of bed and checked that the bleeding had stopped. She washed in the bidet and found a glutinous mess on her thigh. She took fright, her heart fluttering. What could it be? When she realised what it was, she washed twice to be sure she was rid of it.

Could she be pregnant already?

They had made a bargain. No children. They had shaken hands on it. Katy pretended to be a modern woman. Children would stand in the way of her career and if she gave up work they would not be able to pay the mortgage. In truth she was terrified of pain, reluctant to be inconvenienced by a screaming brat and concerned that she might pass on her disease.

Getting out of bed, she had inadvertently pulled the duvet off her new husband.

'Weren't men ugly.'

She went to the window and pressed her naked torso against the glass, her soft breasts and slack stomach soaked up the cool.

'Miracles and sex, especially sex, are overrated.' She liked to talk when nobody was listening, it prevented contradiction and Katy hated being contradicted.

'Save yourself, save your most treasured possession, for what?'

It had not been hard to take a pledge of celibacy. Boys revolted her and men were worse. There had always been some dirty old man pawing at her. She was one of those girls who men fancied their chances with, being plain they were doing her a favour.

Mayor Swan, a miserable man who was at his happiest grumbling, cornered her in the committee rooms. Unused to smiling, his evil leer struck her as funny. He chased her round the committee table, her merriment hindered her getaway and he caught her in a corner. He put his arms around her, and leered before clamping his mouth on hers. He reeked of tobacco and she bit him.

'You minx!' he tried to laugh it off. 'You should know that mature men are more considerate in bed.'

Saving herself, for what, two minutes of clutching? And it hurt like the devil. What possible pleasure could be gained from that?

As for the miracle, she wanted no part of it. A lot of foolishness over nothing. People were funny. The more she thought about it the less sense it made. God; nobody had seen or heard of anything provable that God existed. You might as well believe in fairies.

'What a load of baloney.'

* * *

Katy ran on, feeling awkward, not used to motion, and her nipples were sore from rubbing against her shirt. She walked a few yards, massaging the pain, then continued running again.

She had waited for Chris to fall asleep before getting dressed and sneaking out. She loved the solitude of the empty night. Just her, the nocturnal jogger, a few bawling cats, a busy fox and a family of laughing badgers progressing through the night. Occasionally she would come across a late bird, men getting furtively out of their cars looking up at bedroom windows for signs of life or courting couples looking sidelong at her passing.

It was a dangerous path, but the park was an essential part of her route. Rapists lurked behind every tree, her heart skulked in her mouth but getting through the gates without incident was exhilarating.

Sweating and sanctimonious, she sneaked back into the house and showered. She lay beside her sleeping husband buoyed with a sense of triumph, wrapped herself in her share of the duvet and fell quickly asleep.

Friends and family persisted with their claims that Chris had married a clone of his mother. He knew this not to be the case.

'One Helena Black is enough for a community.'

Chris could not deny that both Katy and his mother were pear-shaped. What was harder to admit was how quickly their marriage was pear-shaped. Neither liked sex very much, but they dutifully attempted to overcome their distaste on a Sabbath eve. This habit dwindled and Katy spent her weekends topping up her Princess Diana scrapbook or doing the general knowledge crossword in the *Sunday Express*.

Although united in their detestation of parents, he and Katy shared little common ground. They were loners because neither had a friend to speak of. Katy's parents were the architects of her isolation and marriage had provided escape. Chris was more enigmatic, and baffled Katy. He did not have a good word for his mother or father but he called his parents often and visited most Saturdays.

'There's no football. Where are you going?'

'I thought I'd pop in to my parents.'

'Why?'

'I don't know.'

Being married gave Katy freedom. She could read without checking on the mood of anyone else in the room or make polite and dreary chatter. When there was football or Chris was busy at the office, doing odd jobs about the house or working in the loft she was left gloriously alone.

Her parents did not want her even having so much as a television in her room. They worried that she would become a hermit locked away upstairs. She was a virtual prisoner, so when Chris came along she saw him as a Trojan horse. He seemed as suitable as any man.

Happy, she set new targets and she indulged several whims to exploit her new found liberty. For no particular reason she decided to slim and decided that running would be a good way to lose weight. She started at the weekends, and embarrassed to be seen in scanty clothing, she napped during the day and ran at night. Within three months she shed four stone.

She borrowed her mother's sewing machine, reduced the size of her clothing and became a skilful seamstress. Tall for a woman, the lost weight transformed her from a pear to a peach. She resisted the temptation to check the slim line Katy Black, but once she did it became a daily obsession. She could not believe her eyes.

The woman in the reflection was a stranger. What she did not discern was that contentment had smoothed over the cracks in her face. The sour mouth, with its turned down corners, had levelled out, the frown that ploughed from ear to ear became fallow and, as her head grew proud, the shadows that clouded her ultramarine eyes were lifted.

No longer was she a frump and she developed a taste for flashy clothes. She surveyed the shelves for weeks before daring to purchase a copy of *Elle* magazine. The title being French suggested the content might be degenerate. No one took very much notice of her purchase and she tried *Vogue*, *Nova* and *Cosmopolitan*. What she read in the latter publication left her dumbfounded.

She could not get up the nerve go to any of the dress shops publicised by these magazines so she tried her hand at copying. She surprised herself with her own creativity, but was too shy to be seen out in her self-made costumes. Her Aunt Sadie gave her two metres of red silk and Katy turned it into a blouse.

'This is too modern for an old cow like me,' said Sadie. 'You keep it, I'm glad the material has been put to good use.'

Waiting in Katy's wardrobe was a black pleated skirt that matched perfectly.

Once she was fully grown, Katy had experienced a problem with underwear.

'Princess Margaret has the same problem,' said her mother.

Katy could not rationalise how the public could know such an intimate detail concerning a royal. Her bulky thighs rubbed together, wearing holes in the gussets of her knickers. Celia tried a multitude of formulas to prevent the inevitable, none of which worked satisfactorily.

Pleased with her new figure, replete with slimmer thighs, Katy bought a pair of daring panties.

'Are these a present?' asked the assistant. 'Would you like them gift wrapped?'

Unprepared to be cross-examined in this way, Katy went as red as the lace, spluttered and nodded wildly. During the interminable wait for the fancy packaging she paced back and forth staring doggedly at the floor. She snatched the parcel out of the assistant's hands and ran all the way home.

Katy was no longer a frump but Chris did not notice. He had acquired a top of the range pair of binoculars.

His conversion of the loft space was making slow progress because access was unsatisfactory. Chris found a folding timber stair on e-bay and travelled to Dunstable to check its suitability. He was able to install it in their semi without any outside help and was very pleased with his acquisition. He could climb into the loft and, with the aid of ropes, pull the stair back into the loft after him.

He was creating a den, set aside for his hobbies and possessions. He had to remove the struts that prevented the purlins from warping and propped them at regular intervals. Cutting and framing completed, he hired an industrial vacuum cleaner and sucked up the dust, sawdust and tile fragments. He then stapled breathable felt to the rafters and paid for the fitting of two velux windows. He covered the floor with tongued and grooved chipboard and left the room in this utility state. He ordered a lining board that had to be cut into two foot strips to get it through the hatch. Once these were stacked on the floor of the loft that is where they stayed.

The workmen who fitted the skylights were given other jobs to do but they made such a hash of fitting a ceiling rose in the bedroom he had to ask them to leave.

The voids around the edge of the attic area were fitted with secret panels that only Chris knew how to access. In these cubby holes he kept his survival kit. A sleeping bag, a roll up mattress, a chemical toilet, a kettle, a primus stove and travelling refrigerator. If need be he could survive up there almost indefinitely.

His hidey hole was properly kitted out and he could indulge his hobby in earnest, spying through the skylight on the neighbouring women. He saw it as a form of bird watching. Patiently he waited, seated at his vantage point, his hide, for a glimpse of the species. He could go for hours without spotting a single living being and dreamed of moving to the coast and owning a house fronting the beach.

Frinton was his ideal location. He had been there as a teenager and saw the girl of his dreams in a black bikini. He expected that if he turned up there tomorrow she would still be sunbathing in front of the beach huts. Those huts were handed down from generation to generation. Mind you she would be over ten years older and moved on from his visual titillation.

He was too mealy mouthed to buy raunchy magazines, but he leafed through Katy's, tore out the swimsuit adverts and kept them hidden in the loft for scrutiny during the slack periods.

An Asian family moved in across the street and Chris was taken with both the daughters. He began a vigil that bore fruit quickly but not the morsel he had hoped for. One of the children was given the box bedroom at the front. After two days watching and waiting he found it had been allocated to the son. The sisters were sharing at the back and he made do watching their comings and goings.

The elder sister, the middle sibling, was extremely pretty and had an active social life. The first time she was collected by a boy in his car he was overcome with jealousy. He assumed his affections were safe for the foreseeable future because he supposed Asian girls would be subject to arranged marriages. There were a stream of callers who whisked her away to goodness knows where and left him pining for her return. The first time she stayed out all night he was suicidal.

Not long after she was presented with a shiny blue Renault Clio her coming and going activities multiplied. He enjoyed a regular routine just checking if her car was on the driveway and made do with fleeting glimpses of her as she set off out.

Tall, thin and unusually elegant, the youngest sister was an unfortunate girl. She walked upright, erect, and Chris was sure she had taken posture lessons. She looked like a mannequin striding a catwalk, gliding to and fro, dressed all in black. The poor girl had a wide nose that had been squashed flat across her face.

Out of the blue, the blue car disappeared and the pretty sister with it. Chris never saw the sister again and suspected she had been murdered by her parents and brother for some transgression of Islamic life. He toyed with reporting her disappearance to the authorities and would have done so if her departure had not changed the sleeping arrangements. Big brother got the back bedroom and youngest sister the front box.

On Sunday afternoons the flat nosed girl posed in front of the mirror. Trying on various combinations of clothing, upon rearranging each fusion and blend she would strip back to her underwear, beautiful shining white, brief and startling against her dark skin.

Chris fell in love.

Chapter Twenty-One

Being podgy and being treated badly by her schoolmates Katy made few friends. It was the same at university and she steeped herself in her studies. Her home life was unexciting and she had little or no expectation of men or marriage. She had no great maternal instinct and now that she had an enviable figure she did not want to repeat the agony of ridding herself of stretch marks. She had contemplated getting pregnant on their honeymoon but only as a legitimate excuse to thwart Chris' sexual demands. But these petered out before she needed to action the ploy.

She loved bedtime, snuggling up in the duvet, warm and cosy, free from her parents and dreaming of nothing much. She did not want a lot out of life. Getting into a crisp, fresh bed at night and waking up dry.

Chris' job sent him on overnight trips in remote parts of the United Kingdom. She was especially fond of Belfast because that was good for two nights. Those nights she would eat an early supper and sleep in the middle of the bed using both pillows.

This allowed her to wake at dawn and run through the morning twilight watching the sun come up.

She did not know how or why it started. Having a bath and going straight to bed dusty with baby powder, she lay gently smoothing the powder into her body as softly as a caress. Helped by *Cosmopolitan's* problem page she discovered the gentle art of masturbation. Now every night alone presented a new thrill.

For a time her hedonism was spoiled. Whenever Chris was away the telephone rang in the middle of the night and awakened her with a start. When she picked up the receiver, nobody spoke and the caller's number was withheld.

'Why are you ringing me in the middle of the night?'

'Sorry,' he said disingenuously. 'Ring you, when?'

'When you're away,' she snapped. 'Checking up on me?'

'Why? What?' He stumbled. 'Who would do a thing like that?'

Katy could see he was innocent and switched her suspicions to his mother. She would take it upon herself to keep a check while her darling boy was away from the nest.

'Nobody gets one over on Helena Black, or her son.'

She called British Telecom and the police but there was nothing they could do unless the calls were threatening or racist.

'We suggest you change your number and go ex-directory.'

They did as was suggested, changed the number and went ex-directory. The late night calls stopped for a month, and when they started again Katy turned off the ring tone at night.

* * *

Chris was obsessed with his Asian girl, spent every waking hour thinking of ways to meet her or spying on her through his peephole. He counted on her unattractive face preventing her finding a boyfriend but worried that her family would arrange a marriage and she would be lost to him. She was a dutiful daughter, kind and thoughtful to her alarmingly decrepit parents, far too decrepit to have teenage children.

It is an outmoded custom on the Pemberton Estate for the youngest sibling to sacrifice their chances of marriage and remain at home to see the parents through their dotage. Chris took comfort from this custom because he was scared he would lose his love.

He used any excuse to go into town shopping in the hope of bumping into her. He was at a loss as to what he would do if they did cross paths but was excited by the prospect. He was not like his brother Gideon, clever at improvising and knowing what was appropriate. He considered a series of phrases that might win her heart in an instant but they all sounded flat or hollow when he tried them out in the loft.

He paid the newspaper bill and was heading back to his car when he bumped into Celia Eddowes and Pamela Riklis waiting at the bus stop.

'Christopher, how are you?'

'Fine, thank you,' he said, careful not to apply a name. He could not bring himself to call her Celia and certainly was not going to refer to her as mother or Mrs Eddowes not in front of Pamela Riklis. 'Are you waiting for someone?'

'The WI has arranged a coach to see Mamma Mia.'

'Have fun,' he said politely, edging away.

'Do you know Pamela Riklis? This is my son-in-law Christopher.'

For reasons he could not understand, Pamela pretended not to know him and they shook hands. Over her shoulder he saw the Asian girl enter the newsagents. She looked more elegant than ever in black slacks and gleaming white sweater. She glanced in their direction and her face displayed more confidence than he expected from such an ugly child. Chris was undaunted, this was his chance.

Politely he made his excuses, and drove his car around the streets searching for the way she walked home, but she had vanished into thin air. Her mysterious disappearance set his mind racing.

Where had she got to? Did she have relations living in the vicinity of the shops? Did she have a boyfriend?

His heart sank. He was depressed for days and kept a prolonged watch on her bedroom window. Closed curtains added to his anxiety.

He got yet another shock when setting off for work late one morning and he had to give way to an oncoming vehicle negotiating slowly through the parked cars on either side. The Asian girl was at the wheel of a brand new bright blue Clio and he had not been aware that she had been taking driving lessons. Inexperienced at tricky manoeuvres, she was focussed on her task, did not catch his eye and did not thank him for hanging back.

A chance lost.

He considered the realities of his infatuation. Would his love accept a white beau? However ugly she was, he was smitten with her, it was not out of the question for someone else to be. Having access to a car gave her unlimited freedom. He must act quickly before it was too late.

His luck turned, he was sent by his company to recheck an

audit of bankruptcy for a jewellery shop in Wyford High Street. The figures were a mess and his head was spinning, he took a breath of fresh air and spotted the Asian girl entering a chemist shop. He waited discreetly outside and followed her to the top of the town. He assumed she was going home and was deliberating on catching her up and introducing himself as her neighbour when she stepped into a doorway and was gone. The door between a pair of estate agents bore a single name plaque, Beck and Fernandez, Solicitors, reception first floor.

He needed an excuse to use the company. Would this guarantee he would meet her? Being so young, she was probably a clerk or secretary. He might get Gideon to arrange an introduction, these solicitors seemed to know each other and lived in one another's pockets.

He looked them up; Martha Beck and Raymond Fernandez. If she knew Gideon, there was bound to be a favour owing.

He phoned his brother, 'Do you know Martha Beck? She's got an office in the High Street, Beck and Fernandez.'

'I've seen a Fernandez in court, lots of gold teeth and a wig.'

'I thought you might know the Beck woman.'

Gideon was quiet for a time. Too quiet, 'Doesn't ring a bell,' he said in a tone that Chris was long familiar with.

'Are you sure?'

'Positive,' Gideon lied.

Whatever dealings he had with Miss Beck were too embarrassing to review. Chris spent a troubled week getting used to this set of circumstances and tried to seek a genuine reason to go to law.

'I could file for divorce.'

When he and Katy became engaged it was decided that Chris should put his flat up for sale. Being prudent, he owned the property outright. When he put the flat in the hands of an estate agent, the agent was anxious about the state of the market.

He suggested, 'Why don't you rent it out? It will help towards your new mortgage.'

'I don't want to deal with tenants,' Chris baulked.

'We take care of that for you,' the agent promised. 'We take care of everything. Damages, evictions, everything. We guarantee you will get your rent even when the place is unoccupied.'

That sold him. How they managed this guarantee did not trouble his conscience. A regular monthly income would soon grow into a deposit for his house in Frinton. He signed the contract for one year renewable, opened a new Building Society account and hid the paying in book in his hidey hole.

The day he completed the audit of the jewellery shop, he came out of the accountants' offices buckling his brief case, which was too full and the lock would not stay. He stopped and dropped to one knee, put the brief case on the ground and completed the job. As he got back to his feet there was a clash of people going in different directions, bumping together and apologising.

Chris came face to face with the Asian girl, gave her his broadest smile and said, 'I'm ever so sorry.' She looked straight through him and went on her way.

Chapter Twenty-Two

During the unsettling period when Ian was hearing strange voices and got the telephone engineers to check his line he had suspected that a serious plot was afoot. With the discovery of Suzanne Marks he had set this suspicion aside, but he was right on the button. The wobbling government were desperate to save their jobs. Six years of mismanagement were coming home to roost. The 'gap' in the opinion polls was widening to a chasm.

'I've got you men together to come up with something radical.'

The Prime Minister looked grave. Eight years had wreaked havoc on his public and private image. His bountiful hair had thinned, his unblemished face was developing a resemblance to the Silverlink map and his tight lips were receding, as was his hairline.

'I'm giving you a free hand, there are no boundaries, I want something that is going to swing the voters 180 degrees.'

These men, permanent secretaries from leading departments, spin doctors and think tank formed a committee secretly labelled the 'executive' and met every day from 8:00am until 8:00pm.

Rumours were rife and the PM ordered the Secret Service to have the rumours quashed. His secret weapon, whatever it was to be, was not getting out until he wanted it out.

It took just under two weeks for the 'executive' to reach a decision. They had come up with four constructive ideas on the first day but the Perm Sec's spent the rest of the time vying. Each wanted their department to be the source of the PM's secret weapon.

Work and Pensions wanted to give everybody a Christmas payout, not just pensioners, the Treasury wanted to reduce Income Tax to 10 per cent and while raising National Insurance to 20 per cent, Trade & Industry wanted to ban imports while allowing foreign companies to set up shop in the United Kingdom. The Home Office, always ahead in the debate, eventually won.

There is a theory, which may be apocryphal, that prison warders become as institutionalised as their charges. The Home Office suffers a similar malaise as a result of meting out rules of law, paying the penalty for dishing out despair. The misery of the convicted, the denied, the deported, the fine line between justice and injustice and the burden of responsibility, weigh heavily. Essentially, the law is too big a subject for men and God is capricious with justice because whatever side of the law you represent your soul is damned.

With his theological training to guide him, Ian could not articulate a fair and sensible policy.

He believed if you stuck to the rules did what your heart and head said, you could not be far off. Carry on regardless, through thick and thin, labour or conservative, dark or light, right or wrong, it would sort itself out in the end.

He was quick to learn the current jargon, hiding behind platitudes was good for business.

Ian was buoyant, having walked the length of Downing Street watched by a throng of reporters yelling questions. He kept staring straight ahead hoping not to trip over a crack in the pavement, smiling idiotically.

This was a 'red carpet' walk as spectacular as the promenade in Malaga, out of the pavilion to the crease at Lords or climbing the steps at Wembley.

'Excuse me, sir. Are you expecting an election date to be announced?'

Ian liked the insertion of 'sir' in the inquiry and his back straightened perceptibly, his tread slowed and he allowed himself a wave to the masses.

The government had completed two terms of flailing, hopeless inadequacy, economic suicide, paranoia, adultery, bribery and corruption, lining pockets, jobs for the boys, in fact the same old same old with different faces dressed up in different packages. Power tended to corrupt and absolute power converted a reasonable man into a complete arsehole.

The PM had called for renewed vigour in selling the party to the country. His address to the cabinet was just like any sales manager geeing up his sales team. If we achieve victory somebody gets a free holiday in Barbados.

Without missing a step the door of Number 10 was opened for him and he was inside, there, where it happens. The hub, the nub, the seat of power, its very air transmogrified him into a close relative of Clark Kent. Around him the stallion that was government hummed, vibrated, snorted with contained energy and he was part of it, a man with reins and a lasso to receive an audience with the jockey in the saddle. Ian Black was a contributor, part of the team that made it work efficiently. A man of substance, if only his brother Duncan could see him now, he would realise how far he had come.

Number 10 kindled a variety of smells. An underlying whiff of polish was adulterated according to the time of day. Early mornings came with a mixture of bleach, coffee grounds and toast. Lunchtime had the breezy balm of a wet day in Ilfracombe and the afternoons were supplemented by rising and subsiding waves of ferrous oxide.

Instructed to follow a gangly man up the winding staircase, Ian proceeded to the Prime Minister's office. Without demur, polite hesitation or knocking they marched in. The PM sprang out of his seat, greeted Ian with a hearty handshake and waved the gangly man away. He adjusted a chair for Ian to sit on and returned to the other side of his desk. Ian was excited and bewildered by this attention.

'I've got a big job for you, Ian,' the PM brushed his upper lip between his thumb and forefinger and then again, in duplicate, as though he had a moustache which he did not. 'Do you think you can handle it?'

'Of course, Prime Minister,' said Ian levitated about fifteen centimetres above the upholstery. 'Nothing is too hot for me to handle.'

'This is a hot potato and no mistake.' Again he brushed his non-existent tache. 'I want you to form a legal committee. Get some appropriate minds, no one who is not malleable. You know the type I'm referring to, *à la* Enoch Powell without the mad eyes, *à la* John Prescott without the lorry driver wardrobe.'

'I know exactly what you mean,' said Ian, without the faintest idea of what he was talking about. 'Strikers disguised as midfield dynamos.'

'Exactly,' said the PM. 'I knew you were the man for the job. From the moment your name was in the hat.'

Imagining his name being used by the powerful levitated him another few millimetres. It was a class 'A' drug that provided kick after kick after kick.

'Ian Black, that's the very man,' said the Prime Minister and tagged on a humourless laugh and returned his attention to the papers on his desk.

Ian was desperately hoping that the meeting was not over because he did not know what he was forming a committee for. When the PM looked up his face was grave and mirthless.

'You won't go unrewarded,' said the PM flourishing a make believe sword and tapping his shoulders. 'Our teams canvassing on the doorstep tell me it will carry the day and I'm relying on you to bring it off. I want that third term.'

'You can rely on me,' Ian was somewhere above cloud nine flying onward to the stars.

Sir Ian Black. Sir Ian Black. Sir Ian Black. How good it sounded.

'I am relying on you. Crest will put you in the picture,' said the PM. 'Get me this radical new law and we can make Britain a better place to live in.'

So that was what this was all about, bringing back hanging just so the party might win the election.

'There is just one reason I would resign,' Ian repeated, making it sound as fresh as ever. 'If hanging is put back on the statute books I will have no other moral option.'

His hands were shaking as he fondled the mobile in his trouser pocket. Sir! Sir Ian Black. Who should he phone? Duncan? Lizzie? Helena?

'I'll start right away, Prime Minister and thank you for giving me the opportunity.'

Ian was almost through the doors when he was called back, 'I don't need to tell you that this is strictly hush hush. If any leaks occur you know where the buck will stop. That PA of yours, trustworthy is she?'

'Sound. I've been thinking she might suit a promotion into the Civil Service.'

'Take care of it.'

'I will, sir.'

'They're waiting for you now,' said the PM. 'Some of the best minds in the country.'

'Where, Sir?'

'In the Cabinet Room.'

Ian blanched.

'Carry on Macduff.'

Ian sat in the holy of holies, a star partly encircled by a half moon of serious men. Crest, hunched and pacing, was putting him in the picture but was having some trouble getting to the point. Ian's moonstruck eyes focussed and searched for a familiar face. A third of the way round the arc sat Lord Justice Christie, with a bad smell under his nose.

Governing is couched in ego. There is the 'man in the street' who claims he can do the Prime Minister's and the Chancellor of the Exchequer's jobs. Their jobs are not easy tasks. When in a tight spot they have to call upon experts to assist them in their decisions and this is where the system comes crashing down. We, the public and they the government readily accept the babbling of egotistical experts. Time inevitably assigns their findings to the dustbin. The title 'expert' seems to be unassailable no matter what prat is on the end of it.

Crest Mornington was a man whom Ian looked up to. Firstly, he was six feet eight inches tall and forced to duck under doorways. His spinal column had lapsed, producing a fine set of round shoulders. Having spent so much time with the PM he had been infected with two of his habits. One was the grooming of a non-existent moustache and the other was flatulence. He was known to the Home Office Staff as the 'killer with the velvet glove'.

'The 'executive',' Crest gestured toward his gathering of best minds in the country, 'have agreed to implement a radical scheme...'

Ian knew he had plenty of time to study his surroundings and let his eyes wander about him. Behind where Crest marched back and forth was a marble fireplace, on either end of which were a pair of brass candlesticks that for some reason were reminiscent of James Cagney films, in the middle was an unremarkable antique clock. The walls were broken up into irregular panels suitable to hang pictures but there were no pictures and in the false light the white decoration had a mushroom tone. The interior designer had grown up on a council estate.

The 'executive' were sitting in lusciously upholstered chairs around a walnut table that showed signs of neglect. There were myriad cup rings and someone had scratched 'MT go home' in the veneer.

'...It is imperative that we present this in the proper way. We must emphasise a humane method and we rely on you to find a suitable doctor, an expert...'

It was here that Ian's attention monitor kicked into gear. Doctor? Why would we need a doctor for a hanging?

'...The last thing we want is to be branded as Mengeles...'

Mengele?

'We want the tabloids on our side. So we have decided to drip feed our intentions in the hope that they will claim credit for influencing government policy. That's not part of your remit, Ian, the spin doctors will...'

Again he gestured in the direction of the 'executive' without completing the sentence.

'...this is a hot potato and we're relying on you to bring it off...'

Where had he heard that before? When was he going to get to the point? Induce Parliament to bring back hanging. Spit it out for goodness sake.

'We were going to encourage the re-introduction of Capital Punishment. We felt there was too much history there. Child crime is on the increase, it is high profile and we need a suitable deterrent...'

It was not hanging. Ian searched the faces for a clue to where Crest's meandering was headed. He could not imagine what was coming.

'We are calling this policy, the Emasculation Act...'

There was an uncomfortable silence, the Civil Servants and the women sat blithely unmoved but the men began fidgeting, squirming in their chairs and crossing their legs.

'Could you elaborate?' Ian spoke for the first time in the holy of holies.

You are a chosen generation, a royal priesthood, an holy nation...

'We will neuter paedophiles.'

There was another rustle and crackle of chafing amongst the peculiar people.

Chapter Twenty-Three

Ian was frogmarched between two burly secret service operatives into a damp dungeon somewhere in the bowels of Downing Street. He was pushed inside and the heavy door was closed with a thud. Ian thought he was alone when an apparition emerged from an alcove.

'My name is Pleury.' They shared a sopping handshake.

As Ian got used to the light he found a bloodless man with a dab of grey hair and wan eyes. '

'There have been far too many leaks of late,' Pleury attempted a smile. 'Don't you agree?'

'Of course,' Ian agreed. 'It's scandalous that there are so many malcontents...'

Pleury held up a bony hand, 'We need time to complete the policy so we are going to set up a smokescreen. I don't think we can prevent rumours or speculation within the Home Office building...'

'No leak will come out of my office...'

'I'm sure that's the case Mr. Black, nevertheless...'

'I can vouch for my staff...'

'Mr Black,' Pleury spoke sternly. 'Let me finish and we can go about our business.'

'But...'

'But me no buts, Black. I'm going to finish what I have to say and you are going to listen.'

Ian, a quivering jelly in the company of women, but rarely intimidated by men, suddenly felt like a schoolboy on the carpet getting a ticking off from his headmaster.

'We are going to lead the Home Office to believe that the legislation you are working on is for the re-introduction of hanging and we are going to call your real purpose Operation Pierrepoint to consolidate. Do you understand?'

'Yes.'

'You will further consolidate the smokescreen by accumulating documentation on hanging and keep a fake file in your brief case labelled Pierrepoint at all times. Understood?'

'Yes.'

'Lastly and most importantly, not one single item to do with the genuine Bill will leave your office. Not even a scrap of litter. You will leave all discarded papers in the bin and our team of cleaning staff will dispose. Understood?'

'Perfectly.'

'You will not speak of it on any telephone.'

'What about my PA...'

'She's already been debriefed.'

Pleury pulled the cuffs of his shirt out of his jacket sleeves and returned to his alcove. The heavy door creaked open. Ian was beckoned by the burly men and escorted out of the building. Downing Street was empty save for a trio of helmeted policemen and a tramp who insisted on sitting against the railings. He and the police were squabbling as Ian skulked away.

* * *

The pile of paper for Operation Pierrepoint was mounting.

Lizzie had another brain-teaser to pass the time on the train ride from Luton to London. How did a deputation reach a decision? It was clear that Lord Justice Christie did not care for her Ian and was purposely hi-jacking the wording. It was also clear that the original document that formed the basis of the committee's findings was faultless but the Lord Justice was determined to change it. He was not alone in placing obstacles and pulling in a worthless direction. Every member of the committee was dead set on getting their two pennies worth on the table however irrelevant. Five weeks of meetings, half decisions and revisions and they were back to square one.

Ian did not seem bothered by the Judge's wilful sabotaging. He thrived on work, no quibble was too small and no amendment too futile, given the chance to fill a sheet of paper with words. Ian was a happy man. For him, this was constructive exercise. Chasing one's tail was part and parcel of the job. It filled up the day.

Sometimes they worked late into the night, after dining on sandwiches with the occasional bottled beer, and if he was sure the building was empty he took Lizzie in his arms and kissed her. It was a heartfelt sexless kiss that infants share. Ian had a problem which he was too shy to mention. The very idea of an embrace sent the blood rushing to his trousers and close contact was bound to reveal the swelling.

Lizzie, a founder member of the Luton Army for the Marriage Bond Society (LAMBS), affiliated to St Lukes, was happy to indulge his restraint. She had pledged her body to the sanctity of marriage. Yet she was experiencing new sensations, lurid dreams of kissing with tongues and awaking soaked in perspiration.

Her work was suffering, her concentration was wandering. Ian would be dictating revision number 113c and she would lock onto his mouth impatient for canoodle. Some of his idiosyncrasies, once upon a time irritated, but were now touching her heart. The nervous tapping of his mouth with his fingers or biro while thinking made her heart quicken and the surreptitious adjustment of his balls was endearing.

As the intensive days passed she cared more about Ian and was feeling a desperate need to touch. She felt it was for him to set the pace.

Not all of her night time picture shows were sexy. One involved a man in a black shroud carrying a scythe pointing a bony finger at her while quoting commandments in a monotone. There was considerable emphasis round number seven with less resonance on the topics of killing or stealing. She prayed for enlightenment but her heart continued to be disobedient and she tried to broker a deal with the creator using Civil Service élan much used in the Oval Office.

There was no sign from above and Lizzie remained in limbo until she accepted the plain fact that she was in love. Genuinely, without lust, well lust did come into it a bit, without too much lust. She fought a battle with impure thoughts, knowing they were a mortal sin. Her chest hurt, her stomach hurt and some place she did not care to acknowledge was continually pecking. Between the crisp sheets of a fresh bed these vaginismus plagued her pre-sleep and awakened her in the night.

The LAMBS sent Lizzie details of a suitor at the beginning of each month. It came with a photograph, potted biography and contact details. Desperate to resolve her torment she agreed to meet Mr. September. If they could not find any common ground she could use him as leverage to force Ian into a decision.

George Joseph Smith was an orphan who spent his formative years getting into hot water. A reformed character, part time lay-preacher he worked as a baker for a supermarket chain. A fitness fanatic, he started the day with fifty lengths of the Luton baths. It turned out he was more like Winston than George Joseph.

Informing Ian of her new relationship threw her deeper into conflict. Ian took the news with equanimity. He excused himself politely and went to the toilet to cry.

What was he to do?

Ian grew up believing he was inadequate and had spent his adult life countering this imagined deficiency. His brother Duncan, three years his junior, was anything but inadequate. The harder Ian tried, the worse matters got. He would cry himself to sleep praying for a transformation. What undid Ian completely was his brother's character.

They played, as brothers do, football in winter, cricket in summer, and Dunk beat him easily. As young as four years old Duncan scored more goals and hit more runs. Ian was humiliated but there was worse to come. A killer blow, gut-rending, shattering, devastatingly degrading, gripped his vitals with every recollection. It had been decades but he could not wipe it from his memory.

Duncan saw his distress and let him win.

Oblivious to his brother's patronage Ian revelled in his hollow victories. He taunted his younger brother, rubbed his nose unremorsefully but Duncan took it on the chin and did not bite back.

Ian was a good student, received constant praise from his teachers. Duncan, a scrawny lad, took his place at Wyford Grammar when Ian was in the fourth year. Ian, appropriately fraternal was soon to be floored by his overblown condescension. In the sports trials Duncan caused a sensation and in his second year got a place over Ian in the school cricket team. It was then Ian recognised his brother's benefaction and his humbling was complete. Duncan was an exceptional child. There was no reason for Ian to be humbled but he brooded because he enjoyed brooding.

As teenagers, Ian took after his father, heavy set, tending toward plumpness. At fifteen, Duncan was over six feet tall, slim and wiry, the school's sporting hero, being scouted by professional football clubs, and had had a trial with the MCC. To make matters worse, Duncan was clever.

Scholastically, a lot was expected of them both. There was talk of special things but Ian's A level results were poor. His parents did not hide their disappointment, having bragged to all and sundry of Oxbridge. Once again, Ian was ashamed and inadequate. His grades were insufficient for his offered places and he had to re-apply. He settled for a course in theology at Oxford Brooks, packed his bags and headed northwest.

University was a welcome escape and he made friends who knew nothing of his inadequacies and developed a self-deprecating humour that attracted people. He made fun of his chosen course but managed a respectable degree. Ian returned home to turmoil and found a modicum of forgiveness. His old school friends welcomed him back as though he had never been away and his brother was rebelling. His parents turned to him to help with their newly disobedient offspring.

Their second son was going the way of the first son for entirely different and less acceptable reasons. To their parents' consternation, Duncan was refusing to go to university. His sporting prowess got him an offer from Churchill College, Cambridge to read philosophy and he would not take it. His parents were distraught and tried desperately to make him see sense.

Duncan was adamant, 'I'm not going.'

'Why not?'

'I've met this girl.'

The arguments redoubled and he brought her home to meet them.

Norman and Rose greeted her sulkily, 'You're ruining our son's life.'

'I agree with you,' she said with her head tilted to one side like an uncertain puppy. 'I want him to go.'

That was the first time Ian knew emotion, his tummy suffered inexplicable jitters and he quickly traced the source. It was that girl Duncan brought home. History was repeating and the final piece of the jigsaw was in place. Duncan had the girl of their dreams.

Chapter Twenty-Four

Ian tried drying his eyes on government issue, an unforgiving substance, had to make do with his sleeve and left the cubicle a new man. Well, almost. That night he paced while Lizzie typed the revisions and with each alternate about-face, walked towards her chair. She wore a top with a low back and he could see the down scrawled on her shoulders and neck. With each swivel he determined to act and with each return swivel his courage failed him. The excitement of this potential daring built to a climax and when he could bear it no longer he stopped. Because of the speed his pacing had accumulated, the suddenness of his halt caused some sort of friction between the underside of his shoes and the carpet. His foot remained transfixed to the floor and his body momentum moved separately, almost severing his leg at the ankle.

He hopped around for several minutes muttering curses under his breath while Lizzie, intent on her work, remained focussed. He went to the washroom and bathed his ankle and forehead. His heart bounding, he returned to the office and watched the keys fly and the words slide across the screen. He placed his hand firmly on her shoulder and bent to kiss her neck, surprised by this major piece of intimacy her fingers froze and she twisted her head to face him, clunking him fiercely on the nose. He bathed his nose and stemmed the bleeding while Lizzie issued instructions and handed him fresh tissue.

Lizzie was as innocent as Ian. She had not been in this situation before and had no instincts as to how to proceed. She expected that when her time came the man would be expert in these matters and guide her. It was obvious that Ian was as inexperienced as she and that endeared him to her all the more.

It might have been the wickedness of being together illegitimately in the men's toilet or it might have been the tenderness with which Lizzie administered his nursing but when they were sure the bleeding had stopped, noses clashed and the corner of their mouths met in unbridled passion. Welded, their limbs and bodies intertwined and they held together as one. It was unfortunate that Ian was so uninformed about French kissing because he misread Lizzie's intentions. She pushed her tongue between his teeth and, inadvertently, he almost bit it off.

* * *

An English teacher called Miss Davis had told Lizzie, to know all, is to be all.

Lizzie had been an extra in the Home Office film. Being ambitious and having just won a speaking role, like so many actors she wanted to do Hamlet and had a desire to direct. That meant learning the business, knowing all the parts and the sum of all the parts.

A condition of her promotion to the Civil Service was to take a crash course on the British Constitution, general protocol and the clandestine workings of the Official Secrets Act.

Her parents had not expected much from their daughter. Academically, there was no precedent. Mrs Borden had left school at fifteen and, until she married, served haberdashery to customers at Bourne & Hollingsworth on Oxford Street. Lizzie showed no potential at primary school and when she did find a brain it was too late. She had been condemned to Cardiff Road Comprehensive, a waiting room for the inert of the town prior to going on to lesser things.

Having acted as typist or PA on every floor of the building, and therefore every level of the Home Office Lizzie had already learned a lot about the system from both sides of the bureaucratic fence. Her journey from ground to top floor had been speedier than a Civil Servant could expect and her learning curve was a short arc. She knew more about the systems foibles than any man, including her boss. Listening without the need to contribute was a help. She owned a natural facility to get to the nub of her subject, studied hard and left nothing to chance.

Lizzie kept two note books for her studies, one she submitted for assessment by her tutor, the other she kept for future reference. In the latter she wrote...

'Decisions are finalised without being able to point a finger at an individual for being responsible if it goes wrong.'

The doyen of the art of dissemination was Frank Jackson Mornard.

He had been much in Lizzie's mind since that Sunday morning in Berkhamsted. She had seen him sporadically, in meetings or along the corridor but since she and Ian had quit the Dog & Duck she had not seen him socially. In these brief sightings Mornard was not behaving in character.

Lizzie had worked with him for eight months, despite the occasional loose hand brushing somewhere on her flank he made no indiscreet suggestions either directly or indirectly.

Mornard was the 'life and soul' type, got himself noticed, instigated a solution and when it was taken up, retreated into the bushes. He only emerged from his hiding place if there was some credit to be claimed. He cut his projects into slices and delegated a piece to his juniors, cloaking their tasks with a hint of dagger. He preyed on their loyalty, encouraging them to keep their role close to their chests. This way he maintained control and, in the event of any slip ups he could point the finger at an individual. Mornard had charm and used his allure to 'keep a tight rein'. He was a clever, if somewhat mealy mouthed man and an accomplished civil servant.

Mornard saw himself as Iago but Lizzie was reminded of Uriah Heap.

Was he hiding in the bushes with Suzanne?

If this was the case, he was behaving out of character. Mornard's victories were always brought out into the open while he explained his role at the forefront.

He was the type to brag about his conquest. So, why the deafening silence? Was he under orders from Suzanne to keep his mouth shut?

Having expressed her own dissatisfaction with Suzanne, her friend had severed the relationship with a simple snip. It was as if they had never been introduced. Suzanne had cut Lizzie free and ignored her existence.

One evening, Lizzie was waiting for Ian to return from a

meeting with Lord Chief Justice Christie at the Hertfordshire DPP. There had been a power failure on the Electric Line and he had phoned to say he was running late. It had been an extraordinarily hot day in the office because the radiators had overheated. Lizzie fancied a long cool glass of shandy and she nipped out of the office to the nearest pub.

Hiding in a corner she sipped her drink and began reading the latest Vidange Tacher. Ian rang again to say that he was going underground and she quickly finished the chapter and emptied her glass. As she made her way out she found her path blocked by Mornard. It was relatively early but he was clearly 'the worse for wear'.

'If it isn't Miss Goody Two Shoes,' he said, his words blurred at the edges. 'How are we today?'

'Fine, thank you,' she tried to push passed him but he stepped sideways, cutting off access.

'How is that friend of yours, the beautiful Ms Marks?' His slur now had bitten corners. He tipped the 'Say No' badge on her jacket lapel with a forefinger. 'Still *virgo intacta*?'

Lizzie, preoccupied with escape, took in his jibe but was unable to apply her mind to his inexplicable questions. 'I'm sorry sir but I'm late for an appointment.'

'Frank,' said Mornard. 'Please call me, Frank. We're out of hours, no need to stand on ceremony. None of that 'sir' and 'madam', frank-ly, my dear, I don't give a damn.'

Had his success with Suzanne gone to his head? Did he see himself as the Playboy of the West End World?

Mornard laughed hollowly and took a long draft of bitter, 'Don't go. Stay and make an old man very happy.'

'Some other time,' she said and feinted to move past and, as he blocked her way again, he bumped softly into the wall, causing his beer to swirl in his glass. With quick reactions he adjusted to save his drink and she nipped into the gap beside his free arm.

* * *

Mornard's tactics were serving Lizzie well in her constitution classes. Their tutorial for the day was the making of policy, its conception, development and ratification.

'Policy that follows in the wake of the unforeseen is the most successful policy because...?'

'It is essential not speculative and the blame has already been apportioned,' thought Lizzie, but waited for her classmates to answer.

In her limited experience, Lizzie saw new policy as a growing child, however well brought up, its rite of passage encountered obstacles. It is allowed to run around the playground. Some policy goes unscathed but some policy falls over, scrapes its knees and is patched up to be sent out to play again. Some policy breaks a leg, develops gangrene and has to be amputated.

It is when policy dies that someone has to take the blame and fall on their sword, however innocent they are of guilt.

She knew enough about the system to know that she must keep this cynical knowledge from her tutors. She let her fellow students raise their hands to ingratiate themselves with teacher and watched them make fools of themselves. Her canny mind guessed that this course included an unspoken assessment of tact and reticence. She was the only class member to score top marks in discretion. Lizzie Borden was making a good impression and putting her scar behind her.

* * *

On the face of it, Ian being offered the chance to organise the 'hanging' committee was an accolade, and the promised knighthood was to be in place before the cat was out of the bag. Nevertheless, this controversial task was like walking a tightrope across the Victoria Falls with only a double edged sword with which to keep balance.

Lizzie suspected his upgrading had blinded Ian to the possible pitfalls. She reasoned that if no one took on these hot potatoes no radical policy would come about, but she suspected that these hot potatoes were dished out to the disposable.

Should she discuss this calumny with her beloved? Was it her place to?

She also reasoned that it was best that the organiser approached the radical policy with the maximum of optimism and decided to keep her reservations to herself.

Scotland Yard sent copies of their pertinent documentation and it took three trips to place the complete works on Ian's desk.

'Nil desperandum,' he said.

At the outset Lizzie acted as coach and trainer to Ian grappling with this Gargantua. She provided him refreshments between rounds and the benefit of her viewpoint from the fringes. Thrown together for long periods, a subtle change occurred. This alchemy cropped up in a book she had read as a child where the hero rode a bicycle over cobbled streets to and from work. As time passed the atoms were hammered against each other and some swapped places. The man became part bicycle and the bicycle became part man.

Lizzie could not help herself, not only did she interfere in the presentation as she was typing the data, she was reworking the whole package.

To prevent the agonies of her weekends separated from Ian she agreed to meet with George Joseph. He insisted that she join him in his fifty laps of Luton baths. She declined, went home and threw herself into her studies, gobbling up snippets of wisdom she might want to refer to in the future.

Lengthy research of her heroine, Margaret Thatcher, compelled her to write an even-handed essay, which she was so pleased with she sent a copy to the *Spectator*. Her treatise claimed that Thatcher, great and glorious to some, heartless, soulless bitch to others. Her successes were destructive, unravelling the knots in which the system had become entangled. The first thing she actually created, the Poll Tax, saw her dethroning and that deadly path to being labelled a grand old lady.

Lizzie was learning that the system repeats itself. History records if policy works, the top dogs take the credit. If it fails, some poor sod has to carry the can. The press, a shabby institution in its own right, will get on its high horse and claim credit for backing the winner or distance itself from the loser. To get to the top and stay there unblemished is a juggling act of mammoth proportions.

This juggling act is made up of a multitude of manipulations. The prime object is getting what you want. To overcome opposite opinion, doubt, and interference without bludgeoning the dissent is an enviable skill.

Ian Black was a maestro, an orchestra conductor who waved his baton with wit to orchestrate his meetings without offence and to keep the musicians on the page. Ian listened to waffle patiently, waited for the players to run out of steam and called for quiet. He would summarise what had been discussed. His précis would push the emphasis subtly in the direction of the Home Secretary's wishes. If they remained out of tune, with infinite patience he would start afresh on a new note.

Lizzie's tutor explained the fundamental requirements to apply this skill, 'You must develop a suitable temperament which is based on long established foundations; tolerance and a complete understanding of 'proper' and total faith that by and large the democratic system works.'

'Is this the Muddle Through Theory?'

'The Muddle Through Theory is a derisive expression used by cynics and the tabloids. We as a democracy are seeking a consensus for the public good. You must avoid these platitudes if we are to muddle through. We have to do so democratically and as fast as possible.'

* * *

'You stubborn fool,' said Duncan and finished his glass of wine. 'You may be my father but I wash my hands of you.'

'It's a waste of bloody time,' said Norman, a mystified frown expanding his voluminous eyebrows. 'And a bloody waste of hard earned money.'

'What the hell do you spend your money on?'

'What business is that of yours?'

The women had disappeared to the kitchen to clear away. Norman, Ian, Duncan and their four boys sat waiting for dessert.

Norman was complaining that Rose had not spoken to him the whole day because of what he had not done. Norman had not acknowledged his wife in fifty years of marriage. Not even bought her so much as a card.

'If you bought her a bunch of flowers just once a year, on her birthday, you would make her so happy she wouldn't nag you ever again.'

Norman's frown grew deeper. He tried but the concept was beyond his scope. 'Where do you get these potty ideas? Rose is a miserable old bat and no amount of flowers is going to change that.'

'Let's have a wager, five pounds to a penny. I'll even buy the flowers for you so that you won't have to be seen in the street with them.'

'What's that to do with anything?' Norman snarled.

'There isn't a woman on earth that isn't touched by a gift of flowers.'

'Rubbish.'

'OK mate, don't do it but don't complain to me that she's forever on your case. I don't want to hear about it.'

'All right you two,' Ian broke in.

'Who asked you?'

'I'm electing myself the referee,' Ian added with a large helping of pomposity. 'I'm the best qualified.'

'No referee nowadays is qualified.' Norman needed to take his annoyance out on someone. 'A bunch of bloody cowboys, the lot of them.'

'It's a difficult job,' said Ian. 'At least you're participating, you know, contributing.'

'Bloody idiots,' said Norman spoiling for a fight.

'Spending your Saturday afternoons or Sunday mornings being sworn at by a bunch of louts,' said Duncan. 'I'll say they're idiots.'

Norman laughed, 'Too bloody right, little men. Those that can, play, those that can't, referee.'

The women came back into the room and placed plates around the table, 'You're not talking football again?' Rose complained.

'It's Ian, Mum,' said Duncan. 'We can't keep him off the subject.'

'I didn't bring it up,' Ian claimed.

'Who started on about referees?'

'Boys, boys,' said Rose. 'Who would believe they're grown men? Who would like crumble?'

'Greatness is the province of little men,' said Duncan, taking a mouthful of pudding.

'What rot,' said Ian.

'What rubbish,' said Helena.

'It was pretty much what dad said earlier, I read that somewhere, greatness is the province of little men.'

'Just because you read it somewhere doesn't give it credibility. You can't say that Churchill wasn't a great man.'

'War's have to have heroes. Wellington was made great by the battle of Waterloo but he was beaten hollow by Napoleon until the Prussians turned up. Churchill was hated by a lot of British citizens and was voted out after the war, so he wasn't everybody's great man.'

'A few ingrates were not why Churchill lost the election. Elections are not won and lost by individuals, they are won by policies.'

In the sullen brooding that followed, the clatter of spoons on crockery created a dark mood. Duncan's cheery voice cut the atmosphere in half.

'When I was doing A levels, Churchill was a part of the course. I read some of his stuff and it's ironic because some of what he wrote would not be out of place in *Mein Kampf*.'

Chapter Twenty-Five

Revision for her Civil Service Certificate was a distraction, but Lizzie was suffering. The disease was the same but the symptoms were changing by the day. Vidange Tacher had not helped. She woke in the night, her sleep broken by vivid and explicit nightmares. There were problems with anatomy and conjugation but the content was obvious and she could not expunge these nightly newsreels.

She read a novel by Ms Tacher called *Beauty is Not Even Skin Deep* and had been drawn into unwitting physical participation in her dreams. She woke in the middle of the night, soaked in sweat, with her nightdress around her neck. So deep was her shame that she avoided her mother's eye, slut was written on the gateway to her soul.

Mornard entered her nocturnal orgies and brought Suzanne along with him. Lizzie ascertained from these fantastic get-togethers that her friend Suzanne was a troubled person and, aside from her translation talents, lacked any coherent life.

Why else would she sleep with Mornard?

Suzanne was a victim, locked into a world where men's tongues hung out in a thirst of wanting. They do not see a woman, they see a possession. At thirteen years old, the staring began and Suzanne did not care for it. Suzanne allowed a boy to escort her along Berkhamsted High Street with his arm about her shoulder. He was there as a bodyguard to pretend that she was spoken for. This boy was so unattractive nobody saw him.

Her parents were of no help to her and, instead of fending off this unwanted attention, paraded her around as though she was an exhibit. At one point her parents encouraged her to give up ordinary school, throw away her talent for languages and go to acting school.

'There's much more money in the theatre than translating French to tourists. If you don't like acting there's always modelling.'

No suitable dependence developed, no relationship was formed. There was always some lesser female who acted as Suzanne's minder and shooed away the fervent admirers.

Lizzie had stood beside the showpiece, stared out at the audience, and watched the startled eyes caught in the headlight that radiated off Suzanne. She was contemptuous of the majority but liked the way Ian addressed her charge as 'Miss Marks'. It was her notion of Old World manners.

After Suzanne's tirade in St James Street Station, Ian did an about turn and Lizzie forgave him the transparent pose he adopted. She listened without comment as he pitied and mocked the remaining lovelorn.

'Miss Marks is merely a doppelgänger, a visual fallacy.'

Where did he get that expression from? It sounded annoyingly familiar.

'Strip away her beauty and you are left with bare bones.'

'Pardon?' Lizzie had a strong flash of déjà vu.

'Being admired and wondered at her entire life. She was a rose, beautiful for a summer, but come the winter she was gone, an empty bud surrounded by prickles.'

'This is a book you've read.'

'Yes,' admitted Ian. 'I found it on your desk. *Beauty is Skin Deep.*'

'*Beauty is Not Even Skin Deep.*'

'That's it,' said Ian. 'Hot stuff.'

'Where did it get to?'

'I put it back where I found it.'

The book had vanished. Lizzie was not shocked that staff of the Home Office had little respect for others' property or that they were sticky fingered. That sort of behaviour went with the territory.

* * *

Ian had to go to Manchester to collate, collect and interview the Northern Office as part of the 'hanging' pretence. He had chosen a Friday so that he could stay over and see Wyford play at

Scunthorpe. Lizzie finished her outstanding paperwork and fancied some company. The weekends were becoming interminable.

The Dog & Duck was empty, save for the redoubtable Coke and Lizzie was that desperate she accepted his offer of a white wine.

'Where is everybody?'

'Everybody?' queried Coke. 'Is me. I wonder if that is grammatical. It is certainly the case and has been for weeks.'

Lizzie assumed that Suzanne and Mornard were cosy in another pub and the groupies had lost their star.

'Weeks?'

'Three or so,' said Coke, 'Soon after you and Black stopped coming.'

Lizzie was vulnerable and the least thing could stimulate a strong reaction. This statement inspired a shiver of fear and panic. Their absence had been noted, which was bad enough, but they were being lumped together. That could be disastrous, especially for Ian. Being lumped together automatically made them an item. She would not have minded if it were true, but to be the centre of gossip when nothing untoward was happening switched panic to self-pity.

If this tittle-tattle had reached the ears of those at Number 10 it would account for Ian's advancement. He had been chosen to organise the Hanging Bill because his hold on his post was already tenuous.

She was about to confront Coke with his implication and stopped. Her mind had run way ahead of the conversation. She must keep cool and lead the man by the nose to a point where she could put matters straight.

'Yes,' said Lizzie. 'We've been given a big project to handle.'

'Emasculation,' said Coke disingenuously, as though this secret work were an inconsequential dealing like identity cards or purchasing the Home Secretary's new car.

Lizzie could not cope with the shock that the 'top secret' project was common knowledge. The more widespread this information the greater the chances of a leak and the greater the chances of a leak, the more vulnerable Ian was.

She excused herself and left, calling Ian on his mobile. It was switched off and she left a message instructing him to call her urgently.

Agitated and anxious, on the train home Lizzie could not focus on her book and found a discarded copy of *The Guardian's* review section and leafed through it to pass the journey. She absentmindedly turned the pages without finding anything of interest, folded it together and laid it back on the vacant seat beside her. Boredom and stress intruded and she searched for distraction. She caught the eye of a mature gentleman who smiled at her inquiringly, she snatched up the arts section and studied each page minutely.

In a corner of the book section, hidden in an article evaluating the bodice ripper phenomenon was an appreciation of Vidange Tacher. Her novels had caught the public's imagination and sales were approaching the million mark. They assessed the literary content by comparing her style to three Barbaras; Cartland, Trapido and Taylor-Bradford. There was a footnote that Radio 4's repeat of the Book Programme that evening contained a feature on the authoress.

Lizzie checked the time, if the train was delayed for only a minute she would not be home in time. She stared out the window praying hard at every stutter in the train's ponderous way.

'Something important,' she said, brushing past her mother and taking the stairs two at a time. In her hurry, she struggled to locate Radio 4 and when she tuned in the programme had started. As she acclimatised to the voices they were talking about a new book written by a man, and the author was in the studio.

Changing out of her work clothes, she half-listened. The man was creating a lot of amusement with his interviewers. She adjusted the volume to catch some of what he said.

'I understand you were a professional footballer, what kind of experience was that?'

'Sobering.'

'Doesn't it provide you with a sense of pride?'

'No.'

The author was being purposely monosyllabic for effect and the presenter, in on the joke, was chuckling. 'You wouldn't care to elaborate?'

'Not really.'

The male presenter gave up on the ex-footballer and segued into the feature on Vidange Tacher. His attitude to Lizzie's favourite author was dismissive and kept referring to bodice rippers as though they smelled of drains. Lizzie thought it unfair to speak of Tacher so patronisingly without her being able to defend her work.

'Ms Tacher has been invited to appear this evening, but nervous of appearing in public declined our offer...'

The female presenter came to Tacher's defence and pointed out that there were elements of the books that were aimed at the females and would be lost on the male population. They asked the guest author to adjudicate.

She listened on the edge of her seat, her ear aimed at the speaker. When the man's name was mentioned again she did not want to miss it.

'I picked up these books just this afternoon and I've only flipped through them.'

'What do you make of these bits and pieces?'

'I would not want to be on the receiving end of a piecemeal review.'

'Please, tell us what you found, however mundane,' said the bullish male presenter.

'Nothing I would label mundane. I can tell you that the writer is an intelligent woman and she describes her problem well.'

'Problem? Only one?' The questioner's attempted irony sounded sarcastic and the interviewee hesitated before speaking kindly.

'I think she is a pretty woman preyed on by men...'

'How...'

'The clues are in the titles. Where Ms Tacher falls down is she writes outside her experience.'

'In what way?'

'She's a virgin.'

'How can you possibly know that?'

'The sex scenes,' the man was laughing at himself. I don't know how, perhaps the books are specially prepared this way but the pages fell open to all the sexy bits. These sex scenes are written by an intelligent woman who has no knowledge of men. They are sheer guesswork.'

Lizzie's mind raced off to all points of the compass.

'...We would like to thank Duncan Black and wish him luck

with his new novel, *Wasted*, printed by Athene Press and available in the bookshops from Monday...'

'Friday week.'

'Sorry, out Friday or Friday week, depending whether you are listening to the repeat...'

Lizzie turned the radio off. Should she telephone Ian and tell him?

'It might not be his brother. Black was a common enough name.'

She decided to wait. One message was enough, best not to call in case there was somebody important in the room with him. She could use the pretext that it was important work but after what Arundel Coke had said that evening she decided to err on the side of caution.

He did not return her call all weekend, adding new ingredients to the suffering of Lizzie's insides. It seemed that Monday would never arrive, but when it dawned it was to prove an eye opening day for Lizzie in many respects, and the possible authorship of *Wasted*, a minor event, was pushed to the back of her mind.

She got to the office before Ian and, while arranging his day's work, found his mobile beneath his chair. Lizzie had fetched coffee early and, Ian unaccountably late, it had gone cold. She returned to the kitchen and found a crowd gathered discussing the unexpected departure of Suzanne Marks.

She had quit without giving notice and moved to the Lake District.

Lizzie later found out that her ex-friend devoted the remainder of her life to the church, eating for solace and comfort. She died at forty-four years of age, a spinster and virgin, weighing twenty-six stones.

Solitarius, Frigidus, Moles.

There was one final intrigue for Lizzie that may have been connected to the enigmatic Miss Marks. Lizzie's copy of *Beauty is Not Even Skin Deep* was returned and left in her desk drawer. The fly leaf was signed with a farewell from Suzanne and dedicated to a kindred spirit.

Mornard, a man of mixed morality, took few secrets to the grave, two of which he kept to save his own embarrassment. One was that Vidange Tacher was a *nom de plume* for Suzanne Marks.

The other was that he, Mornard, had touched Miss Marks' universal wound but had failed to complete the sex act. Her clitoris had the dried consistency of spoiled putty and throbbed frenetically like a nervous tic.

The sales of Ms Tacher's fourth and final book failed to match the three previous novels. The critical world works in an unspoken consensus. The male presenter of the Book Programme passed the word along and the literary establishment closed ranks on Ms Tacher. It was not cricket for a virgin to write bodice rippers. Lizzie thought the fourth book every bit the equal of the first three.

Even though she knew Duncan Black was attempting to be fair, Lizzie blamed him for Tacher's demise. He had not been very polite about another of Lizzie's favourite authors, describing Miss Cartland as a 'dinosaur dressed as lamb'.

In fact, Duncan Black was quite wrong about the sex scenes in Ms Tacher's novels. She gave her male characters androgynous names such as Terry, Evelyn and Simon, gave them ambiguous lifestyles and never referred to their anatomy because all the characters in Ms Tacher's works were women.

The other tumultuous events of that Monday morning put pay to any intention to inform Ian of his brother's publication.

Chapter Twenty-Six

September proved to be a heartless month and mistook itself for December. Chris and the weather were bitter. His Asian goddess moved out, the front bedroom remained empty and Chris was broken-hearted. She seldom visited her family but he kept watch, intending to follow her and discover where she was living.

He mooned about for weeks, utterly forlorn, heartsick. Everything was suffering, his appetite, his work and his health.

Suicide was not out of the question. He had tried it before, cutting his wrists with a bread knife. The instrument was unwieldy and blunt and his wounds left him well short of death. He was sixteen and bereft of all hope. Overshadowed by his brother, unloved by his parents, he fell into a depression. Fog closed in on him and he saw only one way out. They found him on the bathroom floor. Helena was angry because her new Jonelle towels were spattered and Ian, busy at the Home Office, was seriously inconvenienced. They put Christopher in care for a month and, by shifting the responsibility to apathetic outsiders, they lost their son forever.

How best to do it? He did not relish his body being cleared away by strangers or family or anybody. He would fly to Switzerland, jump into a ravine and remain iced for centuries. Nobody would know he was dead. Nobody would search for him. It was a simple and efficient solution.

'I might be eaten by rats.'

Chris believed that rats eked out food from unlikely places. Being eaten by rats was a chilling prospect too vile to contemplate. He could blow himself to bits like that poor architect. What if he took up the Moslem religion and became a suicide bomber? That might sit well with the Asian girl.

If he blew himself up he might hurt some innocent bystander or splash someone with blood and guts. That would not do at all.

There was always the gas oven but whose? He and Katy were all electric.

He would lie awake, the dawn light streaming through the gap in the curtains. Katy was terrified of total dark and would keep checking that she had not gone blind. The howling wind and the driving rain clawing at the windows provided the proper atmosphere for dreaming up ways of death.

Out of ideas, his attention span waned and he studied the light fitting Katy had chosen for the bedroom. Could there be another person anywhere who could like such an object. It was horrible. In the shop it had been labelled 'end of range' and was smothered in dust. It was the one item the shop keeper was resigned to never getting rid of and in walked Katy.

It was a plaster cherubim without genitalia decorated in gold leaf. Held up by a chain attached to its bum it glided through the air with genteel fingers aiding its effete balance. There were glass crystals dangling from wrists and toes.

The odd job men had started to fit the hideous object and had trouble locating a joist. There was a gaping hole alongside the ceiling rose that had not been repaired. That hole might prove useful someday and he had made no effort to get it repaired.

When Katy expressed a liking for the cherubim in the shop, Chris had said something derogatory and she had made a scene, shouting loudly for everybody to hear.

'What do you know? You've got no bloody idea.'

He could hire an aeroplane, fly out over the Atlantic and bail out without a parachute. The sharks would get him but that was preferable to rats.

At his most abject he induced Gideon to purloin a gun. His brother owed him a considerable amount of money and numerous other favours. Gideon stole a Webley of moderate calibre from Hertfordshire's version of the Black Museum. The murderer had used one shot and there were five bullets left in the cartridge.

Afraid that he would botch the job, Chris needed to find somewhere to practice shooting. He wanted to put the gun in his mouth, pull the trigger and be sure of oblivion.

Chris was saved from his irrevocable intention by a run of good fortune. It was his birthday and once again his heart was bursting with joy. He found new love, he found a source of sexual satisfaction and he was promoted.

The gun was hidden in the lower section of his tool box, stashed in the loft.

Getliffe & Quinn were pleased with his progress and Chris' leg-up included an increase in salary.

'They're grooming you for great things,' said Ian when Chris announced the news.

His new role would require him to travel further afield. He provided Katy with a series of dates when he would be in the Near and Far East and she duly noted them on her calendar. Excited that some of these trips included the weekend, she made plans for prolonged stays in bed.

On his debut trip she shorted the electrics. Every appliance in the house had been shifted into the bedroom and the fuse could not cope.

'Who to call?'

There was no point in calling her father and less point in asking Chris, who was somewhere over Africa by now. She had a bath by candlelight, doused herself in powder and spent three glorious hours rubbing it in. She was interrupted when Chris called to say he had arrived safely.

'Why don't you ring Gideon?'

Gideon rang the bell and waited in the darkness. He reached up and flapped his hand across the field of the security lamp but it did not flicker.

'What a fucking lumber,' he muttered, 'Bloody nuisance.'

A pair of high heels clacked along the pavement and he twisted round to see if they were worth a look. A woman in her mid-thirties wearing a fawn overcoat, with sleek legs and dyed hair glanced at him as she went by. He gave her his biggest grin but the light was poor and she walked on without acknowledgment.

He rang the bell again and, remembering the broken fuse, rapped at the door knocker. A woman opened the door.

'Excuse me, is Katy in?'

'Don't be so bloody stupid,' said Katy.

'Katy?' said Gideon, goggling his eyes. 'What the fuck's happened to you?'

As with the passing woman, she ignored him and went inside. Gideon was not deterred by either rebuke.

Never take 'no' for an answer. Women never know what they want until you give it to them.

He followed her in and shut the door after him. She opened the cupboard door, thrust a torch in his hand and left him to it. He switched on the lamp and pointed it here and there. One of the buttons on the circuit breaker was proud of the rest and he saw what was required of him. He clanked around for a few seconds and went in search of his sister-in-law by torchlight.

She was standing beside the mantel piece dressed in T-shirt and track suit bottoms in readiness to go running. The candles shone upwards, casting elongated shadows on her face, dramatising her features. Her eyebrows looked double thick like greasepaint and her thin mouth full. Her usual dull demeanour was striking in the theatrical light.

'Is there a screwdriver?'

'I suppose,' she shrugged, 'in the garage?'

'I'll check,' said Gideon.

The more unsuitable the partner, the more Gideon enjoyed the sex. Forbidden fruit was the best fruit. He drew the line at his mother. There was nothing Oedipal in his make-up. It had not occurred to him before to make a play for his sister-in-law, she was plain and fat. Three months had brought about an amazing change. What accounted for this turnabout? Sex?

Funny how those virgins in the 'save yourself societies' ended up as nymphos. He could not imagine Chris as a sexual athlete, certainly not bonking enough for her to lose fifty pounds in weight. Perhaps Chris was a dark horse?

He faked a search for a screwdriver and returned to the cubby hole under the stairs. He pushed the circuit breakers back in and the lights came on.

'There,' he said. 'Everything should be OK now.'

Her expression held the usual unveiled disgust she kept for him. 'Thank you,' she murmured ungratefully, making no move to welcome him or ask him to leave. She just stared at him with unremitting distaste.

He moved closer, intending to intimidate her into a decision but she remained steadfast.

'Would you like to sleep with me?'

His suggestion induced swift action and his face stung before he was startled. Once he regained his equilibrium, he slapped her back, full on the face, the crack rattled the windows.

He expected tears but there were none and he could not quite translate her surprised expression. His handprint discernible on her cheek, her eyes were dispassionate and she turned her back to him. This was his instruction to leave. He hesitated, gauging whether she would change her mind, then strode out the house slamming the front door behind him.

'Women, fuck the lot of them.'

He laughed to himself out loud because that was his primary intention.

* * *

Lizzie had no appetite but went downstairs to pick her way through her parched dinner. Her wannabee 'busy' mother retrieved the overcooked meal from the oven. Bogged down by unwieldy oven gloves she struggled to separate the plate used as a cloche. She juggled agonisingly and at the last moment saved it from crashing to the ground.

Katy would have upbraided her mother for her clumsy actions but Lizzie's heckles were motionless. 'Can I help?' she said kindly.

'I can manage,' said mum, clearly offended.

Lizzie prodded at what appeared to be least arid section of the meal and ate a mouthful. Her mum was watching for her reaction to the food, expecting another sleight to be levelled at her mothering skills. She was ready with her counter.

'Whose fault is it that you come home at all hours?'

Lizzie was too clever for her, 'Nice,' she lied, stretching her mother's incredulity to its limit, but flooring her prepared argument.

'This came for you.' Mum handed her an envelope. 'It was that nice boy, Paul something. I met his mother in Pricebusters. He's got ever such a good job. Even your father likes Paul.'

Paul was a lemon faced boy, overwhelmed by his mother who still treated him as though he were eight years old. On cold mornings he would allow her to put on his gloves, sometimes on the doorstep in full view of the street. He wrote articles for Luton FC that were regularly printed in the fanzine or the match programme and knew the players to speak to. That was why her father liked him.

She stopped to chew a particularly stultified piece of meat pie and opened the envelope. It contained a computer printout from the 'Say No' society. Lizzie held up a photo to the light to get a clearer look and was taken aback. While reading Tacher's last novel she had adopted an image of the male character from a man she had seen in *Cosmopolitan* and this photo was a good likeness.

Untidy, blonde hair covering his ears, washed out blue eyes and an optimistic twist to his lips. It was a man created in Lizzie's own image. This coincidence was due to Tacher's excellent powers of prose, because the male character was based on the infatuation the author had for Lizzie. The sex scenes in *Beauty, A Curse* were a written record of fantasies Suzanne had dreamed up, in which Lizzie violated her body.

The image she used for the hero of *Lizzie Loses Her Heart* was Ian Black. Studying the contents of the printout brought on a twinge of infidelity. She placed the sheet back in the envelope and, just to please her mother, consumed the rest of her dried food.

Still her mother found room for complaint. 'If you carry on like this you'll get an ulcer.'

Another pain and another grievance for her mother to add to her ever growing list.

Lizzie changed into her night things and joined her parents in front of the last of the telly. Sliding her legs under her she pretended to watch, laughing when they laughed but slightly after the joke, like an out of sync movie.

Her mind was elsewhere. She would give Ian another chance because she could see Cupid hovering over him. Was it his sense of duty that was in the way? Why had he called that evening from the wedding? He had been flirtatious and she had expected more on the Monday but that was the end of the affair. He must have been intoxicated, if not by the wine then by the occasion.

In the coming weeks he would be swamped and may not be alone for the foreseeable future. There was a dinner at the Mansion House and he was going with Mrs Black.

'I'll have it out with him.'

Tears welled up in her eyes and she pretended to blow her nose. Perhaps she should give up on him. No matter what the mitigating circumstances, it was breaking a commandment. Fear of the consequences should have pushed everything else aside. Why not meet the man in the envelope? What had she to lose? He had a kind face and could make a good father for her children. She would be thirty-five soon, her clock was running out. Marrying the envelope would make her parents happy. She checked on her mother and found her as preoccupied as she, watching her and not the telly with a frown, wrinkling her wrinkles.

That night she awoke naked and found her nightdress and knickers flung into far corners of her room. Standing naked with the light on she inspected her body critically. There were full breasts with rose nipples, a flat stomach, smooth, swelling thighs, tobacco coloured hair and a seam with no hare lip but the palate remained uncleft.

Chapter Twenty-Seven

Getliffe & Quinn were brokering a deal at a quarter of a per cent of transactions that should nett them a dividend of £1 million per month. The funds had to be kept in a Middle or Far Eastern location and that attracted the antennae of HM Customs & Excise. It had taken an eternity to convince this authority of the legitimacy of the scheme and the worthiness of the parties involved and that no money laundering was taking place. Having been given a clean bill of health, no bank would touch the deal because of clause 12 (b), until a compromise was reached with Deutche Bank on September 24th, Chris' birthday.

The preliminary contract was signed, Chris was sent for and, while he sat, Getliffe & Quinn circled his chair.

'We are entrusting you, Christopher, with an important objective.' Getliffe, five feet three inches was towered over by his partner who was five feet four. 'You must follow instructions to the letter.'

Quinn nodded dramatically. He had forgotten to apply the adhesive to his toupee, the nodding caused the covering to slip down his forehead.

'There must be no mistakes.'

'This exercise, to date, has been a steeplechase. It would be a shame to fall at the last hurdle.'

'A disaster.'

'We're relying on you to pull it off.'

'Go forth...'

'And multiply...'

'A quarter of a per cent.'

'Will you do it for us?'

Chris was eager to get away from the early winter weather and his own melancholy, happily agreed to go. 'Where?'

'Jakarta.'

'Take your wife along,' said Getliffe. 'All expenses paid.'

'Thank you,' said Chris. 'I'll put it to her.'

In the event he did no such thing. Over his birthday supper, sausage and mash for him, Weight Watchers chicken *à la* slim for her, he told Katy of the his urgent trip, which set her mind racing.

'When are you leaving?'

'I'm booked on the midnight flight, the red eye.'

Unprepared, what arrangements could she make at this late hour?

She stood at the bedroom window, watched him leave and remained staring at the space vacated by the taxi long after it had gone. Struggling to recall the chain of events that had sparked the problem, incapable of sitting still, she wandered from room to room, switching lights on and off. She sat on the bed with the cherubim, bright and fairy, flicked the switches of both bedside lamps, plugged in the supplementary heater but the lights kept burning. Disappointed, she picked up the television remote and pressed the on button causing a flash, a distant bang and darkness. She sat in the dark, smiling.

She changed her clothes and riffled through her diary for the telephone number.

'Hello, it's Katy. Chris had to go away at short notice and I've blown the fuse again. I was wondering...'

The front door knocker sounded, Katy opened her housecoat, removed her bra, stepped out of her panties and re-buttoned her housecoat. When she opened the door, and seeing how she was dressed, Gideon's irritation evaporated. They stood in the hallway, face to face, at arm's length. She gauged the distance, adjusted her position and thwacked him across the face. He returned the compliment and she spread her arms invitingly. He obediently undid her housecoat and she let it drop to the floor. Naked, she took him by the hand and led him upstairs.

Chris arrived at the airport and found a swarm of disgruntled passengers surrounding the British Airways information desk, muttering. The workforce had called a wildcat strike and all flights were delayed. The departures board stated that the flight for Jakarta was delayed but no revised time was posted. He found a seat at the edge of the mob and waited patiently for an announcement.

* * *

She lay on the bed and raised her bottom in the air. Gideon smacked her firmly on one side but she wiggled her bum more insistently and he smacked the other cheek more fiercely, eliciting a plaintive whimper and producing a bloom on her skin like a ripe peach. He gave her time to recover and slipped out of his jacket and shirt, then slapped the original side with as much force as he dared. The whimpering tickled his libido.

He continued undressing between blows, unsure when this section of foreplay was to culminate. He was naked, his penis bursting out of its skin and she turned onto her back and welcomed him. He slipped inside her drenched genitalia and she moaned with pleasure.

This was going to be a doddle, thought Gideon.

Fucking for him was easy, being so detached from the concept of making love he was able to restrain his climax. His sexual pleasure was in the pain he inflicted on his female partner in helping her reach orgasm. He teased and withheld, prolonging the distress. It was the sound of suffering that spurred him on.

With this fluent lubrication, his motion was gloriously efficient but inconceivably there came a change. Somehow he was no longer in control. Some involuntary impulse had triggered the seed of a climax. Whatever he tried he could not stem the inevitable. Why? Why? Why?

It was the pain.

He tried to distract his thoughts and undo what had started. Katy was in no hurry. She was thriving on the torment and hurting him to reciprocate pleasure. She tore at the hair on the back of his head, stabbed him with a knifelike fingernail and clawed at his bum.

Delicious pain was making him panic. He was not going to hold out, she was near but he could not prevent his own, as he softened he kept plunging. He wanted to give up but her urgency gave him a second wind. Her cry sheered through him like a knife. It sounded sweeter than a Paul McCartney ballad. Finished, they remained locked together, joined at the hips, his shrivelled member clasped inside her.

This was the first climax he had experienced involuntarily and he was astounded by its velocity. He tentatively moved to separate but she clasped him tighter, her legs holding him in position. They lay that way, without speaking, breathing sweet breaths into each other's ears.

* * *

The muttering was increasing in intensity and volume. Chris opened his mobile and scrolled up his home number, but on checking the time he decided it would not be fair to wake Katy.

'What should he do?'

The flight was still not allocated a time and he was unsure whether to wait much longer. It was probably best to go home and try again tomorrow. He went to the news stand intending to buy *The Times* but had to make do with the *Mirror*. He started the crossword. If they had not made an announcement by the time he had completed it, he would leave.

'One across, "Sworn declaration", four letters.'

'We are sorry to announce that because of industrial action all flights are cancelled from Terminal Three. We apologise for the inconvenience.'

'Fucking hell.'

'Oath,' Chris said quietly and wrote in the answer.

The mutterings, like an approaching aircraft, grew into a deafening roar. Stoically, Chris grabbed his suitcase and scurried out to the taxi rank.

'How much to Wyford?'

The cabbie consulted a chart, 'A hundred nicker.'

'How much?' asked Chris but did not wait for an answer. He hurried to the bus stop and jumped on a waiting bus, which was labelled, Cambridge via Wyford. Seated at the back he sent Katy, Gideon and Mr Getliffe texts informing them of the delay and his predicament, asking them to text back.

* * *

The silence had not been broken for over an hour, Gideon lost in thoughts of womankind. He peered through the gap in the curtains where the moon was full, haloed by a rainbow, peeking through a tuft of cotton wool. The sky around it was freakishly bright, smiling yellow like poorly kept teeth. Gideon craved a cigarette but knew Mrs Clean would not allow it.

He felt warm and comfortable in the wake of his new wisdom, revelling in the relaxation with the softness and smell of a woman close at hand.

Thwack!

A stinging slap to his thigh signalled that they were to go again. He entered her sodden orifice with their mouths clamped until they came together. He was disappointed only because he had stifled a woeful plea but could feel her climax in the paroxysms of her throat.

Chapter Twenty-Eight

The bus sped smoothly along an unlit ribbon of motorway, its progress occasionally hindered by a cluster of huddling lorries keeping company in the dark. Throaty and clogged, they sneezed as the air was driven out of their brake mechanism. Hypnotically Chris watched the cats' eyes on the verge marking his way. So mesmerised was he that he did not hear his mobile phone ringing until the voice message kicked in. He pressed the missed call button and saw Mr Getliffe's name and number and immediately pressed call back.

'Chris, old chap, you got the message?'

'No,' said Chris.

'Where are you?'

'On the bus home.'

'Good, good, you got the message then,' said Getliffe and rang off.

Chris pressed message recall and listened, 'Chris, old chap, been a hitch their end. Best get yourself home until it's sorted.

Chris turned off the mobile, pressed his head against the window and watched the cats' eyes snaking their way homeward.

* * *

'Where's Chris,' he thought to ask at this late stage.

'Indonesia.'

'Where?'

'Indonesia. Some big financial deal.'

'I should be going soon,' he said half heartedly.

She planted her mouth on his, their tongues wrestled and jaws locked tight. Just as he sensed the tension on her neck might cause it to snap from his frenzied pressure, she sought out his prostate gland, causing his dick to spring to attention. The slapping was more protracted this time and laid face down, she groaned incessantly. Bored, and getting sore hands he sought a new way to inflict pain. He ran his nose across her bottom and bit her in the plumpest, softest section. Momentarily she froze and emitted a strange noise. He bit her repeatedly and the noise increased. He forced her to turn over and bit her inner thigh. Their coupling reached a manic intensity, she came with the scream of a wild animal and clasped him with her legs until he did. He was not going to make it, but she bit him on the neck and shoulder and ear and neck. His climax mixed with the searing pain was so fierce it drained the last remnants of his strength.

Gideon had been a wild stallion, proud, free and now he was tamed. Katy had contained him. She held fast in the saddle, despite his wild contortions, his spirit was broken.

Exhausted, they fell into a deep sleep. Laid across the duvet, their bare limbs entwined, moonlight streamed over them defining their curves like a callow abstract.

* * *

The bus circled its way round Wyford Station, Chris dragged his wheeled suitcase through the lemon twilight, the busy wheels spun and hummed over the flags. The streets were deserted. Every so often a car would speed through the peace, and with a swish was gone, leaving the night more tranquil than before.

He chose a path home through the park, relying on moon glow to see his way. He followed the dog walks trodden down at the rear of the houses in Woodside. The tree-lined avenue screened the moonshine sporadically and he had to tread cautiously from moon puddle to moon puddle.

Stepping out onto a lengthy stretch of clear ground, he could hear noisy activity coming from someone's back garden. He knew there were badgers in the park because on quiet nights you could hear them, cavorting, barking and chuckling. The sounds were muffled so he concentrated, holding his breath.

He moved closer to the source. It was not badgers or any other nocturnal creature, but human comings and goings.

175

Whatever was going on was coming from a summer house at the bottom of one of the gardens close to where his Aunt Emma lived. He strained his ear to be sure he had the right house and gently tried the back gate. The gate, which would normally be bolted, was ajar. He crept forward and peeped in the window.

Spread-eagled on a mattress was a girl and on top of her a huge man with cropped hair, a collage of graffiti and a spotty behind which was plunging up and down at a steady rate.

As Chris adjusted to the murk, he saw the girl's face. It was his cousin Amy. He waited for them to finish in the hope that he might get to see more. They finished in a frenzy of hurried breath and dressed silently. Chris watched as she put on her clothes. She was more rounded than his Asian goddess and he was intrigued by the coquettish way she presented herself.

Afraid of getting caught, he crept away.

* * *

Spent, the sleeping couple barely moved. A noise alerted Gideon and he awoke with a start. Since puberty he spent a large part of his life looking over his shoulder. It was an essential part of the fun. He leaned on an arm and listened, all was quiet.

Katy, her sleeping face in repose, without malice, without the judgemental, without a sneer, was stunningly pretty. He played his lips on hers as delicately as an artist applying the last brushstroke.

'I should go,' said Gideon listlessly.

The room was warm and cosy, he would stay for five more minutes. He fell into a deep sleep and as his steady breathing filled the air, the drone and clatter of a tugged suitcase came into earshot. It made its way closer and closer but Gideon did not wake.

Part of Katy's plan was to fix the security chain in place. Was it over confidence? Was it complacency? Was it the pull of desire and expectancy? Chris put his key in the door, twisted and pushed but as the door opened it caught on the latch.

'Now what am I going to do? She's put on the safety.'

In tugging the key out of the lock, the mechanism passed the obstacle and a relieved Chris stepped inside. He put his suitcase in the cubby hole, extinguished the candles and partially undressed before mounting the stairs. He entered the bedroom, moonlight streamed through the gap in the curtains bathing the entanglement of limbs on the bed with milk. On discovering the identity of his wife's companion he went back downstairs, dressed, rescued the suitcase and went into the garage.

He hid the suitcase between the dustbins and re-entered the house. He went back up to the box room, let down the loft ladder and climbed into the loft space. On hands and knees he crawled to the corner where the tool box was hidden. He pulled away the stacked pieces of wood that masked his secret cupboard and lifted out the box. Opening the rusty flaps made a penetrating screech. He searched in a shoe box and found a half filled spray can of WD40. He sprayed the hinges and edges of the flaps and, with his heart beating loudly in his ears, pulled them apart. Patiently, he did the same with the inner flaps and extracted the Webley pistol. Pointing the gun at the velux window he stared down the barrel and aimed a shot at the moon.

* * *

She dreamed of a threatening shadow, it cowered in doorways and alleys, as it stepped out from the gloom Katy woke with a start. The shadow remained a mystery. Gideon, sprawled across the bed, one arm across her thighs, breathed heavily with his mouth open.

Katy investigated his body, ran her palm over his flawless back and backside, savouring the texture of his skin and shape of his bottom. The tips of her fingers dwelled in the creases. She cupped his testicles in her hand and considered squeezing. The idea formed a paradox in her head. She would enjoy hurting him but it was Saturday and they could have uninterrupted sex for another forty-eight hours. She wanted more sex. Her vagina quivered with longing. She wanted him inside her again, more teasing, more torment, more delicious pain.

Instead of squeezing she caressed his balls and tickled his groin either side of his scrotum. The fondling had the desired effect. She toyed with his penis, fascinated by its softness, empowered by its gradual inflation. He moaned and she gently massaged his grief.

'I can't,' he confessed.

177

'Just get inside me,' she instructed. 'Fill me and lay quietly.'

He did as he was told and they lay joined and still for a time, but she grew impatient and his torture began again. Relentless, inhumane, greedy, he would be of no use to her this time. He was wrong, he could not stop her and he could not pull out.

'Surely not, surely not, I'm going to...Please, quickly, so I can be done with this...It's agony...I can't go on...I can't stand anymore...God, I'll never do this again, I promise...Someone, please...Put me out of my misery...Please...Plee...aaa...eese.'

* * *

Chris felt the weight of the pistol in his hand, how good it felt, powerful, an instrument of justice. He got to his feet and moved to the ladder but the sound of distant voices gave him pause. He checked that the safety catch was on and put the gun down carefully. He rolled up the mat placed in the centre of the room and lifted a small panel cut out in the chipboard floor. Taking the binoculars from the lower section of the tool box he applied them to the unrepaired hole next to the ceiling rose.

For the second time that night he watched a couple complete. His wife and his brother fell into a troubled sleep and when he was sure it was safe Chris returned to the garage. He opened his suitcase and took out a change of clothing because his underpants were filled with come.

Chapter Twenty-Nine

Gideon had his regulars. There were a handful of women, mostly married, who hankered for good sex. They rang him up every now and then, booked into a hotel and spent a pleasant evening.

He never had them back to his flat. Never shit on your own doorstep.

Interspersed with the regulars he carried on an affair or two. He liked clandestine, liked, 'we know but you don't' and knowing looks across a crowded room. The more dangerous, the better he liked it. Sex without risk was tame.

Gideon liked noise, the noisier the better. He liked dishing out suffering to women, if not in bed, then out of it, by withdrawing his favours, by dumping his latest flames. Once he had tired of a woman he had no compunction about dropping her. He enjoyed hurting, the harsher the break, the better.

Some cried, some threatened revenge and the cunning ones were stoical. Some sensed the pleasure he got out of breaking up and saved their disappointment for a private time. The revengers were his biggest problem and the younger girls the most spiteful. Lately he had confined his activities to mature, preferably married, ladies.

He was scarcely through the doors of the Hertfordshire Prosecution Service when he was warned of the fierce reprisals coppers meted out on their unfaithful wives. It was not long before he took up with Sarah, a forensic chemist, whose husband was a copper, and sex with her excited him more than usual. Then there was Mrs Hay, who he had pulled at Chris' wedding. She lived in a posh house up in London and they did it on the living room carpet. He shagged her listening out for a car on the gravel driveway.

Shame about Auntie Pauline. He would like to give her one. She was the only aunt that ever took an interest in him – her and Auntie Dolly.

Chris spotted Dolly Churcher's name in the local rag when her husband died. Gideon remembered the old fella coughing his heart out with a large canister of oxygen by his chair. As he coughed Dolly applied the yellow plastic face mask to his mouth, adding to the cadaverous pigment of his gaunt face.

Gideon wrote a letter of condolence and delivered it by hand. Dolly had gotten old but her memory was intact and the affection with which she greeted him renewed the irritation in old wounds.

'Darling boy, you've grown so handsome,' she took his hand and clasped it warmly. 'I'll bet you've broken a few hearts.'

'You bet,' he said, and a few hymens.

'How is Christopher getting on?' she patted the cushion on the sofa beside her. 'Sit yourself down and tell me everything. Don't miss out a single detail. Tommy, get this handsome boy some tea, we've got so much catching up to do. So much...'

When Mr Churcher died, her son Tommy made her move in with him. He and his wife lived down in Weybridge and Gideon visited her every Bank Holiday armed with a large bouquet. Tommy and his wife did not seem to mind, he always rang beforehand to make sure she was well. Tommy's wife claimed Gideon's visits bucked Dolly up no end.

They had long run out of things to say and Gideon made up stories to please her. She loved to hear about the wedding and he promised to bring her the album, if it ever got printed.

She made him tea, told him what a naughty boy he had been and he pretended he had not heard it before. It was telling how she did not ask after his parents. On August Bank Holiday he borrowed a half dozen of the proofs of Chris' wedding for Dolly to see.

'What a pretty girl,' said Dolly. 'I can see that they're made for each other. Chris looks as happy as a pig in shit.'

Tommy made signs of an apology but Dolly carried on obliviously.

There was a picture of his parents which she studied long and hard, then she put the photograph down and took Gideon's hand in her own. 'There is love out there,' she told him. 'Look hard and you will find it.'

He thought better than to explain she was wrong but she was onto his intransigence. As Gideon kissed her goodbye she cupped his face in her hands.

'Love will heal you,' she said with damp eyes. 'I promise.'

Tommy escorted him to his car when he left and explained that her mind had lost control of her tongue.

'Her heart is very weak and her kidneys aren't working properly.'

Gideon was emotionally spent and today's visit had keyed him up more than ever. Making his way home from Weybridge in the car allowed him time to recuperate. He could not concentrate, pulled off the main road and travelled along a country lane somewhere in Surrey until he came across a pub. He swerved into the car park, stopped in a distant corner and switched off the engine.

He fancied talking but what he had to say would sound weird to a stranger, even weirder to a friend. He flipped open his mobile then closed it again. Thought about having a drink, but did not care for drink that much. He was pushing thirty and did not know what he wanted out of life.

'*Love will heal you.*'

He did not like drink or drugs, did not want marriage or children, his job was boring. He liked driving fast. That was one good thing about Hertfordshire Prosecution Service; he could intercept his speeding fines. Well, Sarah could, she showed him how to cheat the computer.

'You had better not upset that little apple cart.'

When he broke up with Sarah he must let her down lightly.

There were always nuisances that would not take no for an answer. He was blunt and candid enough but they kept calling. He only gave out his mobile number and, seeing who was calling, he torpedoed the calls he did not want. Some of them tried to get clever and duck under the radar by using a strange phone or withholding the number. He made it an ironclad rule, a call that was not identified with a name was cut off.

'*There is love out there.*'

There had been no fatherly talk about the facts of life in Gideon's childhood, just the pessimistic assurance that, 'Son, there is no such thing as love.'

He was barely sixteen when he made his first attempt to break from the emotionless strait jacket he called a mother. She was not only a control freak but a freak in control. A friend, Alex Ellis, helped him run away, letting him use the upper section of his bunk bed. Gideon had bottled out and sent Alex to collect his clothes.

His mother lobbed a black sack out the bedroom window and spoke in a most un-Juliet tone, 'Tell the little toerag he won't get one over on me and I won't have him back even if he comes crawling.'

He went home eventually, he had no choice. It was not the authorities that had demanded reconciliation, nor his parents for that matter. He doubted his father had noticed his absence. It was Mr Ellis who insisted, after he caught his lodger plugging Mrs Ellis. This time the black sack was hurled out the front door.

Gideon could no longer recall the parting words, only the thrill he got when Mr Ellis entered the room. Ruth was right on the edge and he had to leave her hanging.

Helena answered the door and had that face on, the one you would happily smash to a pulp. He lowered his eyes, shoved past and slouched up to his room. He would get her some day and then she would be sorry. How was another matter, whatever the evil cow did, somehow she came up smelling of roses.

* * *

Gideon lifted up the collar of his jacket, raised the zip to its highest point and slipped into a pair of gloves. He let down the hood of the car, flicked the ignition and gunned the motor. He pulled onto the country lane and headed for the distant hills that sheltered the redundant politicians that his father knew. The wind and engine roared in his eardrums and the cold deliciously bit his face. He steered the car along the narrow path, faster and faster, half hoping he would confront a car coming in the opposite direction. Picturing a near head on collision, would he stop in time, that heart dropping, adrenalin firing moment of possibility and excitement.

The headlights swathed hedges and scared rabbits. Smoothly, at a breakneck pace he approached a T-junction. Resisting the temptation to brake he waited until he could see the give way lines before switching pedals. The tyres left black skid marks in their wake and the car stopped half way across the nearside lane of the main road. He crunched back into gear and roared towards the looming shadows, climbing as he went.

Mile upon mile he drove, his cheeks growing numb. A car heading towards him announced its imminence with a glow, revealing a silhouette of trees and fences. Bushes huddled together, hands on shoulders as though they were in the front row of the scrum. The glow grew into a sudden flare of blinding light and was gone.

He soaked up the solitude, slowed the car and swivelled the wheel into a narrower country lane. The slim corridor and steep hedgerows caused the engine noise and the exhaust fumes to bounce and spin back into the car, filling his nose and mouth with carbon monoxide. He liked the smell of burning fuel. It beckoned him toward paradise.

The car burst out of the corridor into a wood and the sounds diminished. Through the wood he was at the top of a hill and across from him was a street sign that read, STEEP GRADIENT – LOW GEAR.

He eased the car out onto the tarmac and perched it in the middle of the road. At the edge of the incline he released the handbrake, put the gear box in neutral and placed his gloved hands behind his head.

The weight of the car rolled slowly down until the incline steepened. Save for the pressure of the tyres rolling on the road surface, the night was silent. Soon the car was hurtling down, gathering speed and Gideon watched the bottom of the hill getting ever closer without any sense of urgency.

How would it be just to let it happen?

His mobile rang. He ignored it.

'You've exhausted my patience,' Ian said. 'I wash my hands of you.'

He had been given his last chance, warned, 'one more scandal' and he would be cut loose. Another scandal was pending. There was no way out of this one. He had really done it this time. He would be better off dead.

'Do yourself a favour, let it happen, be done with it all.'

He glanced at the speedometer, ninety mph and rising. He would have to make up his mind soon.

Quick.

Quick!

Quick!!!?

Would he ever know love like Dolly promised?

A deer loomed out of a vanguard of poplar trees, did not respect the green cross code and stepped out into the road. Unruffled, Gideon adjusted his body and touched the brake lightly before applying stopping pressure and coming to a halt. Gideon and the phlegmatic deer exchanged glances and the animal proceeded on its way.

He opened his mobile and checked the missed call. He played the message but there wasn't any reason for the call other than a declaration of undying love. 'Stupid bitch.' He shut the phone and headed home.

It was just before Christmas, when he telephoned Tommy for his Boxing Day visit that he found out that Dolly had died in November. They had no way of contacting him and Tommy apologised for not letting him know.

It was at that moment that Gideon learned that he did know love. He found a gaping hole had been left in his life. He broke down and cried

* * *

Ian passed the florist on his way to the office for three weeks deliberating whether to buy a bunch for Lizzie. It was all very well giving flowers but Ian could not find a logical pretext for such action. Sending a bouquet for a baby or wedding would be appropriate, but Lizzie would make the arrangements. Giving flowers without a suitable reason was open to misinterpretation.

They accumulated articles and essays, spent hours browsing in the British Library seeking out justifications for their case. Ian was a meticulous reader and years of practice allowed him to digest the pertinent facts and discard the chaff in a single viewing. Working round the clock, they produced the first draft in just two weeks. It read like a thesis for a post-graduate degree. It was Ian's magnum opus.

'You best get home or you'll miss the last train,' said Ian.

'I'm happy to stay,' said Lizzie.

'I'll finish up,' said Ian. 'You've done wonders, thanks for everything.'

Emotion was running high but Ian, who should make the move, dithered. She had given him the opening but he was set on delivering the papers to the Prime Minister's office and extra-curricular activities must wait. Everything must be in its proper place and in the proper order.

'I'll see you on Monday,' he said, anxious to get to work. 'No need to be here at the crack of dawn.'

She closed the door, soft and disappointed. Greedily, Ian ate the printed words on the pages before him.

As their project reached its conclusion, Ian had been feeling groggy. During the last days he got home, ate his dinner and fell asleep in the armchair. Helena left him to it and went to bed alone, and he awoke in the blackness with a crick in his neck or pins and needles.

He ought to go home now but so near to the end of the project a couple more hours and the weight would be off his shoulders. He could deliver the papers without a final read through but he was meticulous. Years of discipline had taught that you could not be complacent.

It was after midnight. His driver was waiting in the hall and, apart from security, there was nobody else in the building. He brewed a strong black coffee and continued reading. As the pages spilled over he got an uneasy sensation that some information was new to him. The prose was close to his prosaic style but was supplemented with a biting energy. He certainly liked the way it read but could not swear he had written it.

'It must be the adrenalin,' he said, swallowing the last of his fourth cup of black, 'The caffeine and the exhaustion.'

He rubbed his eyes with both hands, blew out his cheeks and, lifting his empty mug, toasted, 'Here's to a job well done.'

It was past 3:00am when he closed the file on what he considered to be a high class piece of work. It was worthy of a KCB any day of the week. He was so excited by its potential that he put it in a 'Top Secret' envelope and instructed his driver to take him home via Downing Street. He wrote clear instructions that it was for the PM's eyes only and handed it to the duty officer.

He lay back in the car, eyes closed, with that heady tiredness that accompanies 'a job well done'. It was a satisfied exhaustion and expectation that stoked up the fire, filling his tired body with new life. He emptied his head and soaked up the car's resolute smoothness.

'Home James,' he thought, 'home to the wife and family. They will be so proud when the news breaks. Sir Ian Black, it has a fine ring to it.'

'Lumpen proletariat?' he said out loud. 'What the fuck does that mean?'

Panic fired the uneasiness into top gear, 'Sorry, sir,' said the driver. 'Was there something you wanted?'

'It's OK Derek,' said Ian hurriedly. 'I was just thinking out loud, sorry.'

Who had inserted that expression into the text? It must have been that legal boffin. He was full of antiquated jargon. Funny that he had not noticed it before, because he insisted on having any legalese explained fully. It was one of Ian's golden rules; 'Best to be sure, take nothing for granted'.

Ian felt uneasy, distinctly uneasy. He felt like one of the three bears.

He fell into bed and a deep sleep, dreamed of farm workers, ploughing and mowing with goitres or bulbous noses or hunchbacks or smothered in warts.

He awoke being prodded violently, 'Will you stop thrashing about.'

'Uhh.' He grunted, turned away from the prodder and slept instantly.

Lizzie stood before him covered from neck to ankle in gossamer, and as he tried to snatch it from her she stepped out of reach, her lumpen proletariats bouncing invitingly, the rose nipples flirting in and out of sight. He chased her down a corridor, up a staircase, across rooftops, she was always eluding him. He stopped at a roof's edge, looked down and was overcome with vertigo. Bilious, he swayed drunkenly and as Lizzie lunged to save him he fell forwards. Down, gliding, down, sideways, on a magic carpet, until he landed abruptly in a fountain. When he awoke, his foreskin was glued to his pyjama bottoms.

Chapter Thirty

Monday morning, sitting among forlorn faces, Lizzie urged haste but the defiant train was indolent. She strained in her seat, wanting to slip into a harness and pull the engine along. Anything she could do to go faster. She had made up her mind. Today was the day. It was now or never. She would give her boss first refusal. If he said 'no' or if he dithered she would contact the Church and arrange a meeting with the handsome suitor in this month's envelope, Elvis Black.

How was that for a coincidence? Mrs Black or Mrs Black?

On the way into the office, Ian was in a buoyant mood. The PM had rung him the previous evening and was full of praise. Sun flamed on concrete and warmed the throngs of determined men and women hurrying to work.

He needed to mark the occasion. Lizzie, what could he do for Lizzie, the girl in his dreams? Without thinking, he stopped at the florist and bought a posy of African violets. Proud, he marched them into the Marsham Street entrance across the foyer and up in the lift. Heads turned, but he was above their stares, he was a man apart.

Lizzie was not at her desk. He felt thwarted and needed to remedy this negative sensation instantly.

'Damn.'

He thrust his way into his office and there she was, dressed in a dark suit leaning over his desk, setting out his post. The skirt of her suit was short. Her long legs and the curve of her bottom looked alarmingly attractive. Visions of her in gossamer were revived and something stirred.

He stepped forward, did a little bow and held out the flowers. Her face changed from anxiety to sunshine. She took the posy in both hands as though it were as delicate as a butterfly and stared at the floor to hide her tears.

'Thanks for the extra hours you put in,' he said, attempting to save the situation.

Their eyes met and he searched for enlightenment, she kissed his cheek, her mouth lingered against his face.

He sensed he was required to make a response. Eventually, she pulled away, smiled sweetly with sad eyes and returned to the outer office. Her kiss lingered and he kept touching the spot where her mouth had been. He completely forgot to inquire after lumpen proletariat.

Duncan had been right about flowers. How was it he knew these things? He struggled to imagine the wherewithal it required and his brain turned to spaghetti. Ian was only comfortable in his work environment. He was like a yachtsman in the middle of the Pacific Ocean abandoning his boat. He would bob in the water, a buoy forever.

The day flew by in a puff of smoke. Ian lost track of time and Lizzie reminded him that Helena was on her way and might arrive any minute. They were attending a dinner at the Mansion House given by the Lord Mayor for the great and good. Ian kept his evening clothes at the office and would change in the toilets. He dressed hurriedly and got his shirt tail caught in his fly, it was so firmly embedded that he had to summon help. That was how Helena found them, Lizzie kneeling at Ian's feet wrestling with his flies. 'I'll take over from here,' said a stentorian Helena.

'Excuse me, Mrs Black,' said Lizzie politely. 'We've come this far. You would not want to chip one of your nails.'

Helena conceded and watched this bizarre pantomime to a close.

'A very sensible young lady you have there, Ian,' she pronounced loudly on the way out. 'I should take very good care of her if I were you.'

They were late and shown to their dining place before Helena could take inventory. During the Lord Mayor's interminable welcoming speech she craned her neck and searched for anyone she might recognise. She would need at least a half dozen celeb's to impress the hairdresser later that week.

She had hoped to be sitting next to someone special, but it was some cricketer or other. Numerous guests came to pay their respects to this grizzly old curmudgeon, one of whom she recognised off the television because of his mop of blonde curls. Ian whispered a name but he did not look impressive enough for the salon.

The curmudgeon ranted on over dinner about the loss of the Empire and the demise of gunboat diplomacy and ungrateful wogs, bloody foreigners, whether they were coloured or not and showed no interest in her list of charity works.

Ian made her switch seats and she started a conversation with a pixie faced girl who sang with a pop group. She wore a red dress which clashed with her hair. The girl's pop career was on hold and she was working for Oxfam.

Despite this creditable side, Helena found the girl annoying fatuous and the more they talked the stronger the urge she had to resist to punch her on the nose. Her silly face could have used some reconstructing.

The girl showed interest in Helena's charity works and listened politely enough. Helena told her how much of her life she gave up for the poor and needy. It was then she discovered that the pop star grew up in Wyford.

It would be a feather in her cap if she could get this person to the WI. She tried to win her over by commending her handbag.

'This old thing?' said the girl. 'I bought it Bangkok or Hong Kong in one of those cheapo markets.'

'Marc Jacobs?'

'I've never heard of him, what does he sing?'

Helena ignored her for the rest of the evening and made a list of celebrities on a linen napkin with a washable eyebrow pencil. She was making a collection of these napkins, place cards and invitations which she kept in her treasure box.

In the middle of the guest of honours address, Ian's pager sounded loudly, causing a flurry of rebukes. 'It's the Prime Minister,' Ian explained. 'He needs me.'

He contacted the PM's secretary as instructed and was to report to Number 10 immediately. Helena, outraged at being left in the lurch, was placated when she found out that she would be chauffeur driven home in one of the Lord Mayor's Jaguar Daimlers with a crest on the bonnet. Ian watched the car drive away. The car had smoked windows and he was unable to see inside that Helena was waving in the Royal manner. She continued to so unabated the entire way to the motorway. She planned a grand exit when the Daimler pulled up outside their house.

The driver stopped on a sixpence at the spot she instructed. It provided the best vantage point for the neighbours. Helena hesitated before disembarking to allow a man walking his dog to draw near. The liveried driver opened the door and as she got out she caught her foot in the hem of her dress and did a half somersault into the gutter.

Lizzie was waiting in the foyer of Number 10 and immediately Ian arrived they were shown up to the PM's private office. The room outside was full of busy faces scurrying back and forth. A path was cleared for Ian and Lizzie to go through. Sitting in front of the PM's desk was Lord Justice Christie. He lowered his eyes, glanced over his bi-focals, gave Ian the briefest of haughty looks and returned to his reading.

'Sit,' said the PM peremptorily and continued on the telephone, turning his head away from his new visitors and reducing the volume of his voice. Ian shrugged a query to his PA and she shrugged back.

'Close the door, Ian,' the PM ordered and Ian was relieved. Being addressed by forename meant all was well.

Ian obeyed and returned to his seat, allowed himself to cross his legs and relax. No mention was made of his dinner suit. 'Your report, excellent work, excellent, the Lord Justice here was most impressed.'

Christie placed the paper face down on the table and flashed another disdainful glance in Ian's direction. He did not believe Ian was capable of doing this report unaided and had told the Prime Minister as much. 'He's a bland sort of fellow. This report has elan. The man is too prosaic to produce such work.'

'Will it sway the committee? That's all I care about.'

'It will help considerably, but they will do what I tell them to do. That's what I'm here for.'

'What about the Parliamentary vote?'

'That's up to the whips, but I suggest you use some of the material in this document to win the vote. There are several points that are well thought out and most convincing.'

'You're probably wondering why I've called you here,' said the PM. 'Based on the findings of your report we're going ahead with the committee and hopefully a parliamentary vote.'

'Sir,' said Ian, desperately wanting to contribute.

'I'm visiting Strangeways the day after tomorrow and I will say a few words to the press and will start hinting at some major changes in law and order policy.'

'Tomorrow afternoon, Prime Minister,' his secretary intervened.

'As soon as that?' the PM said, 'I want a few words to take with me. You know the sort of thing, hard hitting but if I change my mind I won't look like a u-turner. Bold but pragmatic, I don't need to tell you.'

'I know exactly...' Ian started.

'You've been booked into a hotel so you can get an early start. Separate rooms mind, I want you fresh and on the job tomorrow, not tonight.' He leered at them and Ian felt his face redden.

Lizzie was sure that the suspicions Arundel Coke had planted in her mind were right. The glint in the Prime Minister's eye confirmed her fears.

When Ian visited the lavatory on his way out his complexion was still the colour of beetroot.

They had adjoining rooms, fitted with an access door. Uncontrollably nervous, Ian lost his voice. They stood facing their room doors heads bowed as if making a prayer before entering. Silently they slipped their cards in the locks and were inside. Ian paced back and forth, wondering what he should do if he were rebuffed, and fearing the possible humiliation. He could not stand another rejection and Miss Marks face loomed inside his head adding to his anxiety.

He could not stand it any longer and went out into the corridor and knocked at her door. He heard her say, 'Come in' and entered to find Lizzie standing in her underwear.

His mouth dropped open and he began spluttering, 'I'm so sorry, I thought you said...'

She stepped a pace toward him and waited, her arms crossed to hide her breasts. Ian saw again that something was expected of him. He placed a hand on either shoulder and kissed her on the mouth, an awkward, sexless kiss.

His concentration had been impaired. Instead of savouring the softness of her lips, he expected her to scream 'rape'. She did not prevent him nor did she encourage or apply pressure in return. She just stood there, no sign of approval, no indication of feeling, merely mouths touching. They pulled apart and without comment Ian left as though nothing had happened.

Ian could not sleep, his reaction to this kiss occupied his thoughts and he tingled in the most unlikely places. It was his duty to sleep so that he would be fresh and alert for tomorrow's workday. He tried to put the kiss out of his mind but each unwanted recollection gave him a glorious thrill.

He got out of bed and knocked softly on the connecting door, half hoping she was asleep and did not hear his gentle rap.

'Hello,' she called with a quiver.

Ian undid the latch on his side and she followed suit. She was dressed in the hotel bathrobe, and her hair was tied back.

'I can't sleep,' he said pathetically.

'Neither can I,' she replied nervously.

'Come to my room,' Ian was amazed at his own daring.

'Give me a minute,' she said and turned away.

Ian got into bed, wriggled out of his pyjamas and laid waiting for her to join him. Then he realised he was still wearing socks and removed those also. The luxurious cotton sheets felt good against his skin and he closed his eyes to savour the texture.

Lizzie entered the room and tiptoed to the vacant side of the bed, she slipped out of the towelling robe the hotel provided and got in beside him. After a brief hesitation their bodies met and Lizzie felt the warm undulations against her own. She let her hand touch his hirsute chest and slide deeper into the forest of hair. Unused to male anatomy, her hand collided with an unexpected appendage which was tumescent. Her hand glided up and down evoking a long sigh and gave her a rush of excitement.

'Oh darling,' she cried and searched out his mouth with her own.

Finding his lips open and his breathing steady, it was then she understood that he was fast asleep. She put her robe back on, adjusted the duvet around him, kissed his sleeping forehead and tiptoed out. She slipped the latch on her side of the connecting door and her tingling body went fitfully to sleep.

Nothing was said at breakfast and, against Ian's better

judgement, they took a taxi to Victoria. It did not do to fritter public money on taxis when there was a perfectly good transport service. They sat silently in the back of the cab looking out of their respective windows and, just before they reached their destination, her hand slipped across the gap and squeezed his thigh.

Chapter Thirty-One

It started with the whistling.

Mornings in the Black house were sober affairs. Helena topped up her mood with black coffee. Ian trundled his way through a stodge of porridge oats which set like cement in his stomach and underpinned his day. They were watching the calories and did not supplement their mealy diet with sugar.

'Breakfast is the most important meal of the day,' said Helena as though this prosaic axiom were her own idea.

Helena was a member of an acetic society, mostly female, who held no joy for food. Knowing you were not sylph-like, someone else must be to blame. That malefactor must be treated with disdain. Today's society needed a scapegoat and the reason Helena was not sylph-like was the fault of food.

'Wicked, wicked food.'

Helena liked quiet in the mornings and this sudden incursion of whistling was testing her patience. Slurping his porridge, crunch his toast, crackling the newspaper at every turn of the page and belching. This cacophony was bad enough, but whistling was the pits. There was no room for happiness in Helena Black's morning.

Following on from this tintinnabulation, Ian would leave for work and Helena would sigh a deep sigh of relief. Her routine could begin in earnest.

Right out of the blue came the whistling, tuneless, erratic, joyful, annoying, whistling.

She tried the 'what do you think you're doing?' face but he was miles away. Then, bright and early one morning he was singing in the shower. That was the last straw.

'Ian showering in the morning, what in heaven's name is going on?'

Helena was so taken aback by this renewal that she lost her place in the week and went to Waitrose/Sainsbury's on the wrong day. Having got over the shock of this unaccountable blip, she again broke with habit and stopped in Phil's cafe, drank four cups of strong tea and ate a mini pack of chocolate bourbons.

This was a world beyond her imagining. Rough men in plaster and paint splatter eating 'bacon sarnies' and 'chips with two veg', voicing the one adjective that was a verb.

'Fucking tasty.'

'Fucking hot.'

A couple, totally out of place in this Gotterdammerung, sat in a corner and held hands. He, a snappy dresser, oldish, bald and sleek, she, half his age.

What were they doing here?

Hiding, that's what they were doing. None of their friends would take tea in Phil's cafe. They were safe from bumping into any known association or prying eyes.

'Ian's having an affair.'

Whistling was neither here nor there. Singing in the shower was conclusive. Helena was amazed Ian knew a song to sing. Showering in the morning was a different matter. Showering at all was suspicious. Ian was having an affair, case closed.

Who with?

It had started raining and gusts of spray flew at the windows of the steamy restaurant. The mottled patches of clear glass became spotted and abstract patterns on the glass were constantly changing. A man by the window drew a heart in a patch of steam, his fellow diner drew an arrow through the heart and they laughed at their cleverness.

Helena's heart underwent no such piercing or a pang of any sort.

You read every day, Cabinet Ministers, MPs and top Civil Servants bonking their secretaries. Hardly any stayed married, hardly any were with their original partners.

Ian was saying that Great Britain had the highest divorce rate per capita in the world. Higher than the USA.

Had he got divorce on his mind?

You read every day that women were attracted to powerful

men, that power was an aphrodisiac, whatever an aphrodisiac was. She had heard of Spanish Fly but imagined it to be an Iberian codpiece. Helena tried to picture her husband as powerful, and stimulating, an aphrodisiac.

She laughed out loud and heads turned to see what the joke was about. Helena did something she had not done for more years than she could remember. She blushed.

The sleek man gave her a charming grin. He was happy and wanted everyone else to be happy with him.

Ian, holier than thou, a man of honour, a man of standards, butter would not melt in his trousers was bonking his secretary. It was as plain as the whistle on his lips.

Helena let her vivid imagination put two and two together but fumbled the balls. Ian and romance, Ian and foreplay, Ian and tenderness, Ian and urbanity, Ian and seduction, Ian and macho. No, no, no, no it was impossible. These speculations were less likely than his fooling with that Lizzie.

'What can she possibly see in him, power or otherwise?'

Surely this Lizzie was too sensible a girl to get involved with an old fogey like Ian. Perhaps she was one of those weird young people, perverted, who like carnal knowledge with the infirm? Apparently some women pitied men and wanted to protect them. Protect them from what? What did Ian need protecting from? It was too silly.

'When he gets home I'm going to give him what for.'

He needed a kick up the backside but she doubted her leg could get high enough. It was getting harder and harder to manage the simplest of stretches. She must cut down on the bourbons.

No way was she giving him a divorce. She would cut off his winkle before that would happen. Then, there would be little point. She laughed out loud again at her feeble pun and left hurriedly before the owners called the funny farm.

When Helena got home she searched through his office for clues of adultery, but there were none. Stymied, she was in dire need of a fantasy. As she puffed her way upstairs she heard the postman but there were more important matters to attend to. She dressed in a purple floor length dress and slipped a red canvas sash over her shoulder. She had stolen this sash during one of her short tenures at school.

You never knew when something might come in handy.

She carried out two trials. First she sentenced Duncan, Ian's brother to be pilloried.

Next up was Ian Black CB, a blackguard of the first water. His crimes were heinous. Possible adultery and, worse, disinterest. She had still not forgiven him for not noticing the house refurbishments she prepared for the *L-O* re-shoot. Ian struggled to see the point of the exercise and created about the bill.

Finding him guilty, she struggled to decide on a punishment for these offences. She could hide his season ticket for the cricket or give his signed photograph of the team to Oxfam but she derived no pleasure from those. She could not deny him any treats because he did not desire any. She then had a brainwave, opened his sock drawer and mixed up the colours, putting a navy with a brown that she knew would upset him.

After passing sentence she went from the court to her chambers, (the en suite), and celebrated. She ran a bath and opened a bottle of cheap champagne left over from the wedding.

In the bath she dreamed of her brother-in-law, head and hands locked in a pillory with a crowd of her friends emptying their dustbins, but it did not satisfy. The wine tasted odd. Maybe she had got some soap bubbles mixed up in it. Perhaps Phil's tea had tainted her palate?

The soak did not restore her soul. Tetchily she started getting out of the bath and slipped on the anointing oil which had collected by the plughole. She clutched at the shower rose to save herself and her shower cap spiralled into a corner behind the pan. Day by day, moving was getting to be chore. It was not fair that she had 'glands' which were responsible for her weight problems. Her sister Emma was a stick insect and did not suffer with glands. God was a fickle beggar.

She rescued her plastic cap, dried and folded it carefully. She would make some quality tea and open a new packet of biscuits. That would make her feel better. Squatting to gather the post left her breathless and she had to sit for a moment. The post fanned out like a hand of bridge and she spotted an envelope that made her tummy loop the loop.

This was a day of contemplation and Helena stared at this envelope with a desire she had not experienced since she was a child, when she saw a fairy costume in the window of Gamages. She drew the insignia close to her face and began shaking uncontrollably.

'HRH,' she said with due deference, savouring the potency of these initials. Her voice reverberated. The acronym of acronyms. She sniffed at its unrivalled bouquet.

The envelope was addressed to Ian, but she had to know what was inside. Should she ring him at the office and get his permission to open it? She pressed his number but cut it off short.

He might be *in flagrante delicto*. Helena had been picking up the Latin from Morse and Rumpole.

She could travel to Victoria and give it to him, but dismissed the thought. She throbbed and itched to know its contents and the torment troubled her shaking hands. She tested the flap with a furtive fingernail. It was not a self-sealing envelope and was stuck fast. She put the kettle on, intending to steam the flap open but as the kettle boiled, it switched itself off, frustrating her to the verge of apoplexy.

Adultery was wiped from her mind.

She found an old poaching saucepan she had not used since they were first married and filled it to the brim. Eventually the water boiled and bubbled, wild liquid spilling onto the hob and sizzling, but it provided enough vapour to loosen the glue. She prised open the sodden flap and eased out the letter.

She read the Queen's message, which increased the trembling to Richter proportions. Helena suffered a body crash and her sphincter failed. She stood, legs clamped together and attempted mini-steps like a Geisha with bandaged feet, sidled just a yard before she knew it was giving out. She parted her legs and clamped a hand over the aperture to stem the flow. A foolhardy move, she felt warm liquid and saw cheap champagne streaming over her Mexican tiles. Helpless, she watched her micturate flow mix with distilled water and concoct a golden rain.

It was salutation to an enduring alliance, Sir Ian and *Lady* Black. This was her birthright, a glittering moment in a special life.

Wyford, a far cry from Venice, but soon to be broadcast across the globe. The article in *L-O* had taken weeks to syndicate and the continent welcomed the miracle. The same miracle that had not aroused much of a following amongst the British ungodly, caused a rumble on the continent. Reverend Waddenham began receiving written requests to witness the miracle and, carried away by the exotic addresses, agreed to visitors.

He underestimated the response and expected the occasional like-minded clergy. Instead coach loads of pilgrims clogged up the streets of the Pemberton Estate. St Marks was filled to bursting and Ian was worried that the extra cost of sacrament would bankrupt the church fund. It was his son Chris who had gained new confidence with his stature at Getliffe & Quinn came up with the enterprising idea of a mandatory donation. Within weeks, the church fund was filled to bursting. Following on from the pilgrims, St Marks was inundated with requests for wedding services.

A trait of the British public that is becoming more commonplace is following in the slipstream of Europe. We entered the Common Market late, too late. We did not join the Euro and we are going to rue the day. The betrothed of Britain joined the continental clamour and St Marks Wyford fast became the Westminster Abbey of the common man.

Chapter Thirty-Two

The telephone rang and Duncan cursed loudly. By the time he crossed the room to pick up the information panel had changed back to date and time.

'Modern technology, I know the date and time, what I need to know is who is the bastard ringing at this hour.' He snatched up the receiver. 'Hello,' he snapped.

'Duncan, is that you?'

It was Solomon. He had explained numerous times that he worked and not to call before midday. Solomon was a member of the 'now' society. Solomon could not wait. Solomon was a Jew, typical of his race, highly intelligent, exuberant and full of *joi de vivre*. He was also tenacious. Like so many of his race when this pushiness drew comment it was lumped together with other criticism of the Jewish fraternity and passed off as anti-Semitism.

Solomon, despite his vast intelligence, introduced him to his fellow race, saying, 'This is Duncan, he's a very nice man for a goy,' without realising how patronisingly rude he was being.

'Duncan is an agnostic...'

'...An atheist. I can't believe in a God that punishes the innocent so remorselessly. No God could have created Africa.'

'The blacks bring their misery on themselves.'

'We Jews have to deal with anti-Semitism on a daily basis.'

'Here we are in our nice middle class surroundings, we do not have to worry where the next meal is coming from or that we have a roof over our heads. We might fall out with our neighbour but that's as tough as it gets. I'm afraid your concerns are an insult to those people.'

'I'm not black. I don't care about blacks.'

'I'm not a Jew,' said Duncan.

'What do you want? I've told you a thousand times I work in the mornings and I want to be left alone.'

'This is important,' Solomon sounded his usual busy self.

'Your daughter got engaged,' said Duncan. 'Mafeking has been relieved.'

'Money wants to talk to you about a film.'

'Money? Robert Money?'

'Who else?'

'Solomon, I'm not interested in film. You sell him the film rights but I don't want anything to do with the script.'

' Duncan, this is no time for scruples. If you do the script and we negotiate a percentage it could be worth millions.'

'I won't do it,' said Duncan. 'I'm sorry. I don't believe the book will make a film worth seeing. The subject doesn't appeal to youngsters. Sell the rights by all means but leave me out of it, please.'

'Meet with the man,' said Solomon. 'Have lunch. He'll pitch you his idea and then you can make up your mind. Do that for me?'

'OK Solomon, I'll think about it.'

As Duncan hung up, Pauline came in with a coffee, 'Solomon?'

'Yes.' Duncan rescued a steaming mug. 'Wants me to do the film script but I'm not sure if I'm capable or want to be bothered. The rewrites, the editing, reading the galleys, I'm sick of the damn thing.'

'I need a lift to town.'

'What time?'

The telephone rang again, the number was not Solomon's so he picked up.

'Duncan, is that you?'

'Yes, Ian,' he raised his eyebrows for Pauline's benefit.

'Is anybody there?'

'I'm here, Ian.'

'I mean with you,' said Ian, losing patience, 'In the room.'

'No Ian, I'm all alone.'

'I thought you might be in the taxi.'

'This is the land line you're ringing,' Duncan shook his head and answered Pauline's questioning look with a shrug.

'So it is. So it is. I've got something to tell you. It's top secret. If any word of it gets out it will be rescinded.'

'What would?' It was Duncan's turn to lose patience.

'I bet you can't guess.'

'If you don't get off the line I'm going to hang up, I'm busy.'

'Too busy for your brother?' Ian waited for an answer, sensing there was not going to be one, continued. 'I'm going to be in the New Year's Honours, guess what as.'

'King of the Zulus?'

'You must promise you won't breathe a word.'

'Cross my heart and hope to die.'

'Sir Ian Black.'

'Congratulations Galahad, regards to Helena, your secret's safe with me.' Duncan put the handset back on its cradle and took the plug out of the socket. 'What time?'

'In about forty minutes,' said Pauline. 'Ian's got his knighthood?'

'Yes.'

'There's a shock.'

'I've got something to finish, then I'd best do some proper work.'

'Aren't you going to give up the cab?'

'Not totally, it's where I get my inspiration.'

'What are you looking at?'

'You.'

'Dunk, don't start that.'

'I'm not starting anything, I was just being nice.'

Duncan had not liked Albert Finney as an actor but had read that the man had refused an MBE as well as a knighthood and went to number one spot in his favourite people poll. He detested David Bowie's music but he admired him as a man for similar reasons.

Ian would explain that he and his brother were as chalk and cheese. Their parents were stuck in a time warp, devotees of a bygone age when England ruled the World and God saved the King. Their father would get in a flap if the *Radio Times* printed the Union Jack upside down. Ian accepted and absorbed this doctrinaire but Duncan went his own way.

Their father, Norman, the image of Ian, was a timid animal. He went to and fro to his job with the council for forty five years, barked behind closed doors or cowered in a corner. He hated intruders and when guests came to visit, he mentally scurried behind the furniture, willing them to leave.

As with so many others, Norman's great moment was two and a bit years of the Second World War. The army forced him out of his shell. The world was subjugated to a fearful conflict but Norman Black was liberated. He had a keen eye and a steady hand and spent two years trying to teach trainee soldiers to shoot straight. He had a strong nostalgia for those delivered times. After demobilisation he went home to his old life and old habits.

Their mother, Rose, was typical of her generation. She knew her place, in the kitchen. Mousey, small and put-upon, never without her 'pinny', she did not have the wit to question her husband's dictatorship. He was her husband and that was the end of the affair.

Norman travelled back and forth to work on the same train for fifty years without making a single connection.

Ian was unblessed with his father's genes. When he got the post in the Civil Service, Norman commended him, 'Son, it's a job for life.' He adopted his father's commuter habits and the only blip in his vigorous routine was his marriage.

How these two met and married was a brain teaser that perplexed Duncan for years until Pauline opened his eyes. He was too close to the puzzle to see Ian's reasoning. Helena was the first woman who showed any interest in him but Duncan fell short of understanding his sister–in-law. She was not only outside his experience but beyond his imagination. Duncan thought that life was for living not a business plan.

Chapter Thirty-Three

Amy sensed her mother had entered the room and did not stir, but the old bag was not fooled. She was going to get a lecture about religion. If she was not careful she would be dragged off to church.

'Jesus died for our sins.'

Her mother did not seem to tire of this platitude. How that man suffered. His pain and misery was worse than anyone else's. Just slightly ahead of her mother in the misery stakes.

Jesus died for our sins. What was it supposed to mean? It was like the silly conundrums Uncle Ian teased her and her cousins with when they were infants. How Hi is a Chinaman and how long is a piece of string? It was as unanswerable as who made God?

If he chose to die to make up for all the sinning that had gone before that would make sense but to die to make up for the sins to come was a nice convenient get-out for the sinners.

How did his martyrdom all those years ago cover the sins committed since? Two thousand years of wickedness is a lot of sin. If he died to eradicate the sins to come then he was giving carte blanche to believers to carry on sinning.

'It doesn't matter much what we get up to because Jesus died for our sins. What a load of…'

Why did one man's death weigh against sin? Thousands of innocent children, babies, died every day. Didn't their lives count? Just this one bloke, Jesus, had got the sole rights on worthwhile death.

'You wait until you are faced with damnation, my girl, you'll laugh the other side of your face.'

'Sonia Green doesn't even go to church and they won the lottery.'

'Money is the root of all evil. Dr Riklis tells me that houses without faith are full of fear. Houses with faith are not afraid of the hereafter.'

Amy did not respond. It was the only way to deal with her mother when it came to religion. It was the only way to deal with her mother on any topic. Just let her rattle on until she burnt herself out.

Emma patiently waited for capitulation but her daughter was made of sterner stuff.

They would not be late for church.

There was the resigned smile when her mother flashed her pious teeth. As she left her stubborn offspring she checked herself in the mirror, adjusted a crease out of her black dress and licked her lips to renew the lipstick's shine.

The front door closed and Amy relaxed. Peace, oh heavenly peace. She would not be surprised if her mother was one of God's messengers, because all the news was bad.

She jumped out of bed and peeked through the curtains. Her mother took her father's arm and they walked toward the church.

Why had he agreed to go today?

Her father's shoulders were rounding, his bulk getting more unwieldy, his fixed smile permanently wan and his step had slowed and shortened. Was the weight of Jesus's burden bearing down on him or was her mother pile-driving him into the ground?

'Wanker,' she muttered.

Sunday mornings were a window of freedom. No vacuuming, no school and no Emma. She brushed her teeth and thought of showering, but decided against. She would save that until her mother returned with a gob full of salvation.

She wandered into her parent's bedroom, opened and closed the drawers searching for unlikely treasure. She had just made the change from primary to secondary school when she happened on a thin green volume by a man named Frank Harris. For a time she had a new respect for her father, but it did not last long. He should have stood up to the old bag more. Amy learned a lot from that thin green volume.

She lay on the bed and looked about her. The room was horribly feminine, pink and fluffy, her mother's teddy bear lay between the pillows. She picked it up and throttled it for a few seconds before putting it back. There was a nude painting without a head on the wall opposite. Amy stripped off and lay in the same pose as the painting's model and compared how well she looked.

Paying close attention to how flat her tummy was she sucked in, then blew out and tried as hard as she could to withhold influence and let her body be natural. She was not sure which of her profiles was genuine, but she was happy with the result.

'Nobody can call me fat.'

That was all some of her friends ever spoke about; weight, dieting, anorexia. 'They should be like me. Regular sex keeps you fit.'

The book on her father's side of the bed was bound in blank yellow paper without a title. She picked it up and flicked through the pages and found pencil marks in the margins. She expected these marks to highlight the sexy bits but they were printing errors.

It was a novel of some sort and she skimmed quickly, looking for the sexy bits. The writer was describing her mother. She finished the paragraph and searched for the name of the author but the book was untitled with no author's name. She opened the book to the beginning.

Amy grew cold and put her pyjamas back on, returned to her own bed and continued reading.

How did this writer know all these things? Was it possible for someone to make themselves invisible, get inside their house and spy?

She searched the room for signs of an intruder and Brad Pitt's vacuous eyes stared back at her. He could have bugged the house. There must be a microphone hidden somewhere. She dropped the book and inspected the telephones, but she did not know what she was looking for.

Could her father have written this book?

Surely that was not possible. She read on until her parents returned from church. As she heard them coming she put the book back where she found it, showered and dressed.

'Dinner,' her father called up the stairs. She ran down obediently and sat quietly while her mother recited grace.

'Who was in church?' she asked.

'Everyone but you,' said her mother dishing out a spoonful of roast potato, cabbage and a slice of beef before handing it to her.

'Not everyone,' corrected her father.

They ate in silence for a time and Amy asked, 'Dad, did you take up writing?'

'No,' he answered abstractedly. 'What makes you ask that?'

'That book in your room.'

'No, I didn't write that book. Your uncle Duncan did.'

'Eat your dinner,' Emma interrupted, her teeth speckled with green. 'Don't go nosing about in my room. How many times do I have to tell you?'

'It's OK for you to go nosing in mine,' Amy snapped.

'I'm the parent. That's my prerogative.'

'That's what you say.'

* * *

Number seventeen was an ordinary semi-detached, but somehow it was prettier than her much larger house. There was a rose bush around the front door with fading red blooms and clusters of bushy chrysanthemums beneath the bay window. Pots dumped haphazardly in the front garden were filled with primroses and pansies.

Through the bay's leadlight windows, she could see a wall of pictures. There was a black taxi parked out front but no sign of anyone being home.

She walked to the end of the road, crossed over and walked slowly back on the other side. Repeating this exercise for a third time, she found herself face to face with Pauline Black.

'Amy?' asked Pauline with a friendly smile. 'Do you want something?'

She had been caught red-handed.

Inside, number seventeen was nothing like home. Emma Telleulin's was a permanent showpiece. Dralon sofa cushions brushed smooth, without a crease. Amy rarely sat down without feeling guilty for spoiling the perfection. Their walls were plain and unadorned, the carpets immaculate but lifeless and the furniture characterless and inert. Her mother was always showing off about her shit stuff.

'We bought this painting in Paris. It cost a fortune.'

'Ben bought that china vase for me for our 20th wedding

anniversary, I picked it out of course, can't trust men to do the right thing.'

Here was welcome, ordered clutter, newspapers flung on the floor alongside a pair of discarded shoes. Books, videos and DVDs piled haphazardly on the coffee table. Plants tumbled out of every corner, a bird screeched sporadically and music blared somewhere upstairs.

'Would you like something, a drink?'

'Thanks.'

'What would you like?'

Toby appeared out of nowhere and smiled a sickly, 'Hello.'

'Look who's paying us a visit.' Pauline felt foolish stating the obvious.

The look on her son's face held a long established want. Why did boys, also men for that matter, drool over pretty women? This girl was not for him, but he was inordinately keen on her. She felt pity for the desperate hunger she saw in his eyes.

They sat quietly around the kitchen table, Toby concentrating on their guest and their guest toying with her half filled glass, waiting.

Waiting for what?

'So,' asked Pauline, awkward in her own home. 'To what do we owe the honour of this visit?'

Amy could not manage an answer, her busy eyes wandered in search of a reply because her motive was not for broadcasting.

Pauline saw her go from face to face, vacant. What she wanted was not there. That left Duncan. What could she want of him? It was then that Pauline saw it all. She had read the book. She had found herself portrayed in the book and that was why she was here.

'Toby, fetch your father. He would hate to miss seeing Amy.'

Toby, knowing this to palpably untrue, looked at her quizzically, shrugged and went upstairs.

Duncan peered at the girl and asked frankly, 'What are you doing here?'

The girl did not notice his rudeness, and said coyly, 'I want to learn to be a writer.'

'You do?'

'Will you teach me?'

Chapter Thirty-Four

Duncan referred to Amy as Lolita, 'She's far more sexually experienced than I'll ever be.'

'Jealous?'

'Pretty, undeniably pretty,' he changed the subject.

They were totally together but she could not ask him, could not broach the subject. Duncan knew her quandary and let her suffer, just smiled and carried on. 'I used to feel like Toby feels, the adolescent longing, wanting to know girl's secrets, the unimaginable beauty inside those clothes you wear. It's part of growing up.'

'She's not for him.'

'Of course she isn't,' said Duncan. 'She mixes in a different stratosphere, where sex is something you do for fun, inconsequential, like picking your nose.'

'You sound disappointed for him?'

'Don't be silly,' said Duncan. 'Why do you try to provoke me?'

'I wish I could answer.'

'Is it the book?'

'That and some other things,' said Pauline, dreading that he would ask for more specific detail.

Often, if he was in the right temper, he would let it go. 'Innocence is life's greatest gift.'

'Is it,' she said, relieved. 'What's the second?'

'Discovery,' he laughed. 'I should speak to Toby. Just you wait twenty years my boy, when Amy's lined and flabby, those delectable legs have swollen ankles and are the colour of corn beef. Her breasts bloated and lumpy, her bum dimpled, her chin doubled, her tummy untucked.'

'She's read the book,' said Pauline.

'That's obvious,' said Duncan. 'She saw herself, and what's more obvious is she saw her parents.'

'She knows somebody understands.'

'I suppose.'

'You had better be careful.'

'I know,' said Duncan. 'I like your idea of her starting a diary.'

'You know what I think?' Pauline looked at him imploringly. 'You should not do this. You're playing with fire.'

'I feel sorry for the poor girl. Knowing that someone understands what she's going through might be good therapy.'

'Don't say I didn't warn you.'

*　*　*

It was early Sunday morning and Ian had eaten an excellent breakfast. He so loved Sundays away from the general delirium, with time to work at his own pace until lunch. Apart from an English breakfast, could there be a better meal than roast beef and Yorkshire pudding? He placed his satchel on his desk and peeped out the window. The sky was clear blue and he stared enviously as a group of smiling men who bundled their golf clubs into the boot of a car and drove away. If only he could spare the time to be out in the sunshine, but there were pressing and important matters of national importance to take care of.

A news conference to launch Operation Pierrepoint was to be held in twelve days' time. Lizzie had a foreboding, 'They should not have chosen Friday the 13th.'

'What foolishness,' Ian thought.

Typical of a female to be irrational. He expected better of Lizzie. The PM's diary was filled and that was the first available date.

He heard Helena's foot on the stair below and his full stomach sank. Ears pricked, he listened hard, dreading that she would come upstairs to talk to him about some irrelevance and spoil his reverie. Why is it women do not care for sport and mock men for their enthusiasm, but can talk in such minute detail about incidentals?

The phone rang and came to his rescue. He heard her solid step retreating.

Lizzie was not like most women. At least she understood the facts of life. Apart from sport and work, what really mattered?

His scanned the faces on his Wyford FC poster, touched the framed CB medal, the framed letter offering his knighthood, and unwound the lid of his Schaeffer. His ritual over, he grabbed a handful of papers from inside the satchel and placed them on his desk.

Reverend Waddenham's dazed face drifted into his head. He did so admire the clergyman's accomplishments, especially how well he had coped since his wife deserted him. His sermons were most interesting, often alluding to one of his parishioners, and were cleverly constructed.

With Emma still wearing widow's weeds and baby Chloe dead for over ten years, his sermon last week told the story of Hannah, Samuel 1, and her promise to God if he blessed her with a child. Unfortunately Emma did not perceive the advice so subtly offered and had remained in a state of mourning. Amy was not exactly in the Samuel mould. L-O might label her a saint but as far as he was aware the opposite was true.

Ian had misunderstood the Reverend's pointed reference in that sermon. His intended protagonists were Hophni and Pinehas, not Hannah.

'*The glory, O Israel, is slain upon thy high places!*
How are the mighty fallen!'

'Yes,' said Ian. 'How the mighty do fall, not just Saul and Jonathan. Those of us that do not overstep the mark remain intact.'

Ian was proud, proud of his family, proud of his life, proud of himself to all exclusion of the proverbial and Charlies' Ecclesiastes. His heart swelled, his chest swelled and his head felt light.

'Sir Ian Black,' he said with a flourish. 'It won't be long now.' He pinched himself violently on the inside of the thigh to be sure he was awake and not dreaming.

'*Tell it not in Gath,*
Publish it not in the streets of...'

'Did the Reverend have wind of his forthcoming elevation and was he pointing him toward caution?'

'Don't be silly, how could he know? It was good to be alive,' thought Ian. 'Everything was right with the world.'

Miles away, he had not heard her approach, and there she was pushing the door open, scything his innards with a sinking feeling. As she droned on, the sinking was replaced by impatience and irritation.

'Can't you leave me alone for five minutes?' he wished.

'Emma had a fire in the summer house. Everything was destroyed, everything. The sofa we gave them and those old kitchen units your parents were going to throw out from the flat in Smith Street. Guess who came to the rescue?'

Gritting his teeth Ian asked, 'Who?'

'Our Christopher,' said Helena puffing up like a pigeon. 'He was coming home through the park and rang 999. If he hadn't done that the whole place would have gone up in smoke, but they managed to save the main structure. It makes you think doesn't it?'

'What was he doing there?'

'I didn't think to ask,' said Helena.

Typical, thought Ian, all the frippery and none of the essentials. Will I ever be rid of her? he wondered.

'I might pop round there later,' she said.

A weight lifted and too enthusiastically he said, 'I think you should pop in, you're good in adverse situations.'

'I might,' she said.

Ian decided on silent tactics to rid himself of her. Would she never leave? He toyed with his papers to give her a hint.

'Humph!' Reluctantly she went away without closing the door, petulantly he kicked it shut.

The top memorandum was from the PM's personal secretary expressing dissatisfaction with Lord Justice Christie. Ian had made a serious error choosing his Lordship. The wording of the legislation complete, the method of administrating emasculation was under debate. Christie was putting a spanner in the works, finding fault with every suggestion. The PM had been informed of the Lord's lack of compliance and wanted rid of him. That was easier said than done.

'Judas,' muttered Ian.

There was a postscript to the memo in the PM's doctor scrawl. As he read the PM's words his Sunday fry up congealed. There was no doubt where the blame for Christie's recalcitrance was being laid.

There was no going back on the knighthood now. In all probability he would not have to put up with the PM for much longer, they were so far behind the polls this Emasculation Act was unlikely to make up enough ground. He and Hay would be re-united soon. What a pleasure it would be, a return to the good old days.

Ian's chest was speared with acid, a bubble of air catapulted into his throat and he belched black pudding.

'Oh my God,' Helena shrieked, 'Oh my good God!'

He thought Helena was downstairs, out of earshot, and Ian's face flamed with guilt for his uninhibited burp. There was another squeal followed by a dull considerable thud. Somebody has died. Ian leapt out of his seat, the chair flying backwards and careering into the wall. He charged, as fast as his portly frame would allow him, to come to his collapsed wife's aid.

'What is it?'

Helena was spread across the bed, revealing dimpled thighs that defied passion. The Sunday papers strewn about and under and she was rolling her head from side to side, moaning, 'I can't believe my eyes.'

'Whatever is the matter?'

'*The Times…*'

'What are you reading *The Times* for? I got you your *Sunday Mail* as usual. It's underneath *The Times*.'

'Look,' Helena pointed with a scarlet fingernail.

'Look where?'

'There, you thick-headed pots. Your brother has written a novel and it's reviewed, there.'

'My brother has written a novel? How?'

'He writes words, makes sentences, sentences become paragraphs, paragraphs become chapters, etcetera, etcetera, etcetera.'

Ian read out loud, 'The first novel by Duncan Black should be classed as a most remarkable work. It shows craft and maturity that usually comes with years of plying the writing trade. What is even more remarkable is that Black, a man of some hubris, claims the novel took four weeks from commencement to completion. Whether this is pure apocrypha we may never know, but this does not detract from this splendid piece of intelligent bravura writing. It lampoons the *Corridors of Power*….'

213

'Enough,' said Helena. 'I've read it.'

'*Wasted*, a novel by Duncan Black. It could be a different Duncan Black.'

'I doubt it.'

'...apocrypha is unlikely because this novel is a satire of how we live a lie and are blind to truth, that lives are wasted immersed in delusion...'

'What's that supposed to mean?'

'I'm not sure.'

'...Black's assured style remains within the bounds of good taste and never resorts to sanctimony or verisimilitude...'

'Sanctimonious?'

'Sanctimonious means believing you are morally superior to other people.'

'I don't know anybody like that, do you?' said Helena genuinely.

'...Our hero, Simon Grundy...'

Chapter Thirty-Five

Ian sat in the toilet, fuming. His mobile in one hand his life in the other. He scrolled up her name and his fingered hovered.

Should he or shouldn't he?

'Lizzie,' he breathed. 'I must see you right away.'

'Where?' she asked, her ardent voice titillated his very being.

She was already there when he arrived, dressed in a thick cardigan and tight fitting jeans. Her legs were long and her narrow hips excited his sporadic libido.

'You look very fetching, my dear.'

Lizzie was a founder member of the Luton Army for the Marriage Bond Society and had to hurriedly leave their AGM to meet with Ian. She was glad to leave. It was pointed out that she was the last founder member still single.

Her feelings for Ian came with a host of new sensations, apart from the lurid dreams and a surfeit of the hots. She would spend her mornings contrite, promising the mirror chastity, apologising to her saviour and praying for enlightenment, but her heart and hips remained disobedient. She bought some one piece pyjamas, a giant babygrow. This worked for a couple of nights, then she began dreaming of *Kama Sutra*-like contortions.

He called and she came running.

LAMBS had taught her restraint and so far she had been content to indulge Ian's reticence but if something did not happen soon she would burst.

She opened her arms and he fell inside, gripping her tightly but keeping his face pinned in her neck. She gently pushed him from her and tilted her head. He pressed his mouth to hers but applied unsuitable pressure at a bad angle, puncturing the inside of her mouth with jarring teeth.

'Ouch!' she squealed.

'I'm so sorry,' he confessed. 'I wouldn't hurt you for the world.'

She pulled him to her and they brushed cheeks. She pulled his hands from around her and placed them on her backside. He almost collapsed with ecstasy. How small and round she was in his palms. His hands investigated slowly and found themselves between her legs. His mind pictured what dwelt there and exploded in a frenzied passion. Without inhibition, their mouths locked open and inexpert tongues splashed.

Ian, always the gentleman, offered his handkerchief to wipe the spittle. He watched as she dabbed, amazed how far his saliva had flung. He took her by the hand and led her to the motorway hotel reception desk.

'Can we order tea for two in the dining room?'

'Certainly, sir,' said the receptionist. 'Just find a table and I'll send the waiter through.'

The dining room was empty but he chose a far corner. He pulled her chair out for her and sat opposite, 'You look so lovely.'

'Thank you,' she said blushing in blotches of dark red.

He changed chairs, sat with his back to the door, took her hand in his. He stared at the floor while he stroked gently. He was silent for a long time, but glad to be in contact Lizzie watched and waited.

'My brother's written a book.'

'I know,' she said and he looked up. 'I heard him on the radio talking about it.'

Lizzie knew she was saying the wrong things but she had to occupy her mind from the turbulent tempest that was snatching her anatomy.

'Duncan and I are chalk and cheese. He was so good at everything, I grew up believing I was inadequate,' his wet eyes met hers. 'I used to cry myself to sleep praying for change. I had red hair.'

'Did you?' Emotion rendered Lizzie's words barely audible.

'I was called copper knob and ginger nut by the other kids but not by Duncan.'

'That's nice,' she said.

'What he did was worse,' Ian spoke with a face Lizzie had not seen before, 'A thousand times worse.'

He swallowed hard, 'He beat me easily at everything,

football, tennis, cricket. I was eight years old and he was five, but he beat me.'

Ian swallowed hard, Lizzie thought he might choke.

'Out of the blue I started winning and I celebrated, boy did I rub his nose in it. Unremorsefully, but he took it, took it without a murmur.'

Ian slumped, pulled her hand to his mouth and pressed his lips to her palm. She had to suppress the urge to demand sex.

'Then I found out he was letting me win,' a tear plopped and splashed onto his wrist.

'At fifteen, Duncan had a trial with MCC and was being scouted by football clubs. I kept my self-respect because I was a good student. The teachers told my parents I was Oxbridge material. I went for an interview at Christ's College but I didn't get an offer. I needed three As for a place at Warwick but I didn't come close to that either.'

Another tear dropped onto his knuckles and slipped between his fingers.

'I felt so ashamed. I hid in the loft for twenty-four hours and my parents were at their wits' end. I got a place at Oxford Brooks to do theology and was glad to get away.'

'You've proved your worth ever since,' said Lizzie. 'They must be proud of you, your parents and your brother.'

'I suppose,' said Ian stifling a sob. 'I made friends in Oxford, friends I still see. They came to Chris' wedding. They knew nothing of my shame, nothing of my brother, nothing of my inadequacy. I made them laugh.'

A supercilious waiter with grubby fingers stood tapping his foot impatiently while they chose what they wanted for tea.

'Is that all?' he asked rudely. It was hardly worth dragging him away from the football on the big screen in the coffee lounge.

'Duncan got a place at Cambridge,' Ian continued. 'They wanted him for his sport as much as anything else...'

'Didn't he go?'

'He chucked it all up for Pauline, threw it in their faces.'

Lizzie was at a loss, she did not understand Ian's stance on his brother's defection. What was it to him if he abandoned the chance of a lifetime ticket to the Polo Grounds? He spoke of his brother as though he were an errant child.

'Perhaps he didn't get the required grades?'

'He got three As. Don't you see, he could have had everything I wanted, but he didn't want it.'

Lizzie was more baffled than ever and lifted his sagging face to help her understand. Ian wrestled free and flopped back into his slump.

'Can I tell you a secret?' He looked about him to be sure no one could eavesdrop.

'Please.'

'I haven't had sex for over twenty-five years, not since I created my son Gideon, and that was one fuck too many.'

Was it the F word or was it the matter of fact way he said it, but Lizzie laughed involuntarily. She knew it was wrong, but her vulnerability was playing ducks and drakes with her good sense.

Ian did not seem to notice.

'Why haven't you?' she asked.

'Why haven't I what?' Ian was bemused and watched the surly waiter shove their tea in front of them without comment.

When he was out of earshot she qualified. 'Had sex,' she said in a hoarse whisper, and Ian seemed not to understand. 'Why haven't you had sex for twenty-five years?'

'I don't really know.' He stretched into a sitting position. 'I haven't had the time. I've been so busy.'

He poured the tea and cut a scone in half and then the promised collapse happened. He placed the teapot back on the table, fell to his knees and put his head in Lizzie's lap. 'I'm so lonely,' he sobbed.

She helped him to his feet and escorted him back to reception. They took a room on the second floor and lay on the bed together, clasped in each other's arms, while Ian cried himself to sleep.

Lizzie lay beside him, her libido doing justice to a deprived nymphomaniac. She stripped and lay naked against her unconscious lover. She needed relief but God was watching. She adjusted her hips and opened her legs allowing Ian's arm to drop between. With a short manoeuvre his comatose hand flopped into place, she took him by the elbow and gently massaged.

The one and only time Ian Black was to assist a woman into achieving pleasure and he was not awake to witness it.

Chapter Thirty-Six

It would not be accurate to say that Ian's pending knighthood had gone to Helena's head or that she had undergone a metamorphosis because the word to describe the change that came over Helena has not been invented yet.

Without telling Ian, she called the bank and had her cheque book reprinted Lady Helena Black. She did the same with her credit cards and took on more credit cards because she loved to see her new name reproduced in different colours.

The joy of this game palled with the arrival of the revised documents. She craved more and joined every society she knew just for the thrill of receiving an envelope addressed to Lady Black. She had no interest in wildlife but became a benefactor of the RSPB, the RSPCA, Battersea Dogs' Home and the Venus Club in Old Compton Street.

She sent off for varioius memberships and every morning waited impatiently for the postman, who seemed to arrive later and later. She wrote to the Post Office to complain about his tardiness and got an apology addressed to Lady Black. This began a series of suggestions and complaints to utility companies, local authorities and government departments.

Helena could not get enough of seeing her name on the envelope preceded by the title. She bought a letter opener to take better care opening her mail and she kept every envelope stored in her treasure chest.

It was then she decided that 8 Brinvilliers Avenue was not a grand enough address and she had a brass plate made with Pemberton House engraved on it. The Post Office reported the change of address to Wyford Council and they sent a representative to call on the Blacks.

A fierce argument ensued because Pemberton House already existed. It was opposite the railway station and housed the small claims court. Helena lost the battle and had to buy a new plaque. She was a happy woman because Pemberton Hall sounded much grander than Pemberton House.

Her trials grew more omnipotent.

As soon as Ian left to confront his brother about the book she dashed upstairs for some judicial work. She sat on the bench at the Old Bailey and Duncan was again on trial for treason. He was sentenced to be hanged. Helena passed sentence wearing a black lace veil, another of her fashion innovations.

Where had he got to?

Helena assumed her post at the window and searched the street both ways for signs of his return. She telephoned Pauline but they had not heard from or seen him. She tried Emma with the same result.

Where had the bugger got to?

For the first time in several days adultery appeared in her mental notebook. She was going to get to the bottom this once and for all.

Since her presentiment that day in Phil's café, Helena had been so busy with her aggrandizement she scarcely had time to check on Ian's affair. She had sneaked his mobile out of his jacket pocket, checked the names and messages, but there was nothing untoward. He was too scrupulous to use government property for personal indulgences. She had ransacked his office thoroughly without uncovering a clue.

There was only one place he would keep secret papers. In that damn case of his. The blasted thing was virtually handcuffed to his wrist. She had spied on the case for a day or two but there was no opportunity to burgle.

Where was it now?

In his hurry Ian had forgotten to wind on the security numbers. Helena tried the latches and they sprang free.

The case had numerous sleeves and pockets, all empty. Amongst reams and reams of claptrap there was no evidence of a personal life. At the bottom of the pile was a legal document tied in pink ribbon. The piece was well thumbed and the corners were curled up or missing. Helena eased the ribbon aside and read the heading.

Making careful note of how the ribbon was tied, she unravelled the knot and lifted out the document. Unused to reading the prosaic she struggled to establish its meaning, but when she did cotton on, her mind raced with the potential.

This was a job for Lady Black.

* * *

When Ian awoke, it was dark outside and Lizzie was dark inside. She wanted more but Ian was implacable.

'I'm so unattractive without my clothes.'

'Let me be the judge of that.'

Reluctantly he did as he was told. It was role reversal. She, the 'virgin', was talking the 'urbane man of experience' out of his clothes. If they had been aware of the uniqueness of their situation they could have patented this role play.

'Give me a minute,' he pleaded as she pressed her hungry hips against his flaccid stomach, the wiry hair scratching burns on his sensitive skin.

She was gyrating uncontrollably, the vacillation of the bed was making him sea sick. No matter what encouragement she applied to his torso, his member stayed obstinately flaccid, and with massaging his penis became invaginate.

Desperate, Lizzie decided on distraction. She had even tried to find the football highlights on the television to get his blood flowing. Ian was set on wallowing in self-pity.

'What about your sons? I'm sure they love you.'

'There fine in their own way but they've got their own lives. In truth I've got nothing.'

'What about your wife?'

'That's rather the point,' said Ian. 'She lost interest in me long ago. She's forgotten who I am, if she ever knew. She's only interested in what I stand for.'

They both studied his reluctant member which would not stand for...

Lizzie made him lie on his face while she caressed his body. With his belly hidden, he was quite pleasant to look at and his tanned skin was silky in her fingers. Her incitement of his erogenous zones was failing, so she tried harder. If she had been worldly she would know that she was barking up the wrong hornbeam. She had not encountered the word dominatrix, let alone understood its implications.

How close she came. He gave her the clue by his compliance to laying face down. One swift slap and Lizzie would have been quids in. Ian was his son's father. His body craved a good lashing and Helena only provided the tongue variety.

Sensing possible success as his breathing grew frenzied she coaxed his genitals, but without warning he propped up on one arm and said, 'I love you.'

It was not what she craved, but it would have to do for now.

'I really mean it.' He sat up, astonished at his own revelation. 'I never knew love existed.'

They embraced tenderly, shared a moderately swamped kiss, excited hands searched and fondled. Blood generated to his recidivist organ but teasingly a tad less than full inflation. He tried to place it in her dolman sleeve but it lolled elusively somewhere near the elbow, shredding her libido.

It was at this juncture that Ian noticed the time on Lizzie's wrist and, in a filibuster of excuses, made a hasty exit. She stayed in the room until past midnight hoping God was busy elsewhere and not watching her jack off.

* * *

Chris was using Katy's running regime to cover his surveillance of his cousin's nocturnal habits. He played possum, faking his breathing and as soon as she was gone, he was off in the opposite direction.

He had pursued Amy from a distance and found the pub where she picked up men. He waited in the car park for her to leave and followed her back to the summer house.

With the loss of the summer house he had to develop his bloodhound skills. Tailing motor cars could be tricky and several times he lost her on route. The impatient ones did it right there in the car park, Amy utilizing the hanging straps to aid them in their rush.

Aunt Emma and Uncle Ben were in no hurry to claim for the fire. He encouraged his mother to hasten the insurance claim and the repairs so that he could resume more convenient spying. Chris fed his mother's ego by getting her on the case.

His plan worked better than he could have hoped, because Helena took the entire matter in hand. She phoned and bullied and demanded and pressurized and moaned and complained and spoke to the senior clerk and the deputy manager and the manager and the claims manager and they sent the cheque off just to get rid of that *bloody* woman.

The payout cheque was based on an estimate provided by Uncle Andrew, whose men completed the job in half the time for half the money.

It was then, Chris offered his services as handy man. He brought along his tool box and started on the finer interior works that could not be entrusted to those rough builders.

* * *

Sunlight was streaming through the window. Pauline, peeking through the gap in the door, watched Amy nosing around Duncan's room. She wore a plain white dress and she could see her white underwear beneath. She had well developed breasts but her bare legs were gangly, the way a fourteen year old's legs should be. Pauline had heard snippets of gossip of the girl's wayward behaviour, tantrums and sulks, rebellions and promiscuity, following on from where her mother left off.

When they were newlyweds they spent weekends at Emma and Ben's. As his inhibitions relaxed, Duncan came down to breakfast in his shorts.

'Isn't he sexy in the mornings?' Emma said hungrily in front of the fleshy and flabby Ben.

These disingenuous flirtations embarrassed Duncan and he took care to assume regular dress.

Because of her promiscuity, Duncan assumed that Emma had a large sexual appetite and that Amy had inherited this capacity. He was wrong, it was not their libidos that craved sex, but the lack of love in their lives.

Now her daughter was intimidating him, flaunting, offering herself. Duncan did not find it hard to come to terms with the obvious fact that this fourteen year old child was more experienced in sexual encounters.

223

He had seen the change from that sweet and beautiful child to a dark eyed fiend. Knowing Emma as well as he did and her extreme reaction to her subsequent tragedy it was easy to guess the source of Amy's problems.

Was she here hoping Pauline would be out? Was she wearing this skimpy dress on purpose? Was it an act of complete innocence? It was when she stood in the direct sunlight that Pauline was positive that she had dressed especially to show what was on offer.

That damn book had brought about this attraction?

Amy had read the book and discovered a kindred spirit, a sympathetic soul.

Was sex the only method by which she could reward him?

Since their son John had left for university, Duncan had seconded his bedroom as an office. The door to Toby's room was opposite. He kept his door open, hoping to catch a glimpse of Amy as she came and went. He could hear everything said in the room next door and understood that his inamorata was chasing his father and accepted that he, Toby, was probably too young and inexperienced to cope with her. Still, he put his faith in kismet and hoped she might become attracted to him. What could he do to attract her attention? When she was expected he played CDs that would make him look cool, hoping to elicit a reaction.

'So,' asked Duncan, 'how is it I can help you?'

Amy pretended not to hear and continued posing in the natural spotlight provided by the Indian sun streaming in the window. Duncan turned his attention to his laptop. She would soon notice his lack of interest in her coquettish flashing. Unfortunately for Duncan, she was not so easily deterred. As he typed she planted herself beside him careful to ensure that her arm and leg were pressed against him.

'What are you writing?' her question paradoxically innocent as she leaned against him.

'A new book,' said Duncan. 'Would you like to read some of it?'

'Am I in it?'

'That would be telling.'

She smelled fresh from soap and felt soft and warm. The front of her dress bulged and with the merest sideways glance, her unfettered breasts were visible. The nipples were that youthful pink that Impressionist painters recorded with stunning subtlety.

'Your book got a good write-up in the papers.'

'Did you read them?'

'My dad told me. Why do you write?' He sensed her move a fraction closer to him.

'I can't really say.'

'For the money?'

'No,' said Duncan with finality. 'Egotism, arrogance and because I can't help myself, those would be closer to the truth.'

'What's egotism?'

'Conceit,' admitted Duncan.

'What's conceit?'

'Vanity.'

'Like my mother.'

'Not like your mother but somewhere in that general direction. There are different sorts of vanity.'

She was now so close to him that if she turned her face towards his their cheeks would be touching. As her head began turning he stepped out of his chair and fetched another for the girl to sit in. He placed it a metre away from his own and unknowingly played into her hands.

She was not fazed by this gentle rebuke and sat back in the chair with the hem of her dress riding up and her legs slightly apart. As they talked, this opening widened slowly, imperceptibly, like Tower Bridge. It was apparent that if he wanted it, his ship was coming in.

Her shapely thighs were healthy, tanned in stark contrast to the clean white of her dress. She slowly rocked her knees back and forth offering glimpses of pale blue pants.

'How come you know so much about people?'

'I think about them a lot.'

'How come you know so much about my mother?'

'I've known her for a long time.'

'Did you ever sleep with her? My mother I mean.'

'No,' said Duncan.

'Didn't you fancy her?'

'I don't like brunettes,' he purposely teased her.

This preference caused her to consider. Her eyes grew busy and her knees still. He studied her extraordinarily pretty face, small features, deep brown eyes and deeper dimples.

225

Duncan was confronted by the age old puzzle. A young man is complacent about the fine texture and quality of women, takes their youth and beauty for granted. When you reached the age where you did appreciate such things, the girls were too young to associate with. Not if you had a semblance of decency.

'I see a therapist,' was her conclusion to her unassailable thought process. 'She doesn't understand my mother like you do.'

'She doesn't know her like I do.'

'Would you help me?'

'How?'

'With my mother.'

'You should write a story, any story, about your mother, knowing that the only person that is going to read it is me.'

'Stop doing the diary?'

'No, keep doing the diary, but write a story for my eyes only. It's good for you to put your private thoughts on paper.'

'What's the point of the story?'

'Once I've read it, I'll tell you.'

Hearing that she was leaving, Toby changed the disc to Tom Waits, and as she came out of the doorway she hesitated and listened. Knowing she was there and was possibly going to acknowledge him, Toby fought the urge to look up. He sat at his computer screen and tapped his foot in time to the music.

'Who is this?' she asked brusquely.

'Tom Waits,' said Toby pretending to tear himself away from the screen. 'Do you...'

'You've got shit taste in music,' she said and skipped out of sight.

Chapter Thirty-Seven

First thing Monday morning, despite the urgency of the PM's memorandum, Ian called in sick. When Borders opened they found Ian waiting outside and he bought two copies of *Wasted*.

He started reading in the car park but by the middle of the third page he had lost his temper and drove home.

'How dare he mock me,' Ian raved at the speedometer. 'I don't care if he is my brother, I'll sue him for libel.'

Caught up in his rant, bursting to get home, he broke the habit of a lifetime and jumped a red light. Unfortunately for Ian, he was spotted by an oncoming police vehicle that was going off duty. It had been a quiet morning and the team had spent their time grumbling over new terms of employment designed by the PM's cost cutting panel, and the incessant demands for paperwork that were draining the Metropolitan life force.

Neither man was in the mood for mitigation.

'Sorry officer,' said Ian. 'I was miles away.'

'If you had been miles away sir, I would not have seen you had jumped the red light.'

'I'm late for work,' said Ian, wondering how to raise his status with due discretion.

'Driving licence,' demanded the policeman in a resigned voice. 'I'll give you a ticket and we can both get along.'

The policeman read the name on the licence, gave Ian closer scrutiny and went to consult with his partner. 'Did you get him up on the computer?'

'Ian Black, 8 Bronvilliers.'

'That's him,' said the first policeman. 'Give us the book.'

Ian watched their conversation, sure that they would discover who he was and let him go with a warning. The policeman leaned on the roof of the car and copied down the details from his licence.

He shoved the ticket through Ian's window, 'You'll be hearing from us in due course. Good day, sir.'

Ian was stunned into silence, put his licence and ticket in his wallet and drove slowly home. Calmed, he locked himself in the toilet and finished four chapters. He rehearsed a severe dressing down of his brother in the bathroom mirror and was upset to find he was clearly losing the last vestige of his top hair. A strong latte helped him through to lunch and get halfway through the book. At each injustice he made a note on a pad of the page in question.

'Why aren't you at work?' Helena asked.

'How can I work?' Ian pushed the book away. 'With this to cope with.'

That afternoon, Helena disarmed by having her husband home on a work day, ruining her routine, sat gloomily watching him, longing for his reading to be over. He had bought the second copy so that they could read it together. She did not care to read, she did not have the attention span. It had been a chore reading the 'hanging' file but that was of some interest. Books were a waste of energy, there was nothing to gain from them. Gossip columns were stimulating. In three short lines she could be transported to another world, a world sparkling with glitz.

Helena's dream was to be sylph-like, with hair down to her shoulders parading on the beach at Marbella. If she had had a daughter she would have groomed her to achieve what she could not. Books did not come into her image of celebrity. Books went on and on about boring things like love, washing and ironing, bringing up children and murder.

She did not want to read about murder or watch thrillers on television, but she would happily murder a few people or have them put down humanely. Any Labour politician and that Jeremy Paxman. Who did he think he was? Most of all she would like to murder that Mrs Twitchin next door.

'If that cat of hers shits on my lawn just once more, I won't be responsible.'

Hardly aware of what he was eating, Ian did not enjoy his lunch. He was collating his notes into a reasoned argument. Always best to be prepared. The gall of the man, he was way off the mark, talking out of his hat.

'How dare he write about me without my permission? What kind of name is Simon Grundy? Why choose that name for my character?'

'I'm coming over,' he said abruptly down the phone to his brother. 'Now.' He hung up, preventing any chance of a denial.

Words tumbled around Ian's brain. Thousands of words gyrated and as they came together, swerved off at a tangent.

'You bastard,' he said and pushed his way inside the door.

He stood in the hallway breathing fire. He was the dragon that adorned the shields of England, or was it Wales? George and the Dragon, it must be English somehow.

'You bastard,' Ian's repeated words emerged in flames.

'Am I?' said Pauline sweetly. 'Why?'

Ian, bright red, his mouth open, but no sound issuing, followed Pauline into the living room. She sat in an armchair and smiled up at him. Duncan, drinking a glass of red wine, sat reading a newspaper. 'To what do we owe this rare visit?'

'I'm always visiting here,' Ian defended. 'I'm your brother.'

'You haven't been here since my 40th birthday party.'

'Surely it's not that long.'

'Oh, but it is.'

Duncan opened the newspaper, folded back the page and began reading. Ian watched, nervously tapping the arm of the sofa.

'I cannot imagine the nerve it takes for you to write about me like this.'

'You think the book is about you?'

'It's set in the Home Office. I work in the Home Office. You are my brother. What else is there to think?'

'I can put my hand on my heart and tell you that while I was writing I never gave you a thought.'

'You're telling me that Mr Grundy is not based on me?'

'Funnily enough, you've caught me out there. I did think of you, but only when choosing the lead character's name.'

'Grundy, what has Grundy to do with me?'

'Forget it.'

Ian had prepared a reasoned argument but was now blundering in the dark. Which accusation should he deal with first? He was inhibited by Pauline's presence. He could not broach his biggest fear with her in the room.

'I want to speak to Duncan alone. Pauline, would you mind?'

Pauline looked to Duncan, who smiled. He would tell her about it later. Pauline closed the door behind her.

'Whether you like it or not, people are going to associate me with this Grundy character.'

'So, deny it.'

'I cannot afford to be associated with infidelity.'

'Why not?' asked Duncan, 'Because Grundy tries to have an affair with the sister-in-law he has been in love with for twenty-five years?'

Duncan was laughing at him. Ian could see the humour in his brother's eyes. Did he know of his infatuation? How could he?

'How did you know about my knighthood?'

'All you lot get knighthoods. It goes with the job. Anyway, it isn't about you.'

He could feel his own bluster as he blurted, 'The whole thing is libellous and I've no doubt you will be receiving a dozen writs before the week is out.'

'The publisher's lawyers have checked the chance of litigation with a magnifying glass.'

'Why did you do it?

'Do what?'

'You've made fun of everything I believe in, everything I stand for, everything I've worked for all my life. What your book does is rubbish my life.'

Duncan, impassive, considered what his brother had said. He stared at some distant corner for a time before blowing out his cheeks and shaking his head. 'If it is rubbishing your life, I did not intend it to. It was simply a bi-product of my intention.'

'Your intention?' said Ian, but could not find a word. 'Huh!'

'Yes, my intention.'

'What is that, pray tell?'

'The man in the street does not have a say.'

'What are you talking about?' Ian was getting heated. 'We live in one of the great democracies.'

'Do we now?' said Duncan, finishing his drink. 'That's your opinion.'

'Don't be bloody silly, of course we do.'

'Suit yourself, but there are things happening out there that are doing damage and you obviously don't have your finger on the pulse.'

'You're just a knocker, a cynic, your type make me sick.'

'How convenient,' said Duncan, 'You've no idea how frustrating it is dealing with the minutiae, if you're a small person with a grievance nobody's listening.'

'Every government department, every borough council has customer services...'

'Ian,' Duncan held up his hand, 'That's precisely the point. Those people are employed to fend off the victims. People are frustrated and they express it in many ways. Do you stop the vandalism? There are those like me who throw their hands up in the air and say, 'Bollocks'. You're not going to win those voters back. I for one will not step inside a polling booth again.'

'Don't you see the danger of that? If you don't vote and others like you, we will be overrun by lunatic fringes.'

'Let the BNP have it. It's what you deserve.'

'I don't know where you get these crazy ideas.' Ian was on the verge of hysteria. 'It's cloud cuckoo land.'

'My publishers think I've got a point. The reviewers haven't been too unkind either.' Duncan offered him the newspaper.

'Is this some sort of revenge?' Ian asked.

Duncan's eyes peered at his brother, 'I don't get you.'

'Are you jealous of my success?'

'The book has nothing to do with sibling rivalry,' Duncan laughed.

Ian jumped out of his seat and began pacing. 'It's not so much for myself that I'm so upset. The cavalier way you portray the police and the army is...' It was his turn to find an object of inspiration, 'Unpatriotic.'

'Is it?'

'What gives you the right to make fun of young men who risk their lives to safeguard our country? Those boys and girls have parents. How do you think they feel when their children are killed protecting you and me?'

'They're not protecting you and me, they're protecting American money.'

Ian was baffled. 'Is this one of your conspiracy theories? You're so naïve.'

Duncan did not answer. His brother considered him naïve. How easily words were used without considering their impact. He vowed to be more conscientious in the future.

'You must really hate me.'

'No,' said Duncan, 'but I don't have much emotion about you that I can admit to. Your constant need to prove how well you've done is more often sad than irritating, but other than that...'

'Sad? That's very nice.'

'You asked for it.' Duncan picked up the newspaper and handed it to Ian, pointing at an article to read. 'That's a big part of my problem.'

'This is Saturday's...'

Duncan gestured for him to read and Ian scanned the page.

'What's wrong with it?' demanded Ian.

'Nothing,' said Duncan. 'It's very well written, but who is he? There are so many of them that can turn a word, turn a brush and turn the public's head; charlatans and chancers.'

'Is that a reason to attack me?'

'You deserve everything you get, Ian. It's the world you inhabit which is losing its humanity. You not only accept and condone it but you contribute to its downfall.'

Ian drove home frustrated and unsatisfied. Once again while sporting with his brother he had lost hands down. Was he at fault? Operation Pierrepoint was nearing disclosure, would it benefit the man in the street and work for the public good?

Chapter Thirty-Eight

Toby's door was open and Duncan leaned against the frame while his son stared intently at the computer screen. 'Want to go for a knock up?'

Toby remained concentrating on the screen, 'You won't take it easy and I'll be too knackered to work.'

'Let's go to the nets then, I'll bowl you a few,' Duncan suggested. 'You should take a break. We could go for a beer.'

'I wish you wouldn't do that,' Toby swivelled his chair to face his father.

'Do what?'

'Tease me.'

'Just because it's the middle of winter,' said Duncan. 'No reason not to think cricket.'

* * *

Warm from the exertion the two men made their way home through the park in silence. Duncan veered towards the further path and Toby, perplexed, hesitated but followed along. Black quickened the pace up the steep incline to the main crossroads and entered the grounds of the Sussex Arms. Inside, in the cool dim, Duncan asked, 'What are you having?'

'Pint of bitter,' said Toby.

'I'll have the same.'

The middle-aged man studied the two of them suspiciously while he pulled the pints. Struggling with a question, he put the glasses on a sodden mat and fingered the price on the till. As he handed over the change he asked, 'Didn't you used to play for Wyford Town?'

Feigning bewilderment, Duncan shook his head, 'Not me.' They carried their drinks to a quiet corner beneath copper hunting horns, ladles and horseshoes. Duncan sipped his drink and let his eyes wander.

'What did you mean by humanity?' Toby copied his father's action and sipped his drink politely.

'What brought that up?'

'I heard your row with Uncle Ian,' said Toby. 'You didn't explain it all that well.'

'That's because I'm not sure myself,' Duncan shrugged. 'Like most things it is made up of a lot of ingredients. I know it when I see it but it is hard to put into words.'

'Try me.'

Toby thought his father was not going to answer. He sipped his drink.

'Humanity is a dying commodity,' he said abstractedly and for a moment Toby thought that was all there was to it. 'There was an incident when your brother was in his pram. Your mother was struggling to get into Smith's and a woman let the door slam on her and knocked the pram over. How John was not hurt was a miracle. That woman was not aware of what she had done and no one came to your mother's rescue, yet once a year we care so much about children we put on red noses and give millions to charity. Does that prove we care?'

Toby shrugged.

'For one reason or another, your cousins are a mess. I'm sure their parents mean well but that just ain't good enough. Nobody has time, so busy chasing money, finding the mortgage payment and success it gives them the excuse to forget how to live.'

'I like Uncle Ben,' Toby objected his motive more for Amy than his uncle.

'He's just like Ian, never home. Your aunts are so fucked up their kids never had a chance.'

'As a kid I hated going to Uncle Ian's,' said Toby. 'The screaming! They don't have a conversation at normal volume. If you asked for a glass of water it was as though you were committing a crime.'

'Aunt Helena's house is not for living in,' Duncan explained. 'It's for show.'

'You're not very nice about her.'

'In the book?'

Toby nodded shyly.

'Those sisters are the antithesis of humanity. They are blind.'

'I don't get you.'

'The Kray twins loved their mum. They were psychopathic monsters but they loved their mum. Those sisters have nothing but contempt for their mother but they visit her every other day. You explain it.'

'How did you get from humanity to mothers? You've got a butterfly mind, do you know that?'

'That's why I like to write. I get my thoughts in proper order.'

'That's not why you like to write, dad,' Toby finished his drink, signifying that he was out of time and wanted to get back to work.

'I don't think I'm going to like this very much.'

'You've got a misguided idea that the reader will take notice. Nobody cares.' Duncan turned back to the window, surveyed the dying light and pushed away the remainder of his pint. 'I've hurt your feelings.'

'Not at all,' said Duncan. 'I was thinking how much more mature my son is than I am.'

Duncan sat in a corner chair warming his arm on the radiator, watching Pauline making dinner. She flittered busily from sink to worktop to hob and back again.

'Toby asked me to explain humanity,' said Duncan. 'I didn't make much of a job of it.'

'It's a big subject and I wouldn't know where to begin. What did you tell him?'

'Most of us think we're humane. We care about children, put a funny nose on and make a donation to charity. Our relatives die in car accidents and we put flowers on a lamp post to show how much we care. On the other hand we care so much for our children we stick them in front of the television to keep them quiet, leave them to the au pair or send them to boarding school. We care about the dead but drive too fast, cut in and out of motorway lanes, pull out of side streets ignoring give way lines, overtake on the inside. Accidents are never our fault.'

'You're using me as a sounding board for your book again,' she scraped a board full of sliced mushrooms into a pot, broke an egg into a glass and beat it vigorously. 'You can sort out your own problems. I've got more practical things to deal with. My mother's run out of clothes and I have to get to the home tomorrow.'

'I'll give you a lift and do some work after.'

'Drop me at the station.'

'No,' said Duncan. 'I should do some work. So why has western civilisation become so self-involved?'

Pauline shook her head. 'Prosperity, dear.' She stirred the beaten egg into the soup and wiped her hands on her jeans. 'If you don't have to worry where your next meal is coming from and you can feed your kids, you become complacent.'

Toby joined them and took the seat on the opposite side of the kitchen table. His mother glanced at him quizzically, 'I could smell dinner was ready.'

'Food.' said Pauline. 'Just like your father. If you didn't have to eat I'd never see either of you. Talking of self-involved, why do you act so petulantly with Ian?'

'I can picture that condescending look of his and I get the purple mist. I know it's stupid but I lose it every time.'

'I should look at yourself more carefully if I were you.' Pauline got three bowls out of high level cupboard and ladled three portions of soup. 'I think this book of yours is to prove how much cleverer than Ian you are.'

Duncan smiled at Toby, 'Is it attack Duncan day?'

'I'm serious,' said Pauline sitting between them.

Duncan dipped his spoon but held it aloft and made a toast, 'To my family, smarter and more mature.'

'I'm right aren't I?' Pauline persisted.

'Could be,' said Duncan agreeably. 'It could very well be. I'm only human after all.'

* * *

Ian arrived at the office and could sense the seismic waves, a prelude to an earthquake. The whole building was quiet before the storm. The news started as a faint whisper, grew to a murmur and crashed through his office door. Lizzie's face, a Venetian mask of white, her eyes sad with his doom. 'You are to report to Number 10 immediately.

There was a car waiting out front and he had to wait outside in deathly silence until the Permanent Secretary joined him. Mornington's greeting was perfunctory and Ian's heart sank. Whatever the problem, Ian's head was front runner for the chopping block. Guesswork was replaced by panic.

What was he to be the scapegoat for?

It had to be something to do with Operation Pierrepoint and if it had been leaked, who could be responsible. He evaluated the committee members, unable to choose a possible mole. He did an inventory of the office and was left with one suspect; Lizzie. Was she the traitor? What could have inspired her to commit such a treacherous act?

Ian had guessed correctly. Lizzie had been treacherous, but he got the topic wrong.

Ian and Mornington were hustled into their audience with the PM and had to wait while he finished his meeting with the Chancellor. They were engrossed in their business and it was an age before it concluded. The Chancellor, a dour Scot, gave Ian the blackest of looks and the PM, a mild mannered man, threw a fit.

Picking out the bones of his rambling rant, Ian gathered that the 'hanging' committee was to be on the front pages of the midday editions. 'I want whoever is responsible for the leak found and sacked within twenty-four hours or you're for the chop.' He placed his index finger close to Ian's nose. 'Get out. I'm sick of the sight of you.'

Ian stood outside the closed door of PM's office, recovering from the tongue battering. As the storm in his ears subsided he was certain he heard laughter but was not sure where from. As the day developed he became more and more certain that the mirth was at his expense.

Finding a mole was akin to finding a needle in a haystack. He did not know where to start.

When he got back to Marsham Street the building was buzzing with rumour and the minutes of Ian's meeting with the PM were common knowledge. Ian had no idea where to start, but Lizzie had plenty of ideas. Perhaps too many.

Ian rang the editor of the *Standard,* and threatened prosecution under the Official Secrets Act, but not only would he not give the source but Ian had the distinct feeling that the newspaperman was also laughing at him.

He closely questioned his PA and she was quick to respond, 'Friday the 13th. Don't say I didn't warn you.'

Lizzie walked the halls and spoke to all and sundry hoping to get an inkling of who was responsible. Various Ministers were interviewed by the media for their views of the disclosure. Those in office condemned the treachery while the opposition deplored the clandestine nature of the committee and deplored the government for using 'hanging' legislation to save a dying party.

A strange tale pinged around the walls of Marsham Street that reached Ian's office mid-week. A woman who would not give a name claimed to have a print out of the forthcoming legislation. She was asking silly money and most of the papers demurred.

It was the reason they turned down her offer that provided the mystery. Those with their ears to the ground understood that the newspapers did not need this unknown woman's evidence because they already had it.

The days passed speedily and far reaching inquiries left them empty-handed, but there was no further pressure from Number 10. News of the proposed Bill made banner headlines and in the coming week the emphasis focussed on the forthcoming election. The proposals fired a public debate 'for and against' emasculation and this polemic completely overrode the need to discover the culprit responsible for the leak.

Was it a phoney war? Ian was perplexed by the lack of flak flying in his direction and Lizzie's canny mind provided a possible explanation.

'The smart word is the leak came from Number 10. They wanted to test the water, get a litmus test of the voting public's attitude. The PM is privately pleased with how events have turned out.'

Ian was glad to hear this hypothesis, but without divulging his private thoughts to his PA dismissed the story as the usual foolish conspiracy theory. No way would Crest Mornington be party to such a dishonourable pact.

Ian's role in the affair fizzled into oblivion. As the days melted away the Sword of Damocles moved on to new pastures. He breathed easily and his thinking became clearer. Certain of Lizzie's loyalty, he deliberated with an open mind, but try as he might nobody fitted the frame.

Lizzie saw Ian's impotence as a sign from the Lord, saving her from mortal sin and stopped dithering about her engagement. She accepted Elvis Black as her fiancée. They approached their spiritual leader to agree a wedding date. Her slate wiped clean, she avoided situations that would rekindle the spark of emotion she felt for Ian and applied for a transfer.

Chapter Thirty-Nine

There is something curiously barren about Christmas morning, heightened since the lifting of Sunday restrictions. It is a unique day in the calendar, in that there are no newspapers and the majority of the country is closed.

It was a long held tradition on Christmas Day for the Black family to congregate at Helena and Ian's house. Everyone was there, Chris and Gideon, Duncan and family, Ben, Emma and Amy, and Helena and Emma's mother, Eunice, who always brought her spinster sister Edwina Bartlett. Jessica and Andrew would pop in for a drink before lunch and swap presents but they made other arrangements for dinner.

A few dusty decorations, a hardy annual tree made of silver foil, baubled and bangled, beneath which were expensively wrapped empty boxes. Around the extended dining table spread with Waitrose's best fare, wearing paper hats and energy drooping, the diners were subdued.

The redoubtable Helena was talking, fighting hard to create a convivial atmosphere, but was losing the battle. She explained to her nephew John that Chris and Katy's wedding album contained few pictures of Chris and none of Gideon. John's weary face grew catatonic.

Each individual was brooding over a preoccupation that had occurred in recent weeks that might soon come to light and was afraid for the future. These inevitabilities, for one reason or another, could not be discussed out in the open and the guilt weighed heavy.

Old Norman was wondering when he could politely excuse himself and fall asleep in front of the telly. Rose was fretting on when her husband would get up the nerve to leave the table. Pauline was wondering how soon they could politely leave.

Helena was struggling to contain her sub-text. The public exposure of Ian's rescinded honour was a week away. Ian was waiting for a discreet moment to disappear and call his beloved to make another attempt to talk her round. Mrs White neé Bartlett had found a man friend but was unsure of her daughters' attitudes to her taking up a new relationship at her age, especially as the man was twenty years younger than her. Her sister Edwina, while attending to their mother's gravestone had spied the secret lovers kissing.

* * *

Toby was embarrassed to admit to what he knew because of the way he came upon the information. He had taken to walking in the night in the hope of bumping into Amy returning from…Christ knows where? His shoelace having come untied, he stopped in the chilly evening and leaned against a lime tree sprouting greenery from its shoulders, stump and thighs. A sharp wind slithered through his clothing and he shivered violently. He was about to continue when he saw Amy returning home, hand in hand with a patchy youth, wearing only a cerise T-shirt, with 'Don't Mess With Me' printed on his chest, to keep out the cold. Even his grey jeans, with holes in the knees, leaked air. Instead of entering the house they veered off and took the pathway into the park. Cautiously, Toby followed.

Oblivious, the couple partook in a game of primitive stimulation. Their artificial horseplay lacked a handy bludgeon. While they cavorted, Toby paused at the corner and was grateful for his caution. From his vantage point he spotted a man spying on the couple from behind a fallen oak. Perched on a branch above the man, silhouetted in the moonlight, sat a puzzled owl, befuddled by the foolish conduct of humans.

Amy and the youth entered the back gate not taking proper care to close it behind them. Toby hesitated, but the man hidden behind the oak was less timid and he tiptoed into the garden. Toby, his heart thumping, careful where he stepped, followed suit. Muffled laughter came from inside the rerfurbished summer house and the spy stood staring in the window. Toby could not see who the man was and decided it was best to leave. His snap decision caused a loss in concentration and, as he stepped away he tripped. His arms flailed helplessly. To maintain his balance he bumped into the gate, which sent it crashing on its hinges.

The Peeping Tom came haring out of the garden at a rate of knots and the patchy youth, bare-chested clasping his grey jeans about his hips, followed after him. Toby took cover behind the oak and contemplated Amy's state of dress. He did not have long to consider. She came to the gate in her underwear and flung the T-shirt to the ground, then closed the gate and shut the lock.

Toby set off home his head full of snaps. Amy, bra bulging with breast and shapely hips in white knickers, a pair of lovely legs, a flash of bottom and a flash of lightning on the small of her back. His cousin Chris' startled face, his eyes filled with terror.

* * *

Ian, despondent, sat behind his desk, which was piled high. Correspondence spilling every which way, urgently awaiting a reply, but words would not come into focus. His office was beginning to notice his lapse, but he did not care. Desperation was mounting and it dispelled fear. Nothing mattered anymore. He might as well be dead. Suicide would be a blessing, at least it would stop the pain. He composed a suicide note, left it on top of a stack of paper and went up on the roof. He peered over the edge of the parapet, suffered a violent cramp and hurried back downstairs.

Lizzie entered his office, placed more paper on the mounting pile and tried to avoid Ian's misery. Head bowed, forlorn, she thought she ought to leave him to wallow and honour her sacred vow to Elvis. She allowed her guard to drop and a flood of emotion touched her heart. She closed the door, squatted by his chair and stared at him with those sad eyes of hers. It was an age before either moved and their lips met doused in tears. It was a kiss so poignant they were poised on the brink of dicky.

* * *

A swirling mist had tail spun throughout the afternoon and as night fell it ran out of energy and flopped, enclosing the town in a black cape. Chris, returning from work up the motorway, saw the black looming on the horizon and pondered where this ominous cloak lurked.

Wyford struggled home through this fearful fog and once in the warm vowed not to venture out. This caused an unprecedented increase in domestic demand on the Pemberton Estate, close to double the usual electrical supply, and the readings on the power station meters were fast approaching red. Technicians were doing everything in their power to avoid a cut but the demand was pushing them perilously close.

Amy was given strict orders to stay at home. She had arranged a date but managed to rearrange. She left a message on her date's answering service.

'I'll meet you in the summer house at ten. My parents will be in bed. Wait by the gate.'

The refurbishment of the summer house had been completed at the weekend. Andrew's work force came and went in a week. Emma and Helena spent the rest of the insurance payout on furniture and fittings. These shopping expeditions created tension. Tension created friction and it was not long before the sisters were at loggerheads. Neither could own up to the fact that they were shopping with separate agendas.

Having secured the insurance payout Helena was determined to see the project through to the end. It was going to be another monument to her matchless indefatigability.

Emma regretted letting her sister get involved. Emma had a lover and problems finding a discreet venue. This home from home was going to be her love nest.

Helena wanted pretty curtains to be tied back at the jambs, material to be delicate and feminine. Emma wanted blankets to be closed and opaque. Helena, not getting her own way, threatened her sister with feng shui.

Emma had begun this affair in the summer and locations for tryst prevented regular consummation. It was not safe to go to his place and impossible at hers. The fire had proved fortuitous and she was going to take full advantage of the windfall. At the insurance company's expense the summer house had been decked out as a boudoir. It was grandly turned out with a four poster bed, kitchenette, spa bath and bidet.

Emma and Ben had been physically estranged since the

discovery of his heart tremor. They were not so very active prior to that. She burnt him out in the early years, initially with her voracious sexual appetite and latterly with her desperation for a second child. When they finally managed to fertilise, the baby was still born and Ben's faltering libido had been res-erected to no avail.

Having struggled through the smog and traffic, Ben arrived home much later than usual, complaining of feeling tired. He would go to bed after dinner and, while he ran a bath, Emma took the opportunity to arrange an assignation.

'Darling,' she whispered into the mouthpiece. 'Everything is perfect for tonight.'

'I was thinking of staying home. Look at the weather out there.'

'You promised, darling,' she wheedled. 'I so want to see you. I'll put the electric blanket on. Wait at the gate at ten o'clock.'

There was an uncertain silence and a resigned voice said, 'OK.'

Chris got home after eight and ate a hurried supper, 'I promised to help Uncle Ben with his accounts this evening. He's got himself into some bother with Customs & Excise.'

'I'll have a bath and get an early night,' said Katy.

'That's probably a good idea,' said Chris. 'I'll sleep in the spare room so as not to disturb you.'

Chris fumbled through a fusion of soupy air, phosphorescent wafts of agitated vapour. Charcoal tinged with yellow staining like smoker's teeth. Unaware of each other until an arm's length apart, he confronted a man walking his dog. They shared a smile and a word or two about the weather. Chris continued on his way.

He found the driveway where Aunt Emma and Uncle Ben lived and rang the front door bell.

'Come in,' said Ben.

'I'm just returning the summer house keys,' Chris jingled the metals.

'On a night like this?' said Ben. 'You needn't have bothered.'

'Who is it?' Emma appeared in the hallway door and Chris could hear music thumping from an upstairs room.

'It's Christopher,' said Ben.

'Come on in,' said Aunt Emma and Ben tugged at is sleeve. Reluctantly Chris let them drag him inside.

'I oughtn't to stay long.'

'You shouldn't have bothered on a night like this,' said Emma. 'I'm glad you came though, we haven't been able to thank you properly for what you've done.'

'Hanging a couple of curtain rails,' Chris said modestly. 'It was hardly a big job.'

'Stay,' said Ben, 'Have a drink.'

'Take your off coat or you won't feel the benefit.'

'Whisky?'

Amy appeared on the stairs, dressed in a T-shirt come nightie with a cat motif and a flash of buff pants with the faintest of dark stains to the front. Chris stared hungrily at her legs and longed for another glimpse of underwear.

They followed his stare, 'Amy, say hello to Christopher.'

'Hello,' she said in a flat tone and turned on her heel, Chris caught sight of a delicious complex of rounds and creases.

Chris had things he needed to take care of but accepted a small glass of best malt and listened politely to his Aunt Emma's inventory.

'Do you like our new acquisition?' Emma asked, standing at the mantelpiece looking up at an unsubtle canvas using flat tones of prime colour. It was an unremarkable portrait of Cafe Society in the Parisian tradition, depicting five women sitting under an awning staring into space.

'Great,' he said with the same enthusiasm Amy showed him.

'You really like it?'

'Yes, very much,' Chris lied.

'We've been meaning to get you a house warming present. Would you like another of the artist's portraits?'

'We've got his brochure somewhere.' Ben got out of his seat and searched among a pile of papers on the coffee table.

Chris was trying to find a polite excuse to leave when Amy came into the room wearing a pink quilted housecoat and clumsy slippers in the shape of pigs. She sat opposite him and crossed her legs. Knowing the exact area his eyes were trained on she hesitated long enough for him to see a substantial amount of buff. Sitting up straight she stared at him with quizzical eyes.

'There you are,' said Ben handing him a leaflet. 'What do you think?'

Amy's presence made Chris so edgy he was afraid to speak, and pretended to study the brochure closely. His stare slipped above the pamphlet and was fixed on the elusive cornucopia hidden by Amy's housecoat.

Chris handed back the brochure, 'Great.'

'Choose one,' said Emma. 'We'll order it for you.'

Chris waited for his heart to return to its proper place before speaking, 'I best check with Katy, could I borrow this?'

'Of course, of course.'

There was an awkward silence and no one was inspired to break it. He took a last glimpse at Amy's legs and got to his feet.

'Would you like one for the road?'

'I just had one,' said Chris abstractedly. 'Thanks all the same.'

Ben and Emma saw him out, 'Putting up two curtain rails took him forever and a day.'

'He's a nice boy.'

'He's a drip.'

Chapter Forty

Chris turned off the street, along the path and into the park, and kept close to the fence until he found the gate. Using his own set of keys he released the padlock and let himself into the summer house. He had been working there the previous week when Amy came calling.

Chris was perched on a ladder screwing when Amy came to the summer house, nosing. Fighting a bout of instant vertigo he continued fixing the curtain rails and they chatted. She confessed that she was looking to start a new life, leave home and set up on her own.

'If I get pregnant,' Amy explained, 'the council will give me a flat.'

'You don't have to go to all that trouble,' said Chris. 'I know of a flat where you can live.'

'I couldn't afford the rent.'

'That won't matter for the time being,' Chris told her, struggling to contain his excitement.

He closed the door and paused, the heating was on and the room was warm. Amy was expecting a visitor. He checked out the wardrobe, this was the more risky of the cubby holes he had prepared and less satisfactory. He could stand comfortably and watch but the spy hole did not provide a wide angle view. The cupboard under the sink had worked out much better.

Where the sink and drainer sat in the worktop he had cut a perfect joint. Easing up the end of the worktop he slid it along the framing, opened the unit door, pulled out the middle shelf and placed it in the neighbouring cupboard. He put on a cap, sat on the open unit's sill, which he had reinforced with joists hidden behind the skirting. He slid backwards into the cupboard and closed the door after him. Inside, he was forced to squat, but by sitting up straight and using the top of his head to push he raised a section of worktop and could see the entire room. Any fear of discovery and he ducked his head down slowly, the flap fell back into place alongside the rest of the worktop with no one the wiser.

This was why putting up two curtain rails had taken forever. He got out his pocket torch and checked the time, 9:50. Should he wait?

'It's not a night for nookie.'

He eased forward and was about to get to his feet when a key was placed in the door lock. Adroitly, he slipped back inside and closed the door softly after him.

A light went on and someone moved about the room closing curtains. This exercise was not as simple as Chris imagined. Dare he raise the flap and take a peek? He might come face to face with Amy and how humiliating would that be. He waited patiently for his chance and on hearing a bathroom tap running he cautiously lifted his head. He could see the entire room bathed in subdued light. Amy stood in the brighter light of the bathroom checking her face in the mirror and dabbing her eyes with water. She came back into the room, removed her housecoat, threw it over a chair and put the front door on the latch. He let the flap drop back on the frame.

Outside, the gate creaked and Chris could hear breathing which may have been his own reverberating around the confined space. The door was pushed open and the lights blew.

There was a minute of frantic silence until voices could be heard inside and outside speaking in stage whispers. The frantic stopped abruptly.

'Who is it?'

'How the fuck should I know?'

There was a quick exchange of hurried oaths, 'Where do we hide?'

'Wardrobe.'

'Turn the lights on.'

'I'm trying,' said a female voice. 'There's no power.'

'Let's forget it,' said a male voice. 'The heating will have gone off and it will be freezing in here. Have you got a candle?'

'No chance,' said the female. 'That's how the fire started.'

'Let's forget it.'

'Just a quickie.'

There was another spate of mumbling and fumbling and frantic breathing. It was reaching a crescendo when someone made a break for it. The man on the bed took fright and they collided.

'Fuck!'

'Whose hand is that?' an outraged voice demanded.

'Uh!'

'Sorry, it's my own.'

'What the fuck?'

'That's the idea isn't it?' someone bemoaned plaintively.

Feet scurried, doors and gates slammed shut, then silence. Chris waited with baited breath for the all clear. No sound came and he lifted the flap. It was pitch black, he could not make out anything and no one stirred. He waited a few more seconds, then opened the door and slid deftly out. He stood and listened some more. Someone was still in the room. He could see no shadow but as his eyes adjusted to the light he saw the white T-shirt with the cat motif. A hand grabbed his sleeve and tugged him on to the bed.

'At last,' whispered an agitated voice, husky with frustration.

He undid his trousers, fell on top of his darling angel and she grunted with surprise. She grabbed him around the neck and adjusted her body to aid his pumping hips. Miraculously Chris held out well, but was going to fall just short of the mark. As he gauged that Amy was getting there his own trigger was pulled. He struggled on, accelerating and yes, she made it.

'Darling,' she gasped. 'I love you.'

Post-coital, feet on the ground, sobered, he realised the legal implications of what he had just done. A thirty year old married man had just come inside a fourteen year old girl without using a condom. He jumped to his feet. Adjusting his costume as he fled, Chris ran for his life.

* * *

The Christmas table was in limbo, on the edge of their seats waiting for the host or hostess to dismiss them. Chris and Toby were ogling Amy's legs and Amy was miles away, too engrossed to think of teasing either of them. Gideon was thinking of Katy and Katy was thinking of Katy.

* * *

Katy got on the bus, took a seat near the exit and breathed deeply. As the bus lurched forward, she regretted getting on. The contents of her tummy whirled into her throat and in a panic she wrestled to extract a Tupperware container she had brought for the purpose. The violence of the bus' progress spoiled her aim and the scatter fell on the lady in front as well as the back of the seat.

The woman turned and smiled with the kindest of eyes. 'Pregnant?' she asked.

Her mouth full of sickly, Katy nodded. She so needed to spit the residual into the receptacle but was too embarrassed.

At the office she emptied the contents into the toilet and brushed her teeth. Sitting at her station she had another attack. Albert Fish, one of the elderly partners saw her predicament. 'Have you eaten something?'

She nodded pathetically. He put her in her a cab and sent her home.

She lay on the bed waiting for the nausea to pass. Nothing she ate or drank helped rid her of the biliousness, and pills made it worse

Nobody but she and the woman on the bus and her pregnancy test knew she was up the spout. She wondered how best to spill the beans. She might do it over Christmas, next week, when she felt better. It would take some explaining, she had not slept with Chris since August.

The acceptance crept up on her. She considered an abortion, but that thought slipped in and out in an instant. She was pregnant and that made her proud, gave her a sense of achievement, but the sickness brought her back to earth. She was terrified at the prospect of pain and was sick of being sick.

It is terrible being a woman and the paraphernalia that goes with it; periods, childbirth and soap operas.

She dozed off and when she awoke the sickness had passed. She thought of Gideon and a need filled her. She found a telephone and pressed his speed dial number.

'Hello,' his voice was expectant.

'I want you now,' she said simply.

'Where are you?'

'In bed.'

'Naked?'

'Yes.'

'I'll be right there.'

Katy lay motionless waiting for his arrival, revelling in the warmth of the duvet. Should she tell him? If she did and he remained true to form he would be off to the races.

Having made wordless and resonant love they lay spent and tingling. Gideon was growing used to these sexual marathons and was gaining stamina, lasting her pace. He had time for one more before he would be missed at work.

While he waited for the signal to begin again, he tried to think of a way of breaking the silence. Whatever occurred to him sounded lame and he remained reticent. To say, 'You're quiet,' as he sometimes did would be ridiculous in these circumstances because as yet, on this bed, they had barely spoken. They had liaised on the telephone and shared a few words in the hall but in that violent bed they had only communicated with hand signals, stretching 'slap and tickle' to new boundaries.

'I'm pregnant,' she said flatly and the words crashed down on him like an avalanche. He was buried alive and battled to escape. A hole opened up in the pile that smothered him and he gasped for air. Free, safe, and serenely calm he propped himself on his elbow. He kissed her on the mouth with as much tenderness as he could muster and rested his head on her tummy and listened for life.

They made love with unhurried fondness and as they finished in sweet unison their mouths remained together, swapping mute words. Their eyes stared a dialogue of understanding and they clasped tightly, each squeezing forcibly like two partially used soaps trying to fuse and create a single bar.

After Gideon had returned to work, she lay beneath the duvet and dreamed of the future. Without the aid of baby powder she caressed herself, clutched at her growing child and asked God to forgive her.

This joy was worth all the discomfort that God prescribed. Not to be alone and to create a thing, a living thing. How lucky could one person be?

Chapter Forty-One

Crashing against the windows, the rain resembled a car wash and Emma, imprisoned, had finished her cleaning regime early and was at a loss. She made a cup of black coffee, re-opened the local newspaper and spread it flat across the table. Without thinking, she opened it to her favourite page, which she had already trawled through carefully on the day of delivery. As most men turn a newspaper over and start from the back page, Emma's reading omitted the sports section and began with Births, Marriages and Deaths.

Not allowing her eyes to take in any annoying data she skipped across Social and Personal and concentrated on the last section. She scanned each name carefully and noted every individual mourner. Letting the names bounce around her head like a computer eking out the slenderest thread of memory or acquaintance. The period before Christmas was historically slow and Emma did not recognize any of the entries or their relatives. Post-Christmas was a busy week for undertakers and next week's issue would have plenty of names to consider.

If she did find the vaguest recollection of anyone associated with an announcement she would send a card offering her condolences. If there was news of a death prior to the funeral and she got word, Emma never missed the chance of a funeral. She did not approve of cremation but attended anyway and used the opportunity to remonstrate with the bereaved.

'You will regret not having a headstone. You need a significant object to focus your loss.'

Mourners listened with polite restraint to Emma's advice while wondering who the hell she was and wishing she was gone.

Emma had taken a training course in grief management at

evening classes and this gave her the confidence to offer advice to the mourners. She felt it was her duty to help the unfortunates and was oblivious of the discomfort she aroused.

She visited Chloe's headstone every Monday and Friday, rain or shine. Her father's grave was thirty yards away but she seldom ventured there.

Having scrutinized the *Daily Telegraph* and the *Wyford Observer* there were no dates to put in her diary and no postcards to write. She sat drumming her fingers impatiently, eager for new business. She could hear the hollow rattling of her daughter going from bathroom to bedroom.

What was she to do about that child?

* * *

Amy had been too young to understand Chloe's dying. Wait until she had a loss to grieve then she would laugh on the other side of her face. It was a pity they had not encouraged a pet, a budgie or gerbil. Losing even a bird she had become attached to might help her understand her mother's grief, have some sympathy and stop adding to her mother's misery with her awful carrying on.

Emma heard Amy come down the stairs and go into the kitchen. Her ears pricked and she frowned. She heard the garage door being unlocked and distant rummaging.

What was she up to?'

Emma resignedly got out of her seat and skipped ungracefully into the hall. Amy, her eyes a mixture of guilt and anger, glared at her mother and slammed out of the house with a semblance of Emma's lost elegance.

Mother stared after daughter, pursed her lips and considered. She looked around the utility area but no clue sprang out. The garage door had not been relocked and the light was burning.

'Typical,' she muttered.

Nothing looked out of place. She lifted the lid of the dustbin and looked inside. None of the black sacks were open. All seemed as it should be. She lifted out a couple of sacks, just in case she was missing anything. There in the bottom corner were two mysterious objects. She had to empty the bin of all the plastic bags, drop the bin to its side and shake the unfamiliar objects into her reach.

Inside a crumpled Boots bag she found a half dozen unused tampons, inside another she found a pregnancy test.

Emma's whole body was throbbing with fear. Her hands shook so violently the test slipped from her failing hands. Dropping to her knees, it took an age for her disobedient fingers to pick up the plastic tube. The test had turned blue. Emma toppled forward, hit her forehead on the concrete floor and passed out.

Emma came too and the side of her body had frozen to the concrete floor. Her hip would not bend and she could not to get to her feet. She pulled herself out of the garage like a beached mermaid. As she recovered, the uncontrollable quaking returned. She was afraid that she was losing control of her body. Some alien source had moved inside and taken over.

Her head swam, her frame vibrated and her legs were numb. She wobbled to the drinks cabinet, got to her knees and gulped a mouthful of amber liquid from the neck of the bottle. The liquid burned her gut and spread the pain. With her head in her hands she drooped and cried. Tears scalded her face with blissful self-pity.

The little bitch had done it to her again.

'Why couldn't I be that lucky,' she howled at the walls. 'God, how can you be so cruel?' Her eyes were flooded and through her blurred vision came Ben's scribbled image.

'She's got herself pregnant,' said Emma.

'Oh God, no,' said Ben.

'The lucky little bitch,' muttered Emma.

* * *

Morning sickness had temporarily become a way of life. With its passing Katy found a neurosis to take its place. What if the baby inherited her condition? She had not told Gideon or Chris of her problem. She lied about her medication, pretending it was contraception. Ashamed of her pretence she was reluctant to share her fears.

She approached her parents and asked their advice. They suggested abortion but before committing she owned up to Gideon. He would not hear of an abortion and arranged a consultation with a specialist. The consultant was skiing over the holiday and her appointment was made for the New Year.

It seemed the day of her appointment would never come. One of the new superior class of exigent, she could not bear queuing or waiting. She needed to know that everything was going to be all right and she needed to know soon. Gideon warned her that her constant worrying might make the baby neurotic and that gave her more to worry about.

Gideon had proved to be truly amazing. Six months ago she hated the sight of him and now...? Now what? She peeked across the table, his attention seemed to be elsewhere but he winked and warmth circulated.

* * *

Ben looked across at his wife and considered what was going on in her head. What was she making of the situation? Would she be seeing Amy's mistake in her own terms? How it would reflect on her. How it would affect her?

When they met, Emma was a spoiled brat and after she lost Chloe she was a thwarted spoiled brat. She had not recovered from the loss and had made it her life's work.

* * *

Head bowed, she fiddled with the fingers resting in her lap, the lap that had sucked the life out of him. She thought she heard a noise of someone approaching and sat up straight, ears pricked. She was a meerkat.

Having been told the unwelcome news, Ben was stoical. Better a baby than cocaine addiction or worse. What had this heartless world done to his daughter? A delicate flower had been tainted by some mystical crop sprayer.

Children used to undergo a period of innocence, now three year olds were subject to marketing. His once adorable child now had the psyche of a charitable whore with no other motivation, no other ambition, than the desire to get her leg under.

What was she seeking?

Love?

If so, he was not absolved from blame. Burnt out and absent, Amy did not get the affection or fathering she needed from him.

Nor was there any emotion for Chloe. He had not only turned his back on himself but on everyone.

A key slipped into the front door and Amy, seeing the two of them waiting, guessed the jig was up. What Ben saw on her face tapped at the door of his perished heart, but nobody answered. Emma was oddly quiet and the atmosphere simmered slowly.

Amy collapsed languorously into an armchair and began wiggling a foot.

'Must you do that?' Emma complained.

Amy lapsed further into the cushions and glared hostility at her mother.

'How long have you known?'

'Dunno.'

'How long have you been chucking tampons in the dustbin?'

'I haven't been counting,' Amy grumbled petulantly.

'How many weeks does it have to be before termination is prohibited?' Ben asked.

'How should I know?' Emma grumbled equally petulantly

'I'm keeping the baby,' Amy announced.

'You are not,' her mother screeched. 'Stupid little bitch.'

'At least it will love me,' said Amy.

Ben was stabbed in the heart and looked to his wife for sympathy, but it was impossible to ascertain what was happening behind her stony face. Amy's statement did not generate a response.

In the quiet, unspoken questions bobbled but Amy's parents were mealy-mouthed. Interrogation would break out when their discussions got heated, but Ben and Emma were afraid of the answers and would rather not know.

Amy alone was calm. She had been putting off the moment but was glad it was happening. She needed to get her arrangements in place. There was the flat that Chris had promised her. It would need a nursery.

'How could this happen?' Emma broke the dreadful silence, 'You're on the pill.'

Amy smiled to herself and wondered if her mother's question was worth answering. What did the truth matter? What's done is done. She could admit to coming off the pill on purpose but what would be the point? She wanted to escape from her mother and this was a way out.

'Jesus died for our sins,' said Emma.

That was the password to Amy's anger, 'Oh my God!' she yelled, got out of her chair and made for the stairs.

'It's our God,' Emma pronounced prissily.

Amy stopped and said over her shoulder, 'You and your God, you hypocrite. You're stacking up more than your fair share of sins.'

Emma reddened. Amy knew, best to let matters rest for now.

'Amy,' said Ben, 'don't go.'

'Leave it,' said Emma. 'Let her stew for a while.'

Amy's knowledge gave Emma pause. Spite was in her mouth, and best it remain there for the moment. Ben, unsure of his wife's sudden surrender, was thrown. She was not behaving as he would have expected, but that was not an unusual experience. What was in that head of hers along with the rest of her lunacy?

Who was the father? Did they really want to know? If it was someone from the Duke of Coxley pub they were better off not knowing. The child might be born with a tattoo and its ears pierced. Ben supposed that Amy had a tattoo secreted somewhere on her person along with the foetus.

Chapter Forty-Two

Helena had widened her correspondence. She ordered a coat of arms, she requested an entry in Burke's peerage and she looked into her ancestry. This genealogist's report had arrived by return of post. She considered suing for defamation, instead she ripped the report to shreds and chucked it in the bin.

Then came Helena's undoing. There was an article in the *Mail* concerning the death of the Queen's favourite corgi, and Helena decided to send a message of condolence. It was hand written on her new letter head and adopted an impertinently familiar turn of phrase. The Queen's secretary took exception to the familiarity and did some investigating.

Helena stood at the window waiting for her daily fix. That lazy man was late again and she started to compose another letter to the Post Office. Over the top of the Twitchin's hedge she saw a dash of luminous colour just as her mobile phone's muffled ring called petulantly from her handbag.

Torn between the postman and the call, Helena stuttered on her feet. Should she or shouldn't she? The ringing was as strong a narcotic as the letters addressed to Lady Black.

She stumbled to her handbag and rummaged hopelessly with the clutter, found the phone, brushed her hair aside and placed the microphone to her ear. Her eardrum was violated by the 'missed call' bleep. In a flash of irritation she flung the mobile on the bed and instantly regretted her foolishness. It hit the duvet on the escarpment where the pillow began rising and bounced in the air, she made a desperate dive to save it from crashing to the floor. Her body slithered gloriously across the satin cover and her outstretched hand caught the descending instrument bang in the palm of her hand. She had a moment of triumph where she was congratulating herself on her agility. Her considerable body weight was in full flight. Without a brake mechanism to call upon, Helena's rite of passage careered on and came to a halt as her head collided with the bedside cabinet.

In that inexplicable instant between happening and realization, Helena said out loud, 'Oh my giddy aunt.'

Then came the excruciating, piercing, burning, agonizing smart. 'Fucking hell,' she screeched, 'that hurts.'

Faster than was sensible, she got to her feet and she was a giddy aunt. Swaying on rubbery legs, fingering her pate searching for blood, she checked her hand and found a palette of reds that added more wobbly to her capricious pins. Somewhere, miles from home, her mobile bleeper let her know she had a message.

Drunkenly, with the aid of the balustrade she made it to the bottom of the stairs. She gathered up the mail from the porch and went into the kitchen. She prepared a poultice of warm damp paper towel and applied it to the head wound. With one arm above her head and the other by her side like a portrait by Archipenko frozen in bronze, she stared for an eternity at the pile of unopened letters.

Once she was sure the bleeding had stopped she got out a silver knife and made two piles of letters. One of those addressed to Lady Black and another of the rest. Three quarters of the way down the second pile she found a letter addressed to Ian that she sorely needed to open. The return address was Buckingham Palace.

The clash and clatter of pots aggravated her hangover. Gingerly she extracted the poaching pan, filled it with water and placed it on the hob. She went back upstairs while it boiled, retrieved her mobile and checked the missed call. Without thinking, she pressed call back.

'What d'you want?' she asked abruptly.

'I need to talk,' said Emma.

'Well talk then,' Helena was getting irritable at the source of her head wound. 'I'm listening.'

'I can't tell you what I've got to say over the phone.'

'Come round,' said Helena abruptly, remembered the boiling pan. 'Hold on, give me...' she checked her wrist, 'twenty minutes.'

'I'm on my way.'

'Twenty minutes,' Helena repeated into the phone and closed it. 'Drama queen.'

The letter containing the announcement of Ian's honour had been easier to open. More spittle had been used to seal this missive and the flap was proving obstinate. Having spent a period on her feet, her giddiness was creeping back. Helena and the pan were running out of steam.

By the time the flap gave way the envelope was drenched and crinkled. Sliding the letter out carefully, she sat down to read it. By the end of the initial paragraph the pain in her head transferred its allegiance to her chest. Helena was initiated into a fresh emotion and started crying. Tears teemed, dark stains striped her face and the front door bell rang.

Before answering the door Helena hid the Queen's letter in the pan cupboard and scrubbed her cheeks. Emma was in full flow before she was halfway inside and Helena could not take in a word she was saying. She was trying to locate her heart which was lodged somewhere between the hem of her pop socks and slippers.

'Sorry,' said Helena gathering herself. 'Let me make a cup of tea and then you can start from the beginning.

'Amy's pregnant,' said Emma hands on hips, jaw pushing forward.

So bloody what, thought Helena. Hardly an unexpected expectation. Amy's carryings on have long been an accident waiting to happen.

'You're surprised?'

'She came off the pill without telling me.'

'Why?'

'What do you think?' said Emma, exasperated. 'She wants to keep the baby.'

'She can't,' said Helena adamantly. 'How would this look to the ladies at the WI? She must get rid of it and the sooner the better.'

'I don't think…'

'She won't want to bring up an unwanted baby at her age…'

'Helena,' shouted Emma. 'You're not listening. She did it on purpose.'

'Got pregnant on purpose? What on earth for?'

'She's got this crazy idea that the council will take care of her.'

Helena's head was full of negative information pulling in opposite directions. Her head ached, the giddiness returned with renewed fervour and she flopped to the ground like a jelly; simply slipped off the plate and plop.

Emma froze, gaping at the glutinous mound slumped on the tiles. She tried to revive her by slapping her face hard. Although this gave her inordinate pleasure it did not bring Helena round. The head wound began seeping again and Emma found blood on her hands.

She dialled 999 but the line was busy.

Panic stricken, she opened the fridge but there was nothing suitable to apply as a poultice except a bottle of milk. She checked the temperature, decided it was cold enough and, instead of soothing Helena's forehead with the container, she poured the contents over her face.

Helena stirred.

When the original letter from the Palace arrived, the Mexican tiles were doused in a golden rain and with the second letter's arrival they were creamed with strawberry milkshake.

Helena came round but remained horizontal, used the situation to think. What was she going to do? That damned letter, it was going to take a lot of her time to put things right and she was anxious to get started. She must get rid of Emma and open a pack of chocolate bourbons.

'Who's the father?' Helena put her question from the floor.

'She won't say. Ben's tried everything, but she won't budge. She says the baby's hers and the father is irrelevant.'

'She's got a point.'

'What if it's one of those ruffians from the Coalpit Lane Estate, smothered with tattoos? It could be congenital?'

'If the father lives on the Coalpit, the baby is more likely to be black.'

'You're not helping.'

'Help me up,' Helena demanded.

'What happened to your head? You're bleeding.'

'It will take too long to explain.'

'What should I do? We're desperate.'

'Give me time to think about it. I'll speak to Ian and he will let me know the legalities.'

She shooed Emma out the door and retrieved the letter from the cupboard. Squinting, she held the paper at arm's length...

Ceremonial Secretariat
Cabinet Office

Dear Mr Black,
  Matters have come to our notice that have warranted a thorough investigation.
  Absolute discretion is required by all participants in the honour system process. It is essential for the confidence of the public and the duty of every individual participating in the honour system not to reveal details prematurely.
  I regret to inform you that you have broken this pledge and your proposed recommendation has been rescinded forthwith.

  Yours Sincerely,
  Sir Charles Russell

Tears welled in Helena's eyes again. Now the tap was released, there was no stopping the flood. What was she to do? Place the blame somewhere else, but where?

She opened a fresh packet of chocolate bourbons, scrunched up the cellophane wrapper and flung it towards the dustbin. It was too insubstantial to travel very far and virtually landed at her feet. She made one step toward it and lashed out with her foot. Emma had not cleared away the milk shake concoction very thoroughly and there was a slippery patch on the Mexican tiles. The foot that should have remained grounded to the floor was now inside the danger zone. Helena felt her foot give way and did a sort of hop that in no way could be described as graceful, but it projected her considerable person onto dry land and she landed safely.

With an exaggerated sashay she returned to her seat and mulled over her problems. Could she fight this? No one had ever got one over on Helena Black before, but this was unknown territory. She had no control. She could get something on this Sir Charles Russell person the same way she put that greasy photographer in his place.

Where to start?

She must scrutinize her magazines and collate a list of every entry. To rifle through every copy of *Country Life* would take her from now to News Years Day.

She googled him.

Chapter Forty-Three

After the episode in the summer house, Chris was rejuvenated. He had proved he was a man. The sound of Amy's climax rang in his ears and he craved more. Inexplicably, she had ceased her nocturnal jaunts.

He spent fruitless evenings parked behind the Duke of Coxley pub. There was plenty of sex to spy on, but not his darling Amy. Where had she got to? He should initiate a meeting and explain what happened on that dark night. She was bound to want more of the same and next time he would bring a prophylactic.

Her absence teased and fired his imagination. Blurred fantasies, re-enactments of his great moment, watching Katy hurt Gideon were stretching his craving to breaking point.

* * *

Chris sat quietly toying with the remains of his Christmas pudding. He had no appetite and was afraid to speak in case he gave his guilt away. He was not supposed to be in the know, but long practiced at snooping he got wind of Amy's condition and was thrown into a panic. First cousins parenting offspring could produce a monster. The baby might have some hideous deformity. He had learned in history lessons that royal families produced an assortment of freaks because of their intermarriage. If the baby was some sort of grotesque, the doctors would be able to establish the source and he would go to jail.

'Prison!' Chris shivered.

It had been generally assumed that the father was one of her casual pick-ups, and as long as everyone supposed the father drank at the Duke of Coxley he was out of the firing line.

In preparation for motherhood, Amy had her hair shorn and she looked more beautiful than ever with her hair cropped. When she smiled her dimples looked deeper.

I must talk to her soon but how and when? She must not go through with the pregnancy. Everyone was against her going through with it. He tried to catch her eye but she was preoccupied. She keeps glancing at something or someone. Who is it? I do wish she would not suck her thumb it makes her look freakish. Are Ben and Emma cousins? Lolita, that's what Uncle Duncan calls her. It's an apt description. Is that who she's watching? It might be.

I must speak to her before it's too late. What am I going to say?

Explain to her that babies born to cousins are deformed. This deformity may be hideous, two heads, twelve toes or some other fault less obvious. Some inner working will malfunction and the child will become a vegetable, doomed to a wheelchair for life.

Being responsible for such a tragedy gave him pause. He must come forward and get the pregnancy terminated. It was his moral duty. He prepared his argument, but no justification put him in a good light. Every predicted conversation ended with the cell door being shut behind him.

He could bribe her with the flat. Get rid of the baby and you can have the flat for free. He would speak to her tonight.

It was once Chris had sweated the fear out of his system that he was able to think rationally. A day of moral strength and self worth crumbled into a mish mash of dismay. He had to cover his backside no matter what the consequences. DNA was undeniable and they could pinpoint the paternity. He developed an idea to cover himself and went to see his brother, Gideon. His brother was in a perfect position to safeguard the father's identity.

It was time to call in favours and Gideon owed him big time. He called at his flat on the way home and confessed. Chris was pleased at how readily his brother agreed to stand by him.

Chris felt an irregular warming towards his sibling and wanted to make small talk like friends. He was tempted to chat about Gideon's affair with Katy but sensed that his brother might be embarrassed. Then there were the explanations of how he knew about their coupling and also as to why he did not mind much.

His shagging Amy would probably salve Gideon's conscience.

If they were committing the same sin it halved the guilt, although he understood that his brother did not go in for conscience on a grand scale.

'No,' thought Chris, 'best to leave it alone.'

Gideon took six cotton bud samples of Chris's saliva, wound them in bubble wrap, put them in a plastic box and stored them in his freezer.

* * *

Modern life is replete with conveniences that are a minefield of subliminal stress. If you possess long fingernails, pressing the pedantic keys of a computer console is a living hell. Having pressed the wrong key undoing your involuntary error causes anguish so infernal it brings on terminal martyrdom.

For Helena, getting to google was loud and expletive. It involved turning the computer off four times, re-booting twice and kicking the desk. When she finally located Sir Charles Russell, there were dozens of the buggers dating back to the Civil War. She scrolled and scrolled and in her agitated search pressed the mouse on the wrong logo and 'signed out' without wanting to. More invective and more kicking, but to her credit Helena had not yet broken a nail, finger or toe.

She whittled it down to two possible Sir Charles Russells and one was the Attorney General. He might be a friend of Ian's? Good switched to bad in a flash. Good, that Ian might know his whereabouts. Bad, that he might explain the reason for the rescinding before she could devise an alternative whipping boy.

'Bugger, he might have told Ian already. These dopey men have these weird codes of ethics. Ethics,' she groaned, 'is the county where letter 'h' doesn't exist.'

Helena sipped a calming cup of milky tea. Who else knew?

Ian did not know that she knew about the knighthood. He had not let on, the disloyal little shit. It was improbable that he would have confided in anyone.

Lizzie?

How could she put the question without arousing suspicion? It would come to her. Who else? She would love to implicate Ian's brother Duncan. How she hated that man. He did not say a solitary word to her that was not disapproving or facetious. Boy, did he have it coming to him. Nobody got one over on Helena Black.

She tested the water and called the Home Office, 'Ian Black's PA, please…Lady…Mrs Black calling?'

'Hello.'

'Hello, dear,' Helena smarmed, 'will my husband be very late tonight?'

'It should be the usual time,' Lizzie said cautiously.

'I was wondering if he had done his Christmas yet?'

'Cards were sent last week and the gifts are wrapped. They're in the corner of my office as we speak.'

'Good, good,' said Helena. 'Did he remember to get something for Sir Charles?'

'Sir Charles Willcox?'

'Sir Charles Russell.'

'He sent the Attorney General a card,' said Lizzie. 'They have little contact and nothing that would justify a gift.'

'I owe Sir Charles a thank you,' Helena lied. 'You couldn't get me his home address and I'll deal with it myself.'

'I'll text you within the hour.'

'Thank you Lizzie.' Helena's smarm now had a dash of 'Aren't I clever?' She breathed on her knuckles and rubbed her lapel. 'I wish you and your family a happy holiday.'

'Thank you, Mrs Black. You have a happy Christmas.'

* * *

She knew the moment they met, and came off the pill. She was a good judge of men and he was the perfect choice to be the father of her child, despite the age difference. She knew they could not be together for a while, not until she was sixteen, but once he knew about the baby they would be a couple. They could meet in secret until she was legal. They could always meet at the flat. Nobody knew it existed.

It was growing in her tummy. Would it be a boy or girl? They would not tell her at the clinic, some bullshit about regulations. Why was everybody so boring about rules? Uncle Ian was forever going on and on about rules and regulations, pompous old sod. He was nothing like his brother. Duncan was sexy.

She wondered what Chloe would have been like. It would have been nice to have a sister, someone to share with, a friend. Someone to stand up with against misery guts, two would be better than one. She gets on my nerves wanting to be my best mate. She's my mother for fuck's sake.

Maybe, if the baby's a girl, she would be like a sister?

* * *

Sir Charles Russell lived in a red brick house opposite Battersea Park, which had been converted to flats by an actor turned property developer. Pell Morey House was a grade two listed building and Sir Charles Russell lived in a slanted two bedroom apartment on the second floor, which faced the angle of the adjoining property. Russell was inclined to sit at his window and long for a river view.

Helena looked up at the house, frustrated and discouraged. The porter was way too smooth for her Wyford wiles and gave a swift heave-ho. She could not see his flat windows from the road and had no way of knowing if he was home.

She was unsure what she was going to say to him. Usually she had her stories memorized word for word, but she expected some esoteric dialogue that she may not be prepared for. She kept her vigil until dark, but no one came in or out. Helena went home and struggled for inspiration. How could she get past the porter? At 6:00 am she was stationed outside Pell Morey House with cash. She accosted the cleaning lady and gave her a bribe. Dressed for her true vocation, Helena entered the portals of Sir Charles Russell's flat disguised as a fledgling fishwife.

'Lena is off sick,' she explained to Mrs Russell in a creditable cockney. 'I'm Eunice.' It was how she saw her mother, a skivvy.

'Forget my husband's study for today, he's busy working.'

Efficiently, Helena dusted and polished the Chinese collection and the Brown Windsor water colours. Her rotation of duties took her by and by the closed oak door, on the other side of which was her one and only chance of salvation.

Helena was giving up hope. She had vacuumed every room twice and was running out of excuses to stay when Mrs Russell, dressed in her street clothes wished her, 'Goodbye.'

'Goodbye, Mrs,' said Helena maintaining her role.

'I must say you are very thorough,' said Mrs Russell. 'I will contact the agency and tell them so.'

'Thank you, Mrs.'

The latch clicked into place and Helena put her ear to the study door. She had been in the flat for two hours and there was no indication that Sir Charles was home.

She knocked lightly.

'Yes,' said a peevish plum.

Helena opened the door and put her head round it, 'Could I get you a hot drink, your lordship?'

'Who are you?' The man asking was typical of Ian's circle of work. Home, dressed in a dark suit, wearing a shirt and tie. His choice of shirt was more daring than Ian's. It was pink with a white collar and Helena could tell that it had not been bought at Marks and Spencer.

'Eunice,' said Helena. 'Lena's off sick.'

'How d'you do Eunice,' said Sir Charles. 'I would appreciate a hot drink. Weak tea with one sugar, thank you. I like my tea weak and my women strong.'

Helena searched the kitchen and prepared tea with shaking hands. What was she to say? Should she offer her body? One quickie and everything back in order. Would he give the staff one? Did he have old-fashioned values and demand squire privileges? Should she come straight out of the closet?

She tapped at the door and entered. Sir Charles was roughly the same age as Ian. He had tresses of wavy black hair with greying streaks. His round face was puffy and he had the obligatory paunch. It was when he stood up to accept his cup and saucer that she saw he was lame.

'What is you do, sir?'

'I work for the Home Secretary.'

'Another of my clients does that. You must know him. A lovely gentlemen, sir, Mr Ian Black.'

* * *

Amy was in love. It was love. She knew men. This was not just sex, this was the real thing. He made love to her unselfishly. It was what Shelaine told her, that mature men knew how to treat a woman.

269

Amy's friends had babies and the Council gave them assistance. She dreamed of being alone with her little girl or boy and spent hours choosing names. Angelina, Brad, Rachel, Bernard, Claudia, Boris, Cameron. She made a choice and recorded it in her diary. Benjamin.

It was not only her father that shattered her dream.

Giving her a load of bullshit about their age difference, he just wanted out, the bastard. It was a proper relationship, no matter what he said. She liked the fact that he was older.

She would show him. If it took a lifetime, she would show him.

Ben waited for the right time, making sure Emma was not there to incite their daughter. He patiently explained the downside of parenthood and cut short every argument with a more devastating point. He won the day, Amy lost her rosy view and her dream of the future was badly dented.

She remained troubled for a time and even agreed to revisit the clinic. The appointment was too late, and she was too far gone for an abortion. The warnings faded and Amy recovered her confidence. The baby's father would come good. He only said what he said to protect her. Once the baby was born everything would be different.

If not, sod the lot of them, she would be fine on her own.

Chapter Forty-Four

It happened so fast she had no memory of how it came about. One minute she was in his study and the next she was on the staircase. It had been going so well.

'Ian Black, a lovely, lovely man.'

'I'm afraid I don't know the gentleman.'

'I'm sure you must,' she said and then despite his disablement, he had one hand on her arm, the other holding her belongings and she was out the door.

Helena was not totally sure, but as he shut the door she thought he said, 'Good day, Mrs Black.'

On the tube ride home, exhausted from the housework, she fell asleep and woke in Upminster, where the driver turfed her off the train. This place was outside her experience and troubled her. Every careworn face was a possible mugger or rapist or both. Increasingly nervous, she struggled to find a safe seat that would take her back to Baker Street.

For protection she sat close to a dowdy couple and the husband addressed her directly without an introduction. The affrontery was equivalent to that which upset the Queen's secretary when she read Helena's letter. Afraid for her safety she put up with the awful man's gall.

The man wore a wretched flat cap with sweat stains on the temples that contributed to making him look old before his time. A gap in his front dentures added to his decrepitude. Reluctantly, she responded to his familiarity, but soon they were chatting away like long lost friends.

Charlie was well informed and had some interesting points of view. He was particularly astute on immigration but more enlightening on paedophiles.

'Chop their knackers off, no messing, sort of thing. That's what they do in them Arab States.'

'Yeah,' said Mrs Charlie, 'Arab States, cut 'em off as soon as look at yer.'

'There's too many dirty old men taking liberties with young birds.'

'Dirty old men,' said Mrs Charlie with an exaggerated nod.

'There's yer Charlie Chaplin and yer Hugh Heffer. It shouldn't be allowed. There ort to be a lor against it.'

They got out at Farringdon to visit St John's and Helena regretted their parting. They left her deep in thought and before she knew it she was the whole way home.

'What a good place for thinking,' she congratulated the underground porter as she handed in her ticket.

Her plan was complete. She would re-seal Sir Charles letter and when Ian read it and was distraught she would jump into action. She would take it upon herself to find out who was responsible. She would arrange a meeting with Sir Charles and he would explain the reasons for rescinding.

'I'm sorry my dear,' he would say. 'It was that book, *Wasted*. The main character Simon Grundy, obviously a pen portrait of your husband, is promised a knighthood. That and the way your brother-in-law lampoons the Home Office, we cannot be seen to condone satirical material damming one of England's principle institutions. So you see my dear, we had no choice.'

'Does that rule out his knighthood forever?'

'No,' Sir Charles would say. 'We will review the situation in a few months.'

'Would an apology help?'

'Oh yes. A full retraction would be best.'

Ian bought the story wholesale. Ian was distraught. Helena had a few nasty moments when Ian was going to see Sir Charles for himself but she nipped those in the bud.

Ian consulted a solicitor and the solicitor consulted a barrister. Ian spent a considerable sum on legal fees, but there was no case to answer. Duncan had been correct when he told Ian that the publisher's legal department had gone through the manuscript with a fine tooth comb and there was no way *Wasted* could either be rubbished or attacked in the courts.

Ian sat glaring at Duncan. He would never forgive him. Everything he had worked for, gone up in smoke. Everything was irritating him. His chest was filled with acid, his cropped hair needed continual scratching and his big toe hurt like the blazes.

Pains always started on the eve of a holiday. Fortunately Riklis agreed to see him that morning. No way could he survive another day with the pain.

The pain in his toe was a dose of gout, but the one chemist open could not fill the prescription. They had had a run on colchicine and none of the other anti-inflammatories they had in stock worked against uric acids.

'You might find a herbalist open, try tart cherry.'

'Everything happens to me,' he complained.

* * *

For weeks the newspapers had been full of the Emasculation Act but it was not until Charlie opened her eyes that Helena took an interest. Public opinion was split down the middle as to whether neutering was humane. More important was the method of implementation.

Castration, as Charlie advocated, was creating a furore amongst the namby pamby liberals led by an MP named Francis Rattenbury. As far as Helena was concerned, what other method was there? She learned a host of new words; emasculation, eunuch, castrati and impoverish. She looked these words up in the dictionary and some excited pleasure.

She resumed her mock trials and dispensed new justice. Devising ways of carrying out the penalty gave her trials a fillip. Her favourite was the *modus operandi* utilised in the old joke about the camel and two bricks. Helena suffered sympathy pain in her thumbs.

Being so busy placing Duncan in the frame for the rescinded knighthood, Helena had overlooked Amy's pregnancy. Emma called, crying at the other end of the telephone. 'She's determined to go through with it. If she doesn't do something soon it will be too late.'

'Too late?'

'Twenty-something weeks and abortion is not allowed by law.'

That night Helena questioned Ian and, fully apprised of the law, it was obvious that the identity of the father was now significant.

Helena, hoping one of the women would suggest clearing away and save her bothering, tapped her plate with her spoon. She studied Amy, who sat slouching, her paltry bump hidden beneath the table. Amy had busy eyes but Helena could not calculate where they alighted. On one occasion she was sure it was Christopher and the next she was sure it was Duncan.

It would be most inconvenient if the father of the baby was a ruffian who frequented the Duke of Coxley. As Helena's will was an exceptional phenomenon she simply decided it was not the case. Amy's vow of secrecy was concealing someone they knew. This idea sat very well in Helena's scheme. She now had to pick someone who fitted the bill and conjure the evidence to convict.

It did not require very much travelling to find the man she wanted to put in the frame.

'It's Duncan, no question.'

Amy had been spending time at Pauline's house and Emma told her that they encouraged Amy to keep a diary. Emma said that it had proved useful in lots of ways but the father of the baby was referred to as X.

Helena made a note she must see this diary at the earliest opportunity. She needed to concentrate.

Absorbed in trifles, she said, 'Excuse me.' Got up from the table and locked herself in the downstairs cloakroom.

'Invite people round and they don't lift a finger,' she complained.

She sat idly staring at the humping pigs hung on the back of the door when a forgotten kiss sprang into her head.

She had seen it in her rear view mirror whilst sitting in the Waitrose car park. Duncan kissing Amy.

'Gotcha!'

* * *

Pauline stirred the soup, but was struggling to bring up the gossip pinging in her head. She did not relish gossip if it had a sting in its tail. Duncan sat in the corner by the radiator, one arm resting on the top, reading Toby's essay.

'Good?' she asked in need of something to break the silence.

'OK, I suppose,' said Duncan. 'How should I know if Hitler was a genius or not? There's far too much publicity about the man.'

'They say we shouldn't forget.'

'Oh yes we should,' said Duncan. 'Put it away and get on with your life.'

'Why has Amy stopped coming around?'

'How should I know,' said Duncan closing Toby's file. 'Given up on being a writer.'

'Did she have any talent?'

'Yes,' said Duncan. 'There's a surprise for you. I pinched some of her phraseology and used it.'

'You're pulling my leg.'

'I am not.'

Pauline stopped what she was doing and opened Toby's file and began reading. 'Has Toby got talent?'

'Not like Amy,' said Duncan, 'Funny that. He's way cleverer than her, but she's got a spark.'

'She's got another spark,' said Pauline. 'She's pregnant.'

'I'm not surprised,' said Duncan without a flicker. 'The cavalier precautions she takes.'

'And how would you know?'

'I don't but she is known to be indiscriminate. I bet she got pregnant on purpose.'

'Where did that come from?'

'Up here,' said Duncan pointing at his temple. 'She's desperate for something to love.'

* * *

Duncan sat in an armchair fighting off sleep. He leaned forward and hid his eyes behind his hand and closed them. He was not sure if he enjoyed Christmas or not. He loved the lights and the break in the bustle but somehow the celebrations always fell short. He liked family but there was always one in a bad mood who spoiled it for everyone else, him included.

He felt a delicious oblivion, when he was rudely interrupted by Ian, who prodded him with a finger and said in a stage whisper, 'I'm going upstairs to commit suicide.'

'What am I supposed to do?'

'Cover for me until it's over.'

'OK,' said Duncan and resumed his rest.

'Don't you want to know why?'

'No,' said Duncan from behind his hand. 'Leave a note for Helena.'

Ian was gone for the best part of an hour and nobody noticed his absence until it was time for charades. Someone suggested a search party but Helena said he was probably working.

'He's useless at charades, let's start without him.'

It was then that Duncan felt a pang of guilt and excused himself. He knocked at the door of the en suite, which was locked on the inside. 'Ian?'

There was a lengthy groan and Duncan felt a surprising relief. 'Dead yet?' he asked.

The next groan was lengthier. 'Go away. Nobody cares.'

'I do,' said Duncan, 'In spite of myself.'

Silence.

The door opened and a deathly white Ian was crouched on the floor.

'What have you done?'

'I took a whole bottle of pills.' He handed Black an empty bottle of codeine.

'And?'

'I threw up,' said Ian. 'Do you think I'll die?'

'I doubt it,' said Duncan. 'You probably won't get a headache this holiday.'

'Do you have to be facetious, you bastard? It's your damn fault I'm doing this.'

'My fault?' said Duncan. 'How?'

Ian staggered to his feet, sat on the laundry basket and put his head in his hands. Duncan saw a scar on the middle of his bald spot and tried to recall what caused it.

Ian belched and moaned, 'God I feel sick.' He rubbed his face with his palm and belched again.

'How is it my fault?'

'My knighthood has been rescinded because of you.'

'You've attempted suicide because you lost your knighthood?' Duncan was incredulous. 'Have you ever had a life?'

'It's what I've worked all my life for,' Ian said thick with self-pity, 'Gone because of your book.'

'Don't be ridiculous.'

'It's true,' said Ian on the verge of tears. 'They think I gave you the background information to take the piss out of the Home Office.'

'Where did you get this nonsense from?'

'Helena...'

'There you are then,' said Duncan indignantly. 'That woman and the truth don't live on the same planet.'

'That's my wife you're talking about.' Ian's righteousness sounded half-hearted even to his own ears. 'Helena spoke to the Honours Office and that's what they told her.'

'I don't believe it, sorry. You want to believe it go ahead,' Duncan made to leave but stopped in the doorway. 'Where did you get that scar on the top of your head?'

Ian fingered his cranium with tentative fingers, 'I don't quite remember. I believe I fell out of my cot. Why do you ask?'

'It accounts for a lot,' said Duncan and disappeared downstairs.

* * *

The day of the Parliamentary vote was dark and overcast. The newspaper headlines ran the gamut from, DAY OF RECKONING, to GELD? FRANK INCENSED, DEMURS to the tabloids' BOLLOCKS TO THAT.

Ian was part of the entourage working behind the scenes to prepare the PM for Francis Rattenbury's expected onslaught. The whips were working flat out, appearing every ten minutes, gauging the result of the vote. It was going to be a close call.

The PM was jubilant when the whips were sure they were home and dry but Ian did not care either way.

Ian had sifted through the list hoping for a reprieve but no, his name was not among the fortunate, not in any of the papers. 'Sir' Ian Black had been torn from his grasp. Not only the knighthood but the other love of his life had rebuffed him.

Lizzie was engaged to be married and had set the wedding day. If that was not bad enough, Elvis arranged the wedding ceremony. It was to be held at St Marks Church, Wyford on February the 14th.

Ian knew he could not compete with this level of romantic flair. His African violets had withered long ago.

Chapter Forty-Five

Gideon's dumb relationship with Katy did not trouble him until he resumed his regular assignations. Having to talk to his dates was daunting. He dreaded those meaningless exchanges. He tried hard to satisfy, but was listless, unenthusiastic or just plain bored. His partners were well aware of his ennui and voiced their dissatisfaction. He feigned illness or injury and gradually these relationships lapsed. There were a couple of defiant saddoes but he kept putting them off. What was left was Katy.

Concentrating on one woman at a time put him under pressure and he experienced stress. He had no experience of love save his surrogate Dolly. Was he in love? He had no way of knowing.

'I'm pregnant,' she had said and a strange feeling crept over him. Those words should have engendered fear and trembling but they did not. They should have set his legs running but they did not. Having discovered that the words did not stimulate a negative reaction he went blank searching for something. What could it be?

What did she want him to do about it?

Did she want him to find a doctor?

Her eyes flickered and he saw that she cared what he thought. She wanted him to be in agreement with her over what they were to do about the baby. That she cared about him as well as a baby. It was then that he realized that he cared about the baby. He cared about another living being and a living being to be. A rush of tenderness swept over him and he kissed her softly. A peculiar flood of emotion spread through him and they made love. It was not fucking, it was making love and wordlessly they completed an unsanctified union.

Overnight, Gideon was a new man. He did a proper day's work, ate proper meals at meal times and his head emptied of futile revenge.

He went shopping and sought a present for Katy. He had no idea what was suitable. Usually he bought his women sexy underwear, cuddly toys or porn films. Now he was at a loss. He asked the shop assistants and found that he was flirting with an attractive blonde girl and dashed from the shop

He bought her a necklace with a silver ring hanging from it, which had 'forever' engraved on the inside face, and he meant it.

* * *

Gideon and Katy's adultery was being carried out during working hours and Chris was deprived of any gratification. He decided to take matters into his own hands and faked a weekend trip to Dubai. The Getliffe & Quinn financial deal was gradually overcoming obstacles and the final trip was pending. He waited for the date to be announced and told Katy that completion of the contract required two meetings, one fake in Dubai and the genuine meeting for the following weekend that had been switched to Jakarta.

In celebration, Gideon and Katy ate a meal together before going to bed. Over dinner Gideon gave her the necklace.

She held it with butter fingers and her clumsy hands touched his heart. It was when she began crying his heart was smashed with a sledge hammer. He kissed her distorted mouth, which tasted of salty tears, and it was the most delicious flavour. Sensing her throbbing body in his arms revived a sweet tenderness and he soaked up her feelings.

Choking and gulping she tried to control her tears but each inspection of the dedication brought a further gush of sobbing, prolonging his pleasure. They sat clutching hold of each other and finally she calmed. Easing out of his arms she wiped her face with those gawky fingers. She took his face in them and struggled to speak, words were stuck in her throat, glued to her tongue. Her tonsils were failing her, syllables were not cohesive, cracked letters separated into the ether. She tried to spit the words into his mouth with a kiss. As their lips joined, she croaked, 'I love you.'

The waited words reached his ears with a thud, his heart gyrated violently, blood gushed and he felt exhilarated by the haemorrhage.

A forgotten pot boiled, in which a tin of jam roly poly danced frenetically amongst the bubbles. Gideon and Katy made long, lingering love. The pan, emptied of liquid, the hob continued burning the underside of the pan, which glowed red and was on the verge of igniting a fire. Reaching in the dark, Katy's elbow connected with the remote, switched on the television and fused the entire house, including the cooker.

Chris was disappointed. From his vantage point in the loft he could hear activity below but could not discern what. He had gone to a lot of trouble organizing this situation and felt he was being cheated.

Hours earlier he had packed a suitcase. He was not sure if it was appropriate to wear a suit in the Dubai climate and preferred not to pack one. He hated his suits getting crumpled. He was sure that the Arabs were less formal and that a jacket and tie should suffice. If he were invited for dinner, would he be expected to dress? No, he decided, if that was necessary he could hire a dinner suit.

These futile deliberations were making him late and he hurriedly completed his packing, including two suits, a grey mohair and a navy worsted. He did not think it necessary to call a taxi. That would be overdoing it. He put everything back as it should be and hurried up the ladder into the loft, dragging the suitcase with him.

He shifted a heavy cardboard box deeper into a corner and placed it carefully on the plywood plinth he had nailed to the joists. He had forgotten his food. He crashed down the ladder, jumped the stairs three at a time and almost lost his footing, saving his balance by barging the wall.

It was lucky he had come back down for the food because he had left his passport on the worktop. He grabbed the pre-prepared bag of grub, checked that he not forgotten anything else and nipped back upstairs. Just in time, as he closed the flap he could hear Katy opening the front door.

'Damn,' said Chris. Unwrapping his cardboard box might have to wait. On the previous occasions when spying in the loft he had suffered untold discomfort.

He prepared the room in readiness for the weekend. He chose a meal for that night's supper and put the rest in the small refrigerator. He could hear Katy coming upstairs and went to his spy hole.

He watched her undress. How pretty she was these days. Pregnancy agreed with her. She had not told him yet. He was looking forward to that conversation. How would she explain it away?

She ran a bath and Chris relaxed. He was to have an hour of sweet surveillance.

Katy cut her bath time short and hurried back downstairs, alerting Chris to the fact that the routine was not to be as usual. Pots and pans began crashing loudly. She was making him dinner. Chris made a mental note to keep his absences to overnight. His wife and brother were supposed to use the time available for one thing only.

Ruefully, Chris opened the cardboard box, sliced the tape with a Stanley knife and cut along the box seams. He piled the cardboard rectangles neatly and taped up the bubble wrap into a roll. While Katy was cooking he read the instructions.

It was a chemical toilet designed to aid paraplegics. It had devices to wash and dry your bum if you wanted but these required fixed plumbing. The seat could be adjusted to any height and could be used anywhere in the house. The chemicals required changing every two days so he would have to go carefully.

He had forgotten the toilet paper.

He opened the hatch and pricked his ears. Katy seemed to be occupied. He lowered the stairs and slipped down onto the landing. He listened again and tiptoed into the bathroom. One of the tiles was loose and its displacement shouted in his ears, but Katy had not heard. He took the spare roll off the toilet cistern, climbed back into the loft, lifted the stairs and shut the hatch.

These games were driving his adrenalin up to new levels. Chris was aware that his clandestine amusement was unorthodox, but that did not bother him very much. He was born to peep. He was happy to accept his niche and was not ashamed.

It was not his fault that he was different. It was his parents' fault.

Outsiders spoke of his father as a 'nice man' a 'gentleman'.

They only saw one side of him, they did not know him like Chris did. He was 'nice' some of the time, when he was wearing his nice hat. His friends thought his father was amusing but Chris could not see the joke. He looked to his father to discover himself and saw weakness and voids.

His father's vision was impaired by many blind spots. He did not possess the wit to understand that there were larger intelligences than his own out there and his ego was so inflated he judged everyone in his own limited terms. Chris had tried to get through but whenever he broached the subject the iron curtain came down. His father's Stalinist attitude to politics was fixed in a personal ideology that had no basis in reality and would not bend.

What troubled Chris most was when his father was confronted by a dissenting point of view, he filibustered, shut out the opposition and hogged the show.

'Daddy's home and he's tired after a hard day's work.' This was the catch phrase of his childhood. It was probably a ploy of his mother's to get him and Gideon to behave.

As for his mother, she was present bodily, but it ended there. For all the use she was as mother she might as well have been a robot. Chris surmised that a robot might be more affectionate.

Boy, did his mother have a mouth on her.

He had been attracted to Katy because of her reticence. He did not want a woman who made demands of him. He was glad she had found a lover. The fact that her lover was his brother provided an extra twist. He was not pleased for his brother. Gideon was a chip off his mother's block and Chris detested him.

What caused his involuntary climax while watching Katy and Gideon making love was the pain Katy inflicted on Gideon. The more she hurt him the more aroused Chris had become. He could not wait for the evening's punishment to begin.

He heard Gideon arrive and it was an eternity before they came to bed. Chris did not approve of them breaking with routine. Dinner after sex would be acceptable. They should at least have given him something to be getting on with.

He peeked out at the bedroom across the street and was saddened to see the empty darkness in the window opposite. He spent the wait thinking of Amy naked and summoning visions of her body. He could not get beyond her face. It was the prettiest face he had ever seen. She had her hair cut short and her face framed in the boyish haircut inflamed him.

Finally they came to bed and dished out more frustration. Their poignant lovemaking, devoid of violence, filled him with envy and they talked afterwards. They talked intimately of a future and promises which did not include him.

'The damn cheek of it.'

Katy reached across the bed for a tissue and the lights fused. He strained to listen, getting angrier and angrier because when they spoke of him they did so in an impertinent way.

They fell asleep, his anger subsided and his eyelids grew heavy. Sure that this was it for the night he placed toilet paper in the bowl to deaden the sound and used the chemical toilet.

Having dreamed of a torrential downpour Katy woke, naked except for the necklace with the ring attached. She caught the ring between her thumb and forefinger and placed it against her lips. She cuddled up to Gideon. Feeling her warm against him, he turned over and they embraced. He ran his hands lovingly over her and she squeezed his backside.

'What's that strange noise?' he asked.

'It's Chris in the loft,' she said, 'snoring.'

Chapter Forty-Six

The Colonial Tea Room was teeming with customers and steam. It was a crisp, bitter January day, the heating system could barely cope and the room temperature was below par. Mouths, teapots and teacups created vapour as the room hummed and hissed. Tin advertising signs, old clocks, bric-a-brac, uninspired oils and assorted antiques hung from every available joist and rail, reminding us of a lost Empire, the Raj and Imperialism. It made you proud, but Helena disapproved and because Helena disapproved, Emma disapproved.

Pauline and Black came here for lunch on market days and she hoped that its quaint ambiance and low key patriotism would appeal to them. She was wrong. They disapproved of the cutlery and to a lesser extent they disapproved of the crockery.

The furniture, a hotchpotch of acquisitions, no chair or table matched. It was hand-me-down and jumble. To Pauline, the purposeful confusion added to the ambiance, but because of their negative attitude, Pauline found herself apologizing.

At each cover was a table setting in readiness with a large plate on a linen napkin. Helena gave her plate a close inspection and screwed up her nose in disgust, making a guttural sound in her throat, and cast a sad glance at her sister. She opened a fresh pack of tissues, gave one a lick of spit and ostentatiously cleaned the plate. When the lunch she ordered was served they took away the show plate and replaced it with her meal on an eating plate.

Eating out with Helena was an event, Emma was an episode and they were both oblivious to the embarrassment they caused. Helena believed that convincing your fellow diners you are a person of substance required complaining about the temperature of the food and the waiting time. Pauline cringed when Helena sent back a gazpacho to be re-heated. Emma treated the staff with the sensitivity you would expect from Genghis Khan.

'Are you sure they do salads?' she whined. 'It doesn't look like a place for salads.'

'We dined at Rules after drinks at the Savoy,' said Helena stealing the limelight. 'Very high class.' She gave Pauline her withering look. 'Ties are *de rigeur.*'

'Is there a British Home Stores,' said Emma grizzling on. 'They do nice salads.'

'Rules do very nice salad.'

'I must try Rules one of these days,' said Emma. 'This looks like an egg and bacon place.'

'That's what I was thinking,' said Helena, 'a motorway caff.'

'Yes madam,' said the waitress, a girl of twelve. 'We do a variety of salads.'

'Where?'

'On the salad page.'

'Is she being rude?' asked Helena.

The infant took their order and smiled before leaving.

'Are you looking forward to being a grandmother?' asked Pauline of Helena, trying to be nice.

Emma went white before realizing where the question was directed. Helena was confounded by the question.

'Pardon?'

'Chris and Katy,' Pauline explained, 'becoming parents.'

Helena was more at sea than ever. 'What had that to do with me?'

A mobile began ringing and frantically the sisters turned out their bags. It was Helena's phone and she pulled back her hair from her ear and she said loudly, 'Helena Black.'

'Yes, dear,' Helena's voice changed from saccharine to indulgent. 'Never mind...Of course I will...Don't you worry, dear...I'll come straight away...Everything will be OK...Straight away.' She collapsed the phone and collected her things together. 'I have to go.'

'What's wrong?'

'Nothing's wrong,' said Helena sharply. 'Ian locked himself out.'

Helena sidled between the maze of tables and was gone, Pauline shrugged and Emma waved a despairing hand.

'What do you make of that?'

'Goodness knows with that one,' said Emma petulantly. 'She might have left her share of the bill.'

Pauline was curious, because Ian was never home at midday on a weekday.

* * *

The plane had touched down in Singapore late and the forty minute stopover was reduced to twenty. They arrived in Jakarta on time and Chris was met by a man in brown livery accompanied by two slaves. They attended to the bureaucracy and got his Visa stamped and his passport checked. His bag was missing from the carousel.

The first class passengers had been met and shunted away. Chris had to wait for the man in brown livery to return. He occupied the time watching the airport staff. The women were extraordinarily beautiful, slim with big black eyes and healthy complexions. He was miles away when the man touched his shoulder.

Stepping out of the airport was the first of many rude shocks. The heat and the humidity clutched his chest so tightly it took his breath away. Struggling to breathe was a monumental task and, having caught his breath, he found he was soaking wet. Perspiration was spilling out of every pore.

This was overtaken by the second shock. Getting into a sleek people mover, the air-conditioning blowing full blast, his perspiration turned to ice. Chris thought he would die of pain and, the panic it engendered. He tugged at his clothing which had adhered to his body. He wriggled and fidgeted but no relief came.

'My bag?' Chris gasped.

'It arrive at hotel,' said brown livery. 'We go.'

An Asian driver in black suit and peaked cap gunned the Espace out of the airport precincts onto a 'road'.

The road was rutted and pitted and Chris found himself being bumped and thrown. He slipped on the safety belt which pressed his icy clothing against his skin. Agonizingly slowly his body warmed and he fended off the cold.

Either side of the Espace was mayhem. An avalanche of eccentric vehicles plummeted headlong. Strange, throaty three wheelers with canvas billowing behind were the local taxis. Each one belched smoke out of its nether region and none could maintain a direct course toward its destination. They weaved and veered, narrowly missing every other haphazard traveller.

Motorcycles carrying five or six passengers, balancing precariously on every available millimetre, bicycles with one passenger on the handlebars and another travelling piggy back on the rider. If it were possible to balance on the mudguard they would do so, but the bicycles were in a poor state of repair and did not own mudguards. The fumes rose thickly up into the constant smog that enveloped the city.

The hotel security was thorough and by the time Chris was shown to his room there was a note explaining that his luggage had been opened and was being cleaned and pressed at Singapore Airlines' expense. He showered, dressed in a toweling robe and sipped a glass of complimentary champagne.

There was a note from his clients that they were waiting in the bar if he would care to join them as soon as he was ready. He notified the desk to pass on the message that he was waiting on his clothes. The meeting was deferred for an hour.

Dressed in his second suit, Chris entered the bar at the appointed time and was escorted to a table in a discreet corner. His client looked like a wax caricature his grandmother had pinned to the newel post in her living room. It was one of a set, Lascar, African, Asian and Arab caricatures made of wax with exaggerated features popular long before any notion of political correctness. This gentleman reminded him of the Lascar, who had been put near something hot and the nose had melted into an enormous blob. He could have been the father of the Asian girl who had lived opposite.

'Christopher, my friend,' said Khan clasping Chris' girly hand between his own gigantic rough-skinned paws. 'My dear, dear friend.'

'How are you Mr Khan?'

'Well, thank you for asking,' he hawked and spat into a silk handkerchief. 'You are well yourself? You are happy with your room?'

'Yes, thank....'

'What is it your father does to keep his family?'

'He works for the government,' said Chris, uncomfortable with his hand being held, 'at the Home Office.'

'I'm the son of a prince,' Khan barked. 'Your bastards Home Office chuck me out. Is your father responsible?'

'Not my father's department,' Chris explained nervously. 'He is working on punishments for paedophiles.'

'Paedophiles?' said Khan, hopefully placated. 'I chop off.'

Thankfully Khan had to let go of Chris' hand to slice a palm of one hand with the side of the other.

'You will come tonight to dinner,' said Khan. 'We will eat and do good business my friend. You will bring money order.'

Chris returned to his room, a worried man. This Khan character was beyond the pale. What should he do? Who should he ask? It would not do to doubt the veracity and character of multi-million dollar clients. Chris had been placed in charge of a money order authorizing up to five million dollars. This was serious dosh.

He had a thorough briefing before leaving and his instructions were filled with warnings of etiquette. Do little and say little, it is the safest path with these foreigners. You cannot be sure whether they are trustworthy, even the honest ones, and they get upset over the least *faux pas*, however innocent. Keep in close contact, report daily and trust no one.

He telephoned Quinn and was put through to Getliffe. 'Did you hear the result?'

'No sir.'

'Wyford 3, Barnsley 0, we stuffed them. How are things your end?'

'I met with Khan...'

'Charming man, loves football. Keep him talking about the Arse and you won't go wrong.'

'I'm to go to his house for dinner tonight and take the money order.'

There was a pause, then Getliffe said thoughtfully, 'I don't think that would be wise. Explain that you cannot sign over until the figures are verified by me or Quinn.'

'He seems to know that I have a money order.'

'Yes, Khan has a lot influence. You'll think of something plausible. We're relying on you.'

Getliffe rang off, leaving the ring tone in his ear punctuated by a knock at the door. He peered in the spy hole and saw a pretty girl in the glass.

Massage sir?'

During the briefing, Mr Quinn offered him extra-curricular advice. 'Apart from TV there isn't a lot to do in the way of recreation. Try a massage.'

Chapter Forty-Seven

Having been sent home early from work feeling ill, their GP could find nothing wrong and Helena gave him a bollocking. Ian not only made a full recovery from this blip but entered an extended period of delusion. He felt light on his feet and no problem was insurmountable, his energy level had been surcharged. He was a new man and everything was right with the world. He was king of all he surveyed. Until...

'Is that emergency,' Helena screeched. 'An ambulance, as fast as you can. My husband's having a heart attack.'

Ian, stretched out on the floor by the bed, struggled to catch his breath, fighting a searing pain like a massive hand clamping his chest. Air stuck in his gullet and refused to move on, oscillating out of reach, torturing his panic button. He struggled to swallow but the mechanism eluded him, increasing the consternation and agony that gripped his ribcage.

'How are you, dear?' Helena spoke to him in that cloying, patronizing tone, as if he were a five year old.

'Shut your fucking trap, you stupid bitch.'

Insults rattled inside his head, his temper flared but ambushed by his failing breath, no words came. Dumb, frustrated and trapped, losing his rag gave a precious moment of respite from the pain.

Helena applied a cold compress to his head, tutted noisily and checked at the window for a sign of the paramedics.

'Today of all days,' she said, nipping into the dressing room to check her hair and make up. She dressed in a tan suit and tried three pairs of shoes before she was satisfied.

Ian belched a noise, a foghorn out at sea, released trapped air and was able to groan self-pityingly.

'Pipe down,' Helena snapped and undid the lid of her lipstick.

She had barely applied any colour when the sirens drew near and went to answer the door with her upper lip *au naturel*.

She let in a pair of luminous men, one with PARAMEDIC and the other with AMBULANCE TECHNICIAN stamped across their backs, and followed them upstairs, their clumsy black boots marking the carpet. In the swirling blue light Ian looked sicker than ever and was sweating profusely.

'What's your name, sir?'

'Ian Black,' Ian gasped.

'Ian Black CB,' Helena corrected.

'Ian, I'm Graham and this is Kenny,' said the paramedic. 'Where's the pain?'

Ian waved a limp hand across his chest.

'We're going to put you on a stretcher, Ian, and take you down to the ambulance. You OK with that?'

'Yes,' Ian was almost crying.

They opened up the stretcher, laid him down and lifted him. Looking over his shoulder the technician led the way out.

While the paramedic carried out preliminary tests, Helena finished dressing. She locked up and tried climbing in the ambulance. She tried either leg but was unable to make the distance.

'Let us finish here and we'll help you up.'

'Where will you be taking him?'

'Wyford General.'

'I want him taken to the BUPA on the Bedford Road.'

'I'm afraid that won't be possible.'

'I don't understand,' said Helena, puffing, inflating, her shoulders swelling as though pumping iron. 'Do you know who you are dealing with?'

'We are the NHS, madam,' said the paramedic engrossed in his readings. 'We have to go to Wyford General.'

'This is Ian Black CB.'

'So you said, madam,' said the paramedic. 'You'll be well looked after at Wyford General.'

*** *

'When am I going to see the doctor?'

'I've explained that he's still working with your husband,' said the night nurse, an Asian lady with Popeye forearms and wide girth, her tolerance being pushed to the edge. 'If you wouldn't mind taking a seat, I will fetch you when he's finished.'

'It's been an age since you last checked.'

'It's not been five minutes since you last asked.'

'You won't hear the end of this.'

'No doubt,' the nurse returned to her paperwork.

With a click of the tongue, Helena turned on her heel and searched through her handbag. She opened her mobile phone and pressed out the memory details with shaking fingers. Agitation and hurry caused her to summon the wrong data causing more tongue clicking. She located the number she was seeking and pressed the call button, pulled her hair back and placed the apparatus to the free ear, only to have the mobile snatched from her hand.

The nurse, with a face like a mouthful of lemon juice, snapped the telephone shut and pointed to a sign on the wall. 'Please turn off your mobile phones'.

On the verge of tears, Helena stood beneath the canopy in the ambulance bay and pressed recall.

'Pam, I need your help,' Helena stifled a sob. 'Ian's had a heart attack.'

Following instructions, Helena went back into the hospital found the lift and, without thinking, pressed the 7th floor button. The doors closed with a clatter that did not inspire confidence and the lift made its way up, rattling and bumping at a ponderous pace. Helena had a fear of confined spaces. She stood stock still, petrified, anticipating a breakdown as it clattered through each floor, hesitating as though it were going to give up the ghost.

At the 5th floor the lift shaft must have been smaller because the rattle and bump was more severe and the lights flickered off. Momentarily the lift stopped and Helena was in darkness. She fumbled at the walls in search of the alarm button but the carriage continued indomitably and the lights stuttered back on.

Helena's plaintive whimper of 'He...e...elp,' fell unnoticed like an autumn leaf.

Alone in the cavernous cubicle Helena experienced real fear. What a night this was turning into. Fear of being trapped, unaccompanied in the dark was worse than being told, 'no'.

Helena closed her eyes and began praying

The lift continued to yo-yo its cumbersome way to the 7th floor, stopped dead and the doors opened with a resounding crash. Gratefully she stepped out into the corridor, deserted and eerie. No sound gave her a clue as to which direction to take. Helena walked into the ghostly void, her heels clacking on the harsh floor. She pushed blindly through doors into another silent vacuum. Halfway along this cavern a gaunt man appeared from nowhere dressed in a green paper suit complete with hat.

'What are you doing here?' The gaunt man had a powerful, dependable voice and solidified vomit down his front that gave off a rank odour.

Helena pressed a handkerchief to her nose, 'I'm looking for Peter Riklis, he's the resident cardiologist.

'He's a cardiologist, not the resident cardiologist.'

'I beg to differ...'

'Riklis is just out of surgery,' said the man softly, exhausted. 'He'll be in the canteen on the floor below.'

'What a nice man for a janitor,' thought Helena. 'There's more to the NHS than I thought.'

She searched for the stairs, found the broom cupboard and the laundry room before finding her way. She stepped side saddle to the floor below and made her way towards a gentle hum where several janitors were drinking from cardboard cups. A large television screen was showing yesterday's news. These tired men, mesmerized by Middle Eastern mayhem, barely noticed her entry.

She watched with them as soldiers and civilians ran in discordant directions and the camera closed in on the dead and bloodied. Medics were attending to the wounded and Helena was reminded why she was here. Medics were downstairs attending to Ian and she was not allowed to know what was going on.

Helena pictured him with his chest cracked open, red meat and giblets hanging out, metal instruments poking around inside and electric paddles reviving his failing heart.

'Is Peter Riklis here?' she asked.

One of the janitors turned around, it turned out to be Peter Riklis.

'I can't tell you how badly we've been treated,' said Helena her head bowed solemnly. 'I'm at my wit's end.'

Riklis was a small man, covered in dark hair. In the shower he looked like the missing link between man and ape, except for the crown of his head, where there was a white spot. He gulped down the last of his coffee. 'If you need me I'll be in A & E.'

Helena began her list of grievances from the beginning. 'I want those ambulance people sacked.'

'The BUPA hospital does not have emergency facilities,' Peter explained. 'If Ian's heart attack is serious taking him there might have proved fatal.'

Helena was not having a good night, unused to being in the wrong or being denied, this was taking the wind from her considerable sails. She decided to sulk and impress the hospital staff with her considerable person. She conjured ways that she might make her mark, more importantly, get her own way. It did not take long to implement her ego.

Riklis went through to check on Ian and found him in bed naked to the waist with the ECG unit rigged up, white discs attached to his chest and wires running every which way to a monitor that bleeped regularly.

'Why hasn't Mrs Black been allowed in?'

The attending doctor took Peter out of earshot. 'Mr Black is very agitated and I think that Mrs Black is the source. I made an excuse and got rid of her. He's calm enough now, if you want to let her through.'

'She can be a bit heavy handed,' said Riklis.

'She's a pain in the arse.'

'What are you intending to do with him?' asked Riklis.

'Give him an aspirin and send him home.'

'No heart problem?'

'It is some sort of breakdown,' said the attending doctor. 'My guess is that it has nothing to do with any malfunction of the heart. Stress perhaps? We get a lot of that sort of glitch down here these days.

'Do me and a favour,' said Riklis. 'Keep him in overnight.'

'Must I?'

'I'll make sure she goes home.'

'I'm counting on you.'

'Darling,' cried Helena. 'How are you feeling?'

'Fine,' Ian replied with guilty eyes.

'We're going to keep him in overnight, just to be on the safe side,' said the attending doctor. 'We'll get you settled right away.'

Helena looked about her, breathed in the clinical air and out came the handkerchief. 'I think I'm coming down with something.'

She drummed her fingers while they waited for a bed, whingeing to Ian about the time it was taking. Finally they were ushered into a ward of six beds, five occupied by sonorous sleepers serenading the moon.

'He's not spending the night in here,' said Helena adamantly.

'Please keep your voice down,' the nurse whispered.

Helena continued unabated. 'He's not sleeping in here. We'll go private. Find us a room, we'll pay.'

'Will you please moderate your voice.'

The attending doctor guided them back out into the lobby, 'Mrs Black, I understand your concern…'

'I doubt it.'

'This is an NHS hospital…'

'Then move us to the BUPA.'

'BUPA does not have the facilities to deal with cardiac emergency,' the Doctor said facetiously. 'Excuse me I have other patients.'

'I don't like his attitude.'

'We don't have private rooms.'

'Create one.'

'What?' the nurse exclaimed.

A bed was made up in the Day Room. Helena stayed to make sure Ian was settled and a taxi was summoned. The hospital breathed a sigh of relief, slipped back into dreamland and the night staff cheered . Helena Black had gone home. Whatever it had taken to get rid of the woman was worth it.

The doctor was wrong. It was a malfunction of the heart. Not of the cardiac variety but the 'Desperate of Wyford' type that was found on the Problem Page.

* * *

Earlier that evening, Ian and Lizzie had booked a room at the Dean Hotel in the Seven Dials. Ian had chosen a Soho venue to be in keeping. They had decided to consummate their love.

Ian signed in at the desk in a cloak and dagger fashion, leaving the receptionist in no doubt as to his intentions. He over-tipped the porter for carrying his empty bag and telephoned Lizzie from the room and gave the room number. She allowed a discreet interval before joining him.

While he waited, Ian removed his jacket and tie, opened his top shirt button, brushed his teeth and sat on the bed watching Sky News. Lizzie tapped softly on the door and he let her in. They sat either side of the bed and held hands through the sports report. Lizzie retired to the bathroom and Ian's body commenced a frenzy. He could feel the blood pulsing through his arteries and veins, rushing to all parts except where he needed it most. His head thundered and roared.

The bathroom door opened and an apparition stood glowing in the light. 'You look fetching my dear,' he said placidly, and passed out.

No amount of flannel or slap could rouse him. She checked his pulse, which was abnormally fast. His breathing was asthmatic and he began frothing at the mouth. This scared Lizzie and she quickly decided what to do for the best. Did the hotel have a medical service? She could find no listing in the room service brochure. Should she dial 999? Again she steadied and considered her options. How would it look if she called emergency and they were found together? Then all became clear. She dressed, packed away her night things and left the room, leaving the door ajar. Once outside she telephoned reception and told them of the sick gentleman in room 613.

She worried all the way home and most of the night without knowing what became of him or how he was. It was the frothing at the mouth that caused most concern. Was he having some sort of fit? Was he epileptic? She need not have worried. He had not rinsed his mouth out properly after brushing his teeth and he was regurgitating the residual of toothpaste.

The hotel was not unfamiliar with such incidents and had an automatic procedure for this situation. Working women often left their clientele in a state of distress. This situation was different in a solitary detail, because the distressed client was fully clothed. Ian was attended to, charged accordingly and put into a taxi. On reaching home, he had suffered a relapse and Helena had dialled 999.

The Day Room remained out of bounds to the television-deprived patients for another two days while the doctors made sure

Ian was well enough to leave. For twenty-four hours Ian was not allowed calls or visitors and fretted that the Home Office would fold without him. On the Sunday, Pauline and Duncan were allowed in and chatted awkwardly while Helena fussed over him.

'What's that all about?' asked Duncan. 'Has he put his hand in the till?'

'What d'you mean?' asked Pauline.

'His eyes are riddled with guilt.'

They continued onto the car park in silence, each engrossed in their thoughts. As Duncan started up the engine, Pauline asked, 'Could Ian be having an affair?'

'Ian,' Duncan laughed. 'No way, he doesn't know which end of a woman is up.'

Pauline was not so sure.

Chapter Forty-Eight

Indonesia and especially Jakarta was the focal point of hundreds of islands and the population varied from saffron to sepia to jet black. Those with English, meaning university students, got to work in the hotels. They intended to accumulate enough savings to escape to Europe or the United States or anywhere under the pretext of furthering their education. Such a man was Ho Lui, who had been assigned to look after Chris' welfare while staying in the Imperial Hotel. Wherever Chris was, whatever the time of day, whatever he needed, there was Ho.

Chris wondered how Ho kept track of him. He checked the room for hidden cameras but found none. Had he been electrically tagged? He decided it must be something to do with the key system. The moment he opened the door to his room Ho was alerted. He would monitor Chris' whereabouts and the cleaning staff would nip into the room, tidy, clean and replace the towels.

Ho was not allowed to fraternize and Chris sought a way to talk to him at length. Ho might help with the provenance of Mr Tajyk Khan.

Chris took every opportunity to gain his confidence, found excuses to summon his valet, offering refreshment and encouraging conversation.

Initially, the man was guarded but gradually he thawed.

He learned that Ho Lui had studied in Paris until his mother was widowed.

With his father gone and his family with no immediate means of support, Ho Lui returned to Jakarta to find work. It was his duty to do so. It was the way things were done.

Ho Lui told a funny story from his time in Paris. While

showering, a fellow student knocked at the bathroom door and inquired as to who was inside.

The student got agitated because Ho answered, 'C'est Lui.'

Ho's mother, brothers and sisters were adjusting to life without their father and Ho Lui was anxious to get back to school. As soon as he had accumulated a suitable amount of capital and his family were secure for the foreseeable future, Ho Lui would return to Paris.

Chris offered to pay him handsomely for information about Khan. Chris checked the bus times and set off to dinner with Khan. Khan lived at the end of the bus line and Chris would have to make his excuses early because the last bus back to town was at 9:30 prompt.

His house was lavish, with a chill factor of minus one centigrade. He was growing used to the efficient air-conditioning, despite a slight touch of bends, he was relatively comfortable.

Khan ate uninhibitedly and talked of Khan, talked of the Arse and talked with his mouth full of flatter.

Khan would not admit to a nationality, as though his origins were a closely guarded secret. Chris doubted that his name was really Khan. He claimed his melded face was the result of a horrendous car accident. Chris could not imagine his injuries being caused by single impact. His disfigurement looked like the work of continuous pounding, and if he had claimed to be a retired boxer Chris would have accepted the story.

When it was time to leave, Khan was blasé. Chris' urgency in catching the last bus was ignored. They would finish their dinner in time-honoured relaxation. Chris, alone in a remote part of the city worried how he would get back to the hotel and did not want to have to ask for a lift. Another dread was waiting for Khan to demand the money order which was in the hotel safe.

During coffee, ragged creatures entered the room and prostrated themselves beside Khan's seat. Back on their feet they salaamed in reverse from the room, muttering words of salutation.

It came time to leave and no mention was made of business. Chris was escorted to the bus stop. It was close to midnight and the 9:30 bus was waiting. Chris got on board, the waiting passengers took their seats and the driver set off back to the city.

Why did Khan pass up the opportunity to talk business? Why had he not mentioned the money order?

Three days of tentative too-ing and fro-ing and Chris, fed up with the twenty-four hour diet of CNN, and disarmed by continual subservience, booked another massage.

A child entered the room and he regretted his foolishness. She had long black hair tied in a pony tail and her slight body was covered in a nurse's overall. She pushed a portable bed into the middle of the room, rolled a sheet of tissue paper its complete length and poked a hole in the paper above the face hole.

Chris tried to mount the bed and maintain his modesty but the height extended his legs' reach, causing the towel to come unfastened. He laid face down blush pink from head to toe.

The girl, named Raki, was Fijian. She spoke very good English and had a smattering of languages, including Arabic. Arab clients liked the young and innocent.

'I twenty-six,' she admitted, and had been a 'masseuse' for eight years. Her other expertise had been learned in a period before legitimate training.

'What expertise is that?' he asked innocently. Her face kept its sweet smile, she made a rude gesture and he went bright red again.

'You nice man,' she said. 'I like you. You should be careful.' She accepted his over generous payment and hurried away with her portable bed.

Chris very much wanted a third massage, more for the company than the rejuvenation. He asked particularly for Raki and paid the extra charges for supplementary expertise. He could not manage an erection and he cried. Persevering, Raki tried to help him but failed. They spent the allotted time he had paid for locked in each other's arms. His nose in her neck smelled the sweetness of her skin and when he dared to kiss her neck she tasted even sweeter.

Chris was as happy as he had ever been. Life was near perfect. He had a love, Amy. As soon as she got rid of the baby she could move into his flat. He had sexual gratification, spying on his brother and his wife. He could not wish for more. Now this pretty girl was supplementing his happiness, and $500 later her persistence paid off. She let him watch her with one of her other punters and later, alone together, she helped him.

301

'You nice man,' she told him. 'I like you. You be careful.'

'How should I be careful?'

'Khan,' she whispered almost inaudibly and put a finger to her lips. 'Bastard.'

Raki revealed the source of his 'valet' Ho Lui's efficiency. There were microphones hidden in the lighting and the telephones.

Ho Lui told Chris about Khan and the men who threw their bodies at his feet. They worked on his land and he paid them well. If one of them died Khan took care of their families, but essentially they were slaves. Without Khan they had no means of survival.

Chris let Raki in and she put her hand over his mouth, led him to the bathroom and turned the shower full on. She put her mouth close to his ear. 'What a patsy?'

'A victim,' he whispered, 'a cuckold or manipulated person.'

'Khan say that you.'

Alone in the room Chris could not think straight, the whir of the air-conditioning unit supplanted itself inside his skull and he could not shake it clear.

He was being set up but had no inkling as to why. Where could he get advice? There was nobody at the office he could trust. His father was a waste of time. Gideon? He would rather Gideon did not know about his predicament for the time being. He knew far too much already. His mother would be the best bet but he could not rely on her discretion. She would go charging head down like a bull in a china shop.

Uncle Ben conducted business abroad. Uncle Duncan had an air about him that inspired confidence. He should call one of them, but from where? He could not make a call from the room, it was bugged.

Raki's 'pimp', was a man named Slim. Slimy Slim, deformed by his trade, was a subservient and unctuous individual.

'How much?' was his sole conversation.

Chris thought about recommending him to the bank.

Slim's gamut of charges went from $20, 'he massage you himself,' up to $100, 'he marry you.'

They met on the escape stairs. Slim was late and Chris, worried he was on the wrong floor, leaned over the railings and went up and down checking for his rendezvous. At the point of giving up, the unctuous man appeared and wanted payment up front.

'One hundreds dolla.'

Khan's plan was to rip off Getliffe & Quinn for five million and split it with another man. They had heard the man's name a couple of times but they could not remember it exactly. Another $100 and they would have the name tomorrow. Chris promised the money on delivery.

'Kite,' said the east's answer to Uriah Heap, pointing upward. 'In the sky.'

'Has anybody seen this Kite.'

'Short man,' said Slim, 'Persian carpet on his bonce. Best silk.'

From his description it appeared that Mr Kite was an alias for Mr Quinn.

The deal was finalized. Getliffe e-mailed Chris his instructions. The money order was to be presented to the bank. London would fax verification of the precise amount to be released and the figures were to be inserted before witnesses. Then Chris was to attend Khan's offices for the signing of the contract and the handing over of the money order. This time Khan was sending a car to fetch him.

Chris asked Raki about the place he was to meet Khan. She became animated wagging a finger and shaking her head. 'Must not go.'

'It is necessary for my work.'

* * *

The bank manager extracted the documents from a large envelope and pressed an intercom button. 'We're ready.'

The door opened, and a kind-faced man dressed in a rumpled suit strode boldly across the floor and took Chris by the hand.

'This is your witness, Mr Black.'

The man's face was dubious with an uneasy smile. His damp palm slipped from Chris' grasp and slid through his waves of dirty grey, but seemingly real, hair. 'My name is Kite.'

Chapter Forty-Nine

Ian was a wreck, no more whistling, no more singing in the shower. Lizzie had handed him a wedding invitation and shown him an engagement ring with a champagne stone. She refused to allow him to kiss her and Ian was a broken man. Typical of his gender, he was not aware of what he had until it was taken from him. His innards churned every moment of the waking hour. Exhausted, he slept fitfully, dreaming of lips and jewellery shop windows.

Try as he might, with his years of machination Ian could not rationalize the break up. He now wanted Lizzie more than ever and love tormented him with unremitting but blissful pain. His knowledge of adulterous unions was limited to theatre and literature of a bygone age. He dreamed of a new life, having given up everything for his amore.

The set was a bed-sitting room off the Cromwell Road set in the late 50s where you needed a two shilling coin for the gas meter. He stood, stage centre, ironing, and a heart torn Helena visited. She begged him to come back home for the sake of the kiddiwinks and criticized his ironing dexterity. He explained away the power of fatal attraction and how it was worth giving up the luxury of Pemberton Hall to share a bathroom with four other families.

His anguish was so pervading that he was prepared to jump into the deep blue sea. In desperation he confessed his overwhelming feelings to Lizzie.

'You can't,' said Lizzie patiently. 'What about your wife? And if you live on the Cromwell Road you'll have to support Chelsea or QPR.'

Ian agreed some notions were unsustainable and more fundamental than love. If he switched allegiance the boys would never speak to him again.

He woke in the night, hearing the wind jeering and the rain splashing against the windows. Palpitating, his throbbing body and soul deliberated on these insoluble conundrums, twisting, turning, thrashing about until Helena expelled him to the guest bedroom. There was the initial step, the first degree of separation. Separate rooms.

* * *

Days later the news broke that a British subject had disappeared in Jakarta. The British Consul was being kept in the picture. Not only was Christopher Black missing, but a money order for five million dollars, authorized by the Deutche Bank, was unaccounted for.

The story was flashed across the world. The front pages of the dailies splashed the story for almost a week, and it remained on the front of the *Wyford Observer* for over a month. 'Is Christopher Black another Nick Leeson?' and 'Is there something in the South Hertfordshire water?'

Ian was prepared to fly anywhere in the world to help, but the British Consulate e-mailed bulletins to the Home Office and these were automatically copied to Ian's Blackberry. No trace of Chris could be found.

The Indonesian police declared him missing, presumed dead, and every corpse that washed up from the ocean for a decade was checked against Chris' DNA, no matter what colour or sex the cadaver was.

Ian, already distressed, was glad of the chance to expose his torment. Friends were surprised by the depth of his grief. Helena, less demonstrative, supplemented her wardrobe with black clothes and a patent leather handbag by Gucci.

Katy was relieved. She did not have to explain her pregnancy.

Ian and Helena received a card through the post. It was a picture of a timber church with a roof of coconut leaves and a wooden cross nailed to the ridge. The location was identified as Fiji and the post mark, St Lucia dated eight days before. Ian looked up St Lucia in an atlas and it was shown as a town in the Fiji Islands. The message was unsigned was written in a childlike scrawl and read, 'Do not despair. All is not lost. The world is abundant with riches.' Curiously all the letters 'e' had a line through them.

Ian notified those who needed to know and kept a photocopy of the card before handing it onto the Home Office forensic team. A search was made in St Lucia by the Fiji police but again it proved to be a dead end.

The bank, embarrassed by the whole affair, wrote off the missing money and the *Wyford Observer* gave up the ghost.

Those close to Gideon were shocked by the changes brought about by his brother's disappearance. Apparently, it got the best out of him. He had stepped into the breach, supported Katy and the impending baby, went to ante natal classes and decorated the nursery.

Many congratulated themselves on being excellent judges of character, spotting the man of worth beneath the toe rag. Judge Christie invited Gideon for lunch and the Hertfordshire Crown Prosecution Service took it as a signal.

'The boy is made of sterner stuff than his father,' Gideon was promoted. Those in the service that he had leapfrogged were livid. They discussed, they plotted and were determined to bring about his downfall.

A satellite of the Home Office, the HCPS was a jealous body and its police force, like its prosecution service, was very much concerned with promotion and the prospects of their pension scheme.

Scheme as they might, Gideon was on a roll and with his success came impermeability. His guardian angel was at the pinnacle of his profession. For the moment, Gideon was unassailable.

* * *

The person most put out by Chris' disappearance was Amy. He had shown her round the flat while the tenants were out. It was white and boring much bigger than she pictured. Chris had disappeared before giving the tenants notice and she had no real idea of how to go about getting it.

She found a letter on the internet that was almost what she wanted. She changed the date and name and gave the tenants a month to quit the premises. She enclosed a stamped, addressed envelope and insisted on an acknowledgement of the notice date. Pleased with her handiwork, she posted the envelope through the door.

Now she had to get to the post before her mother, who could not be trusted not to open her mail, but no response came. She went to the flat to confront the tenants but they laughed in her face and shooed her away. She went to the estate agents representing Chris to explain his revised wishes and they did much the same.

Amy continued to withhold the identity of the father of her pending child. Emma and Ben wanted a termination but Amy insisted she was going through with the birth.

'How do you think you're going to manage?'

'My friend Shelaine...'

'You're not having any babies in this house. So where and how are you going to live?'

'That's all taken care of.'

'What? You're a child, underage. People get arrested for letting girls of fourteen stay in the house by themselves. Can you believe her? She lives in cloud cuckoo land.'

'Amy,' said Ben, feeling desperately tired. 'You have to be sensible.'

'I am being sensible.' Amy was defiant. 'You just don't listen, you never listen.'

Emma confided in her sister about this impasse and Helena offered to talk to Amy. 'Children don't talk to their parents. She's more likely to tell an outsider.'

'If you're sure you don't mind?'

'I'll be only too happy to,' said Helena. 'I'm thinking of applying to be a magistrate or a JP.'

'What's that got to do with it?' Emma was having second thoughts. 'We want her to have an abortion.'

'I thought you wanted to know the father?'

'Let's get rid of the damn baby first,' said Emma. 'I don't give a shit about the father.'

'Has she given you any clues as to who it might be?'

'I'm not interested Helena, can you get that in your head? It's probably some yob from scrubbersville with tattoos, a wife and three kids.'

'That doesn't make sense,' said Helena. 'If that was the case she would have told you, knowing that you wouldn't want to follow it up. She's concealing the father because you know him.'

'Where did that come from?'

'I saw her with someone,' said Helena.

* * *

Amy made a last ditch attempt to get the father to see sense and do the right thing. She spelled out her case and sent him an e-mail but he did not even have the courtesy to reply. She walked along the canal, trying to summon up courage to jump in. Everybody was against her and life was not worth living. She would get rid of the baby to spite him.

'The crummy shit,' she spat into the murky water. 'I hate the fucker.' She kicked out at an innocent duck, which collided with a swan. The angry swan chased Amy along the towpath, hissing.

In fear for her life, Amy did not look back, ran all the way home without stopping. Gasping for breath in the kitchen, she said to her mother, 'I want to get rid of it.'

Emma, overjoyed, embraced and congratulated her little girl, then launched into a prayer of thanks. Amy, unused to blessing, cried gratitude into her mother's paltry breast.

They made an appointment at the clinic and that provided another bombshell. It was too late. Amy was too far along.

'What if we go private?' asked Emma.

It was at this point that the trainee magistrate stepped in. She had discovered that there were legal precedents at their fingertips.

'Was Amy raped?'

'I hardly think so,' said Emma. 'What if she were the rapist? Would that do?'

'I'm not sure. What would work best is if the father were an older man. If Amy was duped into sex. Apparently that's a sort of rape.'

'How old?'

'I'm not sure, but I have a suspect and he would certainly be in the right age group.'

'Who?'

'Duncan.'

'Duncan? Don't be daft!' Emma shuddered. When she was young, she had offered herself to him, got in to bed beside him, naked, and he threw her out. 'He's not the type.'

'I saw them kissing,' Helena snapped, 'as bold as brass.'

'Where?'

'Never you mind,' said Helena. 'What we need is a bit of evidence, just enough to incriminate him. The rest will take care of itself. There's no smoke without fire.'

Emma had lost track of Amy's diary. She had not taken much care of it early on, but recently the diary went missing. Emma searched her room, but without luck. She tried the spare room and the garage but came up empty-handed.

Desperate for a solution, Emma allowed Helena to talk to Amy. 'As long as I can be in the room.'

'What would be the point?' Helena complained. 'She's much more likely to tell me something if you're not in the room.'

Emma conceded that one, but was nervy. Her sister was capable of anything. Emma was certain that there was no trick low enough for Helena to pull just to prove she was right. She might even bribe Amy to back up her theory. She certainly had it in for Duncan ,but then, there was always someone.

* * *

Nobody but Amy and Helena would ever know what went on between them, but they returned to the clinic for an appointment with the resident doctor.

'This is a legal matter. The only circumstances that a termination would be allowed is if there was a breach of the law. You were not raped were you?'

Dr Plum was a caring man with an abundance of flutters. His sympathetic blue eyes waited patiently for an answer and his mouth moved incessantly in his grey beard, aiding Amy to form words.

Amy considered, and her cautiousness about answering gave the notion to the doctor that this might be the case. Her mother had no such illusions, but was prepared to fall in line.

'You must think about this carefully,' said the doctor. 'If you accuse somebody, the police will become involved.'

'It wasn't rape exactly.'

'What d'you mean?' Dr Plum leaned forward to keep the facts private.

'I don't like to say,' said Amy unusually coy.

'Would you prefer to tell me in private?'

Emma, dumbfounded, watched her daughter acting out another stranger. Without protest she agreed to wait outside.

Conspiratorial, the doctor checked the door was closed properly and sat with his ear close to the girl's mouth. Glancing at the door, she whispered, 'I was talked into sex by an older man.'

'How old?'

'Much older, my uncle.'

'Your uncle!'

'Yes,' said Amy with fearful eyes. 'My Uncle Duncan.'

* * *

Ben paused outside the bedroom door and listened, half hoping that Amy was asleep and he could leave it for another time. He breathed deeply, knocked and waited.

'Come in,' said that butter-would-not-melt voice, Amy pretending to be fourteen years old, pretending to be her age.

Without any sense of impropriety, Amy was strewn across her bed in her underwear, resting after the operation. His daughter was blessed with a wonderful physique and any red blooded man would be attracted to her perfection.

He threw a housecoat over her long legs. 'Cover yourself up, I need to talk.'

With unusual obedience she did as she was told and sat up to pay proper attention. He wanted to smack her phoney face. This uncharacteristic cooperation was further proof that she was lying.

'I am going to ask you a question and I want you to tell me the truth. I promise that if the answer is the right answer then you will not be punished. I promise with all my heart.'

Amy looked at him quizzically and shrugged, 'I don't get it.'

'This story you've made up about Uncle Duncan being the father of the baby. Just tell me who the real father is and I promise nothing will happen. Nothing.'

Ben could see that she was going to persist with the lie. Her face was feigning hurt innocence but her eyes were busy elsewhere, weighing up the facts, gauging whether the truth was beneficial. Quickly she shrugged a snap of the shoulders, 'I can't help the truth, daddy.'

'Daddy' ripped and slashed his vitals. The phoney little cow. Did she have any idea of the misery that she would cause by this ridiculous masquerade?

'I want you to be aware of the consequences of what you are doing. If this goes the distance and you give evidence in court and *the* lie is uncovered, you will regret the humiliation for the rest of your life.'

It was there that he lost the battle. Saying 'the lie', instead of 'a lie' hardened her resolve and she stuck to her story. She might have given her father what he wanted, but he was putting Duncan's welfare before her own and that was a mistake.

'If you persist with this lie, you are going to hurt a lot of innocent people. Can you live with that?'

It was too late for discussion, Amy's path was clear.

'No way would Duncan have sex with you. He would certainly not have sex with you without taking proper precautions.'

Amy smiled at him sadly, implying the contrary.

'You are going to hurt a decent man with this nonsense. Duncan is a good and decent man.'

Amy shook her head with sadness in her eyes. There was no more to be said.

Chapter Fifty

Emasculation or similar was the word on everybody's lips. It had been the major talking point in the media since the beginning of the year and was only relegated from the front pages by Christopher Black supposedly absconding with a small fortune. On the day of the parliamentary debate the bookmaker's odds were five to four for a yes vote and four to five for no. If a public vote was an influence, the vote would not be close. The majority for 'yes' would be overwhelming.

If the ayes had it, a third term would not be out of the question. Intimations of capital punishment had been trickle fed into the build-up.

'If this policy proves to be a deterrent, we will seek to make more radical changes to the judicial system,' said a government spokesman.

'Condoning this kind of barbaric practice in a civilized society is the thin edge of the wedge,' said a mealy-mouthed liberal.

Ian was a sad spectator. He waited unemotionally while the human typhoon whirled around him. Whips cracked, speakers waffled and voices were raised. Ballot papers were to hand and were waved as the debate raged. Ian was so detached from the outcome he could barely keep awake.

Lizzie was gone. His love was over. He had been asked to represent the elders at her wedding but Ian, a bad sport, deferred to Lord Justice Christie.

The result was about to be posted, the whips appeared and stood before the Speaker. It was a photo finish. Standing in the vestibule with one eye on the television screen, not a single nerve in Ian's body jangled, and his mind wandered to other channels. Visualizing places his hands had visited and images he would not see again. Lizzie's welcoming arms were open to greet him.

The Commons returned to its stalls all sides braying, unbridled and barnstorming. The blinkered, the free spirits, the shires, the must hangs, the greys, the rum reds, the never say dies, the come argue, the lost sorrels, the pals of mine, the thoroughbreds, the thorough in-breds, the thorough shits winnying and snorting to the last fence, smoke rushing from their nostrils, but the 'nays' had it by three votes.

* * *

Toby had just joined them to watch a film his father had been going on about. His father was always promoting some obscure film or book or music. He was not so good on music, but Toby enjoyed most of the odd films his father went on about.

The credits began and there was a ring at the front door bell.

'Who the fuck is that?' asked Duncan.

'I'll go,' said Toby.

He returned with a tall man accompanied by a police woman dressed in uniform with a check hatband.

'Good evening, Mr and Mrs Black, I'm Detective Inspector Lightbourne and this is PC Baker.'

'Is something the matter?'

'John!' said Pauline.

'John?' asked Lightbourne. 'Who's John.'

'Our son,' said Pauline.

'No, nothing to do with John,' said Lightbourne. 'It's Mr Black I've come to see.'

'Won't you sit down?'

Lightbourne was six feet four inches tall and had joined the force believing it was a place for tall men. His thirty years' experience had borne down on his shoulders, which were markedly rounded. It looked as though he had carried heavy weights for long distances.

PC Baker was a matron with no hospital to go to and her government issue shoes did not flatter her Queen Anne legs.

'Don't I know you?' said Lightbourne. 'Weren't you hanging around the police station last summer?'

'Yes,' said Duncan. 'I was getting atmosphere for my book. Your Chief Constable very kindly gave me permission.'

'Yes,' said Lightbourne with a raised eyebrow. 'I think the

permission came from somewhere high up. Don't you have a brother at the Home Office?'

'I asked the MP John Hay to put a word in for me. He's a mate of mine. What is it you wanted to see me about?'

'I've read your book as it happens,' said Lightbourne. 'In the course of duty you might say. You weren't too polite about policeman.'

'Is that why you're here,' asked Duncan, 'to reprimand me?'

'I must admit there was some truth in your book,' Lightbourne dropped his head sadly. 'Not many coppers have got a vocation, but the public is getting harder and harder to cope with. You didn't put that in your book.'

'It's in the one I'm doing now,' said Duncan. 'You're making me nervous Inspector, would you please get to the point.'

'I'm making you nervous?' said Lightbourne gunning an interrogative eye. 'Have you something to be nervous about?'

'Just the one thing,' said Duncan, pausing for effect, 'your being here.'

Lightbourne grimaced and said to Toby, 'You better excuse yourself, sonny. Mrs Black,' he opened his hands offering her the chance to leave.

'They can both stay,' said Duncan firmly. 'I've got nothing to hide. Is that the correct phrase?'

'I don't think this is a matter for levity,' said Lightbourne. 'Do you know a Miss Amy Telleulin?'

'Yes,' admitted Duncan. 'She's been visiting us quite a lot recently. What about her?'

'She's just had an abortion.'

'I don't see what that has to do with me?'

'She says you were the father.'

His declaration had varying effects on those gathered in the room, which Inspector Lightbourne noted keenly. PC Baker's pastry face went golden brown with bile. Pauline placed her hand to her mouth and wondered at her husband. His son Toby laughed derisively and Duncan look devastated. Lightbourne had expected righteous anger. That was the reaction of the innocent and guilty alike. Duncan shook his head.

'Revenge?' he said, as though asking himself the question. 'Why?'

Lightbourne watched Duncan's face as the man digested the implications, and worked out his response in double quick time. 'This has got to be settled by DNA, right,' said Duncan. 'You're here to check my DNA with the foetus.'

'I'm glad you're being so co-operative.'

'Get on with it,' said Duncan angry at last. 'I want this crap over with.'

'If you'll accompany us to the station, the pathologist is waiting.'

* * *

Pauline had never seen Duncan so rattled. He was laid back, nothing fazed him, but today he was manic. He could not keep still.

'It's late.' she said. 'We should go to bed.'

'I can't.' His voice had a strange ring. 'I couldn't sleep.'

He sat down, wriggled for a minute and got up and paced back and forth. Pauline watched and wondered. Had he screwed that little girl? Was he lying? He had plenty of opportunity, and she threw herself at him. From the moment she came here her intentions were obvious. She was a pretty little thing. Any man might be tempted.

'If you aren't the father, what are you worrying about?'

'Shit like this sticks. There's no smoke without fire and all the other platitudes. I want it over and done with.'

'You're acting the way you criticize others for. You just have to be patient. You'll hear all in good time.'

'That's very easy for you to say. You're not the one being accused of interfering with little girls.'

This observation and the way he expressed it took Pauline by surprise. On the Tuesday after they were married, her sister, Sheila, had emigrated. Her parents were orphaned in a matter of a week. They were hopelessly lost without their daughters and applied pressure on Pauline. She was young and inexperienced and had expected the early days of her marriage to be an idyllic honeymoon. Instead it was a miserable drama in which she was forced to adopt her parents as surrogate children. When she broke down under the pressure, Duncan, whose parents gave him space, refused to help.

'It's ridiculous, ignore them.'

When she refused, he responded sharply, 'I don't want to know. When it comes to the last you are on your own. You might as well get used to it now.'

Some situations were beyond help from outsiders. So began her separate lives, the one she shared with him and the one she shared with her parents. Duncan distanced himself from this second life.

It was his turn to come to terms with a separate life. Only he could know the truth for sure and he had his conscience to deal with. She could not imagine him lying to her, but he was in a corner. The lawyer told him that, if convicted, the sentence ranged from five to seven years. Duncan went as white as a sheet.

If he was innocent she expected more anger. More outrage at the injustice. He had not spoken of going to the girl and getting the truth out of her. He was friendly with Ben and Ben liked him, but he had not suggested they challenge Amy. In so many respects his behaviour was the opposite of what she expected. She translated these deviations as guilt.

Duncan, as though writing and re-writing a novel, replayed scenes that had been and scenes that might have been and scenes that might be, over and over in his head. Polishing, refining, adding and in each culmination the denouement was different.

What truly frightened Duncan was what he had written in his books. What he predicted would happen was close to actual events. Amy getting pregnant and he being accused of siring the child was close to the subject of his sequel novel to *Wasted*.

He had written the opening chapter and last chapter. Then honed both chapters until he was sure they would meet the approval of his editor, and they had. For weeks he had been drafting the middle section and now it was being written for him.

Was this another Wyford miracle? Was this a downside phenomenon to counterbalance the happy miracle that occurred on Chris' wedding day?

Behind Duncan 's laid back and self assured exterior there was an Achilles heel. Twenty-five years into their marriage, Pauline was just now getting an inkling of this weak spot. Had it come with age or had it always been there without her noticing?

Duncan was fixated on his balance of luck. Whatever games Duncan indulged in he was subject to the worst luck and he complained about this unfair treatment. Privately, he was relieved. It was redressing the balance. In most of life's pursuits he was extremely lucky. He had made a perfect marriage with a beautiful woman who was also a kindred spirit. That piece of luck he weighed against forfeiting the chance of Cambridge. He felt that three years of separation from Pauline would be pushing his luck. He might lose her by being apart for so long and he was not prepared to take the chance. That decision had paid off. He got more pleasure having a son at Cambridge than from being there himself.

Had his writing success created an imbalance in his luck ratio? What worried him more was that, having created an injustice in the novel, some omniscient essence was toying with his future. Was this mischievous Supreme Being's power an irrevocable force?

He was too ashamed to admit this crackpot theory to Pauline.

She knew him well enough to know he was holding back. There was only one way she could interpret this concealment. Guilt.

Toby watched his father's suffering and suffered with him.

Chapter Fifty-One

By looking inside himself, Duncan speculated on his fellow men. They simply wanted to be left alone to pursue their hobbies and obsessions. Golf, fiddling with the car, football, a pint with their mates at the local. They were all a great escape. A woman's role is to mock or disapprove. The worst punishment a man can suffer is being organised by his spouse.

Duncan saw a pit of his own foolishness. Losing a cup final lingered longer than winning one. Being spoiled, being thwarted occupied the mind far longer than the joy of winning. Men were certainly capable of evil, sometimes on a grand scale, but Duncan had a counsellor in his cab with a portfolio of a hundred murderers. Ninety-nine had been sexually abused as children and the hundredth had been locked in a cupboard as punishment. It took a lot to push a man to extremes.

What was harder to reconcile was the facile evil perpetrated by certain women, which was more commonplace and more mundane. Was it revenge for subjugation? Was the prospect and duty of keeping the family united too daunting a responsibility? It had always fascinated Duncan that in most households it was the wife that insisted on piety and instigated church. Few women had time for hobbies or obsessions to distract them; collecting thimbles, china pigs, china cats, china houses and china plates was an extension of shopping, and these collections needed regular dusting.

What was at the root of Amy's wickedness? Was it merely a whim?

Duncan perceived that most people, male or female, did not know what they truly wanted. Once they had what they thought they wanted, it soon lost its magic and they started to crave an alternative, and so it went on. It was like eating a bowl of peanuts;

318

the first nut had the most flavour and you finished the bowl trying to repeat the impact of that initial nut.

Was Amy punishing him for some unwitting crime?

In Duncan's estimation, the White sisters were evil and nasty with it. It was not that they just craved being the centre of attention, they demanded adoration, casting themselves in the role of a deity. As far as Duncan could tell, there was no precedent for this in the sisters' mother. Outwardly, she appeared to be a sweet woman, as much in awe of her daughters as he was.

Now, Amy, a chip off the block, was dishing out vituperation. Whatever his crime had been, the punishment did not fit.

* * *

Amy was well enough to get out of bed and go back to school, but she could not be bothered. She lay on her back trying to summon an erotic episode, but she was not in the mood. She put her hand inside her pants and attempted to stimulate some means to break out of her ennui. Her subtle fingers failed to stir any diversion.

She sighed mournfully, turned on her face, pummelled her pillows and burst into tears. It was gone and there was no going back. Her chance of escape was gone. Why had she agreed to it? If only she could go back and stick to her principles.

It was all her fault. She was jealous. Who else had got a mother who envied their daughter for getting up the duff? She was one in a million that bitch.

'Bitch, bitch, bitch,' she pummelled the pillows until she was exhausted, but the anger did not linger and slowly the desolation returned.

The emptiness was barren and consuming, as though the life that was severed from inside was spreading throughout her whole being. A wasted life was eating her, feeding its forsaken soul by consuming her. Nibbling patiently, regenerating itself like an atom. Expanding, it would grow inside her shell like a chicken in an egg and when ready burst free. She, the shell, would be discarded and a new life would take her place.

The air in the room bore down, she was being forcibly pinned to the bed by an invisible blanket, squeezing, pressing, and as much as she struggled there was no escape. Would it ever let her be?

'Please,' she begged. 'Leave me alone. It wasn't my idea, they made me do it.'

Momentarily her words released the pressure, slowly but surely the pressure restarted, implacable and unremitting.

'Jesus died for our sins,' she announced, and some air was let out of the air bag, giving her room to move, but it filled up again and pinned her down. She was being ravished by a phantom.

* * *

As Duncan emerged from pathology, PC Baker accosted him. 'Inspector Lightbourne would like a word, sir.'

In pursuit of their inquiries and pending the results of the DNA test the Inspector wanted a statement. This exercise put Duncan's teeth on edge. The law required a pedantic mockery of the English language that horrified.

'You should get hold of her diary,' said Duncan. 'That's bound to have the identity of the father in it.'

'How would you know that?'

Duncan explained how Amy had read the book and, having found someone who understood her predicament, came to him. She used the pretext of wanting to learn to write and his wife suggested a diary. She showed him the early entries, but they were getting too personal. Not wanting to read her diary he started giving her ideas for stories and that's when her ambition to be a writer fizzled out and she stopped coming round.

'You never met with her outside your house?'

'Never.'

'What would you say if I told you we have a witness that saw you kissing Amy in the street?'

Duncan was floored and panic prevented him thinking straight. Open-mouthed he shook his head, unable to imagine such a possibility.

'When and where did this happen? Do you have a location? A date and time?'

Lightbourne consulted his paperwork, 'Barrow Weald, last summer, mid-morning.'

As he calmed he recalled bumping into Amy outside Phil's cafe. 'She was with her mother that day, visiting a counseller.

320

They could not find the address and her mother was in the cafe telephoning. I gave Amy directions and kissed her goodbye. It was an avuncular kiss,'

'Avuncular?' said Lightbourne, and Duncan regretted using a flash word. He was pleased to have an explanation and was showing off.

'It was not an assignation,' said Duncan and quickly corrected, 'date.'

'I know what an assignation is,' said Lightbourne, and Duncan knew he was not endearing himself to the policeman.

On his way home, doubt triggered a schism in Duncan's confidence. His game of luck decided that the situation was going to stack against him and he began preparations to extricate himself from this accusation. He comforted himself with the DNA results being conclusive, but the thought was there and would not go away.

He pushed this evidence aside and began a constant review of what had been said and by whom. Over and over in his head he reconsidered, adjusting, tweaking, taking a lateral position, and having completed the exercise, he began going over the same ground, adding and subtracting. What started as a minor swirl, a basinful of water exiting a plughole, grew into a whirlpool.

* * *

As the days passed, Amy's depression lifted and anger seethed into its place. She plotted revenge on her mother but tired of this game. Her mother had always abused her privacy, going through her things while she was at school, but she found a safe hiding place for her most precious secrets. While Emma was out, Amy retrieved her diary from under the refrigerator and resumed entries, noting down her innermost thoughts. That gave her pleasure, seeing her head in writing and reading it over and over. Somehow the words on the page gave her life meaning.

Alone in the house one afternoon, having finished her day's entry, she hid the diary on her bookcase and did a tour of the house. Starting with fridge, she had no appetite, and there was nothing on daytime television raunchy enough to take her fancy. She flicked through the adult channels but did not know the code number.

The girls on display bolstered her vanity. She went back upstairs and paraded in front of the mirror in her new bikini. The bottom was cut away and her bum looked good in the reflection. She was much prettier than those television women. They were going to Marbella this summer, where she would wear the new bikini, and at night she would go clubbing.

Feeling a chill, she dressed and lay on her bed, but quickly grew restless. After a few face contortions she wandered into her parents' room. On her father's bedside table was the novel that had sparked her writing ambitions. She bounced across the bed, punched teddy on the nose and opened the untitled book.

It was different. Had Uncle Duncan written the second book already? She opened to the front page and began reading. She heard her mother's car on the drive and finished the page, smoothed out the duvet and went back to her room. She lay on the bed and allowed her annoyance to fester.

'I'll show that dickhead he can't screw me over.'

* * *

Toby knew his father could not have had sex with Amy, because whenever Amy was there, he was in the house. He purposely hung around, sitting in his room with the door open in full view of the staircase. Apart from seeing her, he could hear everything that was said. If what she said had happened it had happened in total silence, and if they made an assignation somewhere else they did it in writing.

He had begun this vigil hoping to catch a glimpse of her as she came and went or hoping beyond hope that she would take a fancy to him.

Amy wore see through dresses and scanty underwear. He heard his mother letting her into the house and hurried to his seat in the doorway. As she climbed the stairs he would be busy at his computer and as she arrived at the landing he would look up and say, 'Hello'. On bright days, the light flooding through the stair window streamed through her dress and silhouetted every curve of her body.

One hot day she arrived in a dress wearing nothing underneath. Toby saw the dark patch around her lower abdomen and spent the time she was there struggling for excuses for another look. He could find no legitimate reason. She was there, naked, save for a loose fitting white cotton frock with blue flowers. With one swift snatch she would be bare and he could get the ultimate vision to box his nightly fantasies.

He heard her propositioning his father, who let her down nicely. He had said 'no' without hurting her feelings.

Could they have met somewhere?

If they had gone to a hotel there would be witnesses. It was then Toby decided that he would help his father. Nobody as yet had explained where this sex had taken place. If Amy gave a location that could be proved untrue that would help his father. Yes, he was the ideal person to face up to her, find out what she was playing at and catch her out in a lie. See her close up for one more time. See that pixie face with dimples, the cropped black hair and that perfect mouth with pink lips. Pink lips that kiss and tell.

Chapter Fifty-Two

Duncan shifted in the groaning chair ignoring the comings and goings. The defeated, the denying, the rabble, claiming, 'I didn't do it. It wasn't me,' repeated so often it had become trite.

Images flickered across Duncan 's blurred vision. Fog was comforting and he let himself remain engulfed. If he let his brain function, depression riddled his soul.

The automatic doors swished open allowing a gust of cold air, and a stain fell across his feet. He showed no interest, concentrating on the smog. It was like counting sheep and achieving oblivion, a blessed relief from the churning.

The breeze brought a waft of cheap perfume that snapped Duncan awake. He looked to the door, saw the shadow retreating and chased it out into the gloomy street.

The police station was surrounded by huge office blocks, eerie in their empty glow, the night lights not reflecting beyond the windows, cast no shadows in the dim streets.

'Amy, please,' he called, but she carried on walking.

He caught up with her at the ramp to the underground car park which swallowed the chequered vehicles.

'Amy,' he said to averted eyes. 'Please talk to me.'

Her face was stony. In the lamplight her skin was the texture of shuttered concrete. 'Please tell me why you're doing this.'

Cast, she stood stock still like a cornered animal, hoping, praying that if she remained inanimate for long enough, the predator would lose interest and leave.

'What are you doing here at this time of night? Have you come to tell the truth?'

For an instant, Duncan had a glimmer of hope. In recent days his emotions were exaggerated. They had slipped into his complacent void and squeezed out his well being. Each new thought, each new chance of status quo torrented in and out of him like floodwater.

If she was not there to confess, why was she there? What would the police want with her at this hour and not accompanied by her parents? A sudden urgency brushed these questions aside. 'If you have come to tell the truth I will help you. I promise that nothing will happen. Just tell the truth and everything will be forgotten. There won't be any trouble. I promise.'

She made no move, no noise, remained frozen with her eyes to the ground, silent.

He pulled her to him and crushed her in an embrace. 'I'll do anything if you end all this. Anything,' he repeated, his voice on the edge of the abyss, his arms tried to make her warm. 'I'll take you to a hotel and love you. I'll give you all the royalties from the new book. I'll give them all to you. I promise.'

He released her and stepped back, her stubborn features were hardening. He was inflamed with rage and balled fists. He wanted to beat the truth out of her. Here and now, once and for all, smash her stupid, stupid face. He could shake the truth out of her. Shake so hard her head would come away. He saw her decapitated head on a plate confessing.

His rage subsided as instantaneously as it started and he cried tears of frustration. Fear and injustice poured down his face and he fell to his knees. Grabbing her around the waist he pressed his wet face against her bare midriff. 'Please Amy, I'm begging you. Please.'

'I read what you wrote in your book,' said a forbidding voice, hollow, resonant, 'it wasn't very nice, was it?'

It was spellbinding, a visitation from a mystic with super powers. With those magic words the spectrum of sufferings drained away. He released her and as though she were a mirage, the next time he looked, she had vanished.

Duncan was in total control, simply because everything that was happening to him was his own fault. He had brought all of this upon himself. She had read what he had written about her and his predicament was his own fault.

In some ludicrous way he was relieved to hear her complaint, her words corroborated his innocence. This revenge was a confession and now he knew why she was punishing him. If only he had recorded their talk, it would all be over.

He would rewrite the Amy section of his new book and send it to her. Pretend that she had read the first draft and that he had thought better of it. That he had distorted her character to heighten the drama. She would understand and it would all be over. It would all be behind him. He returned to the police station, exonerated.

While he waited, he borrowed pencil and paper and began the amendments. Once again he had control, his fate was in his own hands. His changes must be subtle. Amy was not a silly girl and she would see through flimsy flatter.

'Mr Black,' said WPC Baker. 'We're ready for you now.'

Light of heart, light of step, Duncan stepped into the hallowed station and followed her along blue corridors. The door was labelled 'Interview Room Two' and he sat calmly, serene, knowing his agony would soon be over. Perhaps they were going to apologise and send him home, a free man? Perhaps Amy had been coming back to retract a previous confession and he had headed her off.

Inexplicably, they began fiddling with the recording equipment and the anxiety returned. A strange, accusing police woman sat in the third of four chairs and he smiled at her, summoning some sort of bad smell.

Lightbourne switched on the machine and announced the date, time and those present. The policewoman's name was Webster, an Irish girl, with a taste for pork scratchings and best dripping.

The tape ran on in silence for a while as Lightbourne sorted his paperwork. 'Mr Black, I am obliged to inform you that we have completed our evidence and we will be charging you for having unlawful sex with a minor. You....'

A bomb exploded inside Duncan 's head and he heard nothing more. It took an eternity for the smoke to clear and the dust to settle. The inside of his skull was blotched and pitted by flying shrapnel.

'How can that be?' asked a distant voice. 'She just told me that it wasn't me.'

'Mr Black, you must let me finish. Anything you may say

might be used in evidence against you. We suggest you wait until your solicitor gets here.'

'I didn't contact him,' said Duncan blankly.

'Webster will do it for you.' The woman got up to leave, and Lightbourne announced her departure and the temporary halt in the interview. Then he switched the machine off.

'She confessed to me,' said Duncan. 'Not a half hour ago. It's revenge for hurting her feelings.'

Lightbourne stopped at the door and shrugged.

'Are you sure you didn't find a diary?'

'We searched the house from top to bottom.'

'What about the DNA?'

'To be frank with you, Mr Black, I believed your story until we got the results from the lab. It's conclusive.'

A second tower came crashing down and Duncan was propelled from a window. As he plummeted he could not catch his breath. He was drowning above sea level, suffocating, on the point of asphyxia. Bewildered, he gasped, 'How can that be?'

Duncan sat waiting alone in the cell while bail was arranged, the police angry because he had not signed a confession. Lightbourne had taken dictation tetchily, everyone present gave off an air of futility because of Duncan's stubbornness. Duncan recorded his side of the story and signed it.

The bud of a fantasy that Duncan had been toying with bloomed into full flower. Amy, the more experienced, more worldly than he, had secreted a drug into his cup. The drug having taken effect, she mounted him. Astride his comatose body she induced the seed that impregnated her. This was the only rational explanation.

Could it have happened?

* * *

Katy waited until she was certain that Chris was gone permanently before going through his personal belongings. As soon as Chris was pronounced dead by the courts she would have to take care of probate, change the property and the savings accounts to her name. She was in no hurry for the legal process to come to a decision. It was more probable that the life insurance company would have the final word on Chris' disappearance and pay off the mortgage. She was happy to wait.

Bored one Sunday afternoon while Gideon watched a televised football game, she let down the loft stair and rummaged around. Chris was too obvious, the room was empty. Even his survival kit was hidden in the voids. She shifted the boards and found the locked cupboards that circuited the loft space. There was no sign of a key.

With a click of the tongue she climbed down and went to the garage to look for burglary equipment. She found a claw hammer, and a small crowbar and returned to the loft. Inside the first cupboard was the chemical toilet, the sleeping bag and the camping refrigerator. In the next cupboard she found the tool box, the leather binocular case and a file of scantily dressed girls torn out of magazines. None of the other cupboards produced anything of interest.

Katy was going to leave it at that but the tidiness left her dangling with doubt. There had to be more. She surveyed the bric-a-brac, opened the tool box and found the gun. She inspected the chemical toilet but no treasure was secreted within its workings, except for a plastic tub of chemicals. Uncomfortable scrabbling on the floor, she got to her feet and checked about her. It took a series of thoughtful pirouettes to see the obvious. Back on her knees, she removed the boxes of nails and screws blocking the fridge door and inside was a fire box, locked with no sign of a key.

Katy was enjoying herself and smiled at Chris' predictability. That key was somewhere in this room, but where? The chemical toilet would have been the expected place but she had checked there. She turned out the tool box, and the boxes of nails and screws. No key was even taped to the inside.

Determined, she went back to the chemical toilet. She was sure that was how Chris' mind would work. She shook the bottle of chemicals, opened the lid, peered down the spigot and the fumes caused her eye to water. Wiping the tears she tried again.

The leather case was heavy, she removed the binoculars and shook but nothing fell out. She put them back and that was when she found the key taped to a lens.

The firebox burst open and glossy papers spilled out. Well thumbed raunchy magazines, a collection of brown envelopes and the deeds to the flat that Chris was supposed to have sold.

Each envelope was clearly labelled in Chris's meticulous handwriting, 'Asian Girl', 'Asian Girl Two' and 'Amy'. Katy opened the flap and found some poor quality photographs of Amy with men. The photographer was focusing on the girl's body and the identity of the men was restricted to a bare bum or a tattooed arm. Inside this brown envelope was a small white envelope, sealed and addressed to Amy Telleulin.

Katy tore it open and read the contents. She screwed up the letter and the envelope and put it in her pocket. She put the spilled contents back in the firebox and returned it to the fridge. She remembered the screwed up letter later that afternoon, ripped it into small pieces and put the pieces in the dustbin.

* * *

Godman, Duncan's solicitor, had arranged bail and escorted him from the station. Duncan walked home through the empty streets listening to his footsteps echoing about him. He walked past his house to the park and looped his way to Ben and Emma's house. The place was in darkness. He stared up at the blank windows hoping to see what, redemption? He needed a portent, a shaft of blinding light like the one at his nephew's wedding. The moon laughed merrily with rosy cheeks and a white scarf to protect its neck from the chill.

He made his way home to tell Pauline that he would appear in court and would be notified of the date through the post. As part of his bail arrangement, he must hand in his passport to the police station. Worst of all, he had to tell her about the DNA test. How would she believe him?

Tomorrow he would type out the changes to the novel, send them to Amy and hopefully put an end to it all.

Chapter Fifty-Three

With the pending trial, family relationships were fractured. Duncan was in no mood for sympathy or any alternative point of view. He locked himself in the bedroom and worked, but whether he was in the room or not the tension was there. Pauline was torn and had nobody to confide in. Speculating on your husband being a paedophile was not everyday conversation.

Toby understood why wives whose husband's were interfering with their children did not come forward. You did not understand other people's predicaments until you were part of one yourself.

His mother had always been a smoker and seeing her in the utility room by the open door, smoke spiraling into the air, was an abiding image of his life. His mother was strongly opposed to littering, but stamped out dog ends underfoot wherever she happened to be without a thought. Filter tips lay scattered on the crazy paving until Friday when they were swept and binned. The pan had been twice as full on recent Fridays. His mother spent a large part of the day leaning on the door frame, sad eyes staring into space and a lit cigarette between her fingers.

'Would you do me a favour?' his father asked him, handing him an A4 envelope. 'Stick this through your Uncle Ben's door.' The envelope was addressed to Amy.

'Sure,' said Toby.

As he made his way to the house he had other plans. He rehearsed the questions he was going to ask and, making sure he had not forgotten anything, had to go round the block twice before knocking. As he made his way down the path his confidence faded.

He rang the bell and as he waited for an answer his nerves jangled frenetically. He wanted to be in control of the situation but his anxiety was not helping. He breathed deeply as the door opened and Amy poked her face through a small gap.

'What do you want?' she asked nastily, her pretty face contorted by a crumpled nose.

'I'm delivering this,' he held up the envelope.

'My parents are out, like, I'll take it, yeah' she said.

'It's for you,' he explained. Confused, her nose unfolded and she was pretty again. She grabbed at it but he pulled it out of her reach. 'Can I come in for a minute?'

Knowing eyes and precocious modified her mouth. Toby stepped into the house, stepping into the breach, accepting the undeniable, he was out of his depth. He was fighting above his weight, and what a mismatch. This was not David and Goliath, it was Goliath and Noddy.

She was wearing a denim shirt with popper buttons and Toby suspected there was nothing underneath. Her long legs, bare and beautiful and her toes were painted slovenly in red blotches. Seeing her that way made him shrivel and she saw it. Although her face remained impassive, her eyes were laughing at him.

'Well?' she scoffed, 'You're in, yeah. Now what?'

The questions were there but his voice played truant. His fractious eyes would not behave and he wanted to see what was beneath the shirt. More than anything, more than his father's liberty, he wanted a look.

Amy knew it all and began teasing him. Without a word she mounted the stairs and provocatively made her way up. He stared, slack jawed, shrinking. 'Come on,' she ordered.

His mind blank, he did as he was told, his eyes transfixed to the hem of the denim shirt, his memory button firing multiple shots.

Her room was horribly girlish, pink with a poster of Brad Pitt naked to the waist. There were fluffy toys and a pair of silly slippers. There were no books and her CD collection was restricted to boy bands. She sat at her dressing table and brushed her hair.

Toby stood in the doorway without knowing what to do. He must ask a question and a question of any sort would do but his vocal chords had deserted him. He cleared his throat and this got her attention.

'All men do that, right. All men have phlegm. Right, some come too quick and some don't but they all clear their throats, yeah.'

Toby decided he did not like her. His dream girl was obnoxious. With her fluff and her pink, she was a cow and not a lot else. What had he done to her to deserve her contempt? 'Where did you and my dad do it?' he asked.

The crumpled nose reactivated and she sneered at him. 'Like what d'you want to know for?' She got out of the seat and sat on the end of the bed, wriggling her backside and slowly moving back along the duvet. 'Well?'

'I just wondered.'

'No you didn't,' she said guardedly in that old-before-her time voice, dropping the street black posture. 'You think you can catch me out, right, smartass Cambridge? Not so smart as you think you are.'

There was a deafening silence, as he waited for the coup de grace.

'This is what you want,' she said, ripping her shirt open and laying back on the bed. 'I saw you watching me, waiting for me to leave. This is what you're after.' She spread her legs.

Toby felt disgust and elation causing his dick to stiffen. It was what he wanted. It was what he craved to see. It was beautiful and disgusting. Despite his excitement and her enticement he felt a sense of pride. He stepped toward her and as she braced, expecting his arrival, he dropped the package on her naked torso and walked out. He whistled to indicate his nonchalance. He whistled, erratically, but he whistled.

Outside, quivering, head swimming with images and doubts. Had she offered herself that easily to her father, would he have had the strength to say no? Was his father as strong as him?

What about his cousin, Christopher? Would he pass up the chance of a shag? What was he doing spying on her? Was this the act of a jealous lover? Should he tell his mother what he had seen? It could be valuable evidence.

* * *

Ben's business commitments were forcing him to visit New Zealand, but he was reluctant to go. He wanted Amy to retract her accusation and did not want to leave Duncan in the lurch.

Amy was implacable. She lay on her bed, her hand beneath her

332

head, facing the wall. Ben sat on the edge of the bed and tapped her shoulder.

'You'll carry this with you for the rest of your life,' he explained for the umpteenth time. 'You have no idea what you're getting into.'

'It's typical of you,' she snarled. 'To believe Uncle Duncan before you believe me.'

'The truth is the truth, no way would Duncan lay a hand on you. The man is not capable of doing a thing like that.'

'That's very nice,' said Amy purposefully obtuse. She rolled over to face him. 'I'm too disgusting to touch.'

'That's not what I mean and you know it. Look how he wrote about you in his book. He understands what you went through because Chloe died. Then he gave you writing lessons. Amy I'm asking you nicely.'

'Go away.'

'You'll regret this. When you are old enough to realize what you have done. You'll see what an unforgivable sin you've committed.'

Amy turned her back on him again. Disappointed, he got up to leave.

'Jesus died for our sins,' she said and giggled.

* * *

Pauline was devastated. Ian had broken the news to her while Duncan was being charged at the police station. She wanted to prepare herself for his return. Angry, disappointed, disgusted, she could not face him and went to bed early. When she heard the front door she pretended to be asleep.

How could he? How could he and then lie about it?

Men, no matter how different you thought they were, they were all the same. She was too revolted to cry. She pictured him with Amy, sharing intimacy, and it tainted her memories. What they had shared was no longer special.

Pauline understood that she did not think the way others thought. She was without an anchor and had spent a lifetime comparing her life to others; how they conducted their lives, how they brought up their children, what they wanted from life and how near they were to achieving their ambitions. Still she could find no common ground. Delving revealed delusion and hypocrisy and making do. She could not live like that.

What she had was Black and now he was gone. No matter how often she was drowning he pulled her out of the water. She liked his moods of remoteness. When he returned it was like a honeymoon. His giving periods were sporadic and she was rejuvenated. Now she felt as inadequate as those she condemned. Her husband was a hypocrite and a liar. He was one of the deluded. In his weak moment he razed her to the ground and reduced her life to rubble.

Down the years, many men had propositioned her and she resisted the compliment. What if she had accepted Gideon's offer? Would she have enjoyed experiencing a young man? She knew she would not. Gideon did not have the largesse, the humanity that Duncan had in abundance. Gideon was a child from a broken home with a point to prove.

Some of her friends remained in marriages that were shattered, love, if it ever existed, carried on in tatters. Now she was among them. Spoiled, cast adrift in a sea of waste, searching for an elusive desert island, searching for a sanctuary that was not a fallacy.

Duncan came to bed and she kept her back to him.

* * *

Amy opened the envelope and took out the revisions. Instinct told her to rip up the pages without reading them. Instead, she left them lying face down for an hour or two.

She heard her mother return home, grabbed the package and locked herself in the toilet. The new writing was a personal letter, a justification. His portrayal of the dynamic between her and her mother was just how it really was this time, the blame was entirely Emma's. How did he know these things? It touched her that he was sympathetic, but it was too late now. He should have thought of this before.

Chapter Fifty-Four

'Mum,' said Toby, 'got a minute?'

She stubbed out the cigarette with a flagrant foot and gave him the full benefit of her dead eyes. He wanted to hold her, crush her to him but lacked the poise.

He told her what had he had seen and done. He did not leave out one part of it, not even Amy's spread legs, which were still the inspiration for his nightly fantasies.

'Chris was spying on her?' Pauline was appalled. 'His wife is pregnant and he is out tomcatting. Men!'

She made no apology for him and struggled to consider what it could mean. What spurred men to carry on like this was beyond her scope? Gideon was the one with a reputation as a sex fiend but it stood to reason that the brother would be in the same mould. It must be in the genes. Although Duncan was nothing like Ian. In worldliness they were poles apart. In fact on almost every topic they were poles apart. Ian would not be able to handle Amy. He did not have the balls.

What could it mean? Did Christopher have a hand in this business? Inspired, her mind raced. Life returned to her eyes, 'I must speak with your father.'

It was assumed that Duncan was working, throwing himself into the revisions of his book. They had hardly spoken since his release on bail and he was surprised to see her. She could not know that he had spent most of the morning staring out of the window at the street, hoping to see Amy with her critique of his revisions.

It was this hope that was keeping him sane. He had no allies left. Circumstances were teetering and they were about to come crashing down on him.

Face to face with him, her idea seemed far-fetched. In her

favourite pose, leaning against the door frame, she struggled to summon an opening.

'I want you to be totally honest with me,' she blurted and, as he was about to interrupt in that infuriating way of his, second guessing what she was not going to say, she held her hand up to prevent him. 'I need to know the truth.' Again his mouth flexed and she waved him quiet. 'I don't want you to speak until I have finished. I need to know the truth. I won't mind if it is not what I want to hear. I deserve the truth. I've devoted my whole life to you. You owe me the truth.'

He made sure she had finished and was ready for his answer. 'I swear to you on everything that matters to me. Which is you, my Dick Morrissey bootlegs and the boys. I did not lay a finger on that girl, I swear.'

'Could it be that your DNA is similar enough to a relative? Could it be that they got a wrong result?'

'Ian,' Duncan was incredulous, 'and Amy?'

Pauline told him of what Toby had seen, so they sat and discussed the possibilities. Could Christopher's DNA be close enough to his own that a mistake was made?

'That would explain it,' Duncan was ecstatic. 'When they told me that the DNA was mine I thought my head would implode. How do we go about this without alerting anyone? We can't ask Ian to shop his own son.'

'Speak to Godman. If anyone will know, it will be a solicitor.'

In the event, Godman did not know but gave him the number of the Hertfordshire Prosecution Service and Duncan rang. He explained what he wanted and the need for discretion without giving a hint of the reason. He stuck to the story he gave to Lightbourne, simply wanting a supervised second opinion.

The need for discretion did not work well because he got a call from his brother Ian. 'I have spoken to the pathologist involved here and there is no mistake. DNA is not a loose phenomenon, tests are extremely accurate and there is no doubt of the identity. The chances of something odd happening are one in a million.'

'Ian,' Duncan was patient. 'You are overlooking one thing. I am not the father of that aborted baby. So, that one in a million must apply.'

A second test was arranged and Duncan insisted on DNA

samples being compared to other members of the family; Toby, Ian and Gideon. Swabs taken of their saliva were placed in polythene bags and Duncan had to wait twenty four hours for the results.

It was a day of anxious happiness. Pauline and Duncan speculated on their future in a cloudless sky before falling into an untroubled sleep.

* * *

Pauline, not a good sleeper at the best of times, lay listening to Duncan 's steady breathing. The sleep of the innocent? How many nights had she lay wondering? Did he do it or didn't he? There were no doubts about the girl's intentions. Did Duncan have the wherewithal to rebuff her? Would any man?

Although she looked well compared to her contemporaries, Pauline was aware she was showing signs of age. Helena, five years younger and always plump, was hardening to stout. Emma's emaciation was cutting deep lines everywhere that showed and the veins on her arms stood out in a gross piping.

Her vitals squeezed and she would have to get up soon and empty her bladder. This was her nightly game. How long could she hold out. It was snug here under the duvet, Duncan 's warmth better than any electric blanket. She manipulated her nightly routine so that he was in bed ten minutes before her. He, aware of her trick, moved over onto the cold section of sheet when she came to bed and let her have the bit he had warmed. Could such a man sleep with an underage girl? No answer came. You never knew the truth. Even when you knew the truth there was a nuance you had overlooked.

They went together to hear the results of the DNA and were made to wait. Pauline listened to Duncan sighing and watched the faces of the police going about their business.

She was sick of the truth, fed up with being objective and seeing things as they truly were. Why had she been selected to be the arbiter of veracity? What made her so sure she was right and most others were wrong?

Practice, she decided.

How problematic it was for the law to establish facts, each party involved offering contradictions, applying their unnecessary spin and muddying the truth.

They were summoned and Pauline saw instantly that the news was bad. Duncan saw it too and his body jumped with nerves, he could not find a place to keep his hands and his legs twitched uncontrollably.

Lightbourne sat silently and fixed a stare on Duncan's fearful face. Pauline, filled with dread, was like a tumbler being fed from a jug until it spilled over. She struggled desperately to keep her dignity and the effort was so intense she had to close her eyes to shut out reality.

'We can find no trace of the diary you claim Amy Telluelin keeps and the DNA tests...' Lightbourne hesitated like a quiz show host and Pauline hated him. Utterly and irrevocably she hated the man... 'are conclusive.'

* * *

Gideon had made an excuse to stay in his flat overnight. He wanted to be fresh for court in the morning. He lay alone in his bed, thinking of what he might have forgotten. His first presentation to the court on behalf of the Hertfordshire Crown Prosecution Service was Regina versus Black. Not a total coincidence; his father's prestige had something to do with his fast track responsibility.

There was a knock at the front door. It was a new neighbour wanting help with the electrics and Gideon showed him how the temperamental fuses worked.

Gideon's flat block had been built by cowboys and he had been investigating their completion certificate. His searches brought several discrepancies to light, particularly with the planning. He had had his fill of Hertsmore Borough Council. The Planning Department was arrogant; a bunch of ill-trained glorified clerks who learned the UDP and reported to a line manager.

Where did they get their airs and graces?

He suspected that there were too many women in the department and made a mental note to keep a proper balance of males and females under his wing. The door banged again, more persistently. Whoever it was would wake up the entire block.

Naked, he got out of bed and put on a robe. The peephole had blurred and he was forced to open the door to find out who it was.

'What the fuck are you doing here?'

338

She pushed past him, 'I had to come.'

'Tonight of all nights.' Gideon was angry. 'Do you want to bollocks the whole thing.'

'Nobody saw me,' she whined, inflaming his temper.

'Must you talk like a five year old?' Gideon held the door open. 'You'd be surprised what people see, I think you ought to go home.'

'I won't stay long,' she whined on.

'Tonight of all nights. '

'I need you,' she pleaded. 'I need you inside me.'

'The trial starts tomorrow.'

'Do you think I don't know that? That's why I'm so keyed up.' She opened his robe and ran her hands across his chest, down the side of his thighs and cupped his testicles gently. 'Come in me.'

'As soon as it's over, you'll go?'

'Cross my heart.'

* * *

Amy came awake, disorientated for a moment, as though in strange surroundings. She had dreamed a dream so vivid on waking she remained in the dream's location. She had been in bed with someone and the light was so dim she could not make out who it was. She smelled his skin but his after shave camouflaged his identity. She felt his body but that gave no clue either.

For some reason she could not leave the bed and open the curtains. The man had an incontinent dog and the floor was fouled with faeces. She waited for dawn, an interminable wait, and while waiting, fell asleep.

In her dream she saw herself sleeping and coming awake with a desperate need to make an entry in her diary. She had to record a momentous event but, having found the book and a pencil, she forgot what she had to say.

A faint light scythed across the room and she leaned over to see who it was on the other pillow. It was her father. The fright this gave her made her jump and she came awake in the pitch black. She let her hand furtively search the bed but she was alone.

Amy had a strong need to know she was safe and went to find

her mother, but the other bedrooms were empty. She checked downstairs, and searched the house again from top to bottom but there was no question she was alone. She surveyed the summer house. In the moonless night, the summer house windows were in darkness. She put on a coat and walked the length of the garden but the summer house was locked shut.

She checked under the refrigerator but the diary was not there. She struggled to recall where she had left it and returned to her room but it was nowhere to be found. Had the police got it? Had they found it in the search?

'Oh my God,' she yelped.

What would she say when they called her to the witness box? How was she going to get out of this?

They could not have found it. If they had they would have questioned her about the entries. She would tell them she made them up. They were pretend entries she had written to impress Uncle Duncan.

Where had Emma got to? The trial was causing her mother a lot of anxiety, but she felt strangely calm. She had her instructions and they were easy to understand. She would not lose her cool. If their lawyer was a man she would have him in the palm of her hand in no time.

* * *

'Just once more,' she said. 'Then I'll leave.'

'That's what you said last time. Fuck off.'

'That's a most disrespectful way to talk. I am your aunt,' said Emma

'That's why I wear a condom,' said Gideon.

Chapter Fifty-Five

On the morning of the trial the police investigating Chris' disappearance returned the postcard. On the way to the Courthouse Ian read and re-read the wording on the card but without enlightenment.

Do not despair. All is not lost. The world is abundant with riches.

The police had written it off as a red herring. They were suspending their inquiries and as soon as the legal time elapsed, Chris would be presumed dead. His record would be clean because Interpol and the Home Office were sure that when they found Taryk Khan they would find the missing money.

'Are you worried about the outcome?' said Ian, fingering the postcard in his pocket while his brother paced the room. 'Justice will be done, you know that.'

'Thanks for coming Ian,' said Duncan. 'I'll manage from here. If you were going to help you should have done it sooner.'

'I know you're my brother, but...'

'If one of your boys was in my place you would...'

'If a son of mine was guilty, I would back the law to the hilt. I have always done the right and proper thing.'

'Like that woman of yours.'

'What woman? There was no woman.'

'Yes there was,' said Duncan. 'There's something else we don't have in common. I'm a prude. I believe in the sanctity of marriage.'

Duncan was a mystery to Ian. It had not been any different when they were boys. They played cards and Duncan knew every card in the pack, even what Ian had in his own hand. Sure that his brother was looking at his cards, he would get infuriated. This little snot was running rings round him.

He fingered the postcard and wondered if Duncan could find a clue in it. He extracted it from his inside pocket and handed it to his brother.

'What d'you make of this?'

Duncan glanced at the words, studied the picture and the post mark closely and handed it back.

'You must be relieved?'

'I don't get you.'

'Chris is alive and well. I'm surprised he has so much wit, in view of his heredity.'

'I don't get you,' Ian repeated, unaccountably irritated.

'The two 'e's are crossed out as a blind. The word 'riches' without the 'e' is an anagram of Chris. The post card is from Fiji but the post mark is St Lucia.'

'There is a St Lucia on Fiji.'

'St Lucia in Fiji is too small a place to have its own postmark. That St Lucia is in the Caribbean.'

'How can you be so positive?'

'We both collected stamps as children. Your album was filled with prints from Woolworths and I would only collect real stamps with proper postmarks. I learned more about postmarks than stamps.'

'Chris is in the West Indies?'

'I imagine he's long gone from there. My guess is that he is back here in Britain or close by, France or Spain. Somewhere an Englishman with pots of money would not be conspicuous.'

'Who are you, Sherlock Holmes?' Ian was angry. 'There is no way a son of mine would steal.'

'Nevertheless, he's alive and the money hasn't turned up yet.'

'Khan is still missing,' said Ian, getting hot. 'You're not pointing the finger at him. My poor boy might be dead and you are sullying his reputation.'

Duncan thought about dropping the subject but that familiar look appeared on Ian's face and twisted his body away. 'Peter Pan,' Duncan murmured. This childish cowering would usually have incensed him, but today it was so trivial that it did not register on his temper.

You're pathetic, Duncan privately admonished himself. You're looking to get riled. You get pleasure from upsetting yourself. Why? You're behaving more as an infant towards your brother than you did when you were children. Are you making up for lost time?

'Khan has not sent a cryptic postcard,' Duncan explained. 'The person who did is clearly in hiding until the fuss blows over. Secondly, I don't believe your grieving the honesty of your lost son as much as his misdoing will reflect on you.'

'I've worked hard to get where I am,' said Ian. 'Fourteen hours a day for twenty years.'

'There are people working fourteen hours a day to keep body and soul together. They're not in line for a knighthood.'

'You cost me my knighthood,' said Ian defiantly. 'Did you know that? That books of yours, taking the piss out of the Home Office.'

'Helena spoke to Sir Charles Russell. He's head of the Honour's Committee.'

'Were you there when the conversation took place?'

'No, how could I be?'

'And you believe her?'

'What makes you so bloody smart?'

'Seeing weakness, hearing lies, smelling the bullshit,' said Duncan. 'Insight is not a blessing, it's a curse.'

* * *

'Members of the jury, my name is Peter Kurten QC and I, with my colleague Thomas Piper QC, represent the prosecution. My learned friend, Mr Ian Hindley QC represents the defence. Members of the jury, this is an extremely unsavoury case ...'

'...Paedophilia is reaching epidemic proportions. It is a blot on our landscape. We must put a stop to it now and we must make an example of those who do not respect the law or basic human standards.'

'I swear to tell the truth, the whole truth and nothing but the truth, so help me God.'

'Your name?'

'Amy Lillian Telleulin.'

'Your age and your birth date?'

'I was fifteen on February 14th.'

Amy was dressed in her freshly dry-cleaned school uniform. Most of the polish on her fingernails had peeled, exaggerating her youthfulness. She answered questions with shy poise.

'What is your relationship to the accused?'

'We're not directly related, yeah. My mother's sister is married to his brother.'

'Do you refer to him as uncle?'

'Yes.'

'Tell us how your situation with Uncle Duncan came about.'

'Like he had this book published and I found it lying round the house. I don't read many books but because he was family, I read it, yeah.'

'Did you like the book?'

'Yeah.'

'Why?'

'Because I was in it, yeah, I was one of the main characters,' said Amy boastfully.

'So the accused had made a study of you?'

'Right, he wrote about me and my family, yeah, how it is. Like I was surprised that anyone knew of my problems.'

'Then what happened?'

'I went to visit. I wanted to find out how he knew, yeah. It made me feel so much better that somebody else knew and, like, I wanted to tell him.'

'So you went to visit?'

'Yeah.'

'How was it?'

'Nice. Auntie Pauline is very nice, yeah. They let me come whenever I wanted. Sometimes Uncle Duncan let me do his typing and printing.'

'Anything else?'

'He encourage me to take up writing. He said it was therputic.'

'Therapeutic.'

'Right.'

'And was it?'

' I suppose it was.'

'Did you find Mr Black attractive?'

'He's cool for an old bloke.'

'How did the sex begin?'

'I used to watch while he was working and I would stand quite close and he would touch my bum.'

'Did you mind that?'

'Not too much.'

'And when did it start getting more intimate?'

'The first time was when Pauline and Toby…

'Who are Pauline and Toby?'

'Pauline's my aunt and Toby's my cousin, yeah.'

'Please continue.'

'They went for his university interview. Uncle Duncan pretended he had some appointment and stayed behind. He drove them to the station and told me to wait until he got back. That was the first time.'

His mouth and tongue worked expertly, his hands found the right spots. She was ready. She spread herself for him. Now, it won't take long, I'm almost there, quick, please, I'm waiting….

* * *

'Would you say you had a good relationship with your daughter?'

Emma was in mourning. She wore a black suit and a hat with a veil.

'She is a typical teenager. We have all the usual conflicts that mothers and daughters have. Overall, I would say we have a good relationship.'

'How would you describe your daughter?'

'How do you mean? Tall, short, medium?'

'No, Mrs Telleulin. What sort of child is she?'

'A typical teenager.'

'*Who is this man?*'

'*This is Clive. Clive this is my mum.*'

Clive, a muscular man, arms, chest and back a tableau of crass artwork, dressed slowly, his eyes averted. He had seen how hungrily the skinny old bag had stared at his todger. Perhaps he should stay and give them both one.

Best be on his toes.

Emma was fascinated by the size of the unwelcome guest's penis. She had never seen anything like it. How could her Amy take such a thing inside her?

'Yes, your typical, average teenager.'

* * *

'Please tell the court your name.'

'Peter Ancome-Walker.'

'Tell the court what you do.'

'I am employed by the Home Office to administrate DNA.'

'You were asked to supervise the DNA sample of the victim's foetus?'

'That is correct.'

'How old does a foetus need to be to ascertain DNA?'

'There has been a lot of controversy in relation to foetus experimentation and because of several private prosecutions that information is currently sub-judicae.'

'Were you able to establish a DNA in this instance?'

'Yes. The foetus was twenty nine weeks, which is certainly formed enough to establish DNA.'

* * *

'I am a psychiatrist,' said Mr Setty, twitching his nose.

'You are an expert on teenage behaviour? asked Ian Hindley QC.

He had not been Duncan's first choice of barrister but being so sure that DNA would exonerate him he had left it too late and Sean Beaney, the Irish wizard, was in court elsewhere.

'Mostly female behaviour, males are less complicated and therefore less interesting.'

Hindley surveyed the jury and asked, 'What is the basic difference between males and females when it comes to a lie?'

'That is one of the principal differences between girls and boys. Most boys will admit to a lie but girls are more dogged. Some will stick to a lie and carry it to the grave.'

* * *

'Your witness,' said Hindley. Pauline stood uncomfortably and shifted her feet and clutched the rail fiercely. She wanted to catch Duncan 's eye and reassure him, but she was too nervous.

'Are you well?'

'Fine, thank you.'

'Are you on any medication?'

Hindley crouched out of his seat, 'I don't see the pertinence of Mrs Black's medication having a bearing on this case.'

'My learned friend will see the bearing quite soon, my Lord.'

'Continue.'

'Mrs Black?' said Kurten, who was conducting the case as though on a crusade. Pauline knew where this was leading and regretted ever agreeing to give evidence.

'Yes.'

'What pills are you taking?'

'Cranberry juice and anti-biotics.'

'For what condition?'

'Interstitial cystitis.'

'How long have you had this condition?'

'A few months.'

Hindley was bent double again. 'How did this information come to light. This is a private matter between doctor and patient.'

'I assure you, my Lord,' said Kurten smugly, 'our source is not the medical profession. This information is of particular relevance.'

'I'll allow prosecution counsel to continue,' said Lord Justice Christie, 'but keep to the point.'

'How long is it since you and your husband have been able to have sex?'

'I don't remember exactly.'

'An approximation will do. A year?'

'A year.'

'More or less?'

'More.'

'Is your husband a fit man?'

'Yes.'

'With a normal sexual appetite?'

'Yes, and as I said he's been particularly understanding.'

'He has not shown any signs of, what shall we call it, deprivation?'

'He has never put me under any sort of pressure. He knows it troubles me and not once has he spoken of it without my bringing up the subject.'

'Do you think that's normal?'

'He's the only man I have ever been with. He has said that he hates having sex if I do it for his sake.'

'Meaning?'

'If I'm not in the mood for sex he would prefer to leave it.'

'What would you call that?'

'Love. What would you call it?'

'So, your husband is a virile man and you have not had sex in over a year. Do you think that an average red blooded man, still in his prime, would be tempted by the availability of a young girl?'

'I am not a man, but I would not be tempted by a young boy. I could offer evidence to that effect.'

'Maybe so, but it's your husband who is on trial here. Have you noticed any changes in your husband recently?'

Pauline considered, because there had been changes in Duncan over the past year. They had been together for so long each blip, however minute, was noticeable. Duncan had withdrawn, locked himself in that room, cocooned. Could she blame him? She did not put so much emphasis on sex. When it happened it was good, if it didn't happen, so what? When she had been pregnant Duncan was biting the doors in frustration. He had calmed down since but he was always the instigator of sex. Was he hiding his frustration from her? She did not know his secret life and thoughts.

'No, not that I can think of.'

'What about the girl's visits, what did you make of her?'

'She was after him from the first.'

'How can you be so sure?'

'The way she was dressed. See-through dresses and no knickers.'

'What did you do, seeing her in this state of dress?'

'Nothing. I trust my husband. My son Toby was revising for his exams in the room opposite. If anything untoward was happening he would have known about it.'

'Did you talk to him about it?'

'He told me what he had heard.'

'I can't ask you to repeat a hearsay conversation, but did your son put your mind at rest?'

'Yes. Duncan always referred to Amy facetiously.'

'Facetiously, explain please.'

'He never used Amy's name but referred to her as Lolita.'

Christie called lunch and in the break Hindley reassured her.

'I've made matters worse.'

'No, you did fine, Mrs Black. In the circumstances, you were quite dignified.'

* * *

'Please state your name.'

'Duncan Lessing Black.'

'Place your hand on the bible.'

'I'd rather not.'

'Mr Black, do you wish to affirm?'

'I don't see the point.'

'Are you an atheist?'

'No, but since this fiasco has started I have lost my belief in everything.'

'Do you swear to tell the truth, the whole truth and nothing but the truth?'

'I never do anything else.'

'Mr Black,' said Judge Christie. 'I would like you to confine your answers directly to the questions and resist the embellishments.'

'Sure.'

'Yes, my lord,' Christie corrected but Duncan ignored him.

'I have just one question for you at this time,' said Hindley. 'Did you have sexual intercourse with Amy White?'

'No.'

'Is that the absolute truth?'

'Yes.'

He was tired. His last fare had taken him south of the river. Most taxi drivers would have made an excuse or refused outright. He was rewarded by a fare back into town, a black boy, and they discussed the loss of spirituality in his community. He dropped him at the intersection between Shaftesbury Avenue and Charing Cross Road and turned off the 'For Hire' sign.

It was a novelty coming home to an empty house and an empty bed. He and Pauline always went to bed at the same time. She dragged her feet in the winter months so that he warmed the bed before she got there. They used to fall asleep touching, but since her illness that practice had stopped. He made a concerted effort not to put her under pressure, hoping that would help with the cure. It was a matter of time before life returned to normal.

He had his writing and he concentrated on that. Not sex, but when it went well it was nearly as good as.

He cleared the mess in the bedroom and tidied his clothes away, showered, got into bed and switched out the light.

He was dozing when she got into bed with him. He was so dopey, the intrusion might have been a dream. Her hands guided him to her soft breast and her bottom, a handful of peaches, the harsh contrast of hair and damp on his fingers. He could sense the intensity in her body. She spread herself ready and pulled at him. He automatically teased and waited, it was that moment that saved him.

'Fuck me,' she implored. 'Please.'

It was her voice that brought him down to earth, that juvenile whimper.

The jury, the men staring at the floor, returned to their seats in the jury box. Duncan had lost all hope long before today. Pauline, John and Toby were not in court to hear the verdict. They were as positive as he was of the outcome. He did not blame them. Why suffer any more shame than was necessary?

'Has the jury reached a verdict?'

'Yes.'

'Is the verdict agreed by all?'

'Yes.'

'What is the verdict?'

Duncan watched Amy's face as the foreman of the jury said 'Guilty'. Not a flicker. An ignorant child that pulled the wings off flies. God how he hated her.

Has the defendant anything to say before I pass sentence.

Duncan licked his lips but his dry tongue scraped no relief. 'Amy this is your last chance, if you don't undo this you will end up like your mother.'

The guards pulled him roughly back as though it was a hysterical outburst. Amy burst into tears and ran from the courtroom.

'That was reprehensible,' said Christie. 'The evidence in this case has been irrefutable and in my view the jury has reached the only possible verdict. I sentence you to the maximum term of imprisonment. Seven years. Take him down.'

'You always were a pompous idiot, John'

Christie could not resist a look at Duncan, who was smiling calmly. He made a joke with his warders and was led down the stairs to the cells. Christie could not help thinking that the prisoner had come out of this case with more gravitas than he. He had certainly behaved in an unusual way for a criminal in the dock. That was the criminal mind for you, unpredictable.

Chapter Fifty-Six

'There are plenty of grounds for appeal.'

'You need to find that missing diary. It's out there somewhere.'

'We'll try. We'll do everything in our power...'

'No you won't. You'll make a few routine inquiries, get involved in another case and forget about me.'

'That's very cynical.'

'That's life.'

A police officer let Hindley out and his brother Ian into the cell, where Duncan was slumped on the edge of the bench. He did not look up.

'I'm suffering from a surfeit of Ians.'

'Chin up.'

'I haven't asked you this for some time, but I would like you to fuck off out of my life. 'Chin up?' You take the art of being a tosser to new realms. Have you any conception of what I am going through? All you can manage is chin up?'

'Do you have to be so rude? I'm only here to help.'

'Well you're not, so please go.'

'I don't want to leave it like this.'

'I can't help you Ian. We're complete strangers. Who are you? Where do you come from? Were you sent here from another planet?'

'Do you have to do that, make fun of me?'

'It's the only way I can stay sane.'

'What's your problem?'

'I've been convicted of rape and I'm innocent. I just had a trial, didn't you notice?'

'I mean with me.'

Duncan lifted his head so that his face was parallel with the ceiling and shook it sadly. He dropped his chin on his chest and sat motionless, oddly tranquil.

Ian did not want it left. Ian wanted what he had been seeking from infancy. He wanted Duncan's affirmation. He did not even want Duncan to concede to him, just the acknowledgement of his...

What?

Yes, Ian you are a success and I am proud of you.

Should he say it? Could he say it?

It would be the mature thing to do, but the words would not come. Ian was here, not to commiserate with his disgrace but to salvage...

Salvage what? Ego? What came first? The chicken or the ego? Where did it start? How did it happen? Ian was credulous and a ditherer and that was why he was suited to the Civil Service.

Did ambition creep up on you? Was it having something to prove? Unhappy at home, did you hide behind your work? It was the best excuse. Work was an unassailable place to hide. It didn't take long to convince yourself that success was what you wanted. Getting a pat on the back gave you self-worth.

Was it worth the sacrifice? Was it worth putting the time in, giving up your life for the job?

It must take some talent to achieve recognition. Not everyone got to the top. The pity was the egotism and arrogance that arose out of success.

Was this a man thing? Wanting to prove you were better than the rest. Was it him that was the problem? Was he what got under his brother's skin? He could help this man find peace. If he was going to help his brother there was going to be a fee.

'Would you like to know what inspired me to write?'

Ian jutted his chin in a petulant show of unconcern.

'The man in the street has no voice. He has to put up with incompetence and apathy, imparted by a set of arbitrary rules.'

'Rules are rules,' said Ian.

'Rules! Our lives are being fettered by rules. You can't smoke in a building. You can't pick strawberries unless you are wearing a suit of armour. You can't take pictures of your children unless suitably attired. You can't erect a shed in your own back garden.

It won't be long before farting becomes a crime. The emission of unlawful methane in an omission zone. Your rules are a pathetic means for the craven to hide behind. What is worse is the condescension with which these rules are implemented, as though it is for our own good. The trouble with you people in power is that you take us for idiots.'

Ian rapped on the cell door and called out of the peephole.

'That guff I just gave you about the man in the street. It's bullshit. I started writing when the sex stopped. It was somewhere to hide, like you with your work.'

'I love my work,' said Ian sadly.

'You've become pompous, egotistical, self-absorbed and the reason I can be so positive is because when I look inside myself I know deep down I am the same. Just for the record,' continued Duncan, 'I did not fuck that stupid little girl.'

The judge had said that the evidence was irrefutable and Ian agreed. His brother had always had a tendency to live in a world of his own and it was clear he had not grown out of it. How could his views be right when they went against the majority? How could the consensus be wrong? Duncan needed to grow up and accept the real world. A good world, the best there had been, and he had helped create it.

* * *

The General Election was set for the first Thursday in May and canvassing was full throttle. Emasculation, even though it had been narrowly defeated in Parliament, was proving to be a pivotal issue. Promises of a revised Bill and another vote were made by the incumbents if they were voted back in. There were hints of the re-introduction of hanging following on and the feedback from the stump was promising for the governing party.

The tabloids were churlish at having their support of the Emasculation Bill denied. That debate had provided juicy headlines for a month. Editors were reluctant to let the matter slip and one of them got the cute idea to find out who was the brainchild behind the Bill. They tried the proper channels but of the usual contacts some were reluctant, the rest were asking for too much chocolate (nb. Chocolate is a euphemism for pound notes in brown envelopes). A skanky reporter was sent to the Dog & Duck to find the man who inadvertently provided them with the lowdown on Civil Service malfunctions.

Coke was in his usual spot, alone, starving for any personal contact. A pint and a half was all it took to get the name.

The article was headlined, 'Emasculation mastermind named'. Ian liked mastermind a lot but was not happy at being exposed to the public. He was unaccustomed to limelight and fending off journalists. He received criticism from unexpected quarters and exceptional praise from an unlikelier source.

When Ian got home that evening, Helena greeted him with something more than her usual indifference. 'I can't express how proud of you I am.' She placed her paw-like talons on his shoulders and kissed him on the mouth, leaving a daub of red streaked across his lips. She followed this up with a bodily gesture of hideous proportions. 'I can honestly say for the first time since I've known you that I think you're… sexy.'

She did it again and Ian's ischemia caused him to shrivel. A hibernating appendage, like a spent rodent, slinked its way to its mousehole and waited for eternity.

* * *

Helena was over the moon, but Gideon was as sick as a parrot. 'You'll regret this,' he warned his father.

Ian went glassy eyed, moved two steps away and began humming. It was that infuriating expression on his father's face that Gideon could not abide. He washed his hands of him. He so much wanted to help, but the shutters had come down, there was no getting through.

Shortly before the baby was born, when Katy was too big to cope, Gideon moved in. It was intended as a temporary measure but the arrangement became permanent. Julius, six pounds twelve ounces, was the apple of his father's eye. If the baby cried during the night it was Gideon who heard and got up to take care of him.

Katy had read the books and was going to breast feed. 'He won't develop sufficient immunities from a bottle.' One suck of her tit and she demanded the anti-lactose pills, 'Uhh, horrible, I'm not putting up with that.'

Gideon did the ten o'clock feed and while Julius continued waking in the night, fed and changed him while Katy slept.

Katy did not know what to make of her unselfish emotions for the baby or the change that had come over its father. She felt proud that she had created a perfect little person that had grown inside her. The bonus was that she had created a perfect little person out of the smarmy git that was her husband's brother.

Gideon's tomcatting days were over. When they were able to resume sex after her confinement, every slap was delivered with an apology. After sex he would lie facing her dewy eyed and they would discuss parenting methods. Arguing their case from what manuals they had read, neither prepared to concede.

After all, a person in love cannot have it all their own way.

Chapter Fifty-Seven

Ian read the front page of *The Times* with a strong sense of fulfilment. He would end his career on a high. The election result was just what he wanted and he would be reunited with his friend John Hay. The new cabinet smiled into the camera and John had his arm around the shoulder of the new PM.

What was adding to his expectations was the rumour that Crest Mornington and the PM did not see eye to eye. They had crossed swords when the PM was a junior minister at Works and Pensions. Mornington was making overtures about retiring and Ian would be in the running for the vacant post. If he got the top job he would be invited to tea with Her Majesty and could ask her personally to re-instate his knighthood.

It had been the highest turnout in recent electoral history, 96 per cent. Unfortunately, there was not a working majority, but government would carry on regardless. Helena brought in the mail, handed Ian a letter and said crabbily, 'Work.'

The envelope bore the HM Prison logo and he used his butter knife to open it. Inside was a hand written note from Duncan.

Dear Ian,

Having had time to consider matters I am writing to you to apologise for the shabby way I treated you after the verdict. I also want to apologise for the shame and humiliation I have brought on you and my family.

You have worked hard to accomplish a glittering career and I sincerely hope my ignominy will not reflect on you.

Your proud brother,
Duncan.

Helena pursed her lips. There were three things she was to take today. The package, the *Diners' Club* manual and what else? She could not remember. She pursed her lips again, applied a thick coat of red lipstick and brushed her hair.

Helena was letting her fringe grow longer.

Ian thought she looked like a scarlet version of the Dulux dog, but dare not express such an opinion.

What else was it?

She surveyed the room for a clue but no inspiration came. Her eyes fell on the bed, where the package had been thrown, and the contents came to mind.

'Dirty little slut.'

Who was the mysterious *Mr X* who had fathered her child? She could not ask Emma because she had promised faithfully not to read the diary. Did it matter? That ingrate Duncan had been convicted, whether he did it or not, justice had been done. That blasted book of his losing her poor Ian his knighthood.

If the truth be told, Amy was a chip off the old block and no mistake. Emma dropped her knickers for a lick of a lollipop. It was flat chest disease. Because she had no breasts she had to prove her sexuality.

Helena tugged down the front of her blouse to check her substantial cleavage. She was a woman, and what a woman.

That was what it was, the copy of the *Wyford Observer* with Ian's interview. She had run off several photocopies and she had promised one to Emma, who was too tight-fisted to buy her own. She folded a copy, put it in her handbag with the package and the book.

On Mondays, Wyford town centre did a slow trade and the BHS staff outnumbered the customers. Helena, spoilt for choice, struggled to choose a table and Emma was late, for a change. She chose a table by the entrance and sat facing the same way, not so she could spot Emma arriving but in case someone of her acquaintance had chosen the same venue and she could be beneficent. Helena prepared herself for Emma's cross examination.

'Did you open the package?'

'Of course not, what's the big secret?'

She could be convincing when she needed to be. No way would Emma guess the truth.

She was still daydreaming when Emma took the seat opposite. 'I'm reporting those men in the car park. Do you know what they want to clean my car? Five pounds? The cheek of it! Five pounds? I gave them a piece of my mind and one of them was extremely rude, swore at me. Would you pay five pounds to have your car washed?'

'We have a man that comes to the house.'

'So, what do you pay him?'

'Six pounds a car.'

'More fool you,' said Emma, as the waitress arrived to take their order. 'Bring me a herb tea in a glass. A glass, mind you, not a plastic cup, and a green salad with nothing on it, no salad dressing or French dressing or mayonnaise like you did last time.'

'I'll have a glass of still water,' said Helena, 'and a plain baked potato with butter.'

'You get a choice of toppings with that.'

'Just butter thank you and plain water, no lemon and no ice. I hate it when they give you ice in these places. There's no room left for the water.'

Emma was going to point out that ice eventually becomes still water, but she let it pass. 'Did you bring the package?'

Helena handed her the *Diners' Club* book with the photocopy folded inside and wanted to open it out to show her sister. Emma was impatient to get her package back and pushed the book aside. She inspected the flap and saw immediately that her sister knew the contents. The package had been opened. She had stapled the top four times, two vertically and two horizontally. All four staples were horizontal. She made no comment. It was what she expected and she had no desire to discuss the contents with her sister.

'What's news,' she asked as she put the package away.

'Not very much,' said Helena, waiting for an accusation of some sort or some thanks at least for hiding Amy's diary during the course of the trial. 'Katy had the baby.'

'You're a grandmother,' said Emma with abhorrence, 'how revolting!'

* * *

Hay had that rush that goes with an exciting new beginning and even the downtrodden Home Office managed a hum of expectation. Mornington introduced the senior office staff and one by one the senior Civil Servants were summoned for briefing.

Ian, still buzzing from Duncan's letter shared that sense of hope that a new beginning provides. Without any given work to do, he tidied his office awaiting his summons to greet the new Home Sec. He was being left until last and surmised the reason was Mornington's retirement announcement.

He rubbed his hands together with glee. 'Yabba dabba doo!'

It had been customary to promote from within the Home Office system because the hierarchy claimed that Home Office quirks were an acquired malfeasance soaked up through years of imbibing.

It was during a previous administration, when the HO was at a particularly low ebb having suffered the setbacks of the Guildford four and Birmingham six overturns. Not so much egg on their face as being smothered in albumen. What Ian wittily referred to at the time as 'eggtoplasm'. They got in some meddling pests, Morrison, Crippen and Le Neve, 'consultants' and 'experts' in the working environment. They hung around the building for eight months, got paid a six figure fee and made matters ten times worse.

Now, like so many worthy traditions that were ebbing away, they had brought in an outsider who the 'experts' said was not bogged down with HO history and could break free of the illusory chains that hampered morale.

Mornington was a fresh face without baggage. He had transferred from Work and Pensions without any foreknowledge of the mysterious workings of the HO had done an exemplary job keeping the department's image intact. Morale had started at a new high but dipped quickly.

The wait became interminable, butterflies careered around Ian's empty stomach. He was too keyed up to eat. He was checking his watch at shorter and shorter intervals and could not remain in his seat. He paced as he did, while giving dictation and the motion generated his thoughts.

What could he do to save morale? This was going to be his lasting monument and would provide the title of his memoirs.

'How I Saved the Home Office.' Not a grand enough heading, 'Sir Ian Black, Crusader.' That had a better ring to it, but was a touch too tabloid. He opened his copy of the *Oxford Dictionary of Quotations* and looked up hero.

Came the hero from his prison.

Ian felt that might be most apposite and looked up the poem, the *Old Scottish Cavalier*.

Like a bridegroom from his room
Came the hero from his prison

Perhaps not.

Hero perish?

No.

God-like hero sate.

What was that supposed to mean?

Hero becomes a bore at last.

Perhaps he had better choose another word for himself

He was checking for the entries under 'crusader' when he got the call. Struggling to remain calm he headed for the Home Secretary's office.

Hay had moved the furniture. His predecessor sat with his back to the window, providing visitors with a view of the Thames. Over the shoulder of the new Home Secretary was a print of Turner's *Dawn after the wreck*.

Ian, pleasantly surprised that they were alone, was confident that Crest Mornington's absence was significant. Ian assumed he had already stepped down and that was why he had been left until last.

He and John shook hands warmly and his secretary came into the room without knocking, 'Excuse us Alan,' said Hay and his secretary did an about turn and left the room, closing the door behind him.

'How is the family?'

'Fine,' said Ian. 'In the pink.'

'We...' Hay began.

'I'm a grandfather, by the way.'

'Congratulations,' Hay got out of his chair and sat on the edge of his desk towering over his guest.

There was a knock and Alan poked his head around the door. 'We have an emergency. Could you spare me a moment?'

'I'm sorry about this,' Hay left the room.

Ian was popping with nervous excitement and got out of his chair to walk off his anxiety. He looked out of the window across London. A pair of seagulls soared over the Houses of Parliament and glided above St Stephen's Tower and Ian's chest glided and soared with them.

He was at the heart of all he surveyed, part of the essence that generated the nation. 'Hero' and 'crusader', Duncan was proud of him, his boys were proud of him and some day his grandson, Julius Black, would follow in his grandfather's footsteps along the Corridors of Power.

On the desk was a file with his name on it. He glanced at the door, lifted the flap and opened the paperwork somewhere in the middle, letting the papers spiral. An unfamiliar letter caught his eye and in his hurry to locate it, the pages would not separate.

It was expensive buff stationery with notepaper headed LADY BLACK – PEMBERTON HALL. It was a consolation letter to the Queen, commiserating the death of her favourite corgi. There was a photocopy of the memo from an equerry questioning the identity of Lady Black and another from Sir Charles Russell recommending the rescinding of his knighthood. Just as the he let go of the file to consider the implications, Hay came back into the room.

Ian was momentarily distracted because Hay's rosy cheeks were deathly white. 'I'm sorry that this conversation has got to be so blunt but I've got a situation to deal with. We're going to have to let you go, Ian.'

'Whaaa…'

'I want to distance myself from the Emasculation Bill. It's not the sort of policy we wish to be associated with. You will get your full pension. I'm sorry but the decision comes from a higher office.'

'The Prime Minister?' Ian murmured.

'I'd best tell you, because you will find out sooner or later. Your Emasculation Act has put ideas into the heads of the prison population. There have been several…'

'My?'

'…What should I call them? 'Incidents'. The prisoners have taken the law into their own hands and have attempted castrations of convicted sex offenders.'

362

'My Emasculation Bill?'

'I'm sorry to be the bearer of bad news but your brother Duncan has been attacked with a razor blade and is in a dangerous condition in the infirmary.'

'What am I going to do?'

'I'll arrange a car to take you to him.'

'I've given my whole life to the Home Office.'

'You can get one of those jobs in the private sector you always used to tell me of.'

Hay waited for his friend to pull himself together but Ian was frozen to the spot. Running out of patience he guided him towards the door. 'I'm sure things will work out for you. Think, you'll have plenty of time for your grandchild. What did you have, boy or girl?'

'Boy…'

'What's the baby's name?'

'Judas…' said Ian from the hollow sepulchre that was the residue of his being.

Hay opened the door and pushed him out. 'Good luck, old man.'

Stunned, Ian set out for the toilets to release his emotions, but found his path blocked by a pair of uniformed coppers. One held his raincoat and the other his briefcase. They escorted him down the back stairs and he was let out of the building. They stood guard at the front entrance in case he attempted to get back inside.

He hid behind a column and put on his raincoat. He waited for the coast to clear and scurried towards the underground.

Hay returned to his desk and sat with his head in his hands. The attractive face of Duncan Black's wife entered his head. What was it she had said? You men should not marry because you abandon your families for your own ambition. It was something like that and maybe she had a point.

'Poor Ian,' Hay said to the room at large. 'Thinks his son can fuck my wife and get away with it.'

Chapter Fifty-Eight

The rules stated that at least three months should elapse before a sacked employee could collect their belongings. Ian allowed an extra month and drove up to town. The government footed the congestion charge.

Down the years Ian had accumulated a significant number of personal files. These would remind him of his contribution and he intended to consult his records to complete his autobiography. He had a shortcut into publishing, having been introduced to Duncan's agent.

'Such a nice man, for a Jew.'

His office had been re-assigned to the junior that Lizzie upset by paraphrasing his work. He did not shake off the kudos Lizzie's revisions accorded him and he was promoted twice on the shirt tails of Lizzie's verve. He was the personification of the new dynamic Civil Service.

The porters handed Ian a cardboard box with personal possessions.

'What about my files?'

'Shredded.'

He managed the box under his arm and walked the halls to say goodbye.

Word had got around that he was in the building and everyone had absented themselves into uninterruptable meetings. He found just one of his colleagues at their desk.

'Arundel, old chap, good to see you.'

'Ian,' said the surprised minion, his face reddening dark around his grog blossoms. 'Sorry to hear you're leaving.'

'Took early retirement,' said Ian and tapped his breast pocket, 'Doctor's orders.'

'Funny you should be here,' said Coke. 'We got a postcard from that girl you had it off with.'

Ian was prevented from denying this accusation as the long man pushed him aside and went out to the typist's pool. He returned with a postcard come photograph of Lizzie, Elvis and their son.

'She left to get married,' Coke explained.

Neither Ian's stomach nor his chest failed him. In recent weeks he had suffered so many disappointments and here was another plunge, but he was inured to pain.

'I bet you can guess the baby's name,' said Coke disingenuously.

Ian did not answer but left the building. He heard a flat voice call, 'Ian' but he did not turn back.

* * *

'I want you out from under my feet,' Helena told him. 'You had better get one of those private sector thingummies you were always bragging about.'

'Yes, dear,' said Ian, wondering when he could sneak off and be with his darling grandson.

He had promised to take Helena to the hairdressers and hid in the office until it was time to leave. Ian was reading Duncan's second novel, which was clearly about the White sisters.

Helena was going to put the matter in the hands of her lawyers.

'That woman who had sued the papers.'

'What woman?'

'That woman who had a child with that nice Mr Parkinson.'

'What reason have you got for suing?'

'I didn't read it, but my friends tell me we have plenty of grounds for going to law.'

'Hasn't he suffered enough?'

'Not in my book. D'you like that? I made a joke.' Ian blanched. 'Anyway, he's not getting anything over on me.'

Since his retirement, Ian was in no mood for reading, but decided to check the veracity of his wife's friends. Reading without searching for references to himself, his impartiality discerned the main character was his wife and the way she was portrayed, warts and all, was not the least bit libellous.

* * *

Ian watched Helena enter the hairdressing salon, then crossed the road. He pushed open the café doors and chose a booth in a quiet corner by the window. He ordered a cappuccino, found a copy of *The Times* in the rack and spread the paper across the table. He scanned the political pages for mentions of his old colleagues and turned to the sports section.

Ian took a swig of piping hot coffee and scalded his tongue. He was constipated and hoped the caffeine would stimulate some action. Sedentary days had changed his body clock. Nothing was as it had been. He had spent years daydreaming of retirement, fantasies of tending the garden or breeding basset hounds and sitting in the Warner Stand.

Now he had the time, the inclination deserted him. He was lacklustre, jaded and bitterly disappointed. There were few offers from the private sector. Wheels within wheels were grinding slowly and the two interviews he had taken were not taking him.

He had joined the Church's Board of Management and was organizing the pilgrims visits to St Marks, and booking in the weddings, but these were falling off. This downturn was hurting the proliferation of hotels that had sprung up around the town when the advent of pilgrims was at its most prolific. Due to the same malicious sprite that dogged Marsham Street, the sun seemed to have disappeared from Saturdays. He spent more time dealing with complaints and demands for refunds, as though he had control of the weather.

'Never mind,' he thought.

He was used to making difficult decisions and getting things done. His constipation troubled him, all that effluent, foul and festering inside.

There was not much to read on the sports pages, so bored, he turned his attention to the window and saw Pauline walking past, her eyes glued to the pavement. The events of recent months had taken their toll. Stooped, head bowed in obloquy, her ebullient gait further reduced with a perceptible shuffle, Pauline had aged a decade in as many months. Her careless clothes matched her dissolution.

Ian felt sad. How he would love to be her knight in shining armour, her hero and crusader. With a kiss on her lips she would

366

be reformed into the princess she once was. They could live out their lives in domestic contentment. If only he were free and had the means to come to her rescue.

Idly, he turned the pages of the paper and found a review of the new D. L. Black. A cold shiver stuttered along Ian's back, he knew he should turn the page but it was like seeing an accident on the motorway. He read the words through a squint.

...Black has a penchant for literary jokes that demean his good intentions. The youngest sister in the Gray family, named Doreen, has removed the mirrors from her house and combs her hair at night in front of a sketch painted of her when she was a teenager. Doreen's evil doings are reflected in her face and she becomes more witchlike. Her face is wizened before it's time and her nose not only becomes elongated but develops a large wart with a hair in it. Another sister is so vain that, not quite anorexic, she starves herself to an emaciated state that we saw during the liberation of Belsen. Black's joke here is that because of the politeness and delusion of modern society few are prepared to point out these transformations and when someone has the courage to do so, the miscreant denies the truth. This is another literary joke. Evelyn Waugh wrote, inside every fat man is a thin man trying to get out. Black's character is a thin woman who looks in the mirror and sees only fat...

He skipped to the end,

...Black's novel is a gloomy view of modern mores that finds no empathy with this reviewer. Quite simply, Mr Black is a miserable bugger.

Two teenage girls, one carrying a baby and one wearing a vest showing off her enormous breasts, took the table behind him and spoke at a volume as though speaking into a mobile telephone. The mother squatted to attend to a child in a push chair and revealed a design of sharp patterns in navy blue ink.

'Giv' us a hand,' said the mother.

Ian returned to the review pages and found another review of a book written by a Black.

Ms Borden-Black concludes, 'It is hard to summarise this constantly repeating syndrome without resorting to frivolity. Lone criticism is shoved into the sidelines by dismissing the critic as a looney (see Chapter VI Anthony Wedgewood Benn) or as the killjoy spoiling the party (see Chapter VII Michael Newell). Only when the press take up the crusade is there a consensus and the culprits are hounded.'

Open government has led to the worming out of sleaze because it sells newspapers. If government is doing a good job these lapses will be overlooked until the time when government is not working to the media's accepted standard.

The hypocrisy here is that in the private sector, including the fourth estate, sleaze, corruption and jobs for the boys, carry on as usual. This hypocrisy is exemplified by two high profile institutions.

Unquestionably, drink is as base a plague as tobacco, but has not been subjected to any public furore.

The Football Association carried out a cursory investigation of the 'bung' scandal. They made a lot of noise and spouted a lot of sanctimony but they scarcely unsettled the dust and the matter has been swept under the carpet. The FA management do not want an irate manager to be singled out by the investigation and have the finger pointing back at them. It is not customary to admit that they all have their noses in the trough.

'Shelaine, you want a latte?'

'Something stronger, I got kind of wasted last night, yeah. I don't think I'm gonna ever come round today. My head's like cotton wool.'

'Fetch me the local rag. Mickey's supposed to be in it. He got another eighteen months.'

The mother fetched the *Observer* and spread the newspaper across the table. 'That's Amy on the front page.'

'Didn't you used to be kind of mates?'

'Right, we still are.'

'Is that the miracle picture? Don't she look awesome. D'you think she'll win that top model thing?'

'I dunno. 'Angel Amy', some hopes.'

'Wasn't she pregnant?'

'Yeah, she got rid of it.'

'Wasn't it some old geezer that got her up the stick?'

'He got seven years.'

'Seven years,' said the voice. 'Yeah, serves the old bastard right.'

'Haven't I told you about that?' said Shelaine. 'The uncle weren't the real father. '

'Nah?'

'She fancied him like shitloads and tried to shag him. It's ever so funny. The aunt and the cousin were away overnight and Amy hid in the house. When he was in bed she got in with him, got hold of his hand and stuck it on her nonny. Guess what he did?'

'I ain't got the faintest.'

'Chucked her out, she got the dead needle. Swore she would get even. Soon after she got up the stick, see, 'cos she'd been shagging her cousin, right, and he's the one who got her pregnant. The real father told Amy because they're cousins the baby might have two heads.'

'Is that true?'

'It's bollocks. Well, I think its bollocks. There's more, not only was the cousin shagging Amy he was also knocking off her mother.

'You're pulling my leg.'

'Honest. One night both Amy and her mother made arrangements to get laid in the shed at the bottom of the garden. The night of the power cut. In the confusion the cousins' brother, who also fancied Amy gave the mother one by mistake and he thought he was the father of Amy's baby. He's the one who was in the papers recently for nicking millions of pounds.'

Ian froze.

'Amy got rid of the baby though.'

'That's why she fitted up the uncle. Killed two birds with one stone. She was allowed an abortion because she was underage and was forced into sex by a much older man.'

'How could she get away with it?'

'This cousin, the real father, works for the filth and he was able to fit up the uncle.'

'So the uncle's in the nick for no reason?'

'Right.'

'Ahh, that's a shame being banged up and you didn't do nuffink.'

'I think it's a right larf. You know the cousin by the way. Cocky bugger, gobby type. Gideon.'

'Ooh yeah, he goes forever that one. How'd he fit the uncle up?'

'DNA.'

'Sa make of handbag ennit?'

'DNA's your body fingerprint. Mickey's had to get photographed, give his fingerprints and his DNA. That's how that Gideon swung it with the DNA. I told you he's with the filth. He was shagging the woman in charge of DNA tests. He kept swapping the uncle's tests with one of his own.'

Ian's nervous system failed him. His head rang and peeled to a cacophony of bells, his insides flooded to his feet. He hurried down to the basement toilet and cleared his bowels.

As he washed, he was overcome with panic and his spinning head fogged. He left the narrow cubicle, crashing the door into the frame. The stairs proved to be as insurmountable as Everest. He staggered out of the café and was accosted by the waitress.

'You haven't paid, sir.'

Humiliation was heaped upon his other shame. He thrust a £10 note in the girl's hand and muttered, 'Emergency.'

He turned and ran, colliding with an inert object and banging his jaw on this misty obstacle. He rubbed it vigorously and checked for blood.

'Ian,' said the blur. 'I'm sorry.'

Out of the dancing shadows Pauline's face came into focus, his blackened soul on his sleeve for all to see. Confronting the nucleus of his guilt, he recoiled.

'Is something the matter?'

Not trusting himself to speak he shook his head. 'I got this letter.' She rummaged in her handbag and he could only think of escape, dream of escape. Hero and crusader, and honour deserted him.

She handed over an envelope which had been torn open and he fished inside for its contents while Pauline led him by the arm to a bench by the fountain.

Bertis Crown, Literary Agents, King Street, WC1
Dear Mrs Black,

We are writing to inform you that your husband is not coping well with his incarceration. He has suffered several acts of retribution that the other prisoners mete out on sexual offenders. He is in constant fear for his life and is unable to eat for fear of having his food doctored.

We are sure a visit from yourself would go a long way towards helping with his diminished morale.

On a business note, Mr Black has insisted that all royalties from Wasted *and his new novel,* White Sepulchres *are to be paid direct to you and he is also prepared to give the credit for the novel to you so that you might get some lecturing assignments from such a credit.*

Please contact us as soon as possible so that we can finalise the legalities of these contracts (which your husband has already signed).

Yours sincerely,
Richard Crown.

Ian, still speechless, faced his sister-in-law, silent tears streaming down her face, her eyes as empty as his entrails.

It was then, for a fleeting moment, he was inspired to be a knight errant. To explain all he knew and give Pauline her life back. It was the briefest of impulses, but as he calculated the consequences the warmth was eclipsed.

'It's a terrible shame,' he touched her arm, wanting something tangible to remember. That impulse opened a shutter and brought a millisecond of clarity. This was the last time he would see her.

Who should he reproach? It was all their faults. They were all to blame. If only they could have lived their lives by the book.

'What do you think I should do?' she asked, searching his face for help. 'Should I go and visit him?'

'You should do what you feel in your heart,' he told her, clearly seeing her disappointment with his answer.

'Goodbye,' she said sadly and moved off towards the Town Hall.

He hoped she might turn around and wave a last farewell, but she shuffled doggedly on, her shoulders drooping and head bowed.

He walked across the precinct and stared in the window of the hairdresser. His wife was being attended to by a young man with effete gestures and she was holding court, her expressive arms flapping every which way.

Tomorrow he would start his memoirs or mow the lawn. Do something worthwhile with his time. He stepped inside the salon and as he drew near he heard Helena say, 'It's almost biblical. I lose a son and his brother steps into his shoes. Takes on his brother's wife and baby. It is, isn't it, just like the bible? My son Gideon was a lost cause but that's water under the bridge. He has become a total credit to me.'